International acclaim for

The Mosquito Coast

"Theroux's talent is indeed considerable . . . A strong and disturbing fable . . . This excellent story . . . is also an impressively serious act of imagination." —*New York Times Book Review*

"Full of paradox, humor, and energy. A send-up of contemporary America and yet a deadly serious commentary."
—**Associated Press, Best Books of the Decade**

"A chilling yarn of survival. Theroux never loses his tight grasp on the lines of suspense." —*Christian Science Monitor*

"[A] splendidly controlled adventure novel." —*New York Times*

"A superbly good book." —*Sunday Telegraph*

"As oppressive and powerful as its central character. It bursts with inventiveness." —*Times* (London)

"A grand adventure." —*Los Angeles Herald-Examiner*

"Astonishing . . . How much do I like this book? Let me count the ways."—**John Leonard**

"Stunning . . . exciting, intelligent, meticulously realized, artful."
—*Sunday Times* (London)

"An epic of paranoid obsession that swirls the reader headlong to deposit him on a black mudbank of horror." —*Guardian*

"Rich beyond compare . . . exhilarating and provocative, funny and terrifying." —*Chicago Sun-Times*

BOOKS BY PAUL THEROUX

The Mosquito Coast

A NOVEL BY

PAUL THEROUX

WITH WOODCUTS
BY DAVID FRAMPTON

A MARINER BOOK
HOUGHTON MIFFLIN COMPANY
BOSTON • NEW YORK

First Mariner Books edition 2006

Copyright © 1982 by Cape Cod Scriveners
ALL RIGHTS RESERVED
For information about permission to reproduce selections
from this book, write to trade.permissions@hmhco.com or to
Permissions, Houghton Mifflin Harcourt Publishing Company,
3 Park Avenue, 19th Floor, New York, New York 10016.

Visit our Web site: www.hmhco.com

Library of Congress Cataloging-in-Publication Data

Theroux, Paul.
The Mosquito Coast.
I. Title.
PS3570.H4M6 813'54 81-6787
ISBN 0-395-31837-8 AACR2
ISBN 0-395-32075-5 (limited ed.)

ISBN-13: 978-0-618-65896-1 (pbk.)
ISBN-10: 0-618-65896-3 (pbk.)

Printed in the United States of America

16 2021
4500824270

To "Charlie Fox," whose story this is and whose courage showed me that the brave cannot be killed. With grateful thanks for many hours of patient explanation and good humor in the face of my ignorant questioning. May he find the peace he deserves on this safer coast. *Naksaa.*

P. T.

1
BANANA
BOAT

1

WE DROVE past Tiny Polski's mansion house to the main road, and
then the five miles into Northampton, Father talking the whole way
about savages and the awfulness of America — how it got turned
into a dope-taking, door-locking, ulcerated danger zone of rabid
scavengers and criminal millionaires and moral sneaks. And look at
the schools. And look at the politicians. And there wasn't a Harvard
graduate who could change a flat tire or do ten pushups. And there
were people in New York City who lived on pet food, who would
kill you for a little loose change. Was that normal? If not, why did
anyone put up with it?

"I don't know," he said, replying to himself. "I'm just thinking
out loud."

Before leaving Hatfield, he had parked the pickup truck on a rise
in the road and pointed south.

"Here come the savages," he said, and up they came, tracking
across the fields from a sickle of trees through the gummy drizzling
heat-outlines of Polski's barns. They were dark and their clothes
were rags and some had rags on their heads and others wide-
brimmed hats. They were men and boys, a few no older than me, all
of them carrying long knives.

Father's finger scared me more than the men did. He was still
pointing. The end of his forefinger was missing to the big knuckle,
so the finger stump, blunted by stitched skin folds and horribly
scarred, could only approximate the right direction.

"Why do they bother to come here?" he said. "Money? But how
could it be money?"

He seemed to be chewing the questions out of his cigar.

It was mid-morning, already too hot for Massachusetts in May. The valley looked scorched from the dry spring we were having, and the shallow ditches were steaming like fresh cowflap. In the furrows that had been torn from one field's end to the other, only tiny palm plumes of Wonder Corn were showing. Not a single bird twittered here. And the asparagus fields, where the men were headed, were as brown and smooth as if the green scalp of grass had been peeled off and the whole baldness steamrolled.

Father shook his head. He released the brake and spat out of the window. He said, "It sure as heck isn't money. These days a dollar's only worth twenty cents."

Beyond Hatfield and Polski's house, and at the top edge of the valley trough, were leafy battlements, some as pale as lemonade froth and others dark bulges and beetle heaps of bush, and stockades of bursting branches that matched my idea of encircling jungle. A few hours before, when we had woken up, the ground had been covered in glitter beads of cold dew. I thought of it as summer ice. I had breathed out clouds of vapor then. There were pouches of cloud in the sky. Now the sun was up high, filling the valley with light and heat that blazed against those men and made them into skinny demons.

Maybe this was the reason that, though I had seen the men before — the savages, in that very place and close enough to notice the way the sun left black bruises on their leather-brown skin — the sight of them had alarmed me, like Father's finger.

"This place is a toilet," he said as we entered Northampton. He wore a baseball cap and drove with his elbow out the window. "It's not the college girls, though they're bad enough. Look at Tugboat Annie over there, the size of her. She's so big it would only take eleven of her kind to make a dozen. But that's fat — that's not health. That's cheeseburgers." And he stuck his head out the window and hollered, "That's cheeseburgers!"

Down Main Street ("They're all on drugs"), we passed a Getty station and Father howled at the price of gas. TWO SLAIN IN SHOOT-OUT was the sign on a newspaper stand, and he said, "Crapsheets." Just the word *Collectibles,* on a storefront, irritated him. And near the hardware store there was a vending machine that sold ice by the bag.

"They sell ice — ten pounds for a half a buck. But water's as free as air. Those dingbats are selling water! Water's the new growth industry. Mineral water, spring water, sparkling water. It's big news — water's good for you! Low-cal beer — know what's in it? Know why it keeps you thin? Know why it costs more than the regular? Water!"

Father said it in the Yankee way, *wattuh.*

He cruised around, getting grumpier, until he found a meter with time left on it. Then he parked and we walked back to the hardware store.

"I want a rubber seal, eight feet of it, with foam backing," Father said, and while the man went to get it, he said, "And that's probably why gas is so expensive. They put water in it. You don't believe me? If you insist there's morality in merchandising" — but I hadn't said a word — "then maybe you'd like to explain why two-thirds of government-inspected meat has substantial amounts of cancer-inducing nitrates in it, and junk food — this is a proven fact — has no nutritional value whatsoever — "

The hardware clerk returned with a coil of rubber and handed it to Father, who examined it and gave it back.

"Don't want it," he said.

"That's what you asked for," the man said.

Father made a pitying face. "What are you, working for the Japanese?"

"If you don't want it, just say so."

"I just said so, Jack. It's made in Japan. I don't want my hard-earned bucks turned into foreign exchange for the sons of Nippon. I don't want to bankroll another generation of kamikazes. I want an American length of rubber seal, with foam — *Do you work here?*" And he cursed, because the man had walked away and begun serving another customer.

Father found the rubber seal he was looking for at a smaller hardware store on a back street, but by the time we got back to the pickup truck he was having fits over what he wished he had said at the first hardware store. "I should have said 'Sayonara,' I should have made a scene."

A policeman had his hands clasped over our parking meter, resting on it, with his chin on his fingers, like a goldbricker leaning on a shovel handle. He looked at Father and sort of smiled hello, and then he saw me and chewed his lips.

"Shouldn't he be in school?"

"Sick," Father said without breaking his stride.

The policeman followed Father to the door of the pickup and hooked his thumbs in his gun belt and said, "Hold on. Why isn't he in bed, then?"

"With a *fungal* infection?"

The policeman lowered his head and stared at me across the seat.

"Go on, Charlie, show him. He doesn't believe me. Take off your shoe. Give him a whiff."

I jerked at the laces of my sneakers as the policeman said, "Forget it."

"Don't apologize," Father said, smiling at the policeman. "Politeness is a sign of weakness. And that's no way to combat crime."

"You say something?" The policeman clamped his jaw and hovered. He was very angry. He looked cautious and heavy.

But Father was still smiling. "I was thinking out loud."

He said nothing more until we were back on the Hatfield road.

"Would you really have taken off your shoes and showed that cop your healthy toes?"

"You asked me to," I said.

"Right," he said. "But what kind of a country is it that turns shoppers into traitors and honest men into liars? No one ever thinks of leaving this country. Charlie, I think of it every day!"

He kept driving.

"And I'm the only one who does, because I'm the last man!"

That was our life here, the farm and the town. Father liked working at Tiny Polski's farm, but the town gave him fits. That was why he kept me out of school — and Jerry and the twins, too.

Later in the day, fixing a pump by the side of a field, we saw the savages again.

"They're from the jungle. Migrant workers. They didn't know when they were well off. I'd have traded places with them. They think this is paradise. Should never have come."

Father had invented the pump for Polski a year ago. It had a sensitized finger prong like a root in the ground, and when the soil dried out, this nerve-wire activated a switch and got the pump going. Father, an inventor, was a perfect genius with anything mechanical. "Nine patents," he liked to say. "Six pending." He boasted that he had dropped out of Harvard in order to get a good education. He was prouder of his first job as a janitor than his Harvard scholarship. He had invented a mechanical mop — you held it tight and it jigged across the floor, then squeezed itself dry. Using that mop was like dancing with a headless woman, he said. He called it The Silent Woman. What he liked best was taking things apart, even books, even the Bible. He said the Bible was like an owner's guide, a repair manual to an unfinished invention. He also said the Bible was a wilderness. It was one of Father's theories that there were parts of the Bible that no one had ever read, just as there were parts of the world where no one had ever set foot.

"You think that's bad? It's anything but. It's the empty spaces that will save us. No funny bunnies, no cops, no crooks, no muggers, no glue sniffers, no aerosol bombs. I'm not lost, like them." He pointed at the savages. "I know the way out."

He touched the different parts of the pump with his fingers, like a doctor examining a baby for swellings, and still he talked about empty spaces and savages. I raised my eyes and saw them. They seemed to be creeping straight out of the wilderness he had just described. We watched them making for the upper fields, and though I knew they were only going out to cut more asparagus, they looked as if they were searching for some fingers to chop off.

"They come from the safest place on earth — Central America. Know what they've got down there? Geothermal energy. All the juice they need is five thousand feet underground. It's the earth's bellybutton. Why do they come here?"

Across the fields they went, the savages, hunched over and flapping. They had huge shoes and tiny tucked-down heads, and as they passed by the woods they scared the crows and started a racket of caws. The birds flew up like black gloves jerked from a line, rising backward and filling out their feathers with each wingbeat.

"No TV where they come from. No Nipponese video-crapola. Pass me that oil can. Up here, nature is young. But the ecosystem in the tropics is immensely old and hasn't changed since the world began. Why do they think we have the answers? Faith — is that what you're saying? Is faith just playing 'Come to Jesus' in A-flat?"

He locked the wrench over the threads of the protruding pipe, then poked the spout of the oil can at the pipe joint and squirted. With both hands he freed the pipe, and he sighed.

"No, sir. Faith is believing in something you know ain't true. Ha!"

He put his short finger inside the rusty trickle in the pump housing and pulled out a brass valve and a gush of water.

"You can't drink the water where those savages originate. It's got creatures in it. Worms. Weeds. They haven't got the sense to boil it and purify it. Never heard of filtration. The germs get into their bodies, and they turn green, like the water, and die. The rest of them figure it's no good there — spiders big as puppies, mosquitoes, snakes, floods, swamps, alligators. No idea at all about geothermal energy. Why change it when you can come here and go to pieces? Give me the wretched refuse of your teeming shore. Have a Coke, watch television, go on welfare, get free money. Turn to crime. Crime pays in this country — muggers become pillars of the community. They'll all end up mugging and purse snatching."

The water was now pouring out of the pump, and the inside circuits ticked and measured.

"I'm not going into Northampton again. It's too upsetting. I'm sick of meeting people who want the things I've already had and rejected. I've had every dollar I've ever wanted, Charlie. And don't mention education. That cop this morning was educated — that Truant Officer — and all he wants is what they have on TV. I wouldn't send that guy out for sandwiches! I've had all that — what people crave. It doesn't work, and it's irritating to hear it praised ignorantly."

He grinned at me.

He said, "It's an imperfect world."

Now he was grinning at his cut-off finger.

"What are the Russians doing while those people are watching TV? They're conducting some very interesting experiments with water. They de-gas it, bubble everything out of it, including oxygen and nitrogen. When they've flattened it they seal it up in Mason jars, like preserved peaches. Put it aside for a while. Then, when they use this water on plants, they grow two or three times as fast — big healthy monsters. Beans climb off their poles, summer squashes like balloons, beets the size of volleyballs."

He motioned to the water.

"I'm just thinking out loud. What do you think? You figure there's something wrong with the rain? Say something."

I said I did not know.

"Figure someone ought to talk to God about rethinking the weather? I tell you, Charlie, it's an imperfect world. And America's in gridlock."

He cupped his hand under the spurting pipe and raised it to his mouth. Then he slurped it. "This is like champagne to those savages."

Smacking his lips he made it seem wonderful stuff.

"Things you and I take for granted, like ice. They don't have it in their country. If they saw an ice cube, they'd probably think it was a diamond or a jewel of some kind. Doesn't seem like the end of the world — no ice. But think about it. Imagine the kind of problems they have with no proper refrigeration."

"Maybe they don't have electricity," I said.

Father said, "Of course they don't. We're talking about the jungle, Charlie. But you can have refrigeration without juice. All you need is suction. Start a vacuum going and you've got refrigeration. Listen, you can get ice out of fire."

"Why don't they know that?"

"No way," he said. "That's what makes them savages."

He began putting the pump back together.

He said, "Must have all kinds of diseases." He gestured with his wrench in the direction the men had taken. "Them — they've got diseases."

He seemed both fascinated and repelled by them, and he communicated these feelings to me, telling me something interesting and then warning me not to be too interested. I had wondered how he knew these things about the men he called savages. He claimed he knew from experience, from living in wild places, among primitive people. He used the word savages with affection, as if he liked them a little for it. In his nature was a respect for wildness. He saw it as a personal challenge, something that could be put right with an idea or a machine. He felt he had the answer to most problems, if anyone cared to listen.

The crows returned to the woods, speeding toward the treetops, then circling warily and plunging to roost.

I said, "Are those men dangerous?"

"Not as dangerous as the average American," he said. "And only when they get mad. You know they're mad when they're smiling. That's the signal, like dogs."

He turned to me and smiled broadly. I knew he wanted me to ask him more.

"Then what?"

"They turn into animals. Killers. Animals sort of smile just before they bite you."

"Do those men bite?"

"Give you one example. Know how they do it? Kill you? I'll tell you, Charlie boy. They hollow you out."

Holler ya out was the way he said it, and when he did I felt as if my scalp was tugged by a hundred sharp claws.

"That's why it would take courage to go there — and not ordinary gumption, but four-o'clock-in-the-morning courage. Who's got that?"

We worked outside until the sky turned the color of flaming Sterno, then started home to supper.

"Admit it," Father said, "this is better than school."

2

THAT NIGHT I opened my eyes in the dark and knew that my father was not in the house. The sense of someone missing is stronger than the sense of someone there. It was not only that I didn't hear his whistling snore (usually he sounded like one of his own original expansion valves), or even that all the lights were out. It was a feeling of lonesome emptiness, as if there was a mummy-shaped hole of air in the house where my father's body should have been. And my fear was that this unpredictable man was dead, or worse than dead — hollowed out and haunting the property. I knew he was gone, and in a worried guilty way — I was thirteen years old — I felt responsible for him.

There was no moon, but even so it was an easy house to search, because there were no locks. Father disapproved of locking doors. I say disapproved, but I mean he'd threaten to hit us for it. Someone behind a locked door was up to no good, he said. He often shouted at the bathroom door, "Don't barricade yourself in!" He had grown up in a small fishing town on the coast of Maine — he called it Dogtown — where door locking was unknown. During the years he had spent in India and Africa he had kept to the same rule, so he said. I never knew for sure if he had been to those places. I grew up with the belief that the world belonged to him and that everything he said was true.

He was big and bold in everything he did. The only ordinary thing about him was that he smoked cigars and wore a baseball cap all day.

I looked first in the bedroom and saw one figure lying there on the brass bed, a humped-up sheet on the far side — Mother. I was sure he was gone, because he always hung his overalls on the bedpost, and they were not there. I went downstairs and through the rooms. The cat was sleeping on the floor like a tipped-over roller skate. I paused in the hallway and listened. It being spring, there was a powerful odor of lilacs and dug-up dirt, and a soft wind. There was a torrent of crickets outside, and one frantic cricket trapped inside making fretful chirps. Except for this cricket, the house was as still as if it lay buried.

My rubber boots were right inside the door. I put them on and, still in my pajamas, I set out along the path to look for my old man.

We were surrounded by plowed fields. The edge of each field was ragged with woods, left as windbreaks. The corn and tobacco had begun to sprout, and though it was easier to tramp between the furrows, I stuck to the path, with my arms in front of my face to keep the branches away. It was not the branches I hated, but the spider webs strung across that snagged on my eyelashes. These woods were full of marshy pools, and the sound that night was the spring peepers, the little slippery frogs, shiny as fish lures, that made such a warbling. The trees were blue and black, like towering witches. Where was he?

I had left the house feeling wrapped in darkness, but the farther I walked the less dark it seemed. Now the land was muddy yellow. Some trees were ash-colored and the upper parts picked out like iron thorns, and the sky was heavy gray. One cloud was the shape of a loaf of bread, and I guessed that the moon was behind it because it had a bright oily look, as if it hid a mill town in the heavens.

After a while I wished that I had not left the house in such a hurry. Was someone behind me? I turned around sharply to confront the smirking skulls on barkless trees or the reaching finger bones from dead branches. That was one fear. My other was that I would step on a skunk and get sprayed with the stink. Then I would have to bury my pajamas in a hole and go back to the house bare naked.

The woods thinned out. I could see single trees against the sky and another row in front of a yellowish field. A pile of boulders told me where I was. This high point had been left because it was impossible to plow. It was narrow and it rose up at the end of the woods, giving the whole thing the look of a ship. From the side, in daytime, it was a schooner with a rocky bow and a cargo on the deck and thirty leafy masts, stranded in the asparagus fields among the windbreaks that looked like islands.

It was mostly asparagus here. The crop was ready, the harvest had begun. It is a funny-looking crop, because it does not grow in furrows. The fields are as flat and smooth as parking lots. From a distance you can't see asparagus plants, but if you go very close you see the spikes — no flowers, no leaves, just fat green candles sticking out of the ground everywhere. From where I was standing I could not see anything but the smooth streamrolled earth, and its dull shine, like a swell in a waveless sea. And beyond those fields the black ribbon of night where I feared my father was.

There were also lightning bugs. They were puny, not bright, less than match flares, dithering on and off and never in the same place twice. They had a light of their own but lighted nothing else and were like dim unreliable stars dying in the darkness.

But a cluster of small lights far off did not die. They fumbled, they were torches, and when I was satisfied that these fires had men beneath them I set off directly for them, across the asparagus fields, kicking over and cracking the spikes, my boots sinking in the dirt crust.

Closer, I could see the high flames wagging all in a row — a procession of people in single file holding torches over their heads, the flames snapping like flags. Their broadbrimmed hats were lit up, but I could not see their bodies. They streamed from a patch of pinewoods where there was an old building we called the Monkey House.

Men with torches marching at midnight across the valley fields — I had never seen anything like it. It was a snake of flame, and I thought I heard a rattling sound, the jacking of beans shaken in a can. But I was more curious than frightened, and I had hidden myself so well and was still so distant that the thing didn't threaten me.

The procession kept to the far side of a stone wall between the crops — young corn there, asparagus here. I had to stay where I was. I imagined that if they saw me they would attack me and set me on fire. This thought, and the knowledge that I was safe here, gave me a thrill. I hunched over and ran to a ditch and got down flat and looked sharp.

Then they changed direction and came toward me. Had they seen me run? My heart almost stopped as the torches tottered through a gate in the stone wall, and I thought: Oh, Gaw, they're going to set me on fire.

I crept backward into the ditch, and as I was in this lying-down position the ditch water started to leak into my boot tops. Pretty soon my boots were full of ditch water. But I didn't open my mouth. One of my father's favorite stories was about the Spartan boy with the fox under his shirt, I forget why, who let the animal chew his belly to shreds because he was too brave to shout for help. Wet feet were no comparison. There were some low vines growing on the ground nearby. I knew my legs were sunk in mud and water, so I yanked at the vines and pulled them over my head and flattened myself against the side of the ditch. I was completely hidden.

The men were close. They were still gabbling — they sounded happy — and I could hear the swishing of their torches, the flames sounding like sheets blowing on a clothesline — no crackle, just the flap of fire. I looked up. I expected to see torch carriers with crazy faces, but what I saw almost made me yell. The man in front was carrying a huge black cross.

The cross was not made out of planks, but rounded — two fat poles lashed together. There were horrible white chopmarks where the branches had been lopped off, like oval wounds on skin. And behind this fellow with the cross, and more scary, was a man carrying a human body, a limp thing, with the head slung down and the feet dangling and the arms swishing back and forth. He carried this corpse the way you heave a seed bag. It was big and soft and heavy, and its parts swung loose in a dreadful way. In the torchlight the carrier's face was yellow. He was smiling.

I did not feel like looking anymore. I was shivering with cold. *You can get ice out of fire,* Father had said. Now I believed him. That fire froze my guts.

I kept my head down and my mouth shut, even though I was muddy and wet and bitten by bugs. I had felt the heat and smelled the torches — that was how close they were. Then they were gone. I looked up slowly and saw their torches flickering in the ship-shaped woods I had cut through myself. The tree branches jumped in the firelight, and this leaping line of hot stripes and shadows crossed to the far side where it settled and glowed.

I crawled out of the ditch and chucked the vines aside and emptied my boots. Then, keeping to the ditch, I sloshed as far as I could, and duck-walked across the asparagus and into the woods. By now the procession was beyond the trees. All that remained here was the smell of gasoline-soaked rags and burned leaves. I was well hidden here. In fact, I could see everything from behind a heap of rocks.

Two of the men were hunched over. They must have been fastening the dead man to the cross, because soon after, in the fiery light of the circle of torches, I saw the cross raised up with a man on it, his wrists bent and his toes sticking down and his head tipped like a jug.

It looked wicked, and I expected the men to be screaming blue murder. But no, it was all quiet, even jolly, and that was worse, like the nightmare you watch happening to you and cannot explain. In all that zigzagging across the fields, I was so afraid of giving myself away and being burned alive that I had forgotten why I was there. But just as I saw the raised cross I remembered that I was looking for my father. The recollection and the sight came at the same instant, and I thought: That dead twisted person is my old man.

I sat there and put my hands over my eyes and tried to stop crying, but I kept blubbering until my head felt very small and very wet. I thought, without knowing why, that I would be blamed for it.

All I could do was watch and listen. I had gotten used to this murky sight, and the longer I looked the more I felt responsible for it, as if it was something I had imagined, an evil thought that had sprung out of my head. Watching it made me part of it.

There was no time to worry. All at once, the men doused their lights. After the fires and the shadows and the lighted cross, there were only shirts and hats — bone-white skeleton rags moving without bodies — and silence, as the men, these rags, foamed toward me.

I picked myself up and ran for my life.

I'm the last man! That had been Father's frequent yell.

It was painful, back in my bed, in the dark unlocked house, not dreaming but thinking. I felt small and shrunken. Father, who believed there was going to be a war in America, had prepared me for his death. All winter, he had been saying, "It's coming — something terrible is going to happen here." He was restless and talkative. He said the signs were everywhere. In the high prices, the bad tempers, the gut worry. In the stupidity and greed of people, and in the hoggish fatness of them. Bloody crimes were being committed in cities, and criminals went unpunished. It was not going to be an ordinary war, he said, but rather a war in which no side was entirely innocent.

"Fat fools will be fighting skinny criminals," he said. "You'll hate one and be scared of the other. It'll be national brain damage. Who's left to trust?"

He sounded disgusted, and in the depths of that white winter he was sometimes very gloomy. One day, Tiny Polski's pipes froze solid and Father was called on to unblock them. We stood in the snow, at the edge of a freshly dug pit, wiring the pipes to Father's "Thunderbox" to thaw them. (This device was his own invention, and he was proud of it — patent pending — though the first time he used it he almost killed Ma Polski, her hand being on an electrified faucet when he turned on the juice.) He watched the pipes heat and throw off vapor. Ice cracked inside, and jostled, and rattled like gravel. He listened with pleasure to the clunking thaw in the pipes, and then faced me at the edge of the snow-crusted pit.

"When it comes, I'll be the first one they kill. They always kill the smart ones first — the ones they're afraid will outwit them. Then, with no one to stop them, they'll tear each other to pieces. Turn this fine country into a hole."

There was no despair in his words, only matter-of-factness. The war was a certainty, but he was still hopeful. He said he believed in himself and in us. "I'll take you away — we'll pack up and go. And we'll shut the door on all this."

He liked the idea of setting out, moving away, starting off in an empty place with nothing but his brains and his toolbox.

"They'll get me first."

"No."

"They always get the smart ones first."

I could not deny this. He was the smartest man I knew. He had to be the first one to die.

Until I saw that marching procession at midnight, and the dead body on the cross, I could not imagine how anyone would be able to kill him. But that night was enough. I was convinced now, and I was alone. The strongest man I knew had been strung up on two poles and left in a cornfield. It was the end of the world.

"I'm the last man, Charlie!"

The dark hours were passing. Soon it would be morning and I would have to face everyone and tell them that Father had predicted it. So I lay in my bed and thought how Father had said that the country was doomed. He had promised to save us and get us away before it was too late. But he was gone, I was too weak to save the others, and in the dream I finally had in the coldest part of the night I was leading Mother and the twins and Jerry through burning fields under a wounded sun and a sky the color of blood, all our clothes in rags, and the smoke, and nothing to eat. They were depending on me, and only I knew, but was afraid to tell them because it was too late, that I was taking them the wrong way.

In the bruised red-black sky was the mocking face of Father, after we had walked and walked, saying, "Where have you been, sonny?"

I covered my eyes. I was still in the dream and aching, Mother and the kids behind me, disaster ahead and no escape.

"Where have you — ?"

I woke and saw his face, sunburned and angry, and sat up because I expected him to hit me — afraid he was dead, then afraid because he was standing over me. His cigar told me I was not dreaming. I was too shocked to cry.

"I had a bad dream."

And I thought: It has all been a dream — the men with the torches, the corpse on the cross, the laughing savages, the wounded sun and sky. I was very happy. The sunlight bleached my bedroom curtains, birds screeched at me.

"You must have been dreaming about poison ivy," Father said. "You've got the worst case I've ever seen."

As he said it, I began to ache. My face felt pebbly and raw, and my arms too.

"Don't touch it. You'll make it spread. Get out of the sack and put something on it." He started out of the room, and as I pulled on my clothes he said, "You've been fooling in the bushes — that's where you've been."

The loose board on the threshold told me everything was normal. I smelled coffee and bacon and heard the twins screaming and was gladder than I had ever been. I went to the bathroom. My face looked like a pomegranate in the mirror, and my arms and shoulders were inflamed with the poison-ivy rash. I wiped calamine lotion on it and hurried to the kitchen.

"It's a ghost," Jerry said, seeing my whitewashed face.

"You poor thing," Mother said. She set a plate of eggs in front of me and kissed the top of my head.

Father said, "It's his own fault."

But it was nothing. After what I had seen, a case of poison ivy seemed like salvation.

"Eat up," Father said. "We've got work to do."

I wanted to work, to carry the toolbox and hand him the oil can and be his slave and do anything he asked. I deserved to be punished. I wanted to forget those torches and those men. I was thirteen years old again. I had felt forty.

Father said, "Meet me in the workshop when you're through."

"Poor Charlie," Mother said. "Where did you get that face?"

I said softly, "I was fooling in the bushes, Ma. It was my own fault."

She shook her head and smiled. She knew I was sorry.

"Ma!" Jerry yelled. "Charlie's staring at me with his face!"

Father's workshop was behind the house. There were mottoes and quotations lettered on pieces of cardboard and tacked to the shelves, and tools and pipes and coils of wire and various machines. Besides motors of all kinds, and a grease gun and his lathe, which gave the workshop the look of an arsenal, there was his Thunderbox and an all-purpose contraption he called his Atom-smasher.

On the floor, about the size of a trunk but resting upright on its end, was a wooden box he had been building and tinkering with for most of the spring. There were no wires in it and no motor. He had put it together with a blowtorch. It was full of pipes, and grids and tanks, copper tubing below and a door leading to a tin box on top. It smelled of kerosene, and I took it to be an oven of some kind, because bracketed to the back was a sooty chimney. Father said we had to get this thing into the pickup truck.

I tried to lift it. It wouldn't budge.

"Want to rupture yourself?" Father said.

With fussy care, and taking his time, he set up a block and tackle on a tripod and we swung this box of fitted pipes into the pickup.

"What is it?"

"Call it a Worm Tub or a hopper. You'll know when Doctor Polski knows."

He took the back road and traveled toward Polski's farmhouse on the tractor paths by the margins of the fields. When we passed the windbreak that was like a ship, I remembered that it was there that I had seen the procession of torch-carrying men. Below that clump of woods I had seen the men gather, and the corpse raised up on the cross. I hoped Father would take the right fork, so that I could satisfy myself — by seeing footprints or trampled corn — that I had not dreamed it. Father turned right. I held my breath.

What was that in the plowed field? A cross, a dead man hanging on it, black rags and a black hat, a skull face and broken hands and twisted feet.

It froze me, and I could not help the stammering whimper in my voice as I asked him what it was.

Father was still driving fast over the rutted track. He did not turn his head. He just grinned and said, "Don't tell me you've never seen a scarecrow."

He thumped the throttle.

"And it must be a damned good one."

I looked back and saw it hanging in the empty field, the old clothes stuffed with straw. Sweat had made my poison ivy itch, and I wanted to claw my face.

"Because it sure has you scared!" And he laughed.

3

THE STORY WAS that Tiny Polski, who had heard about his inventions, visited Father and pleaded with him to come to Hatfield. We lived in Maine then, not Dogtown but in the woods. Father was trying a year of self-sufficiency, growing vegetables and building solar panels and keeping us out of school. Polski promised money and a share in the farm. Father did not budge. Polski said he had unusual problems because he wanted, by mechanical means, to lengthen the growing season, even make it a two-season farm. It was a good area to raise kids in. It was safe, a happy valley, miles from anywhere. So Father accepted. That was the story he told me. But I knew better. Things had not gone well for us in Maine. Father had refused to spray insecticides on the vegetables — the worms got them before they could ripen. Rain and storm raised hell with the solar panels. For a while, Father would not eat, and he was taken to the hospital. He called it The Buzz Palace, but came out smiling and said, "I didn't feel a thing." He was healthy again, except that now and then he forgot our names. We drove to Hatfield with nothing. He liked starting from scratch.

It was impossible to think of Polski, or anyone else, as Father's boss. Father did not take orders. He described Polski as "the runt," called him Roly, and Doctor Polski — but "Doctor" was pure sarcasm, to frustrate any friendship. He believed that Polski, and most men, were his inferiors.

"He owns people," Father said. "But he doesn't own me."

Polski was waiting for us on his piazza as we drove in. His eyes were gray and as hard as periwinkles. He was older than Father, and small and plump, and looked full of sawdust. He wore a checkered shirt and clean Dubbelwares and a belt around his middle that bunched his bib overalls into two bags. His Jeep was shiny, his boots were never muddy, there was no sweat stain on his hat. He did not smoke. He was always dressed for dirty work but never got dirty. We had not been inside his mansion, but whether this was because Father flatly refused to enter or because we had not been invited, I could not say. Maybe Polski knew better than to invite Father in and hear one of his speeches about crapsheets or cheeseburgers. I had looked through the windows and seen the polished table and the cut-glass vase of flowers, the plates in a wheel-row on the hutch, Ma Polski's busy back as she stooped and tidied. None of it said welcome. And Ma Polski looked like part of the room.

"Nice day," Polski said.

"You bet," Father said.

"Hope it's like this on the weekend. I got something doing on Saturday."

Sumthun doo-un on Saddy was what he said. But Father did not comment. He was excited. He had driven with impatience, he was eager to show Polski the hopper he had made, his Worm Tub. He was proud of it, whatever it was. And yet he was still sitting in the pickup truck, chewing his cigar.

"Got a match, Doctor?"

Polski screwed up one eye and rocked a little on his heels. The question baffled him. He said, "You come all the way over here for a match, Mr. Fox?"

"Yup."

"Be right back." Polski said his *r*'s like *v*'s — vight back, vemember, vobber, veally, vong. It was his lower lip catching on his front teeth. He went inside.

Father studied my rashy face and arms. He said, "You've got the mange. I hope you learned your lesson."

He hopped out and set up the block and tackle behind the truck. "We're going to knock his boots off," he said. He swung the Worm Tub onto the driveway. "We're going to straighten his hair."

Polski returned with a box of big kitchen matches and looked at the Worm Tub and said, "Pretty small for a coffin."

"I wonder if you'd do one more little thing for me," Father said. "I need a glass of water. Just a small glass of regular water from your faucet."

Muttering "a glass of vegular water," Polski entered the farmhouse. I could tell from the way he said it and how the door banged shut that he was getting exasperated. When he brought the water out and gave it to Father he said, "You're a mystery man, Mr. Fox. Now let's get volling."

"You're a gentleman."

Now Polski looked at me for the first time. "Poison ivy. You're crawling with it. Ain't that something."

Hearing *crawlun* and *sumthun,* I stepped back and touched my face in shame. I had been fooled by a scarecrow. And I had figured it out. It made sense to put scarecrows up at night, so the birds would not know. Was that my lesson?

"What is it, anyway?" Polski was saying to Father.

"Tell you what it ain't," Father said, opening the door of the wooden box and revealing the metal compartment with its hinged flap and the rubber seal we had bought in Northampton. "It ain't a coffin, and it ain't a piece of diseased meat. Ha!"

He picked the flap open and said, "I want you to tell me what you see inside."

"Nuthun."

"You're the witness, Charlie."

Polski laughed. "Only his eyes are all swole shut."

Father tipped some of the water out of the glass, seeming to measure it in splashes until there was about an inch left. He put the glass inside the metal compartment, closed the flap, closed the door, closed the hasp, then lit a match.

Polski said, "Don't tell me you're going to cook that glass of water."

"I've got better things to do."

"Likewise!"

Polski moved his lips after this. He was boiling.

Father said, "You won't be disappointed."

"What's that stink? Kerosene?"

"Correct. Range oil. Cheapest fuel in America."

"And smelliest."

Father said, "Opinions vary."

This made Polski gobble. "And you say you're not cooking anything?"

"Not exactly."

Father was enjoying himself. He worked at the back of the

wooden box, where the tubing and the heating element were. Worm Tub was a good name for this crate of pipe joints. He had lighted a wick that was fed and moistened by a spout on the fuel tank, and adjusting the flame he sent bats of sticky soot out of the chimney. There was a gurgle inside, the sound a hungry stomach makes, but apart from this surge of discontented squirts in the tubes, nothing, no motor and not much heat.

"Does she burp or fart?" Father said. "That's what you're asking yourself."

Polski grunted with embarrassment and clicked his eyes and looked impatient as he fussed his footsoles over pebbles. Heat, loose weeds of it, were growing blackly out of the chimney. Polski backed away.

"If them pipes are sealed, she'll blow up," he said. "Pressure."

"Hide in your house if you want," Father said. "But she's got a full set of safety valves. Reason she's smoking is I've got her turned up full blast. For demonstration purposes." He snatched at his visor. "She can take it."

He looked proudly upon it, and he seemed so certain of it, so carelessly confident, that I half expected it to wheeze open with a boom of flame and explode in his face. We had had other explosions. "Just testing," Father would say. The workshop ceiling was scorched, and Father had not lost the tip of his finger opening a can of tuna fish, as he sometimes claimed.

Polski said, "If I ever wanted to cook a glass of water, I'd shove it on the front burner. Only I never veally wanted to voast a glass of water."

Polski looked at me for approval, and then turned gloomy when he saw the column of greasy smoke. His head turtled into his shoulders, and he squinted, awaiting the bang.

Father winked at me. "Like the way she purrs?"

"Vumble, vumble," Polski said.

"Not a wire anywhere," Father said, walking slowly around the box. "She's not connected to anything. I've got nothing up my sleeve. No moving parts, Doctor. Nothing to wear out. Last forever."

"Just the ticket for my chicken coop," Polski said, and he looked at me. "During the winter. It'd keep the birds warm as toast and laying vegular if it didn't kill them with fumes."

"He's a great kidder," Father said. "The fumes can be rectified.

It's all a matter of fine adjustment. I only want to show you what she's capable of."

"I'd say she's capable of putting skunks out of business."

Polski cleared his throat, then spat, and toed dust onto the medallion of spittle.

Father said, "How's the old asparagus?"

"Too damn much of it. It's this dry weather. It's shooting up in this heat. It's mostly all vipe. I've got more than I can store."

Mowah than I can stowah.

"Sell it, then," Father said.

"They'd like that."

"Everyone likes asparagus."

"The market's glutted," Polski said. He filled his jaws with spit and used a jet of it like a reply. "I wouldn't tell you what I'm getting for a pound. I'll be selling it by the ton next. Or giving it away."

"That's the idea."

"I'll be in the poorhouse."

"Sure you will," Father said.

"You too, Mr. Fox."

"I've been there. It's an education."

Polski said, "The cold store is chock-a-block. I want you to look at the fuses later on. I don't know how much they'll bring back today, but if it's more than a couple of truckloads I'm in trouble. I mean, we're all in trouble. Last year, I couldn't cut it fast enough. I was making a dollar a pound some weeks. This year it's vuining me. I'm buried in grass — "

He went on complaining this way and spitting and angrily nuthuning and sumthuning and kicking dust until finally, in what was almost a shout, he said, "I guess that glass of water must be good and cooked by now!"

Father said calmly, "Wouldn't be a bit surprised."

"Mind opening it up, Mr. Fox? I've got work to do. Show me whatever you're going to show me."

Father turned to me. "He wants us to open it up."

Polski was gobbling again. "You talk to him, Charlie. He won't listen to me."

"Don't plow with my heifer," Father said.

Drawing harsh bellyaching breaths, Polski said in a suffering voice, "For pity sake, Fox, will you see if this thing's emulsified!"

Father sucked on his cigar. He tasted it. He swallowed. He puffed and blew a smoke ring into the windless air. It was a blue hoop, it grew handles and pedals and a rider, it cycled away. We watched it slant toward the fields, pulling itself apart like a sinking comma from a sentence of skywriting, filling Father's pause with visible delay.

"Here we go," he said.

He unfastened the door and plucked open the metal flap, and without stooping or looking inside, he took out the water glass, flourishing his arm like a magician. He handed this to Polski, who bobbled it from one hand to the other, blowing on his fingers.

"Hot potato," said Polski. "I mean cold." He blew at his neat fingertips. "She ain't cooked. That's for damn sure."

Father said, "Go on, pour it."

Polski tried. He turned the glass upside-down and shook it. "She won't pour." He smacked the bottom. "She won't come out."

"Ice," Father said. The word allowed him to grin and hiss at the same time.

"Ain't that sumthun." Polski was impressed in spite of himself.

The Worm Tub was still glugging and squirting softly through its guts, the sooty smoke still rising. It looked comic and potbellied, like a fat boy with his coat open, puffing a stogie.

Polski warmed the glass in his hands, then jerked out the disk of ice and lobbed it into the rose bushes.

"I should have known it was an icebox," he said. "I should have expected it from you."

"But where's the juice?" Father said in a taunting way. "Where's the electrical cord?"

"Range oil you said."

Father said, "You mean, I made ice in a firebox?"

"So it seems."

"And range oil is dirt cheap. She's an energy saver."

Polski said, "I've got work to do. I'm buried in grass."

"Want to know how she operates?"

"Some other time."

"Stick your hand in that locker. Feel how cold she is. It'll take your fingerprints off. You've never seen anything like it."

"No," Polski said. "But I've heard of them. You've invented sumthun that was invented thirty years ago." Polski started to walk away. "It's like coming to me with a toaster. 'Look, no wires. And the toast pops up.' Fine, but it's still a toaster. And that's still an ice- box. You can't invent an invention."

"It's perfection!" Father said, and Polski winced at the word. *Puf- fection.* "I perfected it. Those other ones were small. Inefficient. Low-grade coolants. They didn't know a thing about coolants until yesterday afternoon. Gas operated. Couldn't make an ice cube if you shoveled snow into them. Ammonia water, lithium bromide. Brine. But this baby" — and he touched it tenderly — "this baby uses a new formula of high-expansion liquid, enriched ammonia, and hydrogen under pressure. She's a scale model. I'm planning to make a huge one. What do you think?"

Polski said, "That's another thing. It's a fire hazard."

"Not if it's ventilated." Father was explaining, not pleading. "Not if it's sealed right. I've got a patent pending on those valves, never mind the rest, never mind the original idea. This is poetry."

"And a big visk." Polski was not listening at all. "A big one would be a big fire hazard. Smoke all over everythun. It'd be a blast fur- nace. If she ever blew, we'd be picking up pieces in Pittsfield. Know where sumthun like this belongs? Some far-off place, where they test A-bombs, where it can't hurt anybody — that's where, far away. Not here, where it'll do damage and frighten the horses. You're visking your life with sumthun like that."

He set his face at Father.

"There's no risk," Father said. "I'm asking you to consider the principle of the thing. A firebox that makes ice. No noise! No juice!"

"Electricity's cheap."

Father smiled at him. "How old are you, Doctor?"

Spouting with his lower lip, Polski cracked a splinter of spit onto the gobbed ground.

"What about in ten years?" Father said. "What then? Or twenty years. Think of the future."

"I won't be here in the future."

"There's America's epitaph. That's criminal. That's monkey talk."

"You can have fires all over the place," Polski said. "I can do without them."

At this, Father sprayed him with laughter. "It's no more than a teeny flame," he said, as if explaining a candle to Jerry, halting his words, half mocking, half teaching. "A pilot light. Get down here and look at it. You can hardly see it. Why, you need more fire than that to light a ten-cent cigar!"

"I can see it's ingenious," Polski said, looking at his watch, which was buried in wrist hairs. "I always said you had veal Yankee ingenuity. But I haven't got the time for that now. In a couple of hours I'm going to be over my head in asparagus. And that's serious."

Father said, "You're not interested in her" — he drummed his finger stump on the lid — "that correct?"

"I'll bet you think it's a gold mine."

"Only a gold mine's a gold mine."

Polski was crunching back to the piazza. Turning, teetering on gravel, he said, "You're not going to get rich on that contraption, Mr. Fox."

Father let a laugh curl his tongue, but his eyes were darkened by the shadow of his visor. He watched Polski go. "If I ever wanted to get rich — which I don't — I'd raise me some asparagus."

"That wouldn't get you rich." Polski did not turn. "Get you an ulcer."

Father hooked his thumbs on his pockets and set his feet apart — a policeman's posture. "We'll leave you to your ulcer, Doctor."

"Don't go away mad, Mr. Fox," Polski called out from the piazza, but he still was not looking. "I told you, it's a fine contraption, but I've got no use for it."

He pulled himself inside his house and said his wife's name, "Shovel" — her name was Cheryl.

Father said, "I'd raise me some asparagus, and I'd hire fifty migrant savages to cut it. That's what I'd do. And, Charlie, you'd have yourself a new pair of sneakers and the best dungarees money could buy." He doused the flame on the Worm Tub, then looked upon it fondly, as if it were a living creature, and said, "That nearsighted turkey called it a contraption."

He smiled and his bright face widened.

"You couldn't ask for a better reaction than that."

I said, "But he didn't like it very much."

"That's an understatement." Father laughed, and shivering out each word, he said, "He positively hated it!" And snorted. "That's ignorant contempt — the stupidest kind of reaction. 'It's a big visk.' But I'm grateful for it. That's why I'm here. That's the sort of thing that gets me cooking on the front burners, Charlie. Just think what would have happened if he'd liked it. Yes, I would have been very worried. Ashamed of myself. I'd have gone back to bed."

Polski left his house by the back door. He climbed into his Jeep and revved it and threw it into reverse.

"Grind me a pound," Father said. "There he goes — old Dan Beavers. Give these wimps an L. L. Bean catalogue and they all think they're frontiersmen."

Now Polski was hurrying over road humps to the upper fields.

"That piece of diseased meat he calls a Jeep is a contraption," Father said, pointing with his cut-off finger. "But this is a creation. You can't buy this with money."

He was so wildly certain of himself there was nothing I could say, and he did not ask. So, without speaking, we loaded the Worm Tub onto the pickup truck.

I said, "It looks like a fat boy."

"This is a little baby. But when we make the big one, that's what we'll call it — Fat Boy." He peered at my poison ivy and added, "Gaw, don't you look awful."

We headed down the road. "Fat Boy," Father said again, and chewed the words like gum. As we drove, I sneaked a glance at him and saw he was smiling. What for?

4

FATHER WAS still smiling as he drove past the field where the scarecrow was, to a little road overgrown with grass that led to a stand of black pines. There was a sign nailed to a stump, NO TRESPASSING, and beyond it the house in the pines that was known locally as the Monkey House.

I had seen it from a distance. I had never wanted to go near enough to look inside. Anyway, as the sign said, it was forbidden. I was fairly sure that some of the savages lived in it, because I had heard radio music coming from it, and sometimes shouts.

Its clapboards had once been white, but they were discolored now and storm streaked. This wooden house looked as though it was turning back into a tree, but a petrified one. None of the windows had curtains, and some had no glass. The only protection it had was from the dark evergreens around it, and it wore some of their drippings of pitch. We drove up the pine-needle path and, closer, I saw that the screen door was slashed and a drainpipe had come loose and was nodding like a daffy weather vane. The gutter, emptying against the house, had left a mossy water stain on the boards. The whole house looked rotting and wrecked and haunted.

"Come on, Charlie. I want to show you something."

I could not refuse. We entered the house together. It smelled of sweat and boiled beans and old laundry and woodsmoke. The wallpaper was peeling off the walls in yellow crusts, and the paint itself was raised in places like blisters.

I said, "They call this place the Monkey House."

"Who calls it that?"

"Kids."

"I'd whale the tar out of them! Don't let me hear you calling it that."

There were no chairs or tables, and the first room was like all the others, mattresses flat on the floor and green army blankets on the mattresses, and little crumbled cardboard suitcases stacked in a corner with rags and socks. The other junk was cut-open sardine cans and bags of bread hunks and empty sour-smelling milk bottles. A transistor radio on a shelf was held together by tape. All through the house were more flat mattresses and more junk, old clothes and hairbrushes and dirty dishes. It was scratched and damaged like a monkey cage. But it wasn't a lively mess — it had a left-behind and dumped look, as if whoever lived there had gone away for good.

"Look at these poor people," Father said. He picked up a dingy blanket and jacked it against the wall. "Look what they own."

Angrily, he started stamping from room to room, as though searching for something he knew was not there. I followed him but kept my distance. He was swinging his arms and motioning violently at the grubby things.

"They come back here at night — this is where they sleep!"

He kicked a mattress.

"Look what they eat!"

Off his toe a sardine can took a frog hop into the hallway.

"Why, they don't even eat the damn asparagus they cut — "

And then I knew it was the savages.

"— though I wouldn't blame them for stealing it."

He clumped noisily to the back of the house and put his head out of the window and gave a sorrowful laugh.

"They take baths in a bucket. They do their business in that shack. Is that fair? I ask you! And you're wondering why they smell like goats and live in this slop and do unmentionable things that only funny bunnies do?"

I was wondering no such thing. What puzzled me was that Father, who always called them savages and warned me to keep clear of them, knew so much about them. He had driven straight to this house and marched right in, without a fear that one of the savages might be loitering in a closet or wrapped in a blanket, and might fling himself at Father and cut his throat.

I said, "I don't think we should be here."

"They welcome visitors, Charlie. It's an old custom of theirs — from the jungle. Be kind to strangers, they say, because you never know when you might be a stranger yourself — lost in the jungle, out of water, starving, or dying of bites. That's the law of the jungle — charity. It's not the cruelty people think it is. There's a lot to admire in these savages. Sure, they welcome visitors."

"But this isn't the jungle," I said.

"No," Father said, "because no jungle is as murderous and foul as this. They traded green trees for this ruin. It's pathetic. And it makes me mad, because they're going to end up being part of the problem."

He had started out of the house.

"I need air," he said.

But instead of driving away, he unloaded the Worm Tub, his icebox, from the back of the truck. He put it on skids and we towed it into the house. Father set it up in the back room, and lit its wick, and put a tray of water inside.

"They'll see this ice and go bananas," Father said.

"You mean, you're just going to give it to them? What about all the work you did on it?"

"You heard what that runt Polski said. He's got no use for it. And we've got a fridge of our own. These people will appreciate it. It won't cost them anything to run. They'll be able to store their food and save money. They can come back from the fields and have a nice cold drink. It'll take some of the curse off this ruin. That's what matters."

He was kneeling on the floor, adjusting the flame.

"Ice is civilization," he said.

He made an admiring cluck with his tongue and teeth.

I said, "They'll wonder who put this icebox here."

"They won't wonder."

We left the old house and its mattresses and mouse droppings, and I felt I had been introduced to wilderness. It lay very near our own orderly house and yet it was savage. It was apart from us. It was empty and alone. It had frightened me, not because it was dangerous but because it was so shabby and hopeless looking. It had begun badly and gotten worse, and it would stay that way, with all its trash — the tin cans and scribbled walls, the monkey scratches on the wood, the rusty wash bucket, the sink that didn't work, the litter of sweepings, the twisted shoes that made me think of twisted feet.

"It's scary," I said.

"I'm glad you feel that way," Father said.

He drove down the road, sighing as he shifted the gears.

"That's America," he said. "It's a disgrace. Breaks my heart."

I was glad, after this, to go into familiar fields and help Father with humdrum jobs. Sweating in the heat, I was itchy again from the poison-ivy rash, but I did not complain. And Father did not mention it. He was sure that I had been fooling in the bushes and the rash was my punishment.

Polski had ten greasy sheep and a small herd of cows. We repaired the transformer on the electric fence that separated them, and unblocked the drain at a drinking trough.

Father said, "There used to be scope in this country for a man like me."

Toward noon, we went up to the big windowless cold-storage building. Inside the thick walls it was cool. There was a stutter from the overloaded circuit, a stillness in the air, and the sharp aroma of asparagus ripening in the dark. The spears were taped into three-pound bundles. Because the tips are breakable and delicate, they are hard to store. These were packed as carefully on the shelves as if they were bunches of live ammunition. It was clear that Polski did not have much spare room, but Father said that it was amazing that Polski stored the asparagus at all, since the demand for it was so huge.

"And will you look at that!"

High up on a hook was a mink coat, probably Ma Polski's, put here in the cold to keep it away from the moths. It was dark gold, and every thin hair shone when Father turned his flashlight on it.

That got Father laughing about the state of the world, human beings sleeping on the floor of a broken-down house, and a ton of asparagus and a mink coat in a tidy air-conditioned room that cost a fortune to cool. It was a horrible joke, he said. The stupidity of people! And if the savages knew how they were being cheated, they would go over and cut Polski's head off and dance away in the fur coat.

He found a fuse had blown from the strain on the cooler. Replacing this fuse, he said "The runt was right. He hasn't got an inch of freeboard here, and they're still harvesting. Mark my words, that man is going to pay us a visit soon. He's going to have things on his mind. He won't remember what he said to me this morning. Some people never learn."

In the middle of the afternoon we were working at the roadside, digging out a culvert that had silted up after the March thaw. It was as hot as it had been the previous day, and Father had taken his shirt off. I steadied the wheelbarrow he was filling. Then I heard voices.

Three children on bicycles were coming down the road, returning home from school — Hatfield kids. I crouched down. I did not want them to see me here, laboring in my old clothes, and my father bent over like a ditchdigger. I was ashamed of Father, who didn't care what anyone thought. And I envied him for being so free, and hated myself for feeling ashamed. The children rang their bicycle bells and sang out to catch my attention and make me feel bad. They didn't know that Father had spent months inventing a fire-driven icebox and this morning had given it away, just like that, and picked up his spade like any farmhand.

I could not look at their faces. They called out again as they skidded past. After a while, I looked up and saw them wobbling on the country road.

Father was still hacking at the culvert — or rather, screwing out the silt with a spade of his own invention that looked like a large shoetree.

He said, "Don't feel badly. You've seen some amazing things today, Charlie. And what have those pipsqueaks been doing? Sniffing glue in the schoolyard, boasting about their toys, looking at pictures, raising hell. Watching TV — that's all they do in school. Ruin their eyesight. You don't need that."

5

POLSKI CAME after supper, just as Father had predicted. The twins and Jerry were already in bed, and Mother was swabbing my rash with lotion. Father was describing Ma Polski's fur coat hung in the cold store.

"All that vanity and expense," he said. "And the foolish woman is more conspicuously ugly when she's wearing it! With those teeth and that coat she looks like a demented woodchuck, who'd gnaw your leg off if you looked at her crosseyed. Imagine murdering and skinning twenty pretty animals, so that an unhappy woman — "

Hearing Polski's Jeep clatter into the driveway, Father stood up and said, "Time to hit the hay, Charlie."

Mother took me upstairs, and inside my bedroom she said, "I've been worrying about you the whole day. Why do you look so sad?"

I said, "I think something is going to happen to us."

"What do you mean?"

"Something terrible."

Mother said, "When you're young, the world looks impossible. It seems big and strange, and even threatening. If you think about it too much, you start to worry."

"But Dad's not young."

Mother stared at me.

I said, "And he's worried."

"No," Mother said. "But he's got a lot on his mind just now. I've seen him like this before — brooding. It gives him wonderful schemes. Someday soon, he'll tell us what his new invention is."

"Something *is* going to happen to us," I said.

"Something good," Mother said. "Now go to sleep, darling."

After she turned the light out, I wanted to pray. I shut my eyes tight, but nothing would come. I did not know how. I thought *Please,* but that was all the prayer I could manage. And the voices down below, the thump of them, made my heart pound. I went to the door and, creeping out to the landing at the top of the stairs, heard Father's hoots.

"You've got me confused, Doc! I don't know whether I'm deaf or blind! This very morning I showed you a working model of a dirt-cheap freezing plant. You turned your back on it and said you had to water your tomatoes. Now here you are, probably missing your favorite TV show, asking me — "

"I told you I was interested," Polski said in a stricken voice.

"I must be deaf as a post," Father said, "because I didn't hear a thing."

"And I'm interested now."

Father said, "Your interest and ten cents wouldn't get me a cold cup of coffee."

I peeked through the railing. Father was goose-stepping up and down the parlor. Polski had found a low stool. He sat on it the way a girl sits on a toilet, with his knees together and his face forward.

Polski said, "The cold store is full after today's cut. What I want to know is, what am I going to do with what they cut tomorrow and the day after?"

Father said, "You can always go on blowing fuses. It'll help pass the time."

"There must be some way of vigging up the barn. I mean, insulating her and fixing up a cooler where the hay is. I could hire the carpenters, but the vefrigeration angle is the problem. If you handled it, that would see us through the harvest."

"I don't get it. This morning I showed you a refrigeration device that was perfection, and all you did was ride off in your jalopy. What was the word you used? Oh, yes, you called it a contraption. I was scratching my head! I didn't see a contraption anywhere! Doctor," Father said grandly, "I am still scratching my head."

"That icebox was a fine idea," Polski said. "But I'm looking for something more down-to-earth. The cold store you made me last year was okay for last year's crop. But this year we've got ourselves a bumper harvest, and we've got to act accordingly. Now don't think I'm looking for miracle vemedies — "

"Insulating a barn is no problem," Father said. "They can slap on an interior wall and blow rock wool through with hose pipes. But there's a lot of airspace in that barn. What? Ten thousand cubic feet — maybe more? You'd have to have multiple-level cooling to get an even temperature, otherwise you'd be freezing some and roasting the rest. Blowers, thermostats, coils. You're talking about a mile of copper pipe, not to mention the wiring and electricals."

"See, you do understand the problem."

"You wouldn't even look at my Worm Tub — that icebox I showed you this morning."

"It's too small."

"A scale model is always small."

"I need something a hundred times bigger." *Sumthun:* Polski had started to gobble.

"You don't understand its application."

"I don't want fires."

"You'll go broke paying electricity bills. Ten thousand cubic feet. How many kilowatts? Cost a fortune." And he repeated, "A *fotchin!*"

"Stop trying to save me money, Mr. Fox."

"It's not the money, it's the wasteful attitude I object to. Doctor, it's sending this country down the tubes."

"I'm not running this country" — *runnun* — "and this is nothing to jaw about. I realize it's short notice, but I need more cold-storage space and I'm counting on you to provide it."

"I keep asking myself — I'm thinking out loud, you understand — I keep asking myself, what's the point?"

"The point is," Polski said, "there's too damn much asparagus this year. That's the point."

"Are you cutting it too fast, or selling it too slow?"

"I'm not selling it at all — other people are. That's why the price is down."

"Listen, are you in the storing business or the selling business? I'm asking, because I don't know about these things. I'm a handyman, not an economist."

Still hunched on the stool, Polski turned his pinched face toward Father and said in a sour defiant voice, "I'll sell when the price goes up — not before. In the meantime, every spear I cut goes into cold storage."

Father said, "That's the lousiest rottenest thing I've ever heard."

"It's business."

"Then it's dishonest business. You're creating a shortage of asparagus — although there is no shortage. So the price will go up — although the price is pretty fair. Well, it's not as bad as sticking up a bank, but it's bad enough. I'd say it was about on a level with robbing poor boxes." Father was now standing over Polski and smiling horribly. "And what do you get for it? A few bucks, a new pair of dungarees, a tin wristwatch that lights up in the dark — maybe a jalopy or two. You think it's worth it?"

"Every farmer worth the name watches the market," Polski said, hugging his knees together.

"There's watching, and there's tampering," Father said. And he became at once ferociously friendly. "Make yourself comfortable, Doctor. You don't have to squash yourself on that. The chair behind you has hydraulics."

"I'm comfortable where I am, thank you."

"Reason I ask is, you're sitting on my foot massager."

Polski jumped to his feet.

Picking up the boot-shaped stool, Father said, "People neglect their feet something awful. See this slot? You just stick your foot in here and wiggle your toes. That gets the mechanical fingers going inside. Funnily enough, it works. Want to do your tired old feet a big favor?"

Polski said no and went to the chair, which was like a dentist's chair. He sat on it almost daintily, but against his will the chair tilted and embraced him, and lifted his legs off the floor, and swung him toward Father.

"Hydraulics," Father said.

Doggedly, his jaw out as if he were having a tooth pulled, Polski said, "I've got a farm to vun and sumthun like twenty tons of produce to sell. I have to do it the best way I can."

"Simple. Sell it and clear out room for more. You make up in volume what you lose in price, and you still come out ahead of the game. That's sounder than strangling the market altogether. But no, you're not interested in that, because you're riding high — using slave labor. Profit? I didn't plumb that chair and make that foot massager so that I could retire on fifty grand a year. I did it because of lumbago and sore feet, and if I'm able to ease someone else's pain, fine. That's the way I'm made. But you want to bluff the market and make a killing. That ain't business — it's robbery."

"I didn't come up here to discuss the ethics of farming, Mr. Fox. I've got a problem and you seem to have the solution, so will you please stop this nonsense?"

Polski had turned green. He was suffering.

Father said, "You were cool to my cooler."

"It doesn't seem practical."

"If you think that, you're out of touch with reality. It's the most practical invention in the world. And it'll run on anything — not only range oil, but methane gas bubbled out of a solution of raw chicken shit, and there's plenty of that around here. Furthermore, although there's a little more plumbing in it, there's absolutely no wiring."

"How long would it take to set up?"

"A jiffy. You said money wasn't a problem."

"A reasonable amount."

"Don't back away," Father said.

"You'd be willing to install a firebox refrigerator, would you? For the overspill?"

Father hesitated before he replied. I had never seen him hesitate before. I guessed he was doing a calculation.

He said, "I sure am tempted to try."

"This is your chance, Fox. You'd be doing both of us a favor."

Father looked up at the parlor ceiling and said, "I see a vast cooling plant and cold store. It's on seven or eight levels, the size of two barns and then some, with your catwalks inside and your reflectors and insulation outside. Looks like a cathedral, with a chimney for a steeple. What's that bulge in the ground? That's your power unit, the main hardware, the worm tubs, the tanks of coolant, the heat supply. All your pipes and tanks are underground, sheathed in lead, in case of nuclear war, accidents, and acts of God. Your chimney has baffles and coils to conserve heat and redirect it back to the main supply, the fire itself — recycling the heat, so to speak. But there's waste heat — there always is — and that's why we have ducts built into the chimney. Now this is blown across a grid, and that's where your incubators come in. That's your battery in both senses — your egg hatchery, your heated runs for young chicks and chickens that are going to supply you with fuel in time to come. Methane gas. Nothing wasted. You've got your refrigeration.

You've got your ice. You've got your heat. Sell the eggs you don't need and have the rest for breakfast. Cool down your vegetables. Use your chicken shit for methane. It's a perpetual-motion machine. Run a duct to your house and you're air-conditioned — cool in summer, warm in winter. Cheap, simple to operate, no waste, foolproof, and profitable. There's only one thing."

Polski had crept out of the hydraulic chair like a raccoon out of an unsprung trap. He was watching Father with a gentle hopeful expression, smiling sadly as Father described this vision of the cooling plant. In an uncertain voice, and clearing his throat, Polski said, "What's that?"

"I don't want to do you a favor. You just want this thing to cheat people and put up prices and starve the market."

I thought Mr. Polski was going to cry.

"You can't make me sell that asparagus." Polski glanced around, as if looking for a place to spit, and still puckered he said, "I only wish I knew what to do with it."

"Eat it."

"You're talking yourself out of a job, Mr. Fox."

"It's better than you talking me into one, seeing as what the job is."

Polski said, "Keep talking. I might have to let you go."

"Careful now." Father crossed the room, fished a cigar out of his humidor, and took a long time lighting it. When it was smoking he stared at it and said, "I'll go where I'm appreciated."

Polski had turned away from Father and now he was talking to his own two feet. He said, "I don't want to make things tough for you."

"People who say that always mean the opposite. That sounds like a threat."

"Take it any way you like."

"Mother!" Father called out. His shout made Polski jump. "He just threatened me!"

Mother, wherever she was, did not reply.

Polski said, "I knew it was a mistake to come over here." He shuffled slowly to the door. I felt sorry for Polski just then, looking so small, with Father trumpeting cigar smoke at him and the little man's wrinkles of defeat on the shoulders of his jacket, and his tiny head going through the door. I had wanted Father to make peace with Polski, and for things to continue as before. Now, I knew, something had to happen.

I went back to my room on all fours, wondering what.

The next thing I heard was Polski starting his Jeep, and Father muttering "Grind me a pound," and then very clearly, like a moo in a stall, Mother's voice.

"You fool."

"I'm happy, Mother."

"What do you want?"

"Elbow room. I just realized it."

"Please, Allie — "

And Father said, "I never wanted this. I'm sick of everyone pretending to be old Dan Beavers in his L. L. Bean moccasins, and his Dubbelwares, and his Japanese bucksaw — all these fake frontiersmen with their chuck wagons full of Twinkies and Wonderbread and aerosol cheese spread. Get out the Duraflame log and the plastic cracker barrel, Dan, and let's talk self-sufficiency!"

"You're talking nonsense."

"Listen," Father said, but I heard nothing more.

6

WHEN FATHER said, the next day, "We're going shopping," I was
sure we were going to the dump. We seldom went store shopping.
There was little need — we grew practically all our own food. Hard
work kept us at Tiny Polski's, and there was a danger in being in
stores during the day — we might be collared by policemen or truant officers for playing hooky from school. "Then you'll be in
school," Father said, "and I'll be in its rough equivalent — jail.
What have we done to deserve that punishment?" Secretly, I wanted
to go to school. I felt like an old man or a freak when I saw other
children. And secretly, I preferred factory-made cakes, like Devil
Dogs and Twinkies, to Mother's banana bread. Father said store-
bought cakes were junk and poison, but I guessed that his real objection was that the few times he caught me sneak-eating, I had to
tell him that I paid for the food with money that Polski had given
me for doing odd jobs. And Polski told me that Father was peculiar,
which was another secret to keep.We bought salt, brown flour, fruit,
shoelaces, and other small things in Hatfield or Florence, but shopping usually meant a trip to the dumps and junkyards around
Northampton, where we helped Father pick through the poisonous
piles of trash for the wire and metal he used in his inventions.

There were seagulls at the dump. They were fat, filthy squawkers,
and they roosted on the plastic rubbish bags and tried to tear them
open. They chased each other, and they fought for scraps, and they
rioted when the garbage truck came. Father hated them. He called
them scavengers. They squawked, and he squawked back at them.

But struggling up the loose hills of bags and crates, with a pitchfork in his hand, and screaming at the birds that hopped around him and nagged over his head, it sometimes seemed as if Father and these lazy fearless gulls were fighting for the same scraps.

"Now there's a perfectly good set of wheels," Father would say, scaring the gulls and forking an old baby carriage out of the reeks and shaking off the orange peels. Other people took things to the dump — Father hoicked stuff out and carried it away. "Some jackass junked that."

But today, a normal working day, we raced past the greenhouses and rose gardens in Hadley, and hurried through Northampton, and sped toward the pike. Mother was in the cab with Father, and I crouched in the back with the twins and Jerry.

"I'm going to look at ten-speed bikes," Jerry said.

Clover said, "We can buy ice cream," and April said, "I want chocolate."

I said, "Dad won't let you. And we're not going shopping — this isn't the way."

"It is," Jerry said. "It's Dad's short cut."

No — we were far from Northampton, in the country. We came to the Connecticut River and followed it. It was wide and greasy and less blue than it was near Hatfield. There were brick buildings on the far side, and soon the city of Springfield. We crossed the bridge and had to hold to the sides of the pickup truck because of the strong mid-river wind. In the river were bits of plastic foam, gone yellow like slabs of ham fat.

We had never shopped in Springfield before. People on the sidewalks seemed to know this. They stared at us standing in the back of the pickup and holding to the roof of the cab. We kept going until we came to a shopping plaza, where we parked — people still staring. Father got out and told us to follow him and stay together. He was in a good mood, but as soon as we entered the K-Mart store he started muttering and cursing.

Mother said, "Are you sure about the hats?"

"You kidding? It's a hundred in the shade. They'll get sunstroke if their heads aren't covered."

We tried on fishermen's ventilated hats and sun hats and sailor hats. The prices infuriated Father. He said, "Baseball hats are good enough," and bought us those.

Wearing these hats, we trailed after him like ducklings in a file. Here, in this one store, they sold everything — popcorn, rubber tires, rifles, toasters, coats, books, motor oil, palm trees in pots, ladders, and writing paper. Father picked up an electric toaster.

"Look at it. Isn't even earthed right. You'd electrocute yourself before you got any toast. You'd be toasted yourself on that faulty wiring — "

He was talking loudly and attracting attention. "Kyanize!" he said. "Congoleum!" I had the idea that the people who were staring at us knew we seldom went out shopping. Father was embarrassing in public. He took no notice of strangers. A few days ago in Northampton Hardware it was, "Are you working for the Japanese?" and I had wanted to hide my head in shame. Today he was even jumpier.

"Call this a can opener?" he was saying. "You'd lose a finger with that, or gash yourself and bleed to death. That's a lethal weapon, Mother!"

We trooped to the Camping and Outdoor Department. A man in shirtsleeves approached us. He had a smooth face and flat hair and did not look like a camper, but he said hello to all of us and winked at the twins and remarked, as everyone did, on their alikeness.

"What can I do for you today?" he asked, and nodded, giving me a better look at his hair. It was combed up from beside one ear and was stuck down in neatly arranged strands across the top of his head, making you look not at the hair but at the baldness between.

Father said he wanted to look at some canteens.

Jerry shaped the word *camping* with his lips, but I mocked him by wrinkling my nose.

The man handed one over. Father put his thumbs on it and said it was so flimsy he could squash it flat if he wanted to. He looked at it closely and laughed out loud.

" 'Made in Taiwan' — a lot they know about canteens. They lost the war."

"It's only a dollar forty-nine," the man said.

"It's not worth a nickel," Father said. "Anyway, I'm looking for something bigger."

"How about these water bags?" The man dangled one by its nozzle.

"I could make one of those myself out of a piece of canvas and a needle and thread. Where's this turkey from? Korea! See, that's it — they've got sweatshops and slave labor in Korea and Taiwan. Little coolies make these. Up at dawn, work all day, never get any fresh air. Children make these things. They're chained to the machines — feet hardly reach the pedals."

He was lecturing us, but the man was listening and frowning.

"They're so undernourished they can hardly see straight. Trachoma, rickets. They don't know what they're making. Might as well be bath mats. That's why we went to war in South Korea, to fight for labor-intensive industries, which means skinny kids punching out water bags and making tin cups for us. Don't get heartbroken. That's progress. That's the point of Orientals. Everybody's got to have coolies, right?"

The water bag now looked like a wicked thing in the man's hands. The man put it away and patted his hair, and we stood there silently — Mother, the twins, Jerry, and me — while Father grumped. I had put my shirt collar up to hide my poison ivy.

"What's next on the list?"

Mother said, "Sleeping bags."

"On the rack," the man said.

Father stepped over to them. "Not even waterproof. A lot of good they'd be in a monsoon."

"They're for use in a tent situation," the man said.

"What about a rain situation? Where's this thing from? The Gobi Desert, Mongolia, someplace like that?"

"Hong Kong," the man said.

"I wasn't far off!" Father said, twitching with satisfaction. "They do a lot of camping in Hong Kong. You can tell. Look at the stitches — they'd fall apart in two days. You'd be better off with a plain old blanket."

"Blankets are in Household."

"And where are *they* made — Afghanistan?"

"I wouldn't know, sir."

Father said, "What's wrong with this country?"

"It's better than some places I could name."

"And a damn sight worse than some others," Father said. "We could make this stuff in Chicopee and have full employment. Why don't we? I don't like the idea of us forcing skinny Oriental kids to make junk for us."

"No one is being forced," the man said.

"Ever been to South Korea?"

"No," the man said, and he took on the hunted expression that people did when Father spoke to them. It was the one Polski had had on his face last night.

"Then you don't know what you're talking about, do you?" Father said. "Let me see some knapsacks. If they're from Japan, you can keep them."

"These are Chinese — People's Republic. You wouldn't be interested."

"Give us here," Father said, and holding the little green knapsack like a rag he turned to Clover. "A few years ago, we were practically at war with the People's Republic. Red Chinese, we called them. Reds, slants, gooks. Ask anyone. Now they're selling us knapsacks — probably for the next war. What's the catch? They're third-rate knapsacks, they wouldn't hold sandwiches. You think we're going to win that war against the Chinese?"

Clover was five years old. She listened to Father, and she scratched her belly with two fingers.

"Muffin, I don't care what you think — we're not going to win that war."

The salesman had started to grin.

Father saw him and said, "You won't be smiling then, my friend. The next war's going to be fought right here, as sure as anything —"

It was what he had said in the winter, those same words, although I thought he had only been ranting. Today he was in the same mood. I almost expected him to tell the salesman, "They'll get me first — they always kill the smart ones first."

He pushed the knapsack aside. "Do you sell anything like compasses, or have I come to the wrong place?"

"I do a complete range of compasses," the man said. He smoothed the knapsack with the flat of his hand and folded it like laundry, giving a little moan as he put it away. He placed a box on the counter. "This is one of my better ones," he said, taking out a compass. "It's got all the features of my more expensive models, but it's only two and a quarter."

"Must be a Chinese compass," Father said. "It's permanently pointing east."

"One of the features is a stabilizing control. When you release it, like so" — he flicked a catch on the case — "the needle swings free. See, that's north, over there by Automotive. As a matter of fact, this compass is made right here in Massachusetts."

"Then wrap it up," Father said. "You just made yourself a sale." He put his arm around Mother. "What's the list look like?"

"Cotton cloth, needles and thread, mosquito netting — "

"Fabrics," the man said. "Next aisle. Have a nice day."

Father said, "We'd be better off in the dump," as we walked away. In the next aisle, he took hold of a length of material that looked like a bridal veil and said, "That's the stuff."

The saleslady said, "Seventy-nine a yard," and snapped her scissors. She was old and trembling, and the way she scissored the air made her seem evil.

"I'll take it."

"How many yards?" Snip-snip. She was impatient. She had light webs of hair on her face and almost a moustache.

"Give us the whole bolt," Father said. "And if you really want to make yourself useful," he added, grabbing a fistful of Jerry's hair, "give this kid a haircut. Put him out of his misery."

But the old lady did not smile, because she had to unroll the complete bolt of mosquito netting in order to measure it and arrive at a price.

We set off in search of other items. I had never seen my parents buy so much in one morning, not even at Christmastime. We left K-Mart and went to Sears and the Army-Navy Store. We bought flashlights and American-made canteens, knapsacks, hunting knives, rubberized sleeping bags, and new shoes for all of us. Spending money made Father cross. He haggled with the salespeople and complained he was being robbed. "I can afford to be robbed," he said. "But what about the poor wimps who can't afford it?" I had no idea why he was buying these things, and it was embarrassing to hear him argue. Even Mother was getting fussed.

At the drugstore, filling a wire basket with things like gauze and ointment ("For our first-aid kit"), he broke off comparing the prices of aspirin and went to the rack of magazines for a copy of *Scientific American*. He was annoyed that it was stacked with girlie magazines, and said, "That's an insult."

"Look," he said, gesturing to the rack, "half of it's hard-core porn.

There are married men who haven't seen things like this. It's news to medical students! Can you believe this? Kids come in for Tootsie Rolls and this is what they see. But ask any grade-school teacher and he'll tell you it's just what the doctor ordered. Charlie, what are you staring at?"

I was looking at a naked kneeling woman on a magazine cover, her smooth shiny sticking-out bum like a prize pear.

"You're basically ogling a nudie," he said, before I could reply. "But get your last look — get your last look. Mother, people bury themselves in this trash and pretend nothing's wrong. It makes me want to throw up. It runs me mad."

Mother said, "I suppose you want them to ban it."

"Not ban it. I believe in freedom of expression. But must we have it right here with the comics and the Tootsie Rolls? It offends me! Anyway, why not ban it or burn it? It's junk, it belittles the human body, it portrays people as pieces of meat. Yes, get rid of it, and the comic books, too — it's all harmful. How's business?"

He was now at the check-out counter, speaking to the lady cashier.

"Just fine," she said. "Can't complain."

"I'm not surprised," Father said. "You must do a land-office business in pornography. They say the retail porn trade is the new growth industry — that, and crapsheets. Must be quite a satisfaction to rake in the bucks that way — "

"I just work here," the lady said, and punched the cash register.

"Sure you do," Father said. "And why shouldn't you sell it? It's a free country. You don't believe in censorship. You read a book once. It was green, right? Or was it blue?"

Hunted, that was how she looked. Like a nervous rabbit nibbling the smell of a gun barrel.

Father paid her for the first-aid equipment and said, "You forgot to say, 'Have a nice day.' "

Outside, Mother said, "You never give up, do you?"

"Mother, this country's gone to the dogs. No one cares, and that's the worst of it. It's the attitude of people. 'I just work here' — did you hear her? Selling junk, buying junk, eating junk — "

"We want some ice cream," Clover said.

"Hear that? Junk-hungry — our own kids. We're to blame! All right, you kids come with me."

He took us to the A & P supermarket, and just inside, at the fruit section, he picked up a bunch of bananas. "Two dollars!" he said. He did the same with a pair of grapefruits wrapped in cellophane. "Ninety-five cents!" And a pineapple. "Three dollars!" And some oranges. "Thirty-nine cents each!" He sounded like an auctioneer as he made his way down the fresh-fruit counter, yelling the prices.

"Aren't we going to buy anything?" I said, as we left empty-handed.

"Nope. I just want you to remember those prices. Three dollars for a pineapple. I'd rather eat worms. You can eat earthworms, you know. They're all protein."

He got into the cab of the pickup with Mother, and we climbed into the back. I could hear his voice vibrating on the rear window as we drove through Springfield. He was still talking when we stopped on the road for gas. We were in sight of the river — it was full and swift, and budding trees overhung it. But it was as gray as bath-water, and rippling like waves in the factory suds were dead white-bellied fish.

The cab door slammed. "A buck ten a gallon," Father was saying to the bewildered man at the pump. The man had a wet wasp in each nostril, and a tag on his shirt said *Fred.* "It's doubled in price in a year. So that's two-twenty next year and probably five the year after that — if we're lucky. That's beautiful. Know what a barrel of crude oil costs to produce? Fifteen dollars — that's all. How many gallons to a barrel? Thirty-five? Forty? You figure it out. Oh, I forgot, you just work here."

"Don't blame me — blame the president," the man said, and went on jerking gas into our gas tank.

Father said, "Fred, I don't blame the president. He's doing the best he can. I blame the oil companies, the car industry, big business. Israelis. Palestinians — know what they really are? Philistines. Same word, look it up. And Fred, I blame myself for not devising a cheaper method of extracting oil from shale. We've got trillions of tons of shale deposits in this country."

"No choice," said Fred, and snorted the wasps into his nose. "We'll just have to go on paying."

"I've got a choice in the matter," Father said. "I'm not going to pay anymore."

Fred said, "That'll be eight dollars and forty cents."

For a moment, I thought Father was going to refuse to pay, but he took out his billfold and counted the money into Fred's dirty hand, while we watched from the back of the pickup.

"No, sir, I am not going to pay anymore," Father said. "Let me ask you a question. Do you ever wonder, seeing what things are like now, what's going to happen later on?"

"Sometimes. Look, I'm pretty busy." He squinted, hunched his shoulders, and backed away. Hunted.

"I ask myself that all the time. And I say to myself, 'It can't go on like this. A dollar's worth twenty cents.'"

"It's worse in New Jersey," Fred said. "I've got a cousin down there. They've had rationing since January."

"There's a whole world out there!" Father cried, pointing with his cut-off finger.

The man stepped farther back, frightened by the finger.

"Part of the world is still empty," Father said. "Most of it is still uninhabited. You eat asparagus?"

"Excuse me?"

"Know why asparagus is so expensive — all vegetables, for that matter? Because the farmers hoard their produce until the prices rise. Then they put it on the market. When they know they've got you, the consumer, over a barrel. They could sell it for half the price and still get rich. You didn't know that, did you? The guys who cut it get a dollar an hour, nonunion labor — just savages and spear chuckers who hoick it out of the ground. It's no trouble to grow — God does most of the work. Next time you eat some asparagus, you remember what I just told you. Oil companies do the same thing — hoard their product until the price goes up. I don't want any part of it. Wheat? Cereals? Grains? We give it away to the Russians to keep the domestic prices up, when we could just as easily be making it into moonshine or gasohol. In the meantime, pay, pay, and get the little Koreans to make us sleeping bags, and outfit the army with Chinese knapsacks — no one asks where — "

At the mention of Chinese knapsacks, Fred said, "Hey, I've got some customers waiting."

"Don't let me hold you up, Fred." Father shook him by the hand. "Just remember what I told you."

On the road, Father put his head out of the window and said, "Did I set him straight? You bet I did!"

There were buds on some trees and tiny pale leaves on others, and a sweet sigh of spring was in the air. Cows stood in some pastures as still as figurines, and sloping down to the road there were small rounded apple trees foaming with white blossoms. I could tell from the way Father was driving that he was still angry, but in all this prettiness — the delicate trees in the mild flower-scented air, and the sun on the meadows — I could not understand what was wrong, or why Father had been shouting. He cut down a back road just before we reached Northampton. Here were some clusters of yellow wild-flowers and the bright blood-color of a cardinal, like a heart beating inside a bush's ribs.

Jerry said, "When we go camping, I'll have my own tent and you won't be allowed in."

"Dad didn't buy any tents," I said.

"I'll make a lean-to," he said. "I won't let you in."

Clover said, "I'm going camping, too."

"You won't like camping," Jerry said. "You'll cry. So will April."

"I don't think we're going camping," I said.

"Then what's all this stuff for?" Jerry said. We were crouched in the back of the pickup with the paper bags and boxes. "Where *are* we going?"

"Just away from here." After I said it I believed it.

April said, "I like it here. I don't want to go away. The summer's my favorite."

"Charlie doesn't know anything," Jerry said. "He's a thicko. That's why he has poison ivy."

Clover said, "I saw him scratching it."

"It's like a disease," April said. "Get away from me — I don't want to catch your disease!"

I hated having to sit there with those silly ignorant children, and it seemed to me as if, with Father driving madly past these beautiful hills and fields and the orchards that were so new with blossoms they had not lost a single petal, we were going to smash into a brick wall. I expected something sudden and painful, because everything in these last few days had been unusual. The kids did not know that, but I had been with Father, and overheard him, and I had seen things that had not fitted with what I knew. Even familiar things, like that scarecrow — it had been upraised like a demon and struck terror into me.

I said, "Something is going to happen to us."

"That makes me feel funny," Clover said.

I did not say what had occurred to me while Father was shopping in Springfield — Father was a disappointed man. He was angry and disgusted. But if he was aiming to do something drastic, he would take care of us. We were always part of his plans.

When we got to the town of Florence, he pulled to the side of the road and called out, "Charlie, you come with me. The rest of you stay put."

We had been here a little over a month ago, buying seeds. Today we went back to the same seed store. It was dry and spidery in the store. It smelled of burlap bags. And the dust from the seeds and husks stung my rash and made it itch.

"You again." It was a voice from behind a row of fat sacks. The man came out spanking dust from his apron. He had deep creases in his face, and his gaze went straight to my poison ivy.

"Mr. Sullivan," Father said, handing the man a piece of paper, "I need fifty pounds each of these. Hybrids, the highest-yield varieties you have, and if they're treated for mildew so much the better. I want them sealed in waterproof bags, the heavy-duty kind. I need them today. I mean, right now."

"You're all business, Mr. Fox." The man took a pair of glasses out of his apron pocket, blew on the lenses, and, pulling them over his ears, examined the piece of paper. "I can manage this." He looked over the tops of his lenses at Father. "But you and Polski have some work ahead of you if you're planning to get all this seed in the ground. It's a little late, ain't it?"

Father said, "It's winter in Australia. They're harvesting pumpkins in Mozambique, and they're raking leaves in Patagonia. In China, they're just putting their pajamas on."

"I didn't realize Chinamen wore pajamas."

"They don't wear anything else," Father said. "And in Honduras they're still plowing."

"What's that?"

But Father ignored him. He was choosing envelopes from a rack of flower seeds that said BURPEE. "Morning-glories," he said. "They love sunshine, and they'll remind me of Dogtown."

What with the sacks of seeds and the bags and boxes of camping equipment, there was not much room for us kids in the back of the pickup truck. I dreaded all the lugging we would have to do, but when we got home, Father said, "Leave everything just where it is. I'll put a tarp over it in case it rains."

"Dad, are we going somewhere?" Clover asked.

"We sure are, Muffin."

"Camping?" Jerry asked.

"Sort of."

"Then how come we aren't packing our bags?" April asked.

"Simply because you're not packing your bags it doesn't mean you're not going anywhere. Ever hear of traveling light? Ever hear of dropping everything and clearing out?"

I was in the kitchen with Mother, listening to this. I said, "Ma, what's he talking about? Where are we going?"

She came over to me and pressed my head against the bib of her apron. She said, "Poor Charlie. When you've got something on your mind, you look like a little old man. Don't worry, everything's going to be all right."

"Where?" I asked again.

"Dad will tell us, when he's ready," she said.

She had no idea! She knew as little as we did. I felt very close to her at that moment, and there was a solution of love and sadness in my blood. But there was more, because she was perfectly calm. Her loyalty to Father gave me strength. Though it did not take away any of my sadness, her belief made me believe and helped me share her patience. And yet I pitied her, because I pitied myself for not knowing more than I did.

In the afternoon, Father seemed relaxed. He made no move to work. He spent two hours on the telephone, a very rare thing — not his heckling, but the amount of time. "I'm speaking from Hatfield, Massachusetts!" he said into the phone, as if he were calling for help. Normally, we would have been out in the truck, making the rounds of the farm, but this afternoon we were free. He told us to go play on our bicycles, and when he was finished on the phone ("We're in luck!") he went into his workshop and scooped up his tools, whistling the entire time.

Around four o'clock, he went into the house. He came out a little while later with an envelope in his hand. He was still whistling. He told me to take it over to Polski.

Polski, wearing rubber mitts, was hosing his Jeep when I arrived.

"Your vash is lookun better," he said. "What have you got for me?"

I handed him the letter. He shut off the hose and said, "I was going to give you a quarter for doing the Jeep, but I couldn't see hide nor hair of you this morning." He ripped open the envelope and held the letter at arm's length to read it. On it were the bold loops of Father's beautiful handwriting — a short message. It hurt me that by not allowing me to go to school, Father was preventing me from learning to write like this. I knew that he had learned this elegant script at school, and seeing it made me feel weak and stupid.

Polski had started to spit and sigh. He said, "I'll be goddamned" and "So that's how it is, is it?"

His face was as gray as old meat. I wanted to go away, but he said, "Charlie, come on over here. I've got something to say to you. Want a cookie? How about a nice glass of milk?"

I said fine, though I would rather have had the quarter for washing the Jeep, or just permission to go away, because Polski's friendliness, like Father's, always included a little lecture. We went up to the piazza. He sat me down in the glider and said, "Be vight back." I looked across the asparagus fields and saw in the goldy afternoon light the river and the trees. Our own house sat small and solemn on its rectangle of garden. It had a gold roof and its piazza roof was an eyebrow and its paint was as white as salt.

Polski came out with a glass of milk and a plate of chocolate-chip cookies. I drank some milk and took a cookie.

"Have another one," he said. "Have as many as you like."

Then I knew it was going to be a long lecture.

He watched me eat two cookies. He seemed to be smiling at the way I crunched them, and I sensed that the crunch noise was coming out of my ears.

He said, "I've been meaning to tell you sumthun, Charlie." He stopped and sat closer to me on the glider — so close I had to put the glass of milk down. He said, "Your father thinks I'm a fool."

I did not say anything. What he said was half true, and the whole truth was worse.

He nodded at my silence, taking it for a yes, and fixed his mouth in a smile-like shape of warning and said, "Long before you were born, they used to hang convicted murderers in Massachusetts. It sounds horrible, but most of them deserved it. There was a man around here, name of Mooney — Spider Mooney, they called him, and I suppose you can guess why — "

I could not imagine why, though the picture I now had in my mind was a hairy man on all fours, with black popping eyes. Polski was still talking.

"— lived with his father. Never went to school. Wasn't much older than you when he started stealun, first little things at the five-and-dime, then bigger things. He made a habit of it. Turned into a vobber. Did I say that his father was a bit touched in the head? Well, he was. Completely hoopy. Shell-shocked, people said. If you screamed at him, or made a loud noise, he fell down. Just dropped like a brick. And he was full of crazy ideas. Some father, eh? When Spider Mooney was about twenty years old, he killed a man. Not just killed, but cut his throat with a straight vazor. Nearly took the fella's head off — colored fella — and it was only hangun by a little flap of skin. The police caught him easy — they knew where to go. His father's house, where else? Mooney was condemned to die. By hangun."

Polski suddenly looked up and said, "That might be some vain headun our way."

He was perfectly still, looking into space for a whole minute, before he picked up the story. Now he was staring at our house, and the house seemed to stare right back at him.

"On the day of the hangun, they tied Mooney's hands and led him out to the prison yard. This was the old Charles Street Prison in Boston. It was six o'clock in the mornun. You know how vuined you feel at six A.M.? Well, that's how Mooney felt, and it was worse because he knew that in a few minutes he was going to be swingun on the vope. They marched him across to the gallows. He stopped at the bottom on the stairs and said, 'I want to say sumthun to my father.' "

"His father was there?"

"Yes, sir." Polski turned his periwinkle eyes on me. "His father was watchun the whole business. He was sort of a witness — next of kin, see. Mooney says, 'Bring him over here — I want to say sumthun to him.' And they had to grant him his last vequest. No matter what a condemned man asked, they had to grant it. If he asked for vaspberry pie and it was January, they had to find him a slice, even if it meant sendun it up from Florida. Mooney asked for his father. The father came over. Mooney looked at him. He says, 'Come a little closer.'

"The father came a few steps closer.

" 'I want to whisper sumthun in your ear,' Mooney says.

"The father came vight up to him, and Mooney leaned over and put his head close to his father's, the way you do when you whisper in somebody's ear. Then, all at once, the father let out a scream that'd wake the dead, and staggered back, holdun his head and still yellun."

Polski let this sink in, though I had braced myself for Polski screaming to let me hear what it had sounded like.

I said, "What did the son say to him?"

"Nuthun."

"But why did the father scream?"

Polski worked his tongue over his teeth.

He said, "Because Mooney had bitten his father's ear off! He still had it in his mouth. He spit it out, and *then* he says, 'That's for makun me what I am.' "

I saw Spider Mooney's wet lips, the blood on his chin, the little wrinkled ear on the ground.

"Bit the old man's ear off," Polski said.

He stood up.

" 'That's for makun me what I am.' "

I stayed on the shaking glider. Polski was done, but I wanted to hear more. I wanted a conclusion. But there was no more to the story. I was left with the image of the old man clutching his head and keeling over, and Mooney pausing at the gallows stairs, and the gray ear on the ground like a leaf of withered gristle.

"Your father's the most obnoxious man I've ever met," Polski said. "He is the worst kind of pain in the neck — a know-it-all who's sometimes vight."

Then, with all the sawdust in him stirring, he added, "I've come to see he's dangerous. You tell him that, Charlie. Tell him he's a dangerous man, and one of these days he's going to get you all killed. Tell him I said so. Now finish that milk and off you go!"

Father was sitting in his hydraulic chair when I got back to the house. He was puffing a cigar. A cloud of smoke, like satisfaction, hung over his smiling face. He paddled the smoke with his hand.

"What did he say?"

"Nothing."

Father was still smiling. He shook his head.

"Honest," I said.

"You're lying," he said softly. "That's all right. But who are you trying to protect — him or me?"

My face was hot. I stared at the floor.

Father said, "In twenty-four hours none of this will matter."

7

THE LAST THING I saw as we drove away from home was a mass of red ribbons tied to the lower branches of our trees and hanging limp in the morning dew. It was the hour after dawn. Everything was furry gray in the warm dim light, except those bright ribbons. They were knotted there the night before by the savages.

We had been at the supper table and had heard voices and the whisking of feet in the tall grass. Father said "Hello" and went to the door. When he switched on the outside light, I saw more than a dozen dark faces gathered at the stoop. I thought: They've come for him — they're going to drag him off.

"It's the men, Mother." He did not say savages.

She said, "They picked a fine time."

Father faced them and waved them in.

The first one, who was tall and turned out to be the blackest of them, slouched in grinning and carrying a machete. I thought: Oh, Gaw. He carried it casually, like a monkey wrench, and he could have simply raised it and dinged Father into two halves if he had wanted to. The rest followed him, slipping catfooted though their shoes were enormous. They wore white shirts, with whiter patches stitched on, but very clean and starched. They mumbled and laughed and filled the room with what I knew was the dog smell of their own house, sweat and mouse droppings, and fuel oil. The twins and Jerry goggled at them — they were frightened, and Jerry almost guffed his supper from the smell.

But the men, even the one with the machete, looked a little

frightened, too. Their faces were bruise-scraped crooked masks, and their hair as greasy-black as a muskrat's tail, or in bunches of tight curls like stuffing from a burst chair cushion. Most of them were dark and hawk-nosed Indians, and the rest were blacks, or near enough, with long loose hands. Some had faces so black I could not make out their noses or cheeks. They looked at us and around the room, as if they had never stood in a proper house before and were trying to decide whether to tear it apart or else kneel down and bawl. Their silence, this confusion, steamed like fury in the room.

Father clumped the big man on the shoulder and said, "What do you troublemakers want?"

The men laughed like children, and now I saw that they were looking upon Father obediently. Their faces were shining with admiration and gratitude. When I realized we were safe, the men appeared less ugly and foul-seeming.

"This is Mr. Semper," Father said. He used his handshake to tug the big man forward. "He speaks English perfectly, don't you, Mr. Semper?"

Mr. Semper said "No," and whinnied and looked hopelessly at Mother.

I knew this man Semper. His was the face I had seen crossing the fields at midnight. He had been carrying the scarecrow's corpse in his arms. Now I noticed he had the scribble of a pale scar, like a signature, near his mouth. I was glad I had not seen the scar that night.

"See if you can find some beer, Mother. These gentlemen are thirsty."

Soon each man was gripping a bottle of beer. Mr. Semper put his jaw out and chewed the bottle cap off with his molars. The rest did exactly the same, gnawing theirs and plucking the caps off their tongues. They took shy slugs of beer and kept their eyes on Father.

"What have you got for me, brother?" Father said.

Balancing the machete on the flat of his hand, Mr. Semper said, "Dis."

"That's a beauty," Father said. He tried the blade with his thumb. "I could shave with that."

Mr. Semper broke into the rapid chatter of another language.

Father understood! He turned to us and said, "They're thanking us for the Worm Tub. Didn't I tell you they were civilized? See, they're real gentlemen." He said something to the men in their language.

Mr. Semper screamed a laugh. His gums were molded marvelously, like smooth wax around the roots of his teeth. He watched Father with fluidy lidded eyes, and when Father passed a bowl of peanuts around, Mr. Semper nodded and split open his lips to mutter his thanks.

The wonder to me was that this crowd of men was in our house at all. For months I had watched them silently crossing the fields, first planting, then, when the asparagus crop was ripe, bent over it and cutting. I was sure these were the men I had seen that night carrying torches in that scarecrow ceremony. The men had seemed savage, their house had frightened me with its stink, their faces had seemed swollen and cruel. But here they were, fifteen of the queerest men I had ever laid eyes on. Yet they did not look savage up close. They looked poor and obedient. The patches on their shirts matched the bruises on their faces, their hands were cracked from work, there was dust in their hair. Their big broken shoes made their shoulders slanty, and their ragged pants made them seem — not dangerous, as I had expected, but weak.

Father said, "They want to meet you."

He introduced us — the twins, Jerry, and me — and we shook hands all around. Their palms were splintery and damp, and their skin was scaly. They had yellow fingernails. Their hands were like chicken feet, and afterward my own hand smelled.

"I've taken the precaution of buying a good map," Father said, and unfolded it and flattened it under a lamp. The men jostled to look at it. "A map is as good as a book — better, really. I've been reading this one for months. I know everything I have to know. Look how the middle of it is blank — no roads, no towns, no names. America looked like that once!"

"Plenty water dere," Mr. Semper said, and traced the blue rivers with his finger.

The map showed a forehead of territory, a bulge of coastline with an empty interior. The blue veins of rivers, lowland green and mountain orange — no names, only bright colors. Father's finger was well suited for pointing at this map as he said "This is where we're headed," for the blunt blown-off finger was pointing at nothing but an outline of emptiness.

"Are you sure you don't want to come with us, brother?"

Mr. Semper showed his teeth, and his nostrils opened like a horse's.

"They'd rather stay here and face the music," Father said. "Ironic, isn't it? We're sort of trading places — swapping countries."

Mr. Semper laughed and clapped his hands and said, "You going far away!"

Father grinned at him. "I'm the vanishing American."

Black veins swelled beside Mr. Semper's eyes, straining the shiny skin like trapped worms, as he crouched beside us and one by one put his long arms around the twins, Jerry, and me.

"Dis fadder is a great man. He my fadder, too." Mr. Semper's grunts smelled damply of digested peanuts. "We, his childrens."

It seemed to me a ridiculous thing to say, but I remembered that Father had been kind to these men, because they were poor. This was Mr. Semper's way of saying thank you for the fire-driven ice-box.

The rest of the men were silent. Father smiled at them and made passes with his hands. Then he mumbled something, and turned to Mother and said, "That's Spanish for 'Don't do anything I wouldn't do.' "

"Talk about leeway," Mother said.

When Mr. Semper had clasped Father's fingers and murmured into Father's face for the last time, and they were all whisking through the grass, Father raised the machete and slashed the air, using it like a pirate's cutlass.

"Allie, be careful," Mother said.

"I'm raring to go!"

"Trading places," she said. "Those poor men."

"That's all they've got to trade — they don't have anything else. And that's just what we're doing. I would never have thought of it, if it wasn't for them. They inspired me."

There was movement outside. The men had paused under the trees.

"But it's a swindle," Father said. "I feel I'm leaving them to the vultures."

It was not until the next morning that I noticed the ribbons the men had tied to the branches. They were cheap red ribbons, but in the gray morning light they looked rich and festive, and gave a touch of splendor to the trees.

Soon I could not make out the ribbons or the house. Our homestead got smaller and slipped down, and the treetops followed it. Then everything was under the road.

Passing Polski's farmhouse, I recalled what he had told me. But the Mooney story confused me. Did his earbiting mean that he realized his father had been cruel to him, or did it prove that criminals don't change, and are still vicious on the gallows stairs? As for the rest of Polski's rant, about Father being a know-it-all and dangerous, I could not deliver that message. Father knew I was lying. *But who are you trying to protect — him or me?* The answer was neither. I was trying to protect myself.

Now, nothing mattered. We were leaving Hatfield. Father had taken his Thunderbox and his Atom-smasher, most of his tools, some of his books, and all the things we had bought — the camping equipment. But the rest, the house and all its furnishings, we left — every stick of furniture, the dishes, the beds, the curtains, Mother's plants, the radio, the lights in the sockets, our clothes in the drawers, the cat asleep on the hydraulic chair. And we had left the door ajar. Was this Father's way of reassuring us? If so, it was a success. Except for some spare clothes in our knapsacks, we had not packed.

Father had woken and said, "Okay, let's go." He hurried through the house without glancing left or right. "We're getting out of here."

Only later it occurred to me that this was what real refugees did. They finished breakfast and fled, leaving the dishes in the sink and the front door half-open. There was more drama in that than if we had carefully wrapped all our belongings and emptied the house.

The house now bobbed up in miniature, between the fields a mile away. It had never looked more peaceful. It was our mousehole. And because all our things were in it, and the clock still ticking, I felt we could return at any time, and find it just as we had left it, and reclaim it.

So I did not mind going, but where were we headed? Because I did not know, the slowness of time made me sick. Once past Springfield, Father stuck to the highway, and cities and towns rose near the exits. We saw chimneys and churches and tall buildings. We got used to buses with dirty windows, and trucks whooshing past, the gusts of fumey wind and the black canvas flapping on their loads. The signs said Connecticut, then New York. We stopped for lunch at a Howard Johnson's. Father said, "Everything this place stands for, I despise," and would not eat. The fried clams didn't even have stomachs, he said, and were probably made out of string. "Cheeseburgers!" he yelled. Then New Jersey. Here were the tallest smokestacks and dingiest air I had ever seen, and the birds were small and oily. People going by in cars, girls especially, gaped at Jerry and me. We yanked down the beaks of our baseball caps so they wouldn't stare. I shut my eyes and prayed for us to arrive. Father's speed on this fast road made me think we were escaping, hurrying away from following thunder, dropping down a long straight road past a landscape that was like a greasy sink. I had never seen flames like these spurting from chimneys. We could hear the *flub-flub* of fiery hair wagging from the black pipes.

BALTIMORE, a sign said, NEXT SEVEN EXITS. We took the third, and saw a shopping center just like the one we had left behind this morning in Springfield, and went through a suburb that reminded me of Chicopee, then entered the city itself. It was a hillier city than any in Massachusetts. The houses and hotels were bricked along sloping streets. On this early evening the twilight glanced from the nearby water, helped by the curve of pinky blue sky — nothing like the customary thickening I was used to in Hatfield, which was a moldy green sundown with shots of gold. Baltimore's milky ocean brightness and its putty-colored clouds magnified a pale overhang of daylight unobstructed by trees. What few small trees I could see were struggling against the wind.

About five minutes later it was sundown, and different. One part of the sky was darkening with gray, the other dazzling red, a heap of claw-shaped clouds the color of boiled lobster shells, cracked and broken in just the same way. This brilliant crimson sky was new to me. I called to Father to look at it.

"Pollution!" he cried. "It's refraction from gas fumes!"

He kept driving, nudging our truck through the traffic, making toward the lower part of the city. He parked in the wind outside a warehouse.

"What are we doing here?" Jerry asked.

Father pointed his knuckle at the top of the warehouse. He said, "That's our hotel."

It was the yellow-white bow of a ship, its nostril-like ropeholes bleeding rust stains. We could not see the rest of the ship, but judging from its bow it was huge. I did not say how glad I was that we had somewhere to stay. It was now dark. I had thought we were going to sleep in a campsite by the roadside.

We walked up the slatted gangway, and a seaman on deck showed Father where we were to go. We four children occupied one cabin, Mother and Father were in an adjoining one. Everything smelled sourly of drying paint. A cubicle with a shower and sink lay between our two cabins. We stowed our belongings under the lower bunks and waited for something else to happen. Morning in Massachusetts, evening on a ship — six hundred miles away. It seemed as if Father could work miracles.

"It's a ship!" Clover said. "We're on a real ship!"

Father put his head into our cabin and said, "Well, what do you think?"

The ship was being loaded. All night the cranes squeaked and revolved, the conveyor belts hummed under us, and through the steel walls of our bare cabin I could hear cargo being skidded into the hold.

We remained tied up at this dock while the cargo — stenciled crates and even cars on cable slings — was loaded. We ate in the empty dining room and during the day we watched the cranes swinging back and forth. There were no other passengers that I could see. And still Father refused to say where we were going. This worried me and made me feel especially dependent on him. I did not know the name of this ship, and no one I had seen so far appeared to know English. We were ignored by the crew. We were in Father's hands.

One morning before we sailed, we left the ship and drove in our old truck through the city, crossing a bridge and heading toward the water where, at the end of the road, there was a beach. Mother stayed in the cab of the truck reading while we walked along the beach, skimming stones and looking at sailboats. Down the beach there was a broken jetty, some rocks in the water and others tipped in the sand.

"The tide's coming in," Father said. He chucked his cigar butt into the surf. "Who's going to show me how brave he is?"

I knew what was coming. He had done this to us a number of times. He would dare us to go out and sit on a rock and stay there until the rising tide threatened us. It was a summer game we had played on Cape Cod. But it was still spring in Baltimore — too cold for swimming — and we had all our clothes on. I could not believe he was serious, so I said I would try, and expected him to laugh.

He said, "You're keeping us waiting."

A wave broke and slid back, dragging sand and pebbles. Without taking my clothes off, or even my shoes, I ran to a weedy rock at the surf line and perched there, waiting for Father to call me back. The twins and Jerry laughed. Father stood higher up on the beach, hardly watching. No waves disturbed me at first. They mounted just behind me, moved past me, and turned to foam and vanished.

"Charlie's scared," Jerry yelled.

I said nothing. I knelt there unsteadily, clasping the rock with my fingertips. It was like a saddle with no stirrups. I did not know if I was calling Father's bluff or he was calling mine. A succession of waves soaked my legs and wet my shoes. A pool formed in front of my rock. Now the brimming waves numbed my fingers.

I was rehearsing an excuse for giving up when, in the sallow late-afternoon light, I saw Father's silhouette, the sun beneath his shoulder. He was dark, I did not know him, and he watched me like a stranger, with curiosity rather than affection. And I felt like a stranger to him. We were two people pausing — one on a rock, the other on the sand, child and adult. I did not know him, he did not know me. I had to wait to discover who we were.

At just that second — Father as simple and obscure as a passerby, doubting me with his slack posture — the wave came. It slapped me hard from behind, traveled up my back and frothed against my neck, pushing me and making me buoyant, then just as quickly releasing me. I trembled with cold and grasped the rock tightly, thinking my chest would burst from the howl I held in.

"He did it!" Jerry shrieked, running in circles on the beach. "He's all wet!"

Now I could see Father's face. A wildness passed across it, like a desperate memory, making a mad fix on his jaw. Then he grinned and yelled for me to come in. But I let two more waves break over me before I gave up and staggered ashore, and against my will I started to cry from the cold.

"That's better," Father said, while the twins whooped at me and touched my wet clothes. But it sounded as if he was complimenting himself, not me. "Take those shoes off."

Father carried a shoe in each hand as we walked up the beach toward Mother and the pickup truck.

"Hey, put the kid's shoes on." It was a voice behind us. "There's glass and crap on this here thing."

We turned and saw a black man. He held a radio against his ear and wore a tight wool sock on his head. He blinked at Father, who was twice his size and still smiling.

Father said, "You're just the man I'm looking for."

The man switched off the radio. He looked truly puzzled. He said his name was Sidney Torch and that he did not live near here. But he had seen some kids breaking glass bottles on this beach, and it was dangerous to walk around barefooted or you would get slashed. But he did not want to start anything, he said, because he was nobody, going up to visit with his brother, and he had never seen us before.

Father said, "I've been meaning to tell you something."

He said this in a kindly way, and the black man, who gave him a sideways look, began to chuckle.

"No one loves this country more than I do," Father said. "And that's why I'm going. Because I can't bear to watch." He strolled along and put his arm around the man, Sidney Torch. "It's like when my mother died. I couldn't watch. She'd been as strong as an ox, but she broke her hip and after a spell in the hospital she caught double pneumonia. And there she was, lying in bed, dying. I went over to her and held her hand. Do you know what she said to me? She said, 'Why don't they give me rat poison?' I didn't want to watch, I couldn't listen. So I went away. They say it was an awful struggle — touch and go — but she was doomed. After she died, I went back home. Some people might say that's the height of callousness. But I've never regretted it. I loved her too much to watch her die."

All this time, Mr. Torch was twisting his radio knobs nervously. I had never heard Father's story, but it was characteristic of him to tell personal details of his life to a perfect stranger. Maybe it was his way of avoiding betrayal, divulging his secrets to people he met by chance and would never see again.

"That's a real sad story," Mr. Torch said.

"Then you missed the point," Father said.

Mr. Torch seemed flustered, and when Mother saw me all wet and yelled at Father — "What are you trying to prove?" — Mr. Torch took gulps of air and backed away.

But Father addressed him again. He had a proposition for him. "Mr. Torch," he said, "I am prepared to sell you this pickup truck for twenty-two dollars, because that's what she cost me to register."

"I just figured your kid should be wearing his shoes." Mr. Torch said this very softly.

Father said, "Or you can swap me your radio. There's one on the truck. I've got no use for it." He put his hand out and the black man meekly gave him the radio.

We drove back to the ship. Mr. Torch sat in the back with Jerry and me. He said, "Your old man sure can talk. He could be a preacher. He could preach your ears off. Tell you one thing, though. He ain't no businessman!" He laughed to himself and said, "Where you guys going?"

We said we did not know.

"That your old man there behind the wheel? If I was you I wouldn't be so sure!"

Jerry said, "My father is Allie Fox."

Mr. Torch scratched his teeth with a long fingernail.

"The genius," I said.

"That's right," Mr. Torch said.

Back at the ship, Father handed him the keys and said he could have the radio, too. He didn't want it after all. We went up the gangway, and that was that.

"Free at last!" Father said. We stood on the narrow deck outside our cabin. The lights of Baltimore gave the city a halo of glowing cloud. The night was not dark, but just a different sort of muddy light. The traffic noises were muffled and nervous. A breeze scratched at the ship's side, and it seemed as though we had no connection with the city and were already at sea. We stared at the portion of dock where Mr. Torch had driven away in our pickup truck.

Mother said, "If the police stop him, they'll think he stole it. He'll get pinched."

"I don't care!" Father said. He was pleased with himself. "I just gave it away. 'Take it!' I said. 'I've got no use for it!' Did you see the expression on his face? A free pickup truck with a new transmission!"

Like the Worm Tub. I just gave it away! Like Polski and the job. Clear the decks!"

But Mother said sharply, "What have you given away? A beat-up truck that was too much trouble to dump. A homemade icebox that stank to heaven. A job that wasn't worth having in the first place."

"That's what I mean."

"Don't pretend to be better than you are."

Father was still staring down the hawser at Baltimore.

"Good-bye, America," he said. "If anyone asks, say we were shipwrecked. Good-bye to your junk and your old hideola! And have a nice day!"

8

WE SAILED from Baltimore on this ship, *Unicorn,* in the middle of the night. The cabin walls vibrated, as if shimmying on the teeth of a buzz saw. My bunk grumbled and nudged me awake. I put my face against the porthole and saw the sloshings on swells, like whitewash hosed over black ice. I heard a foghorn moan, a bell buoy's clang, and a spray like pebbles hitting a tin pail. The steel door rattled, but none of the kids woke up. In the morning, we were in open sea.

And there, in mid-ocean, the ship came to life. The dining room was full at breakfast — the other three tables occupied by two families. One of the families was very large. After we introduced ourselves, the grownups said good morning to Father and Mother and the children made faces at us. We were quiet strangers, they were noisy and seemed right at home here. They acted as if they had been on the *Unicorn* before. They were the Spellgoods and the Bummicks.

"You're Mr. Fox," one of the men said to Father on our first day at sea. "You've already forgotten my name. But I remember yours."

"Of course you do," Father said. "I'm much easier to remember than you are."

That man was the Rev. Gurney Spellgood. He was a missionary. At each meal he led his family — two tables of them — in a loud hymn, giving thanks, before they fell on their food. The Bummicks' behavior was odder, for this brown-faced family of four always argued, and as their voices rose in competition they would begin to holler in another language. Father said it was Spanish and they were half-and-halfs. On the afterdeck one day, Mr. Bummick, who was hoggishly fat, told Father that what he had always wanted to do was bust a window in Baltimore, then run aboard the ship and sail away. "They'd never catch me!" Father told us to stay clear of the Bummicks.

Apart from the Spellgoods' prayer meeting, which was a daily affair, we seldom saw these people, except at mealtimes. At dinner on the second day, the nine Spellgoods were not at their tables.

Father said to Mr. Bummick, "What's become of our hymn-singing friends? I suppose they're seasick — feeding the fishes, eh?"

Mr. Bummick said no, they were with the captain. It was the captain's practice to invite his passengers to take turns eating with him.

"That's funny," Father said. "I was thinking of inviting the captain to eat with me. But I decided not to. I don't like the cut of his jib."

The Bummicks stared at him.

"Just joking," Father said.

He never smiled when he told a joke. In fact, he sounded especially grumpy when he tried to be funny. It was embarrassing to know he was joking and to see the puzzlement on other people's faces.

The next night, the Bummicks ate with the captain.

"I guess he's forgotten all about us, Reverend," Father said to Gurney Spellgood. "I'd much appreciate it if you said a prayer for us."

"The last shall be first," Rev. Spellgood said. He folded his hands and smiled.

Father said, "Some."

"Pardon?"

" 'Men will come from the north and south, and sit at table in the Kingdom of God. And behold, *some* of the last who will be first, and *some* of the first who will be last.' Luke."

Rev. Spellgood said, "I was quoting Matthew."

"You were misquoting," Father said. Up went his blasted-off finger. "Matthew says many, not some. But the best part is in chapter nineteen. 'Everyone who has left houses or brothers or sisters or father or mother or children or lands, for my name's sake, will receive a hundredfold, and inherit eternal life.' "

Rev. Spellgood said, "That is my watchword, brother. You have understood my mission."

"And yet I can't help noticing," Father said, waving his finger at the two tables of Spellgoods — there was a granny there, too — "you haven't left anyone behind." Quickly he added, "Just joking."

But after this, Rev. Spellgood tried to engage Father in discussions about the Scriptures and include him in the prayer meetings on deck. The next morning, Rev. Spellgood stopped him as he paced the deck with his maps. I was nearby, fishing from the rail.

Father said, "We don't look like much at the moment, Reverend, but time and experience will smooth us down, and we pray that we will be polished arrows in the quiver of the Almighty."

"Ezekiel?" Rev. Spellgood said.

"Joe Smith," Father said, and he laughed. "Prophet and martyr and founder of one of the twenty richest corporations in the United States."

Copperations was the way Father said it, with a quack of pure hatred.

Rev. Spellgood faced the ocean and said, " 'Thou didst walk through the sea with thine horses, through the heap of great waters.' "

"Hosea."

"Habakkuk," Rev. Spellgood said. "Chapter three."

"That's chloroform," Father said. But missing the quotation stung him. He turned on Spellgood and in front of his big family he said in an annoyed voice, "But how many pushups can you do? Hah!"

The Spellgoods were silent.

Father said, " 'Of making many books there is no end, and much study is a weariness of the flesh.' Ecclesiastes. Besides, I've got other weenies to roast." And he went back to his maps.

It was from one of Rev. Spellgood's daughters, a girl named Emily, who had a chinless ducklike face, that I found out where the *Unicorn* was headed. It was now hot and sunny. Three days out of Baltimore and it seemed that spring had become summer. The crew walked around without shirts. I spent most of the day fishing.

Emily came up to me and said, "You never catch anything."

"It's too hot," I said, because in the past I had always fished in brooks and in shady sections of the Connecticut River. "The fish go to the bottom in hot weather, and don't eat."

"If you think this is hot wait until you get to La Ceiba," she said.

"Where's that?"

"It's where you're going on this boat, silly. In Honduras."

It was the second time in my life I had heard that name, and it had the sound of a dark secret.

Then a young Spellgood boy joined us. Emily said, "This kid doesn't even know where we're going!" They both laughed at me.

But it was worth being mocked to find out where Father was taking us. And now I understood the business with Mr. Semper and the men. They were from Honduras. Father was trading places. On the map outside the radio room, Honduras looked like the forehead of land on Father's map, but smaller, now like an empty turtle shell, side view, with fingerprints all over it, and La Ceiba a polka dot on the coast. That town was almost worn away from being touched. And pins on the map showed our progress from Baltimore. The last pin was parallel with Florida, which was why we were so hot.

The sea was as level as a rink — green near the ship and blue far-off. There was no breeze. The deck was a frying pan, and some of its paint had blistered from the heat. I kept fishing.

Emily Spellgood would not leave me alone. She was about my own age and wore pedal pushers. She said, "It's a whole lot hotter than this in La Ceiba. You've never been there, but we have. My father's real famous there. We've got a mission in the jungle. It's really neat."

I wanted to catch something, to show her up. I payed out my line and watched the flocks of seagulls that followed us. They hovered goggling over the stern, they bobbed in our wake, they dived for scraps that were sluiced out of the galley. They never settled on the ship, but they would scissor lumps of bread out of my hand if I held it to their beaks. Father hated them. "Scavengers!" But they gave me the idea for fishing. I had seen several pluck mackerel-sized fish out of the sea behind the ship.

I used bacon rind on my hook — no float, and only enough of a sinker to let me fling the line out and troll. Emily stayed in back of me saying, "It's called Guampu, we've got a fantastic motorboat, and all the Indians — "

My line went tight. I jerked it. There was a human scream among the gull squawks. I had hooked a bird. The hook must have been halfway down his throat, because when he flew up he took my line with him, tugging it like a kite string and screeching. He beat his wings hard and tried to get away. He plunged into the wake of the ship, then came up again overhead and made as if to fly off. But when the line went tight he tumbled in the air and made pitiful cries. The other gulls fluttered foolishly around him, pecking at his head out of curiosity and fear.

I let go of the line. It whipped across the water like a trout cast, and the big panicky bird flapped over the waves dragging fifty yards of fishing line from his beak. He did not fly far. A little way off, he flopped into the water and sat there splashing his head like a farmyard duck and raking his wings against the sea.

"You killed him," Emily said. "You killed that poor bird. That's bad luck — and it's cruel, too! I thought you were nice, but you're a murderer!" She ran down the deck, and later I heard her yell, "Dad, that boy killed a seagull!"

For the rest of the day, I walked around with an ache in my throat, as if I had swallowed a hook.

Father said, "Kill one for me, Charlie" — how had he heard about it? — "but don't let anyone see you."

The next time I saw Rev. Spellgood, he looked at me as if he wanted to throw me overboard. Then he said, "Have you said good morning to Jesus? Or do you just do pushups like your dad, and turn your back on the Lord?"

I said, "My father can do fifty pushups."

"Samson could do five hundred. But he was wholesome."

That night it was our turn to join the captain for dinner. I had set eyes on him only once before this, when he was wearing his captain's hat. Without it, and in his khaki clothes, he looked like any farmer, a little sour and shorthaired, about Polski's age. He had no neck, so his ears, the lobes of them, reached his collar. His blue eyes had no lashes, which made him look as if he doubted everything you said, and gave him a fishy stare, like a cold cod on a slab. He had a small narrow mouth and fish lips that sucked air without opening.

His dining room had a low ceiling, and the fittings were so darkly varnished they looked pickled — pickled shelves, pickled wallboards, and a pickled wooden chest that said CAPT. AMBROSE SMALLS on its lid.

Captain Smalls was talking to another man when we entered the room. They were at the table, bent over some charts, and the man, whose shirt and hands were greasy, snatched his cap off when he saw us but kept talking.

"It's got to be the welds," he said. "I don't see what else it could be across there. Unless that pump is losing suction. You think we should seal the bulkhead?"

"It's number six — one of the biggest," the captain said. "Better check the ballast tanks. You say it's bad?"

"At the moment it's just a condensation problem."

The captain stood and squared his shoulders. "These good people are hungry. See me later."

The man rolled up his charts and sidled out of the room.

Father said, "Instead of drowning your problems, why not teach them to swim?"

The captain pressed his mouth shut and regarded Father with his flat lashless eyes.

"Got a leak in your tub, eh?" Father frowned — he was joking.

The captain frowned fishily back at him. "A bilge pump's acting up on the port side. Nothing for you to worry about. It's my problem."

"Must be a gasket in one of the cylinder heads," Father said. "Sea water's hell on gaskets. Perishes the material, even your so-called miracle fibers. All this heat. And gaskets don't stand for neglect. They'll just die on you. But that's all right — we can swim."

"No cylinders — it's a centrifugal pump. And we're not even sure it's the pump," the captain said. "Please sit down."

Father jerked his napkin open by snapping it like a piece of laundry. He tucked it beneath his chin, giving himself a bib. Jerry and the twins did the same, but I put my napkin over my stomach, as Captain Smalls had done. Mother put hers on her lap. Father glanced at me and smiled, because I had imitated the captain.

"Must be the vanes," Father said. "Or it could be the motor. I wouldn't advise you to seal the bulkhead. It'll just fill up and you'll get so complacent you'll shut off the pump. That would set up vibrations. Sympathetic vibrations. They'd shake your teeth loose, raise hell with your ship — "

"Your soup's getting cold," the captain said. "This your first visit to Honduras?"

Father spooned soup into his mouth and did not reply.

Mother said, "It's more than a visit. We're planning to stay awhile."

"Ever been there before?"

Father said, "I met a savage who lived there once. And I once ate a banana from Honduras. That tasted mighty good, so I figured why not migrate?"

But the captain ignored him. He said to Mother, "In most ways, Honduras is about fifty years behind the times. La Ceiba's a hick town."

"That suits me," Father said. "I'm a hayseed from way back. But we're going to Mosquitia."

Mother stared at him. It was news to her.

"That's the Stone Age," the captain said. "Like America before the pilgrims landed. Just Indians and woods. There's no roads. It's all virgin jungle."

"America's verging on jungle, too," Father said, and frowned again.

"And swamps," the captain said. "They're so bad, once you get in, you never get out."

"It sounds perfect," Father said. He seemed genuinely pleased. "You know it like the back of your hand, do you?"

"Only the coast, but that's bad enough. You wouldn't catch me inland. Some of the crew come from those parts. One's in the brig at the moment. I'll pay him off in port and he won't set foot on another ship again. A lot of those fellows give me headaches, but I'm in charge here."

"Must be nice to be king of your own country," Father said.

The captain stared at him, and yet I was sure that Father was serious and paying him a compliment.

"Gurney Spellgood's got a mission there. His church is somewhere upriver."

Father said, "I think his theology's shaky."

"What line of business might you be in?" the captain asked, annoyed by what Father had said about Rev. Spellgood.

But Father didn't reply. He hated direct questions, like Where are you going? What are you doing? and What's it for? We never asked.

Mother said, to break the silence, "Allie — my husband — used to be quite interested in the Bible. He and Reverend Spellgood were discussing it. That's all he means. He's the only person I know who actually invites Jehovah's Witnesses in the house. He gives them the third degree."

Father said, "I've tinkered with it, in a general sort of way. It's like the owner's guide, isn't it? For Western civilization. But it doesn't work. I started wondering, Where's the problem? Is it us or is it the handbook?"

"And what will you be doing in Mosquitia with this fine family?" A direct question. But Father faced him.

"Growing my hair," Father said. "You might have noticed I have long hair? There's a reason for it. I've done a lot of traveling, but I like to keep to myself. It's hard in America — all those personal questions. I can't stand answering them. What does this have to do with hair? I'll tell you. It was the barbers who always asked them the most. They used to give me interviews. But after I stopped getting haircuts, the questions stopped. So I guess I'll just go on growing it for my peace of mind."

"We had a fellow like you on board a few years ago. He was planning to spend the rest of his life in Honduras. He went ashore. We took on our cargo. It was pineapples. The fellow came back with us. Couldn't bear it. He lasted two days."

"Don't you wait for us," Father said, "unless you want your pineapples to rot."

The captain said, "I brought my family along on one run. They spent a few days up in Tegoose, and then visited the ruins. It was a nice take-in."

"I don't feel we're going to ruins so much as we're leaving them," Father said. "And speaking of bitter and hasty nations, just before we came down to Baltimore we had a little shopping to do. We went into Springfield, one of those shopping centers that are more like shopping circumferences. We were buying shoes, and when I paid the bill I looked through the stockroom door where there was a bulletin board for the employees. A slogan's written on it in big letters. It says, 'If you have sold a customer exactly what he wanted, you haven't sold him anything.' A shoe shop. It made me want to go away in my old shoes."

"That's business," the captain said.

"That's ruins," Father said. "We eat when we're not hungry, drink when we're not thirsty, buy what we don't need, and throw away everything that's useful. Don't sell a man what he wants — sell him what he doesn't want. Pretend he's got eight feet and two stomachs and money to burn. That's not illogical — it's evil."

"So you're going to Honduras."

"We need a vacation. If we'd had the money, we would have gone to the island of Juan Fernandez. But we didn't want to sell the pig."

Mother laughed at this. She often laughed — she thought Father was funny.

"My family's grown up," the captain said. "My wife's happy where she is, which is Verona, Florida. And this ship is my home. But I've put into a fair number of ports — the East Coast, Mexico, Central America, through the Canal and up the other side, and I'll tell you, give or take a few palm trees, they're all the same."

"That's a kind of fear," Father said. "When a man says women are all the same, it proves he's afraid of them. I've been around the world. I've been to places where it doesn't rain and places where it doesn't stop. I wouldn't say those countries are all the same, and the people are as different as dogs. I wouldn't go if I thought they were all the same. And if I was a ship captain I'd stay in my bunk. I expect places to be different. If Honduras isn't, we'll go home."

"Gurney sings its praises. Bummick works with the fruit company. That's another story, but he must like it or he wouldn't stay."

"If there's space we'll be happy. We ran out of space in America, and I said, 'Let's go!' People don't normally say that. Ever notice? Americans never leave home? People say they want a new life. So they go to Pittsburgh. What kind of new life is that? Or they go to Florida, and they think they're emigrating. Like I say, I've done a lot of traveling, but I've never met any Americans who planned to stay where they were, apart from a few cripples and retards, who didn't know where they were. Most Americans are homing pigeons, and none of them has the conviction to do what we're doing — picking ourselves up and going to a different country for good. I suppose you think it's disloyal, but a man can only take so much. Me? I feel better already on this ship. That's why I'm telling you what I couldn't tell anyone back home. If I'd said I was leaving, they'd call me an outlaw. Americans think that leaving the States for good is a criminal act, but I don't see any other way. We need elbow room, so we can think. Right," Father went on — and now he was laughing — "as you probably noticed, I think with my elbows!"

All the time, the twins, Jerry, and I were jammed against the wall, our arms bumping as we ate. The twins had crumbled crackers into their soup because the captain had. But they had not eaten theirs, because it looked like swill. And Jerry, who hated sausages (Father always said they put horses' lips and cows' ears into them), hardly touched the main course, except for a few peas. The kids were also kicking each other under the table. I was so ashamed of them, I ate everything that was put in front of me by the black waiter. I was at the captain's end of the table and he complimented me, saying I had quite an appetite and I was going to grow up to be a big fellow and did I have a hollow leg?

He said to me, "If you like, I'll show you the bridge. I've seen you fishing from the stern. We've got sonar. You can spot fish on the screen and you'll know the right time to use your line. Want to come up?"

I asked Father if it was all right.

"You heard him, Charlie. The captain's in charge here. This ship is his country. He can do as he pleases. He makes the rules. All these men and bilge pumps are his, whether they work or not."

"I fly the Stars and Stripes, Mr. Fox," the captain said. "I don't run my country down."

"Nor do I," Father said.

The captain drank air slowly, then said, "I heard you doing it."

"I don't have a country," Father said. "And someday soon, neither will you, friend."

Mother said, "Captain, I'd like to go below decks and see the cargo holds, the engine room, and where the crew is. The children would be interested. It would be a good lesson — they could do some pictures of it."

"See, we're educating these kids ourselves," Father said. "I wasn't happy with the schools. They're all playgrounds and fingerpainting. Subliterate teachers, illiterate kids. The blind leading the blind. Of course, they'll all turn out rotten — it's despair."

"Home study has its limitations," the captain said.

"Ever tried it?" Father said.

The captain said the public schools were fine by him, and "I've never had any grief with the school system."

Hearing this, Father reached to one of the shelves and pulled a book out. He put it in Clover's hand. He said, "Open it, Muffin, and read what you see."

Clover opened it and read, "Compass error is sometimes used in compass clackuations as a sah-speficic term. It is the al-alga-alga-breek sum of the vary-variations and dah-viation. Because vary-variation depends on gee-geographic location, and dah-der-viation upon the ship's heading — "

"That's enough," Father said, and snapped the book shut. "Five years old. I'd like to see a school kid do that."

Clover smiled at the captain and put her hands on her belly.

"Smart girl," the captain said.

"Take this energy crisis," Father said. "It's the fault of the schools. Wind power, wave power, solar power, gasohol — it's just a sideshow. They have fun talking about it, but everyone drives to school on Arab gas and Eskimo oil, while they jabber about windmills. Anyway, what's new about windmills? Dutch people have been using them for years. The schools go on teaching worn-out lessons and limping after the latest fashions. No wonder kids sniff glue and take drugs! I don't blame them. I'd take drugs, too, if I had to listen to all that guff! And no one sees how simple it might be. Hey, I'm thinking out loud, but take magnetism. Ever hear anyone talk sense about magnetic energy?"

"Generators have magnets in them," the captain said.

"Electromagnets. They need energy. That means fuel. I'm talking natural magnets."

"I don't see how that would work."

"The size of a Ferris wheel," Father said.

"They don't come that big."

"A thousand of them, on a pair of wheels."

"They'd just stick together," the captain said.

"I'm way ahead of you," Father said. "You set them at various angles, over three hundred and sixty degrees, so there's a push-pull effect with the alternating magnetic fields."

"What's the point?"

"A perpetual-motion machine. The point is you could light a city with something like that. But tell anyone about it and he looks at you as if you're crazy." Father faced the captain, as if defying him to look at him that way.

Mother said, "Allie's an inventor."

"I was wondering," the captain said.

"Strictly speaking," Father said, "there is no such thing as invention. It's not creation, I mean. It's just magnifying what already exists. Making ends meet. They could teach it in school — Edison wanted to make invention a school subject, like civics or French.

But the schools went for fingerpainting, when they could have been teaching kids to read. They encouraged back talk. School is play! Harvard is play!"

"The captain is offering you some coffee, Allie."

The captain held the coffeepot over Father's cup.

Father said, "Ain't that always the way? You get on to a really serious subject, like the end of civilization as we know it, and people say, 'Aw, forget it — have a drink.' It's a funny world. I'm damned glad we're saying good-bye to it."

"You won't have a coffee, then?" the captain said.

"No thanks. The caffeine in it makes me talk too much. Hey, I *like* this banana boat! I'll just go back to my cabin and smoke a joint."

I thought the captain's eyes were going to burst.

"Just joking," Father said.

9

THE *Unicorn* was moving more slowly now. I knew it from the pins on the map. I told Father this, and he said, "You keep an eye on those pins, Charlie. I've got my hands full, hiding from Gurney Spellgood and his gospelers. He prays for me to join him — I pray for him to leave me alone. We'll see whose prayers get answered."

Later that morning I was looking at the clustered pins when Emily Spellgood jumped behind me and said, "Why aren't you fishing?"

"Don't feel like it." I walked out to the deck.

She followed me, saying, "Where do you come from?"

"Springfield," I said, naming the biggest place I knew.

"I never heard of Springfield," she said. "What's their team?"

What was she talking about? I said, "It's a secret."

"We're from Baltimore. Baltimore's got the Orioles. That's my team. They almost won the World Series. I'm wearing a new bra."

I walked to the stern.

"I know why you aren't fishing," she said. "That seagull you killed took your fishing line away. You deserved to lose it, because you're a murderer. You murdered an innocent bird, one of God's creatures. They're good — they eat garbage. My father said a prayer for that bird."

I said, "My father said a prayer for your father."

"He's got no right to do that," she said. "My father doesn't need any prayers. He's doing the Lord's work. I bet you don't even have a team."

"Yes, I do. They're on television."

"What's your favorite TV program?"

This stumped me. We didn't have a television. Father hated them, along with radios and newspapers and movies. I said, "Television programs are poison." It was what Father always said.

"You must be sick," Emily said, and I felt that Father had let me down, because I did not know what to say next.

Emily said, "I watch *The Incredible Hulk, The Muppet Show, Hollywood Squares,* and *Grizzly Adams,* but my favorite is *Star Trek.* On Saturday afternoon, I watch the 'Creature Double Feature' — I saw *Frankenstein Meets the Space Monster* and *Godzilla.* They were real scary. On Sunday morning we all watch *The Good News Show* and sing the hymns. My father was on TV, on *The Good News Show.* He read the lesson. He lost his place and had to stop. He said the lights hurt his eyes. TV lights can give you a wicked burn — that's why all the people are red. I'll bet your father's never been on a TV show."

I said, "My father's a genius."

"Yeah, but what does he *do?*"

"He can make ice with fire. I saw him."

"What good is that?"

"It's better than praying," I said.

"That's a sin," Emily said. "God will punish you for that. You'll go to hell."

"We don't believe in God."

This shocked her. "God just heard you!" she shouted. "Okay, who made the world, then?"

"My father says whoever it was did a bad job and why should we worship him for making a mess of things?"

"Jesus told us to!"

"My father says that Jesus was a silly Jewish prophet."

"He wasn't Jewish," Emily said. "That's for sure. You must go to a real dumb school, if you think that."

I did not want to talk about school — or God either — because I only half-remembered the things Father had told me.

Emily said, "We study communications at school. Miss Barsotti teaches it. She's got a new Impala. It's real neat — white, with red upholstery, and air-conditioned. It gets eighteen miles to the gallon. She gave me a ride, in the front seat. Our school in Baltimore has two swimming pools — one's an Olympic-sized. I've got my intermediate badge. That day — the day of the ride — Miss Barsotti bought me a Whopper and a Coke. She says her boyfriend's bionic."

This speech left her breathless. I had no school, no swimming pool, no Miss Barsotti. I looked over the rail, into the green slab of ocean, and thought, If this is the kind of creep who goes to school, Father's right. But she knew things that I did not know, she moved in a bigger and more complicated world, she spoke another language. I could not compete. She demanded to know my favorite movie star and singer, and though I had heard Father dismiss these people as buffoons and clowns, there was no conviction in my voice when I repeated what he said. She wanted to know my favorite breakfast cereal — hers was Froot Loops — and I was too embarrassed to say that Mother made our cereal out of nuts and rolled oats, because it seemed makeshift and ordinary. She said, "I can do disco dancing," and I was lost.

I said, "Your father's a missionary. You don't live in Baltimore at all."

"Yes, we do. My father's got two churches. One's in Guampu — Honduras — and the other one's in Baltimore. The Baltimore one's a drive-in."

"What kind of drive-in?"

"There's only one kind — with cars, outdoors. The people drive in and pray — but on Sunday mornings, when there's no movie. Gosh, you're stupid. You're like a Zambu."

Emily Spellgood was from that other world that Father had forbidden us to enter. And yet it seemed glamorous to me. It was something you could boast about. It made our life seem dull and homemade, like the patches on our clothes. But if I could not have that life, then I was glad we were going far away, where no one would see us.

I was saved by Captain Smalls. He walked out to a balcony on the top deck and said, "Come on up, Charlie. I want to show you something."

"I'm going to help him steer the ship," I said, and walked away from Emily Spellgood.

On the bridge, Captain Smalls showed me the compass and the charts. He let me hold the wheel and he demonstrated the sonar — schools of fish showed as shadows and bleeps. Two decks down and still at the stern, Emily stood at the rail. Near her were two crew-men, one hosing water against a cargo hatch and the other swabbing with a mop.

I said, "My father invented a mechanical mop. You sort of dance with it, but it works all by itself."

"Your father seems quite a fellow."

"He's a genius," I said.

"He'd better be," the captain said. "You know where he's taking you?"

"Yes, sir."

"See the man on that kingpost on the foredeck?"

The man was on the top of an orange pillar, brushing white paint on it.

"The reason he can do that so good is because he's half monkey. They practically live in the trees where he comes from. Some of them have tails. Ain't that right, Mr. Eubie?"

Mr. Eubie was at the wheel, but not moving it. He said, "They sure do, Captain."

"That's where you're all going — where he comes from."

I looked hard at the hanging man, and I could see his resemblance to the men at Polski's.

"The Mosquito Jungle," the captain said. "Some people there have never seen a white man or know what a wheel is. Ask Rever-end Spellgood. If they want to eat, they just climb a tree and grab a coconut. They can live for nothing. Everything they need is right there — free. Most of them don't wear any clothes. It's a free and easy life."

I said, "That's why we're going."

"But it's no place for you," the captain said. "Picture a zoo, except the animals are outside, and the human beings are trapped in cages — houses and compounds and missions. You look through the fence and you see all the creatures staring in at you. They're free, but you're not. That's what it's like."

"My father will know what to do."

The captain said, "Tegoose is pretty bad, but at least it's a city. I wouldn't send my family alone into the jungle to get bitten alive and grinned at and yelled at."

"We won't be alone," I said.

"I hate bugs," the captain said. "You'll never see a bug on this ship. I don't stand for them. But your father must like them a lot. Snakes, beetles, bugs, flies, mosquitoes, mud, rats." He shook his head. "And stinks."

The telephone rattled. Captain Smalls answered it and an inhuman voice on the line jabbered at him. He said "Yep" and hung up, then spoke to Mr. Eubie. "We've got some weather ahead." To me he said, "We might be in for a blow. You better run along now, but you come back and see me."

At lunch, Father asked me what the captain had said about him. "I'll bet he's been running me down, eh?"

"No," I said. "He just showed me his sonar."

"I wonder what else he got for Christmas."

Jerry said that one of the younger Spellgoods had told him about scorpions. You died if they bit you. Clover and April had spoken to one of the crew members. Clover said, "He taught us 'grassy-ass.' "

Father said, "I got bitten by a scorpion once, and I'm still here. And I speak Spanish like a native. And as for sonar, Charlie, I've read up on it, and I could teach that captain more than he could learn!"

"You're paranoid," Mother said, and left the table.

"She's mad about something," Father said. Then he looked at us. "Do you think I'm paranoid?"

We said no.

"Then follow me."

He led us to the afterdeck. Rev. Spellgood had just begun preaching from his usual place on a winch platform. He stood there, under the cloudy sky, his hair blowing sideways, squawking to his assembled family. But seeing Father, he jumped down and welcomed him. Father said we were busy. Rev. Spellgood said he had a present for him — a Bible.

"Don't need it," Father said.

Spellgood thought this was funny. He cackled and looked over his shoulder at his family. "You need one of these, brother," he said, and showed him a book covered with dungaree cloth.

"Keep it."

"This is the newest one," Spellgood said. "The Blue-Jeans Bible. A whole team of Bible scholars in Memphis translated it. It was designed by a psychologist."

Father took it and turned it over in his hand. Then he held it between two fingers as if it were soaking wet.

"There's a Spanish version, too. We use them in our parish. Those people appreciate it. The other ones, with the gold leaf and the ribbons and all the begats, used to scare the wits out of them. That's for you, brother."

Father showed it to us. The dungaree cloth was real, stitched over the cover, and there was a little pocket riveted onto the back.

"Take a good look, kids," Father said. "This is the kind of thing I've been warning you about." He handed it to Rev. Spellgood, saying, "Your kingdom is not of this world, Reverend. Mine is."

"May God forgive you."

Father said, "Man is God."

We continued past the hatches on the afterdeck to where the tall steel pillar was. The booms we had seen swinging cargo from the pier in Baltimore were secured, each by six thick cables. Father said these were the shrouds. They held the booms in place, he said, and were attached by blocks to the top of the derrick.

"The kingpost," I said.

"Sorry, Charlie. The kingpost."

"That's what the captain called it."

"Well, if that's what he called it, that must be its name," Father said. "That there's a davit, and those, as I said, are shrouds. I wonder how high you could climb on those shrouds. Think you could make it to the top?"

The skies — three portions now — were purple and pale yellow and smoked. The wind was streaked with flying spit. Clouds had drifted into gatherings of old-fashioned hats, with peaks and plumes, and the sea no longer looked tropical. It was harbor-colored and streaming with chips of froth, and seemed pushed from below by shapes like whales' shoulders and sharks' fins.

"Think you can do it, Charlie?"

As the ship rolled slowly, I saw the post and the booms and the shrouds that held them, cutting back and forth. But looking up like this nauseated me. I told Father I felt seasick. He said to look at the horizon awhile and I would feel better.

"Seasickness is just a misunderstanding in the inner ear."

"*Jee-doof!*" Rev. Spellgood's voice traveled to us in drawling pieces on the wind. "Loave . . . the Load's marcy . . ." And the wind moaned in the shrouds the way it did in Polski's fences on winter nights, the loneliest sound in the world, air sawing a thin cry from a wire.

I said, "It might rain."

"Water never hurt anyone."

Jerry said, "Charlie's scared."

"Charlie isn't scared," Father said. "He's studying the shrouds for handholds, aren't you, son?"

"There's a ladder on the post," Clover said.

"Any fool can climb a ladder," Father said. "But those shrouds — if you climb those, you'll be hanging right over the water."

"Up here?" I pointed to where they crossed the deck.

"No," he said, "on the outside." He gestured into the spitting wind. "That's the fun of it. Boys your age used to do that all the time on the great sailing ships."

He was testing me, as he had on the beach near Baltimore, where he had challenged me to sit on the rock. The kingpost was no higher than elms I had climbed in Polski's meadow, but the roll of the ship and the streaming white-chipped sea made my guts ache.

I said, "My foot hurts."

"Use your hands."

In a whisper, I said, "Dad, I'm afraid."

"Then you'll have to do it," he said, "because doing it is the only way of not being afraid of it. Or would you rather join those Holy Rollers and forget the whole thing?"

The Spellgoods had started a hymn, which the wind twisted into a slow-fast grunt-groan.

There were no crosswires on the shrouds. They were simple and thick — six cables angling up to the blocks at the top of the king-post. If I shinnied them, I'd be dangling. But I saw a better method. By shinnying part of the way and then setting my feet against the far shroud I could move vertically, like walking up a wall by holding a fixed rope. It was possible.

"You're delaying," Father said. "You're just getting more scared."

"The captain might yell at me."

"So it's that fruit you're afraid of!"

Jerry said, "Let me try it, Dad."

"You can go after Charlie."

That was my incentive. In order to see Jerry try and fail, I would have to do it first. I kicked my shoes off and climbed to the lower blocks that held the shrouds to the ship's side. I pulled myself up. Father said, "Good boy." A few feet more and I was looking at the top of his baseball cap.

The wind pressed me, and the gulls, like rags gone mad, screeched at me, as if in revenge for the one I had killed. And I could hear Rev. Spellgood's high voice, leading his family in the hymn. I was only eight or ten feet up, but already the wind was as strong as on a hilltop, for the deck was sheltered by the canvas on the rail. I hoped Father could see my pants flapping, and how the wind dragged my legs out as I climbed. Halfway up, I turned and set my feet against the far shroud and wedged myself there to rest my arms, like a spider in a crack.

I was staring directly down at the sea. It was boiling under me, mostly suds, and some of the spray reached my feet. The shrouds up here played a different tune in the wind, a lonelier cry, because they were closer together. And the roll of the ship made me swing. It was the first time on this ship I had been cold. The movement and the cold sickened me, so I stared at the sea awhile. The weather had gotten so bad it was impossible to tell where the water met the sky, and this made me feel sicker. It all looked like old blankets. Gulls kept screeching at me from high up on the post, slashing at the cottony mist with their beaks.

Braced against the shrouds and trying to walk horizontal, I started off again. The shroud cables were greasy, and my hands and feet slipped in the gunk if I moved too fast. The next time I looked down, Father was tiny. This little figure on the deck was making me do this! And he wasn't even looking! I struggled against the slimy cables in the high wind and saw that I had only six feet to go. But this was the hardest part — the shroud cables were bunched together and I could not fit between them. I could see clearly the wheels in the blocks and the manufacturer's brass plate, speckled with salt, bolted to the top of the kingpost.

Now the whole white ship was pitching and rolling in a hilly black sea. I felt I could not climb any higher. I held on tightly and had another dread — that I would not be able to get down. I could only fall. Miles away, on the whitened water, a dark hooded cloud pushed like a demon through other clouds of shabby yellow. I did not know whether the spats of water hitting me were rain or spray, but their pelting frightened me and froze my hands.

"Attention!" It was the captain's voice coming over the loud-speaker. I was surprised to hear it above the wind. "Rodriguez and Santos to the afterdeck. Wear your life jackets and bring a line. Mr. Fox, stay right where you are!"

I thought he meant me, and hung on. The next thing I knew, a black man was kicking his way up the shrouds beneath me. He wore a yellow life jacket, and a rope was strung out behind him. One thing pleased me — he was climbing just the way I had, shinnying first, then bracing himself against the cables like a spider. His eyes were wide open and he was breathing hard. He appeared just under me, put his arms around my waist, and plucked me off, not saying a word. Then he wrapped his legs around the shroud and slid down, dangling me over the water like a sack of feed. His tight grip and his dog smell were worse than the sight of the sea frothing beneath us. The black man passed me to another man on deck, and that man placed me gently at Father's feet.

The captain meanwhile was shouting at Father and not waiting for answers. *Who do you think you are?* and *Are you trying to kill that boy?* and *You've got no right —*

But Father had crossed his arms. He defied the captain with a kind of deaf-man's smile.

"Have you got a hole in your head!" the captain yelled.

Father uncrossed his arms and looked unconcerned.

"If you want some excitement, you're going to get it, because we're in for a spell of bad weather. But if you give me any more trouble like this, I'll put you all ashore at San Juan. Now you remember that, Mr. Fox." He turned to me and said, "That was real stupid, Charlie. I thought you had more sense."

Father did not speak until the captain had stalked away. Then he said, "If you had climbed a little faster he wouldn't have seen you. By the way, you didn't make it to the top."

Jerry whispered, "Crummo."

I wished then that I had fallen off the shrouds and into the sea and drowned. They would have been sorry. And I had half a mind to throw myself overboard, but one look at the water frightened me.

It was only three in the afternoon, but the sky was blankety gray and the sea swells layered with the chips that were beaten to spittle and moved as slow as paste along the rolling slopes. I staggered, but it was not from the scare I had got on the shroud — Jerry and the twins were staggering, too.

Father said, "There's something wrong with this vessel. Look."

He took a shuffleboard puck and set it on the deck upside-down, on its shiny side. It trembled across the deck, hit a davit, and bumped a railpost on the side.

"The ship's going up and down," Jerry said.

"Just down," Father said. "She's yawing. If she was rolling properly, that shuffleboard pancake would slide back. But she's just setting there."

Clover said, "The deck's all slanty."

"She's listing," Father said. He looked up at the bridge and grinned. "That's why he's all het up. You want to go up there and ask your friend what's wrong?"

He was talking to me. I shook my head. I didn't dare face the captain after what he had said to Father about my climbing the shrouds. The captain didn't understand that this was a game we often played. And if I had done it better, Father would not have been caught and yelled at.

"He doesn't want to ask the captain," Father said. "How about you kids? You want to go up there and hear what he has to say?"

Clover said, "I want to ask you."

"That's my girl."

Mother came down the deck in her yellow slicker, holding the rail. She said, "One of the men just told me there's a storm coming. You'd better get inside — it's already rough." She looked at me. "Charlie, you're covered in grease!"

"He was climbing the shrouds — on my orders. He came down on the captain's orders."

Mother looked helplessly at Father, and with real agony. I thought she was going to cry.

"Don't you turn on me, Mother."

"Get them inside," she said.

Father said, "The problem isn't the storm — it's the ship. I imagine he sealed that bulkhead after it filled up. Couldn't pump it out. What's the weight of a gallon of water, April?"

"Eight point three three seven pounds," April squeaked.

Clover made a pouting face. "I was going to say that."

"What with the weight of a full bulkhead, and a heavy sea, some of the cargo has shifted. If the port-side pump's crapped out, he can't counterbalance by filling or emptying the ballast tanks. It's basically a pump problem. So we've got a list of about twenty degrees. See the deck? It's all uphill. You could ski down it." Father looked at me. "Some captain he is — can't keep his ship on an even keel!"

The Spellgoods were on their knees near the winch platform that had become their open-air church. They wore pointed rainhats, and the row of them looked like a picket fence.

"Come over here, brothers and sisters!" Rev. Spellgood cried. His wet hair was glued in a strip across his nose. "Pray with us awhile. Pray for the waters to subside."

"This is nothing," Father said. "It's going to get a lot worse. This far south? Probably a hurricane — probably already got a name, like Mable or Jimmy."

"Pray for the hurricane, then," Rev. Spellgood said. "Prayer is the answer."

Father honked at him. He told him to do something practical. He said the ship was listing twenty degrees and yawing.

"Prayer is practical! Prayer is an air-mail stamp on your love letter to Jesus!"

But Father went on honking and pushed us through the cabin door. He said, "Gurney's a frightened man. His Blue-Jeans Bible's got a rip in the seat of its pants. He doesn't know what's happening, so he's praying like it's going out of style. *I* know what's happening — bulkhead full, cargo shifted, list to port, a yaw. That's a solvable problem, if you have the know-how. Nothing to *pray* about. But I'm not in charge here — you heard the man. I'm a paying passenger, and I intend to play gin rummy until they ring the dinner bell, unless that's busted, too!"

He seemed very pleased, having figured out what was wrong with the ship. In the hours before suppertime, he was the only member of the family who did not look green. He even suggested a game of Ping-Pong, but the table was slanted so badly it was impossible.

At dinner that night, after the hymn of grace ("God who gave us Jeedoof's weal, Thank we for this preshuss meal" — I knew it by heart now), Rev. Spellgood made a speech. He stood up crookedly, like a man with a backache, because of the slant of the room. Though he faced his family and spoke to them, what he said was loud, and I knew he wanted everyone to hear.

This is what he said. There was once a storm at sea, and the passengers on a ship in that fearful storm were seasick so bad the stew was half knocked out of them. They were rolling on the floor like pigs, screaming and crying. All day long the storm raged and they thought Mister Death was paying them a call. Then one of these sick people saw a small kiddo who wasn't seasick and he asked the kiddo, "Kiddo, why ain't you sick, when everyone else is puking their guts out and the sea's so terrible awful?" The kiddo ups and says simply and innocently, "My father is the captain." That kiddo believed, that kiddo trusted, that kiddo was different from all the pukers and spewers. The others were rolling around in misery, moaning and doubting and sick as dogs, while this kiddo was happy as a cricket. That kiddo had a valuable thing in his heart. He had faith. "My father's the captain."

That was the Christian way, Spellgood said, but his words got lumped up. He looked green and held on to his chair and pretty soon he took himself off, I think to guff. By this time, the soup had slopped out of everyone's bowl, and the dining room was silent, except for the clatter-clink of china.

"It's a nice story," Father said. "But you're green around the gills, Charlie, so I guess you don't trust that captain — ah, look who's here."

It was Captain Smalls. He looked irritated, as if he had come through the wrong door, and he did not sit down. Rev. Spellgood sneaked in after him and looked sorrowfully at his food.

The captain made a little speech. We might have noticed the weather had changed. But we would ride it out and he hoped no one would be fool enough to go out on deck, let alone climb the rigging. Here, he put his fish eyes on Father. Yes, he said, the storm was moving northeast and we were sailing southwest along the storm's path. If we moved quick enough, we'd pass through it before it got too strong. If we were slow, we'd be smack inside it. Bad weather wasn't anything unusual, but sensible precautions should be taken, like staying off the rigging and not doing damn-fool things on deck. And all glass bottles and objects should be stowed. He finished by saying, "As you know, I have no more control over the weather than a fish."

We surprised him by laughing hard, because after saying that he put on his fishiest face and gaped his mouth like a haddock.

Mr. Bummick told him he would put his loose bottles away. He explained that they were just hair bottles and jelly jars and tonics.

"And I'll empty mine," Father said. "But meanwhile what about the ship? You can control that, can't you?"

All eyes in the dining room moved from Father to the captain. The captain said, "I am controlling the ship, Mr. Fox."

Now the attention was on Father. He turned to us and said, "I need a round object."

His hand went to Jerry's face. Manipulating casually, Father pretended to squeeze a Ping-Pong ball from Jerry's mouth. The Spellgood children were amazed, and Mr. Bummick's whole tongue drooped out in astonishment. But we had seen Father's party magic before — the card tricks, the disappearing ring, the way he won at Up Jenkins. Father, forbidding all entertainments, had had to become all entertainers.

"Thank you, Jerry," he said. "But I was going to say, Captain, how do you explain this?"

He placed the plastic ball on the table. Off it went, *pock-pock-pock,* between the soup bowls and across the surface, and *pucka-pucka-pucka,* onto the floor, and *pippity-pippity-pip-pip-pip* through the captain's legs, and *pook* against the wall near the Bummicks, where it stuck.

"Someone could break his back if he slipped on that," the captain said. "Be crippled for life."

"That Ping-Pong ball's out of harm's way, and it's staying there. Why? Because your ship is listing twenty degrees or more. Is the bulkhead full of water? Has the cargo shifted? Faulty pump? Having trouble filling your ballast tanks to counterbalance the uneven weight? I don't know. I'm just thinking out loud. But if you're controlling the ship, why isn't she on an even keel? We've been walking uphill all afternoon, and if anyone breaks his back, Captain, it's not going to be that Ping-Pong ball — no, it's going to be because he went ass-over-teakettle on your slanted decks, and I'd like to know the legal position if I end up paralyzed on account of your seamanship."

The captain looked at the other tables, instead of ours. "She'll even out," he said. "I've got two men working on it."

Father said, "Why it's listing so much it's parted my hair the wrong way! It's making the Spellgoods sing off-key, and the Reverend starts in his prayers with 'Amen.' My kids can't swallow, the blood rushes to their heads when they're sitting down. It's so slanty, my wife scratched her ankle thinking she was scratching her ear!"

Mr. Bummick held his ears and laughed so hard he brought on a coughing fit.

"He thinks I'm joking," Father said, frowning. "I'm only telling the truth. I have to do everything upside-down or it won't work. I dropped a coffee and it came back and hit me in the face. I feel like an astronaut. My stomach thinks I'm in Australia."

"That's enough, Mr. Fox," the captain said, but Mr. Bummick was still laughing and coughing.

"And look," Father said, holding up his finger stump. "Your ship's so topsy-turvy I cut myself shaving and took half my finger off." Quickly — because of the gasps of horror: it was a very ugly finger — he said, "Just joking."

The captain turned his back on Father and said, "Don't worry, folks. Everything's nailed down."

He walked to the door. His walking proved Father's point. One shoulder was higher than the other.

Father said, "I'm not nailed down, Captain."

"I can arrange it so you don't move a goddamned inch, Mr. Fox."

Father said, "I appreciate that, Captain. But I've been studying the degree of list on your ship, and my observations lead me to conclude that she's yawing."

"How so?"

"Oh, because the hull's center of lateral resistance is nearer the bow than the ship's center of gravity? Because she's veering, never mind the sway and surge? Because I don't think we'd have much luck in a heavy sea?"

He stopped talking just as a wave hit the port side, dragging the dining room sideways and flipping more soup out of everyone's bowl. The captain tottered and had to hold the doorhandle for balance.

"That sort of thing," Father said. "Now this is no time to be proud. We know it's an imperfect world. The innate stupidity of inanimate objects — isn't that how it goes? Gurney Spellgood's prayers aren't working. I think God's trying to tell us that he'll help us if we help ourselves. It's no good saying 'Don't worry,' because this is the Caribbean and — correct me if I'm wrong — this is where little storms grow up into big bad hurricanes. That's not a jumbo jet passing the porthole — that's the wind."

The captain said, "You're holding up dinner, my friend."

"Shucks," Father said — I had never heard him say "shucks" before — "no one's going to keep it swallowed long enough for it to matter. But I was saying, I think this ship is listing. Am I right?"

"It's a small problem of weight distribution."

"The Ping-Pong ball hasn't moved, so let's call it a list. It's hard to slide cargo uphill, isn't it?"

"We'll winch it."

"He admits it's shifted," Father said.

"It's a small problem."

Windborne rain sizzled against the porthole glass like a spatter on a griddle.

"All the better," Father said, "because I have a small solution. My guess is that it's a pump problem, bulkhead sealed with a few tons of the Gulf Stream, no way of redistributing the weight. Captain, I think I can help you."

"I doubt it."

"I'm sure of it. I'd like to participate. And if I can't straighten out this ship — if you're not happy with my work — you can put me and my family ashore at the nearest port."

"It might be Cuba." The captain passed his hands across his mouth. Was he smiling?

Father said, "That prospect surely ought to tempt you."

The captain was silent. At the porthole the wind and rain were like burning sticks. Finally he glared at Father but addressed the others. "You people are witnesses. If this man's wasting my time, he's going to pay for it."

"You've got nothing to lose."

"You're the only one around here with anything to lose. You and your family — God help them."

"These people are bricks."

"Mr. Fox, you're on. See me after dinner and I'll give you a chance. But you'd better eat well, because by morning you might find yourself in a strange country, where they eat people like you for breakfast."

Captain Smalls went out and slammed the door. There was silence, and no one knew where to look.

Father said, "What did I say about this ship being upside-down? All the letters in my alphabet soup are backwards!"

But no one laughed. The storm had worsened, and now everyone knew why the ship was leaning. The rest of the meal was served quickly by staggering waiters, holding their trays in two hands instead of on their fingertips.

The argument afterward, which I heard from the in-between toilet, was about me. Father wanted me to come along. "It's an education," he said. But Mother said no. She did not want me staying up half the night and maybe banging my head in the engine room. Father said I knew more about fixing pumps than those savages, but he did not mean it; he wanted someone to keep him company. He didn't like working alone. He needed a person there to hear his speeches. I would not have been much help with the work; my hands still hurt from climbing the shrouds.

Mother said, "You got us into hot water, Allie. Now you can get us out of it" — speaking to him the way she might speak to Clover.

"It's the captain who's in hot water," Father said, confident as ever. "Ordinarily, I wouldn't have offered to help. I'd like to see him laughing on the other side of his face. But I'm concerned for the safety of the passengers, and I think it's time this ship made some proper headway. Here's my toolbox. Where's my baseball hat? I can't do anything without my baseball hat."

Before he set off — and he looked the way he did as he went to work each morning at Polski's — he put his head into our cabin and said to me, "Got a message for your friend?" Without waiting for an answer, he ducked into the passageway, bumping his toolbox against the wall with each shake of the ship.

Then I knew he was doing this for my sake alone, because the captain had invited me to the bridge, because I had admired the sonar, and because the captain had yelled at him in front of me, "Have you got a hole in your head!" He had already proved that he could outquote Gurney Spellgood, and he was more than a match for Mr. Bummick, but now he was trying to outcaptain the captain.

I did not doubt that he would succeed. I had never known him to fail. People sometimes misunderstood Father, because he frowned when he joked and he laughed when he was serious. He also gave you information you did not need, like "These are davits." But those of us who knew him never doubted him. If there was one thing Father did not know, it was this: he did not need to prove himself to us. At the time, I thought he enjoyed taking risks. Yet what is a strong man's risk? He was fearless, so we were safe. I was the boy in Rev. Spellgood's story — I believed in Father. I was not afraid.

All night long the ship received the shock of waves and wind, and the sound was like the tumbling of flinty boulders against the hull. I hit my head against my bunk frame, and Clover and April cried. They woke me up to tell me they could not sleep. I listened to the rough water. It sometimes seemed as if it were sloshing across the floor and down the passageways and we were under the sea. All night in my dreams I drowned. And the morning was dark, the ship still pitched and rolled. But it did not strain anymore. Its rolling was an easy movement — not the sudden stages of dropping, all the waves hitting one side, and the downwardness of decks. It was a freer unhooked motion, a seesawing spank that sent my pencils slowly back and forth on our cabin table.

Father was not at breakfast. Rev. Spellgood led his family in "God who gave us Jeedoof's weal" and the Bummicks ate in silence. Mother cracked her boiled egg with the back of her spoon as if she wanted to give it a concussion. She said, "At least Dad doesn't make us sing."

But he came in singing. The dining-room door opened and Father entered, still wearing his baseball hat. His face was pale and whiskery and there were finger-smears of grease on his nose. He sang,

> *Under the bam,*
> *Under the boo,*
> *Under the bamboo tree!*

"Amen, brother," Rev. Spellgood said.

"You can call it the power of prayer, Gurney, but I call it hydrostatics. Gaw, I could eat a horse."

He told us what he had done. He had worked until midnight repairing a pump. "The bushings were shot," he said. Then the bulkhead had been emptied of seawater. But this had only corrected the list slightly. Supervising the crew ("It was fun — like being back at Polski's and chewing the fat with those savages"), he had had them redirect the pump and empty a ballast tank and then winch back the shifted cargo containers. "One had a new Toyota in it — a huge great stupid Landcruiser, one of these Nipponese nightmares." They had not finished the job until dawn, but the ship had gained speed and had stopped yawing.

"Your friend the captain went to bed about four, when it was touch and go." Father winked at me. "Couldn't take the strain. What did I tell you about four-o'clock-in-the-morning courage?"

The waiter brought him coffee and eggs. Father spoke to him in Spanish. The man listened, clicking his teeth.

Father then said to us, "I told him he's got nothing to worry about. I've fixed everything down below. It ought to be clear sailing from now on. As for me, I'm going to hit the hay. Smile, Mother."

"I was thinking about that poor old captain. You know, you can be an awful bully."

Father put his elbows on the table and whispered, "It was wonderful the way the men were following my orders. Once I got that pump working they were on my side. Mother," he said — and his white face frightened me — "I could have started a mutiny down there!"

With Father asleep, the ship was quieter, and throughout the day the clouds softened, the storm abated, and Rev. Spellgood's voice and the gospeling were now louder than the wind in the shrouds. When the sun came out it was tropical, and it scorched all the dampness from the ship. Late that afternoon, Father appeared. He was shaved and tidy and went for a stroll on the afterdeck. Both the Spellgoods and the Bummicks asked him when we might arrive. Father discussed various possibilities. He basked in their praise and he called the crewmen by name and joshed them in Spanish.

Captain Smalls remained on the bridge. He did not invite anyone to eat with him. In fact, we never saw him again.

"He's just ashamed," Father said. "It's only natural. I suppose he thinks I've got a college education."

Emily Spellgood followed me from deck to deck. She gave me a fishing line she had stolen from one of her brothers. Father had managed to impress even this boastful girl. I spent the rest of the time fishing, with her behind me. I caught a few flat bony ones, and one with stiff upright fins like wings, and one as purple as a pansy.

Emily said, "I have to go to the bathroom."

My face went hot. I pretended there was something wrong with my fishing tackle and began to fuss with it.

"Do you have a girl friend, Charlie?"

I said no.

"I could be your girl friend."

She looked so sad and plain and lonely. And she was a few inches taller than me. I said all right, but it had to be a secret.

She touched my leg and squeezed. It was the first time a girl had ever touched me, and my leg jerked so hard I thought it was going to shoot out of its socket. She widened her eyes and in a whisper said, "Now I'm going to the bathroom to think about you."

She ran away, and I waited. I thought my poison ivy had come back, I was so itchy. I could barely see straight to fish. But the next time I saw her she was praying near the winch platform.

That was the day we arrived at La Ceiba. The sea was flat and green, and the land behind it was a range of mountains, black and blue, with clouds hanging on them in smoky rolls. We sailed toward the pier and the clouds sank farther down the mountains and into the racks of trees, revealing a ridge of peaks, some like the spiky backs of monster lizards and others like molars.

II
THE ICEHOUSE
AT
JERONIMO

10

SEVEN PELICANS with dark freckled feathers flew low over the green sea in formation like a squadron of hedge clippers. Father said, "I hate those birds." There were gulls and vultures, too. "There's something about a coast that attracts scavengers," he said. There was a cow on the beach, and railway boxcars on the pier, and the low town of La Ceiba looked yellow and jammed. Hundreds of men met our ship, not to welcome us but to quarrel with each other. Everything was backward here. Father said, "You kids can go on ahead — you've got your knapsacks," but we were so alarmed by the heat and noise we waited for him to finish with the passport official and load his tools and seed bags into a black man's cart. Then we followed with Mother, who seemed to be holding her breath.

The Spellgoods, still gospeling, were met by a troop of black girl choristers in pink dresses and tipped-back straw hats. The Bummicks were hugged by people who looked just like the Bummicks — a boy, a woman, and two old men in khaki. There were wooden motor launches tied up at the pier, taking on crates of dried soup and sacks of rice. They had canvas awnings instead of cabins, and names like *Little Haddy* and *Lucy* and *Island Queen*.

I never saw so many people doing nothing except sitting and standing and calling names. But where the pier met the main road, they were selling baskets of fruit and greaseballs wrapped in green leaves. There was a fat black woman in a torn dress with a white cockatoo on her shoulder. She wore a dirty pair of blue bedroom slippers and was selling oranges. Father bought six oranges and said to us, "How much were these at the A and P in Springfield?"

Clover said, "Thirty-nine cents each."

"And I just bought six for a quarter. I guess we came to the right place!"

Father plunged through the crowd, and Mother said, "I love him when he's happy. Look at him go."

He hurried to the beach, and when we caught up with him he said, "I can't see anyone invading this town. I really can't imagine landing-craft on this beach. Can you, Mother?"

"Why would they bother?"

"That's what I mean."

He said he wanted to walk down and feel the sand between his toes. The black man remained on the road with our belongings in his cart. He looked as if he was used to waiting. We walked past a long low building that faced the ocean. In front of it, on the beach, a boy with a rifle was watching two other boys digging a deep pit in the sand. Father said the diggers were prisoners — that low building was the Central Jail.

"In the States, jailbirds like them are watching TV, so don't tell me digging holes is torture. They're just burying their grievances."

The cow was ambling slowly toward some shacks, her hoofs sinking in the brown sand. I had never seen a cow so skinny, and what was a cow doing here? Nearby, a dog was gnawing the skull of what looked like another dog. The sea was brown, the lazy waves flipped plastic bottles, and rags, and hacked-open coconuts onto the blackish sand. Standing at the rail of the *Unicorn,* I had seen this beach as dazzling white, but up close the digging prisoners, the cow, the dog snarling at the skull — all these and the stinking air gave it the atmosphere of a crusted and crazy jungle shore. The Mosquito Coast, Father had called it — it was a good name. Barefoot people watched us, but no one swam in the water. One man down the beach threw a limp round net into the low waves. Then he dragged it out, shook its sinkers, and held it in his teeth while he untangled it. And he threw it in 'again. I watched him do this eight times — not even a minnow. It was more washing than fishing. We could hear people calling out on the pier, and the clang of the ship's booms. The *Unicorn* lay yellowing in the setting sun. I was sorry we were not still on it.

We trudged past the man with the net to where the shacks were banked against the beach. People lived in them, though they were no better than woodsheds and would not have done for chicken houses because of the loosely slatted boards and leaky-looking roofs. But humans were in them, cooking and sleeping — I saw their fires and their hammocks. Walking was hazardous here because of the shacks. From each back door there was a furrow of black water stretched across the sand — slime, suds, and worse, spewing into the sea. The beach was their junkyard and the sea was their sewer.

Mother said, "Allie, I've seen enough."

But walking back to the road and our cart in the twilight, we heard music. We saw a boy with a flute stumbling toward us. He played a warbling sundown song. It cast a soft spell on the beach, as purply-blue as the sky over the sea. It was a strange song, with a trickling melody, and it sweetened the air like raindrops. The boy was a shadow, and his flute no bigger than a twig, but the song was an invitation for us to stay a little longer on this Mosquito Coast. It had in it a promise and a plea, liquefied like the freshet of chirps from an oriole in a leafy tree.

Then he was gone and there were sharp voices in the sudden darkness. I was afraid. We were so far from home. Father and Mother walked ahead of us, holding hands and whispering. We children followed and I thought, What now?

Jerry said, "It's junk, it stinks, it's crappo, I hate it."

"Don't let him hear you," I said.

We entered the town at night, under the bright barnacled moon, and it was magic — the halos on old lampposts, the solid buildings, the sheltering trees, the half-deserted streets, and the snuffle of traffic. We went to a hotel, and from our bedroom the town was like velvet. I imagined the whole place to be made out of green pillows, creepy-quiet and cool. I dreamed of meadow grass and rolled over, put my arms out, and flew in buttery light over places I knew. I could often fly in my dreams — not high, but high enough so that people had to watch me with upturned faces. It was a lovely night and coming at the end of that stormy sea voyage, it was like arriving home.

But in the morning, birds I could not name yattered against the windows, and in the darkness of the dusty room cracks of sun showed in the shutters. I opened the shutters and saw that the town was burst open by the sunlight. It was cracked and discolored and mobbed by people actually screaming above the braying car horns. There was no magic now, nor even anything familiar. The smells and sounds were an idiot argument I could not win, and it was so hot I could smell the old paint on the windowsill. I had been fooled, and hated the sight of it. It had taken so long to get there — even if we left now it would be days before we could get back to our own house.

Mother and Father were in another room. We kids looked out of our own window at the town of small stores. There was a heavy whitewashed church across the palm-tree park in which men in hats were standing, doing nothing. The radio music in the street — the street! — was so loud the noise seemed to heat the air. I remembered the dismal beach, the boy prisoners shoveling sand, and one up to his shoulders in the hole. I had expected trees, jungle, stillness, and flitting birds. Father had promised us something better than home, not this dusty place. It was like a nightmare of summer ruin, a town damaged by sunlight.

The hotel smelled of its carpets and its kitchen. The room in which our four beds were stuck was a bare cell, but on one wall was a colored picture, probably cut from a gas-station calendar, of a New England scene — woods, a pond mirroring a green mountain, and a red canoe on the pond. Whoever cut it out and pasted it into the frame knew that it was prettier than this town. Jerry said, "It looks like Lake Wyola."

Father roused us. He blew cigar smoke into our room and said he was famished. "He's still happy," Clover said. But as we approached the hotel dining room for breakfast, we heard singing — "God who gave us Jeedoof's weal . . ." It was the Spellgoods, they were also staying here, singing with bowed heads over their helpings. Emily stopped scratching when she saw me. The dining room of this hotel was like the dining room on the *Unicorn*, the Spellgoods at two tables, we at ours, and some Bummick-like fruit-company workers at other tables, all starting breakfast.

"Here you are, Mr. Fox," Rev. Spellgood said. "I guess the good Lord intends for us to team up after all! If you're going to be in the area any length of time, you scoop up your family and pay us a visit. You'll find us in Guampu, doing the Lord's work."

"The Lord hasn't mentioned Guampu to me," Father said. "I wish He would get in touch, though. I could give Him a few pointers if He's planning any other worlds. He certainly made a hash of this one."

Rev. Spellgood said sadly, "Friend, there's a lot of work to be done."

"So I noticed."

"You never did tell me what you're aiming to do here," Rev. Spellgood said.

"You're absolutely right, Gurney. I never did tell you." With that, Father sat down, and we had breakfast, which was mashed beans, like red clay, and a small square of damp goat's cheese, and a heap of hot tortillas.

Father said, "We're getting out of here."

"This town?" Mother asked.

"This hotel. Half the people in this room are packing guns. Even old Gurney's got one — he's wearing a pistol under his shirt. So much for putting on the whole armor of the Lord. I've been outside. It's all soldiers and shoeshine boys. I don't know which is worse, them or the missionaries."

Across the room, Emily Spellgood was staring at me.

"I don't see why we have to hang around," Mother said. "We could be on the road."

"There aren't any roads — that's the beauty of this country," Father said. "But we're not the Swiss Family Robinson, and we're not squatters. I'm going to buy a piece of land, cash down. I don't want any of these gunslingers giving me the bum's rush or stealing my soul at gunpoint. After that we'll be on our lonesome, and I don't care if — oh, Gaw, here he comes again."

It was Rev. Spellgood, leading his family out of the dining room. He winked at Father and said, "Guampu."

Emily sneaked behind my chair and whispered, "I'm going to the bathroom, Charlie."

"Charlie's blushing!" Jerry said.

We moved that very day in pelting rain to another hotel, called The Gardenia, at the eastern edge of La Ceiba, on a sandy road next to the beach. Still the rain came slapping down, tearing the leaves off the trees. It was straight, loud, thick, and gray, and it stopped as quickly as it began. Then there was sunlight and steam, and a returning odor.

The Gardenia was a two-story building covered with stucco in which cracks showed through the faded green paint. Its long piazza faced the sea and gave us a good view of the pier, where the *Unicorn* was still tied up. That ship was my hope. Men's voices and the racket of conveyor belts and bucking freight cars carried across the water. During the day, we were the only people at The Gardenia, but at night, just before we went to bed, women gathered on the piazza and sat in the wicker armchairs drinking Coca-Cola. Later, there was music and laughing, and from our room I heard men and shouts and slamming doors, and sometimes glass breaking. I never saw this crowd, though I was often woken by it — by tramping feet and songs and screams. In the morning, everything was quiet. The only person around was an old woman with a broom sweeping the mess into a pile and taking it away in a bucket.

The manager of this hotel was an Italian named Tosco. He wore a silver bracelet and pinched our faces too hard. He had once lived in New York. He said it was like hell. Father said, "I know just what you mean." Tosco liked Honduras. It was nice and cheap. You could do anything you wanted here, he said.

"What's the president like?" Father asked.

"He is the same as Mussolini," Tosco said.

This name darkened Father's face, and with the shadow of the word still on it, he said, "And what was Mussolini like?"

Tosco said, "Tough. Strong. No fooling." He made a fist and shook it under Father's chin. "Like this."

"Then he'd better keep out of my way," Father said.

Father spent part of every day in town, and while he was there, Mother gave us lessons on the beach, under thundery skies. It was like play. She wrote with a stick on the damp sand, setting us arithmetic problems to solve, or words to spell. She taught us the different kinds of cloud formation. If we chanced upon a dead fish, she poked it apart and named each piece. There were flowers growing beneath the palms — she picked them and taught us the names of the parts in the blossoms. Back in Hatfield, we had studied indoors, to avoid the truant officer, but I preferred these outdoor lessons, studying whatever we happened to find on the beach.

She was not like Father. Father lectured us, but she never made speeches. When he was around she gave him her full attention, but when he was in town she was ours. She answered all our questions, even the silliest ones, such as "Where does sand come from?" and "How do fish breathe?"

Usually when we returned to The Gardenia, Father was on the piazza with someone from town. "This is Mr. Haddy," he would say. "He's a real old coaster." And the prune-skinned man would rise and creakily greet us. There was nothing Juanita Shumbo didn't know about rearing turkeys — she was an old black woman with red eyes. Mr. Sanchez had splashed up and down the Patuca — he was tiny and brown and had a crooked mustache. Mr. Diego spoke Zambu like a native, Father said, and he made that man sneeze a Zambu salutation. There were many others, and each of them listened closely to Father. They were respectful and seemed, sitting nervously on their chairseats out of the sun, to regard him with admiration.

"He's wonderful with strangers," Mother said. But the strangers made me uneasy, for I had no clear idea of Father's plans, or how these people fitted in. I wished I had Father's courage. Lacking it, I clung to him and Mother, for everything I had known that was comfortable had been taken away from me. The other kids were too young to realize how far we had drifted from home. Except for the *Unicorn,* still at the pier, the past had been wiped away.

Coming back from the beach one afternoon, we saw Tosco at the hotel, talking to his Chevrolet. He asked it questions and called it improper names. He stood near its radiator grill and shouted and cuffed it and finally rocked it with a kick.

"She stupid," he said, wagging his foot in pain. "She no want to go. She hate me."

"My husband will fix it."

And that evening, with one of his new friends — it was Mr. Haddy — Father did fix it. He said machines had bodies but no brains. Mr. Haddy stared, as if Father had said something wise. Tosco was so grateful for the repair work he said we could use the car anytime we liked. The next day, Mother said she wanted to take us for a drive, while Father was occupied in town. Were we going to Tela? Tosco asked. No, Mother said, we were going east, toward Trujillo. Tosco laughed. He said, "You will come back soon," and gave Mother the keys.

"Which road do I take?"

He said, "There is only one."

We drove through town and at once I could see that it was both richer and poorer than I had guessed. There were chicken huts, like the shacks on the beach, but also large houses and green lawns. The best of them were surrounded by fences. That was the strangest thing to me, because the Connecticut Valley was a land without fences, except for horses and cows. It reminded me of what Captain Smalls had said about Honduras being like a zoo, only the animals were outside and the people inside the cages. But so far, we were outside.

From this town road we came to the flat main road and turned left. We went less than half a mile before the road became rutted and filled with broken rocks. Ahead was a bridge across a river. It was a railway bridge, but there was no other. Cars took turns using it. Mother waited and then drove along the planks and railway tracks of this girder bridge. Below us, women were washing clothes in the cocoa-colored river.

Beyond the bridge, the road gave out entirely. It was a wide mud puddle that seeped through the door frame, then a narrow track, and finally not a road at all, but a dry creek bed in which the rocks were higher than our front bumper.

"This is the end of the line," Mother said.

We were a mile from The Gardenia.

We tried other roads. One ended at the beach, another at a river-bank — the same riverbank as before — and a third became a quarry, which was part of a mountain. At the end of two of those roads, skinny barking dogs jumped at our windows. It was a town of dead ends.

"I'm not giving up this easily," Mother said. We drove toward Tela, on the road to the west. The mountainsides were full of slender palm trees, and beneath them, where the land was flat, there were banana plantations and grapefruit trees and fields of spiky pineapples. Mother stopped the car, so that we could study the way bananas grew, but when we got out of the car we saw a congregation of vultures in the tall grass of the road's shoulder. They were bald-headed and watching a dog chewing the pink ribs of a dead cow. The dog had eaten his way under a rugflap of skin. The cow must have been hit by a car, Mother said, and the carcass pushed into the grass. Every so often a vulture would jump out of the flock — there were twenty-three in the congregation — and snatch at the hanging strips of meat and try to gouge them away. But the dog, growling and chewing, kept the vultures waiting, and most of the time these horrible-looking birds stared like witches in skullcaps. Their wings were like dragging skirts.

Farther along this road we saw a dead dog. Five vultures were tearing at a hole in his belly. The vultures shuddered their wings and hopped aside to let our car pass. Then they returned to the dog's body. Clover and April said it was making them sick, and could we go back? So we did, without seeing Tela.

That was Honduras, so far. Dead dogs and vultures, a dirty beach, and chicken huts and roads leading nowhere. The view from the ship had been like a picture, but now we were inside that picture. It was all hunger and noise and cruelty. Next to this, the grapefruits hardly mattered, and the sunshine only made it worse. Was it for this Father had swept us away from home?

Back at The Gardenia, Father was sitting on the piazza with another man — not one I had seen before. Seeing Mother, the man stood up unsteadily, and when he spoke, spit flew out of his mouth.

"I am talking to your husband," he said. "He is crazy."

"Crazy like a fox," Mother said.

There was a crack of thunder and a sizzle of rain on the roof. It was sudden and straight down, making poke marks in the sand.

"This is the prettiest woman I see in my life," the man said.

Mother said, "You're not very old. Maybe that explains it," and took the kids away.

"Stick around," Father said to me. "Meet Mr. Weerwilly. We're talking real estate."

"Good, good," the man said.

"This is my oldest boy, Charlie."

Mr. Weerwilly cocked his head at me and said, "But I am German, so I call you Karl. You know what, Karl? This man is crazy."

I looked at Father. He was grinning. I said, "No."

"Yes! He is crazy! I tell him this is a rotten country. He says he likes it very much. This is crazy. You know, Karl, this is the last colony in the world, and I am one pee-sant in it. How many Germans here? Not more than twenty. But sousands of Americans — sousands!"

"Not in Jeronimo," Father said.

Mr. Weerwilly said, "He sinks Jeronimo is wonderful. This is crazy. He doesn't know Jeronimo. Jeronimo is not wonderful. It is better than La Ceiba, that is true. Four hundred dollars for one acre? It would be much more here."

"You heard him, Charlie," Father said, and set his eyes on Mr. Weerwilly.

"When the road comes up, the price comes up," Mr. Weerwilly said. "I have no money. I am a pee-sant. I have to sell you my land." He began to laugh. "But what can you do in Jeronimo?"

"I can do what I want."

"You do not want very much."

I hated this man, I hated his loud voice. His thick tongue crowded his mouth and interfered with his words. He snatched at my knee and spit flew off his blubbery lips.

"I am working with my hands alone," he said. "The fruit company has machines. If I want to clear some land or thumsing I use a machete. The fruit has bulldozers. The fruit can spray insecticides from helicopters. Me, I have a little pump. The fruit pays the worker too much — two *lemps* a day. What can I do? For a stalk of bananas I get one *lemp* — one dollar only. One cent for an orange, and a grapefruit — one cent." He gargled his beer and said, "That is why I am starving. *Ptooi.*"

Father said to me, "He's not starving. He's got my money in his pocket."

"You are crazy," Mr. Weerwilly said.

I said, "I think I'll go inside."

"You go, Karl," Mr. Weerwilly said. "Bye-bye."

"Stay where you are," Father said to me. "Ask him if he's got my money in his pocket."

I began to ask, but Mr. Weerwilly made an ugly clownish face at me and squeezed my leg. "Know why I like this man, Karl? Because he hates the fruit. And because he is not a missionary. And he can make sings."

"Songs?" I said.

"Sings!" Mr. Weerwilly said. "He tells me how I can carry water up to my terraces. Even my friends don't tell me that. So I like him. Also, he pays cash."

"You're the witness, Charlie," Father said. "Remember that."

"But we are different," Mr. Weerwilly said. "You are an American imperialist. You take my land. I am a poor Communist, just a little pee-sant. I have to sell you. Now I have my house and some few trees."

Mr. Weerwilly went on talking. He repeated himself and lisped and spat and drank beer. The time passed slowly. Why did Father insist that I sit here, with the rain spattering around us?

Mr. Weerwilly said, "But I know why you are taking that pretty woman and those children to Jeronimo. Because you are crazy."

"You heard the lady," Father said. "Like a fox."

"And here you can buy food for nothing. You wear a shirt only. You can get a girl for five *lemps*."

"Watch it, Weerwilly," he said, and gave the man a wild grin.

Father pointed angrily with his blown-off finger and made Mr. Weerwilly flinch. I suppose the man mistook Father's blunt finger on the fist for the barrel of a gun. Mr. Weerwilly's hand went to his shirt.

Father said, "Charlie, ask the man where his contract is."

I asked this question.

"Sank you," Mr. Weerwilly said. "You help me to remember this sing." He took an envelope from inside his shirt and let it plop on the table.

Father tore it open. But I was not looking at him. I was staring at Mr. Weerwilly. When he parted his shirt to remove the envelope, his hand had brushed a black leather holster that was strapped across his chest.

"He is in such a hurry."

Father said, "It looks like a Harvard diploma."

"Spanish," Mr. Weerwilly said.

"I can read," Father said.

I could not take my eyes off the holster bulge in Mr. Weerwilly's shirt.

"He sinks I cheat him."

Father read it closely, frowning, pushing his finger stump across the page. Then he said, "It's been a pleasure to do business with you."

Mr. Weerwilly finished his beer and belched. He stood up and gripped my hair and twisted my head so that I was facing him. He smiled at me in his ugly way and said, "Perhaps he is not so crazy."

Then he laughed, touching the bulge in his shirt.

When he had gone, Father said, "Thanks for sticking around, Charlie. Isn't he a sad case? He was drunk. I didn't think he was going to give it to me. He could have walked away with my money." Father folded the paper and returned it to the envelope. "He was playing hard-to-get."

I said, "He had a gun."

"Correct. He thought he had the drop on me."

"Weren't you frightened?"

He took my hand tenderly. His own hand was hot and gummy and trembled over mine. He said, "Nope."

He let go and reached for the envelope.

"I got what I wanted."

"Some land?"

"Jeronimo," Father said.

"A town?"

"Wipe that grin off your face," he said. "It's a small town."

The rain squittered on the roof and beat on the hedge of hibiscus flowers, making the blossoms nod. It blackened the sand and drummed on Tosco's Chevrolet, and thunder boomed on the inky sea.

"Still," Father said, "I'll be the mayor."

We sat until the rain let up, then Mother and the kids joined us, and Tosco served us our dinner here on the piazza.

Jerry said, "We saw a dead cow," and told Father how a dog had been eating it by the roadside, watched by vultures "with beaks like potato peelers." Clover and April described the dead dog on the road, and the vultures there, jostling to peck pieces out of the carcass. Clover said, "They kept on beaking him until it made me feel sick."

"Father's not impressed," Mother said.

"I can't bear those birds."

Mother told him about the roads, how you drove on ruts and trenches, how you had to cross a railway bridge on the slippery tracks and loose planks, and then it was too rocky to go any further; how one road led to a quarry and another to the sea, and how the roads were not roads, and how after less than a mile you came to trees, or a dog, and usually a dead one. The roads led nowhere.

"I'll drink to that," Father said.

Clover said, "And people go to the bathroom on the street. Yes," she protested, because April had started to giggle. "I saw one!"

"That's good for the rhubarb," Father said.

"All we saw was bananas," Clover said.

"He's still smiling," Mother said.

"Tell them the news, Charlie."

I said, "Dad bought a town."

"A small one," he said.

"You're joking," Mother said.

"Here's the deed," he said. "And I can show you the place on a map. The name's right there in black and white — looks about the size of South Hadley. A drunken German sold it to me. He tried to grow bananas there, but lack of transport made the whole thing uneconomical. Anyway, he was probably drunk as a dog — I wouldn't send him out for sandwiches. He was glad to get rid of it. Best of all, the whole thing's secret. There's no road, and no one goes there. There's a few savages, but apart from them, only sunshine."

Jerry said, "I'll bet there's a dead dog there."

"Maybe a live dog," Father said. "But no dogcatcher. No policemen, no telephone, no electricity, no airfield — nothing. It's about as unimportant as a place can possibly be. That German was damning it, but it all sounded like praise to me. You talk about starting from scratch. Well, Jeronimo is scratch."

"How do we get there?" Mother asked.

"Don't confuse me with trivial questions," Father said. "But I've said enough. Except for that German, there's not a single soul between here and the Land Office who knows where we're going. From that point of view, it's better than a desert island." Up went his finger stump. "Mum's the word."

Just then, a car drew up to The Gardenia and parked in a puddle. Four women in bright dresses got out. They had long black hair and carried handbags. They walked across the piazza to the bar at the end. I recognized their laughter.

"Here come the ladies of the night," Father said. "This meeting is adjourned."

Tosco approached Father as we were leaving to go to our rooms. He thanked him again for fixing his car, and repeated that we could use it anytime we wished.

"You're a gentleman," Father said.

Tosco said, "But you don't need a car now, eh? I hear you buy Jeronimo." He kissed his fingertips. "Is beautiful, Jeronimo."

The nighttime noise was worse than usual, and it racketed almost until dawn. Then I looked across the sparkling harbor to the pier and saw that the *Unicorn* had sailed.

The disappearance of the white ship left me feeling helpless and half blind, as if a handy thing had been tricked out of my head. It was hope. I had felt safe because the ship had been there — we could go home. Now I felt abandoned.

After that, I never left Father's side. I made every excuse to accompany him into town. I sat patiently in stores and warehouses while he bought equipment he said we would need in Jeronimo — hardware, he called it, pipes and fittings. The fruit company was selling it cheap, he said. I did as I was told and usually found myself squatting in the shade of a tree with the man named Mr. Haddy, while Father — inspecting racks of copper pipe or old boilers — gave his junk dealer's speech about taking this scrap off their hands and saying he didn't have the slightest idea what he was going to do with it.

"Seems a shame to throw it away," he said, and acted as if he pitied them for having it and would do them the favor of removing it.

I had heard all this before, but still I stayed near him. Our last link with America was broken with the sailing of the *Unicorn*. Father had been partly right when he accused me of siding with Captain Smalls — I had felt that old man would take care of us, and I had sometimes felt the same about Tiny Polski.

But now Father was in sole charge. He had brought us to this distant place and in his magician's way surprised us by buying a town, and half a warehouse of copper pipe, and an acre of old boilers.

"These are the raw materials of civilization," he said. But I did not care about that. I just wanted to be near him. I feared the recklessness of his courage and I remembered the German and the gun. *If he dies,* I thought, *we are lost.* Whenever he was out of sight, I got worried and did not stop worrying until I heard him whistling, or singing "Under the Bam, Under the Boo." He noticed me tagging after him. Often, he stooped over and said to me, "How am I doing?"

I said fine. But I did not know what he was doing, or why. I only knew that whatever it was, he was doing it among the savages.

11

"WHAT YOU taakin about?" Mr. Haddy said. He was frogfaced and so bucktoothed the two front ones were bone-dry from sticking out. "The water is camera in the night."

"Not where I come from," Father said. "It's the same, day or night. So let's go."

Mother said, "Whose boat is it, anyway?"

Mr. Haddy was still protesting to Father. "I don't say *you* water is camera in the night — I say *this* water. Is mighty rough in the day, and sometime she rain like the devil. But in the night she a baby."

He licked his words lazily and spoke in a flat voice, with hiccups of emphasis, and he lapsed into Creole when Father became unreasonable. "No bin yerry, dat the way it is? Tonda pillit me!"

"Just get us out of here," Father said.

"Besides," Mr. Haddy said, "it take us the whole entire day to load up this dum cargo on me lanch."

"Shake a leg then!"

"And she mightna fit," Mr. Haddy said. "All them iron wares."

"We'll experiment."

Mr. Haddy looked at Mother. "You man is a good one for spearmints, Ma."

It was not hard to move our belongings from The Gardenia to the pier where Mr. Haddy's launch, *Little Haddy,* was moored. The bags of seeds, the camping equipment, the toolboxes — we trucked them over in one trip. But the boilers and pipes were another matter. At last, this heavier cargo came in a boxcar from town, trundling along the main street rails of La Ceiba and down the pier, gathering a procession of people behind it as it went.

"This spearmint bound to sink me lanch," Mr. Haddy said. "She gung sink it, she *gung.*"

The *Little Haddy* was a wooden motor launch with a steering wheel inside a flat-topped booth at the stern. It had forty feet of open deck, part of it shaded by a canvas awning. Rubber tires hung over its hips for bumpers. Its paint was peeled and chipped and showed gray salty planks. Green fur grew on the hull below the water line, and it was altogether the sort of boat I had seen scuttled on mud flats or overturned above the tidemark on the Massachusetts coast. Even its ropes had the bleached and flimsy look of junked lines. Some of its deckboards had sprung up and freed the caulking, and in many places it was smeared with tar. The hold was so shallow Mr. Haddy had to kneel and bump his head to stow our gear, and it was quickly filled. The rest — the boilers, three of them, and the pipes — was to be roped to the deck. Each time something was hoisted on board, *Little Haddy* groaned and settled lower in the water and seemed to blow its nose.

The people from town who had followed the boxcar stood in its patch of shade and watched Father and Mr. Haddy loading. Father knew several of the onlookers by name. He joked with them in Spanish and English. Less than a week in La Ceiba and already he was known in a friendly way, respected even, although no one on the pier made a move to help him truss up this cargo and swing it onto the launch.

Father howled from the effort of lifting, and said, "They don't care if I rupture myself."

"But you could stay here, Uncle," one of the watchers said.

"I wouldn't stay here for anything," Father said. He guided a bundle of copper pipes onto the deck, where they broke apart and clattered against the wood.

"She a nice place, La Ceiba."

Father said, "No place for kids."

"So many kids here!"

"Why is it," Father said, walking toward the people and letting the sweat dribble off his face, "all these people growing fruit, picking it, wrapping it, loading it, canning it, and everything else — why is it they're all so damned puny? I'll tell you why. They do everything but eat it! I've never seen so many shrimps in my life. Skin and bones, that's all I see. Admit it, you're weaklings."

The people laughed and sort of cowered in the shadow of the boxcar. The noon sun beat on the iron pier, and at the end of it, where Jerry and the twins were playing, the pier was watery from the heat shimmer and as wavy as the sea. Pelicans drooped on posts, the shoreline blazed. Here, sunlight came down hard and jangled against the sand.

"It's a company town," Father said. "A one-crop economy and a one-company crop. You can keep it. But I'm not going to let my family starve here."

"We not starving," one man said. "We strong folks fo' too-roo."

He was a big man, with a rag tied around his head, and green tattoos on his arm muscles, and even in his bare feet was taller than Father.

"You're funny-bunnies and shrimps," Father said. "You eat too many hamburgers, you polish your rice, you use white sugar. What you people need is vitamins. You" — he said to the big man, as he poked him in the chest — "you need lead in your pencil."

The man laughed out loud. He didn't mind Father's abuse. He flexed his muscles for the crowd.

"Okay, Samson," Father said. "Want to do an experiment?"

"Another spearmint," Mr. Haddy said, "and we still ain't loaded me lanch."

"How many pushups can you do?" Father said to the man.

"Sumsun!" yelled another man.

The big man said, "I could lift that tub nah."

"Sure you can. You could scream it up and tip it over and probably manage to take all your toes off. But how many pushups can you do, ape-man?"

Mother said, "Be careful, Allie."

Mr. Haddy took her aside and said, "That big feller don't wuth a dum bit of good."

"Clear a space," Father said. "Give this gentleman air."

In the middle of the ring of onlookers, who shouted encouragement, the big man started. Father squatted in front of him and told him to touch his chin and keep his back straight. Father counted as the man cranked himself up and down. Then the man fell flat with a grunt and could not raise himself again.

"Twenty-two," Father said. "Not bad, but look at him — he's incoherent." He hugged Mother and said, "My young bride could do that many before breakfast."

The man rolled over and picked himself up. He was narrow-eyed from panting, and he looked slightly crippled from the strain.

"Hold these," Father said. He handed me his baseball cap and his cigar.

"Puppysho," Mr. Haddy said — puppet show. In Creole it meant silly or foolish.

Father rolled up his sleeves and got into position on the pier, the ramp of his back already soaked with sweat. Pumping his arms rapidly, he did twenty-two, while the onlookers counted. He stopped a moment, grinned at the big gasping man, and did twenty-eight more. "Fifty!" he said. Then he did twenty-five more. When he stood up, his face was red and he was winded, but he said, "That's seventy-five for starters. I could do lots more, but there's work to do."

They loved him for that, and when he went back to loading the launch, eight men came forward to help. They spent the rest of the afternoon shifting the hardware with Father and Mr. Haddy.

"It's a funny thing," Father said to Mother. "They're helping me because they think I'm strong. If I was weak they wouldn't lift a finger. You'd think it'd be the other way around. And you're wondering why these people are savages?"

"I wasn't wondering," Mother said, and went to collect the kids.

"On the other hand," Father said, "it doesn't matter if a fellow's a savage, as long as he's a gentleman. Remember that, Charlie." Then he boarded the launch, chuckling to himself.

Night fell. The town was kinder looking. Small lights burned on the pier, and windows shone in the harbor offices. The palms, so spindly and ragged during the day, had feathery heads, and these dark umbrella plumes sheltered the cozy buildings. Some blood-red sunset streaks were still bent across the mountains to the west. The town was tucked beneath. It lay flattened, a pool of tiny lamps in the darkness, and some dim spangles glimmered from the lighted huts on the mountainsides.

Jerry was yawning miserably on Mother's lap — he was too big to be comfortable there — and the twins were already asleep under the awning. It was ten o'clock. It had rained twice since mid-afternoon, and still the lightning flashed on the sea in sudden bursts. It seemed cruel to have to leave the town at this late hour. We were an early-to-bed family, and it was way past bedtime. I envied the people in the houses I could see — the ones at the windows and even those I imagined swinging in hammocks in the shacks next to the beach. It did not excite me to be on this narrow boat and listening to the sea flopping against its wooden hull, I sat on a box and shivered. Mother lay down with Jerry and the twins — they were all in sleeping bags. I looked ashore. I did not want to leave here.

The motor had been stuttering slowly for the past hour. Mr. Haddy lifted a trap door, reached inside with a long-handled monkey wrench, and brought a loud rat-tat from the engine that made the broken deckboards shake. The gasoline fumes choked me.

Father said, "I've seen eggbeaters with better motors than this. Listen to it misfiring. Call that integrity?"

"What are those birds?" I said. I had been watching them since sundown. They had small sharp bodies and flat wings and careered around the pier's lights, darting like swallows.

"Some sort of nocturnal bird," Father said, but he had not looked up. He was still frowning at the engine noise.

"Them's bats," Mr. Haddy said.

Hundreds of them — enough to darken the lights. Now I was eager to shove off in this boat.

Father went forward. He said, "We're about ready, Mother. I made you a coffee on the cookstove."

"I've been ready all day," she said. "The kids are asleep."

Mr. Haddy whistled fuzzily through his buckteeth. He said, "Yerry me, Ta Taam?" and a man who had been sleeping on the pier rose up like a disturbed insect and untied the ropes and threw them onto the deck. Mr. Haddy blew out his cheeks and jammed a lever down — it was an iron stick in the wheel house, like a gearshift on a tractor — and Ta Tom gave the boat a push with his foot. We were off, making for the black sea.

"Yep. Them's bats," Mr. Haddy said.

He leaned out of the wheel house.

"Wish we was gung to Utila," he said.

I asked him why.

"It's only two hours. Santa Rosa's ten." He hung his long fingers on the wheel.

I said, "I thought we were going to Jeronimo."

"Jeronimo's in the jungle. You don't see no lanches there. Just fellers with tails."

"Don't interrogate the man," Father said. "Mind if I take a turn at the wheel, Mr. Haddy?"

Mr. Haddy did not budge from the wheel. In fact, he tightened his grip on the spokes. He said, "Against regulations."

"Which regulations?"

"Of me lanch. I'm the steerer, you's passengers."

"Take a walk," Father said.

Mr. Haddy stayed where he was.

Father said, "I know every lunar star in both hemispheres. I'm master of the quadrant and sextant. I could take a meridian altitude of the sun from its reflection in a tar bucket."

"Regulations," Mr. Haddy said.

Father said, "And how many pushups can you do?"

This made Mr. Haddy laugh. But he did not let go of the wheel. He crowded it and put his nose against the dirty glass of the wheel house.

The echo of our engine reached us from the palms on shore and rang against La Ceiba's iron pier as we rounded it to head east, into deepest night.

Father said, "We've got gas, we've got food, we've got all our stuff. Plenty of drinking water and no perishables. I'm damned glad to be going. No offense, Mr. Haddy, but that town is no place for children."

We looked back. Even our little distance had leveled the town and drawn it fine. It was a shallow puddle of light beneath the shadows of mountains and the mops of storm-silvered cloud.

"You know where you gung, Fadder."

"Mr. Haddy, we're going home. Give me the wheel and we'll get there in one piece."

Mr. Haddy hugged the wheel and steered us through the moonlit corrugations of sea. Father sighed. He licked a cigar — it was a long Honduran cigar. He had a whole basket of them. He set it alight, and the flame that spurted from its tip showed his fiery eyes to be burning on Mr. Haddy.

"First deep-sea boat I've ever seen without a compass aboard," he muttered. "Lucky thing I brought mine. But I'm not telling you where it is."

There were small huts along the shore, flickering like lanterns under the tall palms. Then a greater darkness and tinier lights, and no shore but a blackening slope of land and sea and scanty flames in the mounting pitch.

"I know what you looking at, Charlie," Mr. Haddy said. "It ain't carkles."

I did not say I was looking at the punctures of light on the shore.

"When I was a little one," he said, staring with me at the shore, "we live back of Brewer's Lagoon. That's where I learn Zambu — the Indian black fellers teached it to me. Along about one night, was a big disturbance in me room, a locomotion, fluttering and flapping. I woke up and called me ma, 'Ma, come quick! Something happen!' She come in with a torch and say, 'Puppysho! You wasting my time — dreaming bout Duppies.' Duppies is your own ghost. Then she went all over gray. 'What that blood on you pilla?' she say, and did she screech. I look at the pilla and it is red. Blood! She axed me was my head all right. It was bleeding, but I couldn't feel nothing."

"Why were you bleeding?" I asked.

" 'Hah!' me ma say, and she stamp on the floor, and a bat as big as a jacketman floops into the wall. After she chase it away, she look again at me head. That big old bat had been sucking my ear and making tooth holes in it. And the blood is squirting out. And they is bat-shoo all over me room. And the bat-shoo smell like mung."

He widened his brown-flecked eyes at me.

"I know what you looking at. Bats."

I had not been, but now I was.

Father was silent, smoking, looking as if he wanted to tear Mr. Haddy's hands off the wheel.

"I know a feller," Mr. Haddy went on. "Bat sucked his toe, while he is asleep. Oh, bats, they just go at you. Big as pillas theirselves, some of them, out there. Down Bluefields way they come big as antsbears, bite through your cloves."

In the dark wheel house I could see his dry teeth, white as paint, and hear him trying to whistle through them.

"Fruit bats," Father said.

"Oh, sure, fruit bats," Mr. Haddy said. "And all the other kinds."

"They eat bananas," Father said.

"But if they ain't get their bananas, they just go at you."

"Tell us about the sharks," Father said.

"I seen some sharks," Mr. Haddy said.

"Big as dogs?"

"Bigger."

Father pointed with his finger stump and said, "That's north, Mr. Haddy."

"I could have told you. I know north like I know me own name."

"Right now," Father said dreamily, "someone over there in America is painting yellow lines on a road, and someone else is wrapping half an onion in a blister of supermarket cellophane, or putting an electric squeezer down the garbage disposal and saying, 'It's busted.' Someone's just opened a can of chocolate-flavored soup in a beautiful kitchen, because he can't get his car started, to eat out. He really wanted a cheeseburger. Someone just poisoned himself with a sausage of red nitrate, and he's smiling because it tasted so good. And they're all cursing the president. They want him re-tooled."

Father was silent a moment.

Mr. Haddy said, "That sure is north."

"There," Father said, facing the darkness, "there's an interior decorator, probably a funny-bunny, standing in the lobby of a bank. He's been hired to redecorate it. The bank is failing. It needs depositors. Maybe a new lobby will help. But the decorator doesn't know what color to paint it, or where to put the geraniums. He says to the banker, 'What do you want this room to *say?*' "

"Not too sure about that," Mr. Haddy said.

"Someone's thinking up a new name for corn flakes," Father said. "Someone else just died of them."

"That ain't good," Mr. Haddy said.

"But we're going home," Father said.

"Ever I tell you bout the tiger and my ma and the yampi?"

"Tell me, Mr. Haddy. But give me that wheel first."

Mr. Haddy said, "I will never give you this wheel. I am the captain, I am the steerer, this me own lanch."

Father was silent. He sometimes gave off a smell when he was angry, and I had a whiff of that now, a little glow of tomcat steam.

"You's a passenger." But Mr. Haddy's voice had lost its boldness.

"If I was the passenger type, I'd be over there," Father said. He pointed north, toward the United States. "Go to bed, Charlie."

I unrolled my sleeping bag near Mother and crawled in. The engine vibrated against my back. The mass of stars overhead was like a swell of sea shiners — a million tiny star smelts drifting dead on the sky tide.

It was darker when I woke than it had been when I turned in. There was a close clammy blackness around the puttering launch, and no stars. The bundle of sleeping bags nearby told me that Jerry and the twins were still asleep. A small light burned in the wheel house.

Father was steering. Mother was beside him with a map, and Mr. Haddy was nowhere to be seen. With his hands on the wheel, and the lantern light distorting his face, Father looked eager and impatient. I asked him where Mr. Haddy was.

"Threw him overboard," Father said. "He couldn't take the strain."

How much did I trust Father? Completely. I believed everything he said. I even looked off the stern, at our foaming wake, expecting to see the teeth in Mr. Haddy's drowning face.

Mother said, "He's kidding you, Charlie. Mr. Haddy's asleep."

"Sent him to bed," Father said. "Gaw, I wish we had one of these boats."

He had a dead cigar in his mouth, and he worked the wheel with spread fingers, his firelit face against the wheel-house window.

Behind him, Mother held lightly to his shoulder, her white hand keeping him back, the way she had restrained Jerry and the twins at the rail of the *Unicorn*. Her face was pale, enclosed by smooth straight hair and without any expression. Her dark eyes mirrored the darkness ahead and seemed to absorb the lantern flame. She was calm, but Father was hunched forward as if straining to break free of her grasp. He had shadows of muscle knots in his jaw, and his face twisted to make sense of the darkness. His eyes shone with certainty, like glints of shellac. He was active and watchful. He did not turn his eyes — he turned his whole head when he wanted to see aside.

Father and Mother remained in this posture, not speaking, for some time, and the longer I looked the more they seemed like a wild man and an angel, and this boat an example of the kind of life we led, plowing through dark water with black jungle on one side and deep sea on the other, and moonless night above us.

But I did not see the jungle until later, after Mr. Haddy woke and told me we were passing the "haulover" at the Guayamoreto Lagoon, just past Trujillo.

Then the darkness, which was like fathoms of ink, softened, became finely gray, and, without revealing anything more of the sea, turned to powder. All around us the powdery dawn thickened, until, growing coarser and ashy, in a sunrise without sun, it threw us glimpses of the soapy sea and the shoreline and the jungle heaped like black rags of kelp. Soon the sun was an hour high on the naked level shore.

"Fadder steering me lanch," Mr. Haddy said in amazement. But he was the only one on board who was surprised that Father had taken charge. "He make himself captain last night. I complain it breaking regulations, but it ain't do a dum bit of good."

I think we were all secretly glad of this, and the fact that Father was steering another man's boat through an unfamiliar sea to a foreign coast was proof that he could do anything.

"Oh, Lord," Mr. Haddy said, as a lightning bolt was printed briefly on the mist. Bearded clouds flushed with light, then faded. There was a dead pause, then a thunderclap, the nearest thing I had heard to a bomb, and soon the sea around us was pricked by raindrops as big as marbles. Dawn streaks and storm clouds met in this wide sky above the tropical sea, the sun pushing the slanting storm to the shore. The rain did not fall evenly. We made our way in the launch east along the coast through these bowed contours of driving rain — now beating on Father's ironware and the whole deck awash, now silent and all the wet boards blackened.

Except for the light swell, the sea was as calm as it had been when we left La Ceiba. The clouds parted — a whole sky of them above the flat sea, moving aside and changing in shape, columns of them, and roofbeams, collapsing and shouldering their way to the shore. The sun broke through and dazzled us. It was fire-bright and very hot, the lower rim of its saucer still dipped in the dishwater cloud, and when it burst upon us it brought steam and stinks from every plank of the sodden launch.

"We be in Santa Rosa for breakfast," Mr. Haddy said. "She ain't far — maybe half an hour. You can almost see her."

"I've got news for you, sir," Father said. "We're going to have breakfast right here. Look what Mother and I caught, while the rest of you were dead to the world — "

He leaned back and drew a line of striped fish out of a basket. Mr. Haddy called them sheepshead fish. They were strung through their gills, five plump ones.

"Now you gut those fish, Mr. Haddy, and Mother will start the cookstove. The kids will clear the deck and we'll have us some real food. Or would you rather put into Santa Rosa and eat last month's beans?"

Mr. Haddy took the fish and started slitting them. Up ahead, Jerry and the twins had crawled out of their sleeping bags and were rubbing their eyes. Mother set out a basin of fresh water, so we could wash, and then she fired up the cookstove (this was a steel barrel, cut in half, with a grid over the top), and she put the coffee on.

"I'll tell you another thing," Father said. "We're not stopping at Santa Rosa."

Mr. Haddy was opening the sheepsheads like envelopes and pinching out tube clusters of gray guts. With some of this slimy spaghetti on his fingers he said, "First you say you ain't want to go to Trujillo, because you ain't want to see no missionaries. Now you make me into a fishmonger and say we ain't gung to Santa Rosa. Nothing wrong with Santa Rosa, for hell sake."

Father said, "I've been looking at the map."

"Fadder and his map," Mr. Haddy said. He scraped the fish as if he were punishing them and punishing his thumb, and sent the tarnished silver scales flying across the deck.

"I didn't say we're not going there," Father said. "I said we're not stopping."

We ate the fish under the foredeck awning because of the occasional squalls. Mr. Haddy cut a fishhead open, and in its brain was a fragment of a clear substance, like glass, a knuckle of it. Father decided to wear it around his neck. "Like a Zambu feller," Mr. Haddy said, and then he told us to look up. There, under long chutes of rain, were a jetty and some yellow buildings and the green stripe of jungle shore. Mr. Haddy said, "That is Rosy there."

It was, Father said, a dark insult on the green Mosquito Coast, no more than ten low buildings and a church steeple. Steam and smoke, red-tiled roofs, and half a dozen kids on a jetty.

"We stop at Rosy?" Mr. Haddy said.

Father said, "I never stop until I get where I'm going."

"If I am steering this lanch, I land back there, Fadder," Mr. Haddy said. He looked at me sadly. The whites of his red-rimmed eyes were stained with brown blotches. We had passed the jetty and the beach. Mother told him not to worry. He said he was not worried, but he was pretty confused.

"Keep your shirt on," Father shouted from the wheel house.

The twins were at the bow. "You can see the bottom," April said. And Jerry hurried forward for a look.

"I ain't even know why I ain't steering," Mr. Haddy said. "I always steered before. Look — that brown surfy water — that is the rivermouth. Now what the man doing?"

There was a break in the shore, and at this wide opening a river current met the rising tide. The surf rushed sideways spilling silt onto sandbars. Further on I could see sticks and branches beating down toward the sea.

Father swung the launch onto this brown inland tide. A fisherman standing knee-deep in green breakers cast his net over the water and waved to us. *Little Haddy* nosed into the current, sending up spouts on either side of the bow.

"This ain't the way, Fadder!" Mr. Haddy cried. He was still seated, frowning near the leavings of our breakfast, the fish bones and bread crusts and coffee cups. "Him no yerry," he mumbled. "Him no keer."

He got to his feet and went to the wheel house to complain.

"Please, Mister. This ain't no cayuka. This is a lanch!"

"Sit down," Father said.

"I'm the steerer," Mr. Haddy said. "I ain't steer up these rivers."

"That's no ordinary river — that's a flood," Father said. "It's funny. First time I saw Santa Rosa on the map I didn't notice the river, and when I did notice it, it looked small. It was the rain that gave me the idea. She's in flood. There's enough water in this river to take us most of the way to Jeronimo."

"It ain't for lanches! We get broke on a rock-stone!"

"He doesn't trust me," Father said.

"If you don't lose me license, you lose me lanch. Oh, my hat!"

The launch had started bucking in the current, throwing the awning from side to side. The old iron clanked and rubbed. "Allie!" Mother cried, as she was soaked by a shower of spray. Now the boat seemed light, and it tipped easily in the surf of the rivermouth. I held tight, fearing that it would go over.

"I can't do this alone," Father said. "I need your help, Mr. Haddy. Now hop up there to the bow and if you see any rocks, you give me a shout. We're fighting the current, so there's no sense cutting the engine down. Now what do you say" — more spray hit the wheel-house window — "are you on my team or not?"

"Another spearmint," Mr. Haddy said. He was not smiling. "Ain't like these rivers. Fellers up there in that jungle — black fellers — they got tails!"

It was the Aguan River, Father said, and on the Santa Rosa bank people had started to gather, maybe thinking that we were going ashore. They carried baskets of fruit, bunches of coconuts, and straw mats. When they saw us heading into the middle of the stream and moving against the floating branches and the debris of broken cane stalks, they sang out, calling us to shore. Their tottering dogs yapped at us, too.

We traveled on, past the settlement that lay behind Santa Rosa, the sloping shacks and the huts on stilts and the rows of overturned canoes on the riverbank. We passed the gatelike entrance of a green lagoon, and pushed on, struggling in the river that brimmed at our bow. It was hotter here, for the sun was above the palms and the storm clouds had vanished inland. There were no mountains, or even hills. There was nothing but the riverbank of palms and low bushes and yellow-bark trees, and the sky came down to the treetops. The high muddy river had flooded the bushes on the bank.

Mr. Haddy hung over the bow with a sounding chain. He was singing sorrowfully and showing us the seat of his pants. From time to time, he called out "Rock-stone to port!" or "Rock-stone dead ahead!" The ocean was astern, and then we turned on a riverbend and it was lost to view, gone with the fresh breeze and the sting of salt and the fish smells. We were enclosed by jungle on the short reaches of the river, and each tree shrieked with birds and insects. They were loud, like the sound in your ears when you eat potato chips. The launch took on a different character. At sea it had seemed dilapidated and very small. But here, furrowing up this narrow river, it seemed large and powerful, its engine booming against the banks, startling the herons and chasing the butterflies aside.

"Look at the road hog," Father said, as Mr. Haddy jangled the chain at a man in a canoe. Mr. Haddy was pointing out birds to Jerry and the twins and catcalling to women who paused in their clothes-scrubbing on the gravelly parts of the bank to watch us pass.

"They never see a lanch here before," Mr. Haddy said.

Mother said, "How far are we going?"

"Until we hit bottom," Father said.

We managed fifteen miles or more, traveling upriver until noon, before Mr. Haddy began shouting about rock-stones all around. He didn't give signals, he just howled. The water was not so muddy here — I could see eels and schools of tiny fish on the gravel bottom. In places there was barely enough room between the banks for the launch's width to squeeze through, and the rapid water slowed us and splashed onto the deck.

It was on one of these narrow twisting canals that I saw the men in the trees. I took them for rooty stumps, strange boulders — anything but men. Their heads were propped on branches, and some were squatting under bushes, black shiny-skinned men. Some knelt, facing away from us. We were so close to them I could not tell Father without their hearing me. Some held sticks and spears and fishnets, but they were silent and did not threaten us.

I went to the bow, where Mr. Haddy was hanging over. He saw them, too — he was staring into the trees. Then an old black man, wearing only a pair of khaki shorts, stumbled from the water to the bank carrying a bucket.

"How is it?" Mr. Haddy said.

He was speaking to the man.

The man dropped his bucket against the mud bank, spilling its contents of fish.

"Zambu," Mr. Haddy said. "Ain't have no tail."

But saying so, he had taken his eyes from the river and let the sounding chain go slack. There was a bump under us — the launch was thumped from beneath and the twins were thrown to the deck. Jerry said, "I bit my tongue!"

The launch turned aside, thrust away by the current, and tilted, tipping over the cookstove. We were stuck fast. At once the engine stalled, and the flotsam of river branches piled up against the hull. Father kicked the smoldering cookstove into the river and it sank in its own steam.

"End of the line, Mr. Haddy," he said. "Ask that gentleman where we are."

Mr. Haddy did not ask. He watched the kneeling man gathering the fish and called back to Father, "This here is Fish Bucket!"

Then as the river scarfed around us, seven or eight men appeared on the bank, all black, with big heads and wearing shorts and carrying nets and sticks. Father jumped from the stern with a line. He was waist-deep in water and scrambling to the bank.

The men watched him securing *Little Haddy* to a tree. They stepped back a little, as if to give him room, although they were thirty feet away.

Father spoke to them in Spanish, in a friendly voice.

They stared. They seemed to understand, but they did not reply.

"How is it?" Mr. Haddy cried from the bow.

"Right here," one of the men said.

Father said, "They speak English?" He began to laugh.

This pleased the black men. They opened their mouths to watch him laugh.

"Good morning, Fadder. My name is Francis Lungley. Kin we help you?"

Father said, "Hey, I've been looking all over for you!"

12

JERONIMO, just a name, was the muddy end of the muddy path. Because it had once been a clearing and was now overgrown, it was thicker with bushes and weeds than any jungle. In other ways it was no different from fifty bushy places we had passed on our walk from the Zambu riverbank that Mr. Haddy called Fish Bucket. It was hot, damp, smelly, full of bugs, and its leaves were limp and dark green, "like old dollar bills," Father said.

Jeronimo reminded me of one time when we were in Massachusetts, and fishing. Father pointed to a small black stump and said, "That's the state line there." I looked at this rotten stump — the state line! Jeronimo was like that. We had to be told what it was. We would not have taken it for a town. It had a huge tree, a trunk-pillar propping up a blimp of leafy branches with tiny jays in it. It was a guanacaste, and under it was a half-acre of shade. The remnants of Weerwilly's shack and his failure were still there, looking sad and accidental. But these leftover ruins only made Jeronimo seem wilder this wet afternoon.

One other thing was a smoking chair in the grass, an armchair, sitting there smoldering. Its stuffings were charred and some of its springs showed and its stink floated into the bushes. This burned chair, useless and fuming, was as unimportant as the place itself, and the only person who was sure we had arrived at our destination was Father.

The twins sat down and bellyached. Jerry's face was red from the steamy heat. Jerry said, "I'll bet he makes you climb that tree, Charlie. I'll bet you chicken out."

But Father had walked into the chest-high bushes. His baseball cap was turned sideways and he was shouting.

"Nothing — nothing! This is what I dreamed about — nothing! Look, Mother — "

Mother said, "You're right. I don't see a thing."

"Do you see it, Charlie?"

I said no.

He was still punching his way through the bushes.

"I see a house here," he said. "Kind of a barn there, with a workshop — a real blacksmith's shop, with a forge. Over there, the outhouse and plant. Slash and burn the whole area and we've got four or five acres of good growing land. We'll put our water tank on that rise and we'll divert part of the stream so we get some water into those fields. We'll have to lose some of these trees, but there's plenty more, and anyway we'll need timber for a bridge. I figure the house should face east — that will give us those hills and the morning sun. I see a mooring down there and a slipway to a boathouse. A couple of breezeways to the left and right of the main house will make us showerproof. The ground's plenty high enough, but we'll raise the house to be on the safe side and use the underneath for a kitchen. I'd like to see some drainage back there — I smell a swamp. But that'll be easy. Some three-foot culverts will do the trick, and once we've got control of the water we can grow rice and do some serious hydraulics. The hard part is the plant. I see it in that hollow, a little downwind. We can take advantage of that fuel growing there — they look like hardwoods. It'll be a cinch to get it off the slope — "

All this time, under the guanacaste tree, the Zambus and Mr. Haddy were putting their loads down. Mr. Haddy pulled his shoes off and frowned at Father's voice. Father went on talking, staking out the house, marking his proposed paths, and dividing the land into beanfields and culverts. We had arrived ten minutes before.

But even Father's booming voice could not make Jeronimo mean more than sour-smelling bushes in an overgrown clearing.

The Zambus saw it their own way. There were hills behind it, and a stream running through it. The Zambus called the hills mountains — the Esperanzas — and the stream a river — the Bonito — and Jeronimo, to their bloodshot eyes, was a farm — the estancia. These grand names were all wrong and imaginary, but they were like the names of the Zambus themselves. The half-naked jabbering man, pointing to the narrow creek and calling it the Bonito

River, called himself John Dixon. It was the fierce woolly-headed one in the torn short — Francis Lungley — who told us the name of the mountains, and the dumbest one, Bucky Smart, who called the rusty hut the estancia.

They could call it anything they liked, but I knew that Jeronimo was no more than a tin-roofed hut in a bush patch, a field of finger-bananas that had collapsed with beards of brown smut disease. Over here a broken rowboat and over there some cut-down tree trunks that no one had bothered to saw into cords. What fenceposts there were had turned into trees again, a row of short saplings that might have been a pigpen, alongside the mud and fever grass and that armchair smoking poison.

Father came back saying, "It's beautiful."

Just then, a scabby black pig hoofed and humped through the grass and ran past us. The Zambu Bucky stood up and made an ugly face at it, as if he were going to murder it with his front teeth. He followed it with his face, then shrugged and squatted on his ankles. He must have been tired — he had carried first Clover, then April, all the way from Fish Bucket.

"That there is a white-lipped peccary," Mr. Haddy said.

"Worry," Francis Lungley said.

"I'm not worried," Clover said.

"That is what these boys call them — worries. It is a name. One here means maybe fifty or a hundred more in the woods."

"Weerwilly must have lived in that shack," Father said. "What a hole. I wouldn't be caught dead in that dump."

"Any case," Mr. Haddy said, looking his froggiest as he turned to Father, "there is some folks already inside, so they save you the trouble."

Football faces in the window of the rusty hut stared white-eyed at us through vines of climbing flowers.

"Morning-glories," Father said, and ran to the hut.

The faces retreated a little as Father picked a bugle blossom and said, "What's your name?"

"Maywit," was the trembly answer.

"He telling him the name of the flower," Mr. Haddy said. "That is the flower, Maywit, not the folks. Folks' name probably Jones. Jones of the jungle. Jones the chicken-man." Mr. Haddy clawed his scalp. "Wish I was on me lanch. But Fadder went and ripped a hole in her bum."

Father was still trying to coax answers out of the hut, but the faces had gone from the window.

We pitched our tents under the spreading branches of the guanacaste tree and built a smoky fire, as Father directed, to keep the mosquitoes away. Mother sorted our belongings and food bags and hung them on branches, out of a rat's reach — we had already seen two. The knapsacks and tents reminded Father of shopping in Springfield. He got Jerry to tell the story of how American camping equipment was made by slave children in China and Japan. Father interrupted and gave his war-in-America speech, but the Zambus laughed in the wrong places.

As we began to eat, Mr. Haddy said, "Here come Jones the chicken-man."

It was the Maywits, carrying plates of fruit — limes, bananas, avocados — and handfuls of cassava, and a calabash of something they called wabool. These they timidly presented to Father, who distributed them to us, saying, "This will keep your bowels open!"

He showed Mr. Haddy an avocado and said, "Two bucks at the A and P. Two *lemps* for one!"

"Butter pear," Mr. Maywit said nervously.

"How is it?" Mr. Haddy said.

"Right here," Francis Lungley said.

"Am naat taakin to you," Mr. Haddy said. "You," he said to Mr. Maywit. "How is it?"

But he was too frightened to speak up.

Father said, "I want you all to meet our friends and neighbors, the Maywits."

They gaped at us, we gaped at them. This family too was a father, a mother, and four children. But the smallest child was naked and being carried like a knapsack by one of the girls. They were our reflections — shrunken shadows of us. The man was short and had brown barklike skin, and the woman was chicken-eyed, and the kids had dirty legs.

"That is you actual name — Maywit?" Mr. Haddy said.

Father said, "Pay no attention to this interloper."

The man said "Ow" in agreement. Then he blinked flies from his eyelids and said, "We was just going out of you house, Fadder." He pronounced it "huss."

"You're not going anywhere," Father said. "You're staying put. I've got some work for you to do."

"More spearmints," Mr. Haddy said, and made the Zambus giggle.

"You want some work?"

The man said he didn't mind. He made wild eyes at his turned-up toes.

"That's your house. You can have it as long as you make yourselves useful," Father said. "I've got a house of my own over there, beyond the culverts and the breezeways, just above the mooring and to the left of the barn, where it meets those beanfields."

Ain't see no huss, someone said softly. The Zambus and the Maywits and Mr. Haddy flicked the bushes with their eyes, searching for the things Father had named. There were no culverts, no breezeways. There was no barn, there was no house or beanfields. Then they looked at his finger.

"Just cause you ain't see it," Mr. Haddy said, "don't mean it ain't there," and had a fit of laughing.

Father was still smiling at those same bushes when Clover said, "Dad, there's some ants trying to get into my tent."

"Ants all over this place," Mr. Haddy said. "Tigers, too. Some of these baboons bigger than a grown-up man. And I step on monkeyshoo on the path."

"Them is wee-wees." This was the chicken-eyed woman, Mrs. Maywit.

"Yep, them's wee-wees." Mr. Maywit pinched an ant in his fingers and flicked it away. He did not do this disgustedly, but gently and with a kind of sorrow.

"You listen to these people," Mr. Haddy said. "They know what they talking. They lives here. Axe me anything bout the coast, but don't axe me jungles."

And this was true. Mr. Haddy was a coastal big shot, his voice snickered and mocked in this jungle. Out of his element, he clowned.

"They carries leafs," Mr. Maywit said. "But they ain't hot you."

Father said, "Tomorrow I'll make a platform for those tents, and some insect traps. I don't want ants and spiders crawling all over my kids."

Mr. Maywit said, "You from Nicaragua, Fadder?"

"He ain't from no Nicaragua," Mr. Haddy said. "What make you say that?"

"They got some trouble there. Last people come through. Had some ruckboos. They was from Nicaragua." He spoke in a slow puzzled way, as if he had just been woken up and was struggling to be interested in his own words.

"We're from the United States," Father said.

Mrs. Maywit sighed in appreciation, and Mr. Maywit said, "That is another place, for true."

Father plumped his hand on the spongy ground. "But this is our home now," he said. "You think this is a foreign country?"

Mr. Maywit shook his head. No, he did not think so.

The air around us was soupy green, like the water in a fish tank, and green shadows rose as the sun dropped.

Mother said, "Do many people come through here, like those people from Nicaragua?"

"Some preachers, Ma," Mrs. Maywit said, staring at Mother with her chicken eyes. "Churcha God. Jove as Wetness. Shouters."

"And Dunkers," Mr. Maywit said.

"And Dunkers."

"If we get any of them," Father said, "I'll show them the door. When we get a door!"

"Never mind," Mr. Maywit said.

The sun was now behind the hills, and though the sky was still lighted, green shadows had crept up to our tree. Jeronimo had more substance in the dark. It had sounds — insect crackle, bird grunts, the river's watery mutter — and these sounds gave it size, and the odors shaped it. At its furthest edge a Jeronimo bird blew softly in a tree.

Father gave a little speech in the filling darkness.

"We came here in three jumps," he said. He told them how we had left home in a hurry and gone to Baltimore, then La Ceiba, then on the *Little Haddy*. He made it sound adventurous, but it had seemed accidental at the time, and not much fun. "What were we looking for? I'll tell you," he said. "We were looking for you."

He named everyone present, even the silent Zambus who had carried the seed bags and metal pipes from Fish Bucket. Somehow, he knew their full names. What was remarkable to me was that he had not slept for two days. He had loaded *Little Haddy* and done seventy-five pushups on the pier and steered along the coast and up the river and then led us all in single file along the path to Jeronimo.

He was strangely energetic and talkative when he had gone without sleep.

Jerry and the twins were asleep. Mother was nodding off. But Father walked up and down in the green firelight and whacked the smoky air and said that he was happy, and had plans, and was glad there were so many people here to witness this historic moment.

He said he did not believe in accidents.

"I was looking for you," he said. "And what were you doing? You were waiting for me! If you hadn't been waiting, you would have been some other place. But you were here when I came. I need you good people, and I've got the feeling that you need me."

Everyone agreed that this was so.

Francis Lungley said, "I go down to that river. I ain't know why. I just have to go. Then I see that old lanch fetch over."

"That is why I looks out the window," Mr. Maywit said, in the same mystified voice. "I ain't know why. I sees this man from Nighted Stays. Standing in the grass. That is why."

Mr. Haddy said, "I have a dream. Bout a man. And this is the man, wearing the same cloves as the man in the dream and a peaky hat. I meet him in my dream."

But I knew that what Mr. Haddy said was a fib. He had told me himself that he had met Father on La Ceiba pier and thought he was a missionary from the Moravian Church. I did not contradict him now, because the mood around this Jeronimo campfire had become solemn.

"I was sent here," Father said. "I'm not going to tell you who sent me, or why. And I'm not going to tell you who I am or what I aim to do. That's just talk. I'm going to *show* you why I'm here. You go ahead and watch. And if you don't like what you see, you can kill me."

Tiredness had made his voice harsh. He hissed this again ("You can kill me"), then let it sink in. There were murmurs. Mr. Haddy scratched his big toe and said he would not dare do such a thing as kill Father, though he was sure hoping to get his launch fixed pretty soon.

Father resumed, saying, "I didn't come here to boss you around. I came here to work for you. If I'm not working hard enough, you just tell me, and I'll work harder. You come up to me and say, 'Mister, you've got to do a whole lot better than this.' I'm working for you people, and you're going to see things you've never seen before. What do you want me to do first? It's up to you."

No one spoke.

"You want some food?" Father said. "You want a bridge and some beans and a paddle pump and a chicken run?"

Mr. Maywit cleared his throat.

"I heard you," Father said. "I'll obey. And those Indians up in the hills are going to look down here and they're not going to believe their eyes. They're going to be absolutely feverish with amazement."

Every listener was transfixed. The only sounds were from the jungle, and here and there a smack when mosquitoes were slapped. Beyond our tents and our little fire, the jungle was black. The blackness screeched, it grunted — it had risen up and wrapped us in its noise and in its sweet-sour folds. The hidden insects were excited and the darkened trees made a sound like brooms.

"Now let's get to bed," Father said, "before we all get bitten alive."

But he remained by the fire.

"Ain't you sleeping?" Mr. Haddy said.

Father said, "I never sleep!"

The next day we planted the miracle beans. Father made a ceremony of it. He lined up the men and had them dig with homemade shovels — planks that Father had planed into blades. Mr. Haddy did not dig. He said, "I ain't a farmer — I am a sailor." And Father said, "He doesn't want to get his prehensile fingers dirty." The men stood shoulder-to-shoulder, stabbing the dirt. It was not difficult. The German Weerwilly had had a garden here — most of his bean-poles were still standing.

By mid-afternoon we had turned over an acre of weeds. Father dragged out his bean seeds. They were called miracle beans, he said, because they were a forty-day variety. The first ones he planted he gave names. "This is Captain Haddy," he said, and held up a bean. "This is Francis," and he held up another one. Then he poked them into the holes. "This one is Mr. Maywit. This is Charlie. This is Jerry — "

He straddled the furrows and when he ran out of names, he planted faster. Half the field was miracle beans, the rest was Wonder Corn and tomatoes and peppers — the seeds we had bought in Florence, Massachusetts. It rained in the afternoon. Father said he had been expecting it. That was part of the ceremony, too, he said.

Mother said to him, when we were alone that night, "Aren't you laying it on a little thick, Allie?"

But Father just laughed and said that it had been his intention to get us out of the States and save us. He had not thought that he would be saving other people as well. Yet that was what had happened. If we had not come here, these people would have been bone-idle, and the vultures would have made a meal of them.

"I want to give people a chance to use their know-how," Father said.

The following day, he asked Mr. Maywit what his occupation was.

"I been a sexton in my time. Up in Limon," Mr. Maywit said. And he explained. "Polish the brosses, make em shine. Set out vesmins. Hang the numbers on the board. Tidy out the pews."

Father looked discouraged.

"Also I kin do some barbering."

"Hair cutting?"

"Cutting and dressing. And ironing hair. And twisting. Heating it flat. And I know how to wax — flows."

Small night rats, called pacas, gnawed through the corners of the nylon tents. We ate the pacas. They were good-tasting, and Father said it was poetic justice. We made a wooden platform for the tents to keep their floors dry and hold the tents straight — the stakes had not held in the wet ground. Down at the river we made a trap that funneled fish into a wire cage, and from a simple roof and frame and some of the mosquito netting we built a mosquito-proof gazebo where we could congregate. These were gadgets, not inventions, but they made life more comfortable, and within very few days I could see the skeleton of a settlement in Jeronimo.

Every evening, the Zambus turned their backs on us and crept into the jungle. Every morning, looking wrinkled and damp, they reappeared. They had a camp there, Father said. Toward the end of the first week, Mr. Haddy left Jeronimo with some of the Zambus. Mr. Haddy did not come back immediately, but the Zambus did, towing log rafts on harnesses Father had made for them. On these rafts were the last of our supplies from *Little Haddy.*

The boilers, the tanks, and the rest of the scrap metal were dragged away and stacked. Some of the pipes Father used for his first real invention at Jeronimo — a simple paddle wheel that moved a belt of coconut cups up a tower on the riverbank and filled a drum with water. The height of the drum gave it enough force to pipe the water anywhere we liked, but most of it went to an enclosed shed that became known as the bathhouse. We washed clothes there, and took showers, and boiled water for drinking, and altogether it improved our lives.

The excess water flowed through a stone culvert and under the bathhouse to a privy at the edge of the clearing, where our latrine stood. The privy was always clean, but the Maywits' latrine was mucky and so fly-blown that Father said, "Anyone who uses *that* throne is Lord of the Flies."

The first invention, a pump made on the spot, was a piece of primitive technology. The Maywits and Zambus were greatly impressed by its flapping and splashing, but they said they could not understand why Father had made such a thing in the rainy season, when there was water everywhere.

"We're building for the future, the dry season," Father said. He said it was a civilized thing to do. "And know why it's a perfect invention?"

"Cause you ain't have to walk down there with a bucket," Mr. Maywit said.

"That's blindingly obvious," Father said. "No, it's perfect because it's self-propelled, uses available energy, and it's nonpolluting. Make one of these up in Massachusetts and they'd have you certified. But they're not interested in perfection."

Some days later, after a heavy rain, the river rose and the paddle wheel was torn off its brackets and rods. Father strengthened it with metal straps and it continued to supply us with water and went on sluicing the latrine.

Each time he made something, Father said, "This is why I'm here."

It was Father's policy that no one should be idle. "If you see me sit down, you can do the same," he said. But he even ate standing up. Part of the beanfield was divided into plots — one plot for each kid, who had to keep his portion weeded. There were other tasks assigned to us, such as collecting firewood and keeping the fish trap mucked out. And when our chores were done we were to gather stones the size of hen's eggs and use them for paving the paths. So there was always something to do, which was perhaps just as well because it took our minds off the heat and the insects. And the uncertainty, too, for though Father said confidently, "This is why I'm here," we did not know why we were, and were too scared to ask.

The work in the first few weeks was mostly land clearing. The process of clearing the land of bushes and small trees revealed more of Weerwilly's activities and uncovered some of the implements he had abandoned. We found a plow and bales of chicken wire and any number of small tools, a lantern that worked pretty well, and an oil drum with enough fuel in it to last us for months. These discoveries filled Father with enthusiasm and convinced him that Weerwilly had failed because he was careless, like the people in America who junked perfectly good lumber and wire. And he said that if the Maywits had been a little sharper, they would have found this stuff and used it themselves to improve the place, instead of playing Lord of the Flies.

One day, following some of the Zambus who were clearing land, I came upon a bird jerking in a clump of grass. But it was not the grass that held it — it was a web, a thick wet spider web, like a hank of wool. I knelt down and untangled it, and I had let it go before I thought to look for the spider. Then I saw it — as big as my hand, and brown and hairy, and matching the color of the fever-grass roots. The Zambu Bucky said it was a Hanancy spider and not only did she catch birds but she ate them as well, and she would eat me too if I was not careful. The bird, a peachy-gray color, was one that Bucky said just came a few weeks in the year. I guessed it was a migratory bird, too innocent to be wary of the spiders in the jungle grass. It worried me to think that we were a little like that bird.

There was everything in this grass — scorpions, snakes, wire, chicken bones, mice, pacas, wine bottles, ant nests, and shovelheads. We cut the grass so that mosquitoes would not have a place to breed, but in the process we often found other useful things. For example, while the clearing went on (it was supervised by Mother, who was infected by Father's desire to shave the whole of Jeronimo and rid us of bugs), Mr. Maywit and Father were digging postholes for our new house. Father kept saying that what they needed was a posthole digger. Later that day, Francis Lungley clanked his machete against a metal object. He brought this thing to Father, who said it was the business end of a posthole digger.

He worked its blades, which were like jaws, and said, "All she needs is a couple of handles and we're on our way."

It took him less than an hour to get it working.

"I needed a posthole digger, and a posthole digger was found. Now I ask you — was this accident or was this part of some grand design?"

The best find in all the land-clearing was a stack of wood, cut into planks. Father said it was the best grade of mahogany — so good, he said, that he had half a mind to make it into a piano. It was too heavy for the house, but he said he knew just what to do with it. It was put aside, and the snakes swept out of it, and it was left to dry.

"Find me some more of that lumber over there," he said, and that same day some more wood was found. The Zambus laughed, because it was right where Father said it would be.

Mother worked alongside the Zambus, wearing one of Father's shirts, with her hair done up in a scarf. This was Father's idea — he said that none of the Zambus would stop working while a woman was on her feet cutting brush. Soon, most of Jeronimo was slashed and burned. It looked as though a battle had been fought there — black land, black stumps, steam and smoke issuing from cracks in the earth. Mr. Maywit's rusty hut stood hanging with morning-glories on an island of its own banana trees. What was to be our house was a rectangular corral of thirty posts sticking about six feet out of the ground. Once the floor was set on these posts, the cooking apparatus was moved to it from the guanacaste tree. This underfloor part of the house became our kitchen.

Some corrugated iron sheets were uncovered in the land-clearing. But Father did not like the look of them, and for a number of days he went upriver with three of the Zambus to cut bamboo. He left early in the morning, and an hour or so later the bamboo in eight-foot lengths would appear, floating down the river into Jeronimo. These were brought ashore by the other Zambus, the Maywits, and Mother. But most of the carrying was done by the river, Father said. He had a genius for simplifying any job.

These bamboos, about five inches thick, were carefully split in

half and smoothed inside to resemble gutters. By laying them over
the roof beams and fitting them like tiles — locking them together
lengthwise and cupping the line of grooves with an overlapping
series laid face-down — a completely watertight roof was made.
Father was so pleased by this, he sang.

> *Under the bam!*
> *Under the boo!*

He made the walls in the same way — we had four rooms and a
porch, which Father called the Gallery. The whole thing had over-
hanging roof eaves, like an enormous birdhouse.

Father was so taken up with the house and the work projects in
Jeronimo that our lessons stopped. Mother said they were neglecting
us. They ought to be spending some time with the kids, she said.
What happened to our education?

"This is the very education they need," Father said. "Everyone in
America should be getting it. When America is devastated and laid
to waste, these are the skills that will save these kids. Not writing poetry, or fingerpainting, or what's the capital of Texas — but survival,
rebuilding a civilization from the smoking ruins."

It was his old speech, War in America, but now he felt he had a
remedy.

The Maywits and Zambus regarded the bamboo house as a
miracle.

Father said, "They don't paint pictures, they don't weave baskets
or carve faces on coconuts or hollow out salad bowls. They don't
sing or do dances or write poems. They can't draw a straight line.
That's why I like them. That's innocence. They're a little touched
with religion, but they'll get over that. Mother, there's hope here."

During the house raising, Father encouraged us to watch him
with the Maywit children. Clover and April got on well with the
Maywit girls — though Clover bossed them by making them recite
the alphabet over and over again — and Jerry played with the boy
called Drainy, who was also ten. None was my age, so this left me
free to help Father, or play by myself.

Drainy was a bug-eyed boy with a shaven head and spaces between his teeth. He had a collection of little cars and toy bikes made
out of coathanger wire. As he was playing with Jerry, I found some
of these wire toys and rattled them along the ground. Father asked
me what they were.

I showed him. They were ingeniously made. They had moving parts, and one resembled in the smallest detail a tricycle, with pedals and wheels.

Father was fascinated by anything mechanical. He sat down and studied them. After he had meditated over them for several minutes and tried them, he said, "These were made by some very sophisticated instruments. See how that wire is twisted and joined? There's no soldering at all, and the angles and bends are perfectly formed."

He looked at me and winked.

"Charlie," he said, "I think someone's hiding tools from us. I had these people all wrong. I could use the kind of precision tools that made these."

He showed Mr. Maywit, who said sure enough, they were Drainy's. Drainy was summoned to the Gallery.

"Where did you get these?" Father asked.

"I make um."

"Take your time, son," Father said. "I want you to show me exactly how you made them. I'll give you some wire. Now you get your tools and make one for me."

Father gave the boy some fine strands of wire, but Drainy did not move. He held them dumbly in his dirty hand, and sucked his teeth.

"Don't you want to show me your tools?"

Mr. Maywit gave the boy a poke in the shoulder.

"Ain't got no tools."

Father said, "So you can't make them after all?"

"Kin," Drainy said. He squatted and took the wire in his teeth, and by chewing it and drawing it through the gaps like dental floss, and champing it like a marrow bone, he formed it into a sprocket and held it up for Father to admire.

Mr. Maywit's excitement made him gabble — "He make em wif his teef!"

Father said to Drainy, "You take care of those choppers and brush them every day. I'm going to need you later on."

13

IT WAS NOT an easy life these first weeks in Jeronimo. It was no coconut kingdom of free food and grass huts and sunny days, under
the bam, under the boo. Wilderness was ugly and unusable, and
where were the dangerous animals? There was something stubborn
about jungle trees, the way they crowded each other and gave us no
shade. I saw cruelty in the hanging vines and selfishness in their root
systems. This was work, and more work, and a routine that took up
every daylight hour. On the *Unicorn* and in La Ceiba, and even in
Hatfield, we had done pretty much what we pleased. Father had left
us alone and gone about his own business. Usually I had helped
him, but sometimes not. Here, things were different.

There was a bell at sunup, by which time Father already had the
fire going and the coffee on. The Maywits always joined us — they
had stopped cooking for themselves the week we arrived in Jeronimo. After pineapple and oatmeal, Father yelled for the Zambus
and told us our "targets" for the day. On Mondays he gave us our
targets for the week: finish the house, or get so many bushels of
stones, or clear a certain amount of land, or cut beanpoles, or dig
trenches for culverts. The Maywits were mainly the gardeners, the
Zambus mainly the landclearers and builders, and the children —
the Maywits and us — the collectors and cleaners.

We did our jobs throughout the morning, and by lunchtime the
heat was terrible — it was now July. Lunch was always hot soup,
because Father had the idea that it was necessary for us to sweat
buckets: it kept us cool, nature's way. Afternoon work was often interrupted by rain, but the downpours did not last long and we were

soon back on the job. All work stopped in the late afternoon, for it was then that the black flies and mosquitoes appeared, and their bites were torture.

Just before sundown we took turns in the bathhouse, washing up. One of the rules was a shower bath every day. In Hatfield we had never kept so clean, but here Father became a maniac for cleanliness. He made us change our clothes every day, too. Clothes to be washed were dumped in a tub, and one of the smells of Jeronimo was this skunk stew of boiling clothes. Mrs. Maywit had always washed her family's clothes in the river, but now she used the tin clothes tub. Father was pleased that the Maywits had begun following our example in taking a daily shower. Only the Zambus remained the same — they steamed like tomcats, as Father did when he was very angry.

In the early days, we spent the dark mosquito hours between supper and bedtime in the insect-proof gazebo. After the house was finished, we sat on the Gallery (also insect-proof) until it was time to turn in. The Maywits often joined us. Mr. Maywit told us about the Indians in the mountains and up the rivers. He liked giving information. He said it was true what Mr. Haddy had told us, about some of the Indians having long tails. He said one tribe of Indians was all giants, and another pygmies.

Mr. Maywit's strangest story was about some Indians he called Munchies. He said that Munchies lived in a certain part of Mosquitia, and he confessed that he had thought, on first seeing us, that we might be Munchies. The Munchies kept themselves hidden in secret cities in the jungle. They had been here longer than the Miskito Indians, or Payas, or Twahkas, or Zambus. But there was nothing to be afraid of in the Munchies, because they were peaceful and virtuous. They were also very tall, and built pyramids, and were in all respects a noble people.

Father said, "You forgot the important part, Mr. Maywit. They're white Indians. Whiter than me — even whiter than you."

The Maywits were the color of instant coffee powder and had burned hair and green eyes.

"You see them?" Mr. Maywit said.

"Dad knows everything," Clover said.

"I know about these Munchies," Father said. "Tell us about their gold, Mr. Maywit."

"I ain't know nothing about no gold."

"They've got gold mines," Father said. "Nuggets as big as walnuts. They hammer it thin and write on it. They roll it and make bangles. Gold dust and gold slabs — ingots a yard wide."

"Haddy tell you this?"

Father said, "Nope. But save your breath, Mr. Maywit. I don't want to hear about white Indians who are angels. I want to hear about the devils from Nicaragua."

"The ones they carry ruckboos?"

"Not only them, but the ones that make things go wrong, give you headaches and toothaches and flat tires, let the mosquitoes in, and hide things that belong to you, so you never find them again. The ones that make funny noises at night and keep you awake and pull your house down and set you on fire." ·

"Never hear of them," Mr. Maywit said. "Where you hear?"

"Stands to reason. If there's golden white Munchies in secret cities, there's got to be horrible devils that do you wrong, isn't that so?"

Mother said, "Allie's pulling your leg, Mr. Maywit. He doesn't mean a word he says. I think that's a darned interesting story about the Munchies."

"But he hear it before."

"Tell me something I don't know," Father said. "Forget the Munchies and the devils. If you believe in them, you never get anything done — spend half your life looking over your shoulder. Personally, I don't believe in Munchies, unless I'm a Munchy." He frowned. "Which is entirely within the realm of possibility."

Jerry said he did not believe in Munchies, and April said it was a silly superstition, like the Easter Bunny and Santa Claus and God.

Mr. Maywit said that we could think what we wanted, but for true he believed in God and so did Mrs. Maywit. They had seen God with their own eyes at the Shouter church over in Santa Rosa.

"What exactly did God look like?" Father asked.

"Like a bill-bird in a cloud," Mr. Maywit said. "That is what Ma Kennywick say."

"So you didn't see God?"

"No, Ma Kennywick see God, and I see Ma Kennywick."

"Up the Shouters," the chicken-eyed Mrs. Maywit said.

"It was a speerience," Mr. Maywit said.

"I'm sure," Father said. "Now tell me something I don't know."

"Know about Duppies?"

I said, "Mr. Haddy knows about them."

"But Mr. Haddy has flown the coop," Father said. "So let's give this gentleman the floor. Go on, sir, you've given us your proof for the existence of God — that is, Ma Kennywick's shouting that the Almighty looks like a bill-bird in a cloud. Now tell us what a Duppy is."

"The Shouters tell me about them, and lots of folks, even Zambu fellers, believe in Duppies. Mainly, Fadder, they is ghosts."

"Of dead people," Father said.

"Of alive people."

"I see."

"Everyone got a Duppy. They is the same as youself. But they is you other self. They got bodies of they own."

"So half the world is people and the other half is Duppies, is that right?"

"Never mind," Mr. Maywit said.

Mrs. Maywit was wringing her fingers. She said, "Cep you cain't ketchum."

"Invisible?" Father said.

"They is here," Mr. Maywit said. "Somewhere. Waitin. They shows up every time to time. But they ain't hot you. Make you shout, Duppies do. That is why Shouters see them. Me, I never see my Duppy."

Father said, "How do you know I'm not your Duppy?"

Mr. Maywit did not say another word. He stared at Father and his coffee-dust face became slack with fear. His eyes grew another rim around the sockets. It was as if at last he understood who this man was, and was about to surrender to this belief.

"That's enough, Allie," Mother said. She spoke to Mr. Maywit. "Can't you see he's joking?"

"Never mind." But Mr. Maywit's voice trembled as he said so.

Father was interested in what Mr. Maywit had said, but he went on joking about Munchies and Duppies. I was sure he believed some of it — it was too good not to believe. Live ghosts! White Indians! And

I knew from past experience that Father was never more mocking than when he was discussing something serious. If someone was fearful, Father joked. If the person tried to be funny, Father quoted the Bible or said, "Haven't you heard there's a war coming?"

He was complicated in other ways. After we got to Jeronimo he claimed that he could go without sleep. He was awake when we went to bed, and he was at work when we got up in the morning. He also said he could go for days without food, and never got sick, and wasn't bitten by mosquitoes. This mystified the Maywits and the Zambus, but I knew he was trying to set an example — if he worked hard and did not complain, the others would have to. Work and lack of sleep did not make him irritable. In fact, I had never seen him happier. And Mother, who loved him in this mood, was happy too.

Now we had a house and a number of inventions that made life convenient. The Zambus, whom we had met by chance on that Fish Bucket riverbank, seemed contented. They walked around in trunks and short-sleeved shirts that Mother had made for them out of sail-cloth. And the Maywits, with Father's help, improved their own house.

Our miracle beans were more than half grown and already had pods that Father said would be ready for picking in a few weeks. The other crops flourished beside the spillways of irrigation ditches. Entering Jeronimo from the Swampmouth path, you saw something that looked like a settlement — houses, gardens, stone-paved paths, and the pump wheel flinging water into the drum. It was the civilized place Father had seen that first day, when all we had seen was tall grass and a mud bank and a smoldering armchair.

I was luckier than anyone. When the twins went down with squitters because of stomach trouble, and then Mother and Jerry, I did not get sick. And I noticed that Father liked me a little better for that. He had a way of insinuating that if anyone was sick he was faking, or at least exaggerating. He never said "He's sick," but always "He says he's sick" or "She claims she's ill."

"I haven't the time to get sick," he said. "If I had a little spare time, I'd probably get sick as a dog!"

One day, Mr. Haddy returned. By then, Father had started building what he called the Plant, which was so far only a large framework of peeled poles two stories high, in the hollow at the back of the cleared land. The boilers were dumped there. We heard the motor before we saw the launch. Father made me climb to the top of the poles to get a look at it.

"Who is it?" he said, sounding angry for the first time in Jeronimo.

"It's the *Little Haddy,*" I said. I could see the torn awning and the little wheel house.

Father was glad about this, but when he got down to the landing he did not like what he saw. Mr. Haddy was not alone. There was a man with him — a white man, carrying a suitcase ashore.

Mr. Haddy explained that he had pumped out the launch at Fish Bucket, and patched it. He had found that without the boilers and scrap metal there was enough freeboard for it to float easily in the shallowest river. After spending two weeks at Santa Rosa getting it properly fixed, he decided to see if he could make it all the way to Jeronimo, by sailing up the Bonito River, where it branched from the Aguan.

"I bring you some real food from Rosy — carkles and conks and wilks." These shellfish were in kegs on the deck. Then he showed us a dead turtle. Its flippers had been hacked off, and its lizard head of beaky bone hung out of its big barnacled shell. "And a hicatee."

But Father was not interested.

He said, "Who's this hamburger?"

"This here Mr. Struss from Rosy."

"How do you do," the man said. He stepped forward onto the mushy bank and set his suitcase down. Then he took his sunglasses off and tried to smile, but his eyes wrinkled shut in the sunlight and gave him a squinched face. He was a bit older than Father, and fleshy, and there was a dark sweat patch on every bulge of his body — moons under his arms, and a belt of wet around his waist. He turned his suffering smile on us. "What lovely kids." He looked beyond us. "And you've made yourself a beautiful home."

"What do you want?" Father said, blocking the path and keeping the man sinking in mush.

The Zambus had put down their tools, and the Maywits had trooped from the garden. There were about seventeen of us here, watching Father and the stranger.

"Mr. Haddy said he was coming up this way. He kindly let me hitch a ride."

Mr. Haddy said, "He a paying passenger, but I do all the steering. He work the sounding chain. He know the way."

"I've been here before. Mr. Roper knows me. Don't you, Mr. Roper."

He was speaking to Mr. Maywit.

Father said, "There's no Mr. Roper here. It's a case of mistaken identity. The heat is making you rave."

Mr. Maywit just goggled and kept his mouth shut.

The man was confused. He put his sunglasses on again and picked at the sweat patches on his shirt and said, "I came here to ask you all a question."

"We're not interested in your questions," Father said.

"You just answered it, brother. And I'm glad I came. Because the question is, 'Are you saved?' And I've got a funny feeling, the Lord — "

"The Lord is up in that tree," Father said, pointing with his finger stump at a bill-bird on a branch.

The man stared at Father's finger, and even adjusted his sunglasses to get a better look.

"Go away," Father said, and gave the man his deaf-man's smile.

"You can't answer for these people here."

"I'm not answering at all," Father said. "As far as I'm concerned, you didn't even open your mouth or ask a question. You're not allowed to. I own this place, and you don't have my permission to come ashore. If you want to talk to these people, you'll have to do it somewhere else, outside Jeronimo. About half a mile due north of here you'll come to a little swamp. That's Swampmouth, the Jeronimo line. Can't miss it. You go there and do all the preaching you like. Start walking, Mr. Struss."

He handed the man his suitcase.

"The Lord sent me here," Mr. Struss said.

"Bull," Father said. "The Lord hasn't got the slightest idea that this place exists. If he had, he would have done something about it a long time ago."

"This river doesn't belong to you, brother."

"You planning to walk on the water?" Father said. "If so, don't say another word until you're midstream."

Mr. Struss looked us over. Flies had gathered on his shoulders and he was breathing hard.

"You know I'm a fair man," Father said to us. "If any of you people want to go with him, I won't stop you. Hurry on down to Swampmouth and listen to what this gentleman has to offer. Anyone interested?"

Mr. Maywit and his chicken-eyed wife looked anxiously at Father. The Zambus had started giggling.

"Excuse me, Mr. Roper, will you please — "

"Shut it," Father said, and Francis Lungley laughed out loud.

Mother said, "You'd better do as my husband says. There are some dugout canoes at Swampmouth, and I'll give you a bag lunch. You'll have no trouble getting back to the coast."

"The Lord wants me here," Mr. Struss said.

Father said, "That's what I like about you people — your complete lack of presumption. But listen, I'm not going to tempt you with martyrdom, so just shove off and don't come back."

A little while later, from the porch of the house, we saw Mr. Struss walking down the riverbank toward Swampmouth. He carried his suitcase in one hand and Mother's lunch bag in the other. He was alone.

Father said, "Imagine that hamburger coming all that way to ask a silly question." He put his face close to Mr. Maywit's and said, "Are you saved?"

"Yes, Fadder."

He then asked everyone else in turn and they said yes and laughed along with him. He asked me and I said yes, but I was at the window and I saw that, hearing us laugh, Mr. Struss glanced up. He looked sick, but he kept on walking.

The days passed. They were sunny, there was little rain, they were muffled by dust. But the nights were furious with the ringing cries of insects, and bird grunts that sometimes rose to screams. The darkness helped us hear the soft splash of monkeys on branches, and the chafing of crickyjeens was like combustion, as if every bush and tree were burning. And night heat was more suffocating than in the day, and made sleep seem like death. It was a dreamless plunge into that riot.

Father spent these days hammering. He did not say why, but his eyes told me that his thoughts were storms. And every man in Jeronimo labored with Father at the plant. It was, so far, only a skeleton, with pipes buckled to poles and men hanging like monkeys to the crosspieces, where they followed Father's orders. It was slow work, and for a long time it did not look like anything at all.

The day after the bean harvest, Father declared a holiday. It was our first day off in six weeks of work. The Zambus shot a curassow and the Maywits brought cooked cassava and plantains and fruit. Father would not allow any of the Maywits' chickens to be killed. "That's living on your capital." We had an afternoon feast in the front yard. Mr. Maywit and Mr. Haddy took turns telling stories about the Mosquito Coast — pirates and cannibals — and Clover and April sang "Under the Bam, Under the Boo."

Father gave a speech about us. We were bricks, he said. He went on to explain all the things you could do with bricks. And he got angry only once. This was when Mr. Haddy praised the food. Father hated anyone talking about food — cooking it or eating it. Fools did it, he said. It was selfish and indecent to talk about how things tasted.

He called this our first thanksgiving.

It was now August. Mr. Maywit said he knew this without looking at a calendar, because the sickla bird had arrived. The bird was shiny green and yellow, and very small, with a warbling song that reminded me of the fluting music we had heard the boy play on the beach our first evening in La Ceiba.

Work on the plant continued. The mahogany planks were hoisted into position and bolted to the poles. The floors told me nothing, but when the sides went up it took on a familiar shape, and before it was finished I guessed what it was.

14

MOST OF THEM, including the Maywits (they had seen one in Tru-jillo), thought that Father had run mad and built a silo.

"Shoo! What green you gung put in it?" Mr. Haddy said, speaking for everyone.

Father said he was not going to put anything into it, and certainly not grain. "But just you wait and see what I pull out of it! And keep pulling! Listen" — he whispered and stared — "this gizmo is sempiternal. It won't ever quit."

It was not the bottle that some silos are, nor was it a thermos-jug shape, and there were no feed bins. It was tall and square-sided. It had now windows and only one hatchway door, twenty feet up and no stairs to it. It was a plain wooden building, a huge mahogany closet raised up in our clearing in the jungle. A box — but a gigantic box, with a tin lid. It was an oddity of such magnificence that it was a thing in itself, like an Egyptian pyramid. Its great shape was enough. It did not need another purpose. But I knew it was the Worm Tub, enlarged a thousand times.

No sooner was it raised than flocks of people came to look. I supposed our hammering was heard in the woods. Father made these strangers welcome. They were hill Indians and Spanish-speaking farmers, and Creoles and Zambus. The Indians did not stay, but the others did — Mr. Harkins and Mr. Peaselee, old Mrs. Kennywick (the very one who had seen God in the Shouter church), and some more. They said that they had watched the house — as they called it — rising. They marveled at it. It was taller than the trees and flat-topped like nothing else around here. They had seen it from far-off.

That was an advantage, their curiosity. Just when Father needed help, these people crept out of the trees and said they were willing. With the finishing of the other buildings and the first harvest and the rest of the crops coming along fast — all we needed — everyone in Jeronimo assumed our work was done. This made the plant — as Father went on calling it — a bewildering surprise. What was it for? What was it doing here?

Father promised more marvels, but there was still wood to add to the structure proper, and still brickmaking to do.

"Where is the bricks, Fadder?" Mr. Maywit asked.

"You're standing on them." Father pointed his finger stump at the ground. "Clay! This is all bricks, just sitting there, waiting to be made!"

There was ironwork, too.

"The Iron Age comes to Jeronimo," Father said. "A month ago, it was the Stone Age — digging vegetables with wooden shovels and clobbering rats with flint axes. We're moving right along. It'll be 1832 in a few days! By the way, people, I'm planning to skip the twentieth century altogether."

There was more plumbing in this than a waterworks, but the building went on smoothly. The new people were glad to do the work and liked listening to Father, who talked the whole time.

"One of the sicknesses of the twentieth century?" he said. "I'll tell you the worst one. People can't stand to be alone. Can't tolerate it! So they go to the movies, get drive-in hamburgers, put their home telephone numbers in the crapsheets and say, 'Please call me up!' It's sick. People hate their own company — they cry when they see themselves in mirrors. It scares them, the way their faces look. Maybe that's a clue to the whole thing —"

Most of the plumbing was bends — enough to make a cow cross-eyed. Some of the bends were the fixed elbows we had brought from La Ceiba, and some we made in the forge. The forge was built with the first bricks, and the bellows (a simple fire was not hot enough) was two paddles and a leather bladder. Father saved his welding torch for finishing off each seal, because he did not want to waste the cylinder of gas. The sight of Father in his welder's mask, his eyes darting in the mask's window, with his gauntlets and his asbestos apron and his fizzing torch, fascinated the onlookers. And he kept talking, even with his mask on.

"Why do things get weaker and worse?" came the echoey small mask-voice, as if out of a conch. "Why don't they get better? Because we accept that they fall apart! But they don't have to — they could last forever. Why do things get more expensive? Any fool can see that they should get cheaper as technology gets more efficient. It's despair to accept the senility of obsolescence —"

They liked his talk, but they loved the spray of sparks and the scabs of dead metal flying. They were astonished to see iron bars soften and drip like tar under the jet of blue flame.

The welding torch was one of Father's toys. There were others — his Thunderbox and Atom-smasher, and even his simpler ones, like the Beaver, which machined and threaded pipes — a hand-operated jaw of his own making with a toothy mouth set off by clamps. They were toys to him, but magic to the others. When he took a rusty pipe, reamed it, bent it, gave it threads, and fitted it with so many elbows it looked like a crankshaft, everyone gathered to watch him. Then he was a sorcerer in his iron mask, transforming a hunk of scrap iron into a symmetrical part for the plumbing that was the stomach and intestines of the plant. He claimed that even with this basic equipment, he could make the simplest rod or pipe into the tiniest computer circuit.

"I could make microchips out of the thickest iron brick around. I could make dumb metal talk. That's what computer circuits are — words and paragraphs in a primitive language. You don't think of computers as primitive," he said — he was speaking directly to Mr. Harkins — "but they are. They're mechanical savages."

He said he was making a monster. "I'm Doctor Frankenstein!" he howled through his welder's mask. He called one set of pipes its lungs, and another its poop shaft, and two tanks, "a pair of kidneys." He always spoke of the plant as "he" — "He needs a gizzard today," or "This will fit straight onto his liver," or "How's this for his gullet?"

Harkins and Peaselee laughed at this and asked Father if his monster had a name.

Father said, "Tell them, Charlie."

I remembered.

"Fat Boy," I said.

Everyone whispered the name.

Jerry and the twins were surprised that I knew something they didn't — not only its name but its purpose, how it worked, and what it would look like when it was done. They showed me some respect and for a while stopped calling me "Crummo" and "Spackoid."

Even Mother was a little curious about how I came to know so much. I told her that I had seen the scale model. I remembered the morning Father and I had loaded the little Worm Tub onto the pickup truck and driven past the scarecrow to give Polski a demonstration — Father happy, then Father fuming, and the wooden chest gulping and producing a disk of ice in a tumbler. I remembered more than that — the rubber seal in Northampton, and the policeman, and Father saying, "No one ever thinks of leaving this country. But I do, every day!" And the Monkey House. And "It's a disgrace."

That was all far away, but seeing this towering windowless building at the edge of the clearing, I understood why we had come here — to build Fat Boy, to make ice.

This was the distant empty place that Father had always spoken about. Here he could make whatever he pleased and not have to explain why to anyone. There was no Polski here to say "Vumble, vumble." Father said, "You look at Jeronimo and you can't tell what century it is. This is part of your original planet, with people to match. And you're wondering why I gave that missionary the bum's rush?"

Father had found his wilderness.

But the people were afraid of Fat Boy. It started with Francis Lungley. He said he heard noises in it at night. Mr. Maywit said it had a smell, not a machine smell but something like tiger breath. "They's bats inside," Ma Kennywick said, which was true. "He got twenty-two eyes at night," Mr. Haddy said, which was not true. They all watched it anxiously, as if it were a dangerous monster. No one would go inside unless Father went first, but Father had a habit of singing inside, and this frightened everyone. Mr. Harkins said one morning that it was gone. We ran out of the house and saw it was there. He said, "It just come back." The Zambus still heard noises in it. They were voices. Witches, they said.

Father told them to calm down.

"This isn't something to be afraid of," he said. "It isn't new. It isn't even an invention."

But they were still afraid.

"It's a marvel, but it's not magic. People call me an inventor. I'm not an inventor. Look, what am I doing here?"

"Spearmints," Mr. Maywit said. He had got the word from Mr. Haddy.

"I'll tell you what I'm doing — what anyone who invents anything is doing. I'm magnifying."

Hammering the shoulders of a boiler, talking as he worked, Father said that most invention was either adaptation or magnification.

"Take the human body," he said. That contained all the physics and chemistry we needed to know. The best inventions were based on human anatomy. He himself had two patents on ideas he had plagiarized from the body — his Self-Sealing Tank and his Metal Muscle. He said there was no better piece of engineering than the ball-and-socket joint in the human hip. Computer technology was just a clumsy way of making a brain, but the central nervous system was a million times more complicated.

"Insulation? Look at fatty tissue!" You had to study natural things. Anyone who took a good look at an alligator or a hicatee could make an armored vehicle. The natural world showed man what was possible. In a world without birds there would be no airplanes. "Airplanes are just magnified sparrows — they're crascos with leg room."

The Zambus stared at Father, and the others listened twitchily to this man who the harder he worked the more he talked.

"What's a savage?" he said. "It's someone who doesn't bother to look around and see that he can change the world."

Everyone looked around and said this was so.

Father went on to say that savagery was seeing and not believing you could do it yourself, and that that was a fearful condition. The man who saw a bird and made it into a god, because he could not imagine flying himself, was a savage of the most basic kind. There were tribes of people who did not have the sense to build huts. They went around naked and caught double pneumonia. And yet they lived in the same neighborhood as birds that made nests and jack rabbits that dug holes. So these people were savages of utter worthlessness who did not have the imagination to come in out of the rain.

"I'm not saying all inventions are good. But you notice dangerous inventions are always unnatural inventions. You want an example? I'll give you the best one I know. Cheese spread that you squirt out of an aerosol can onto your sandwich. That's about as low as you can go."

Ma Kennywick's laugh went *heck-heck,* and Mr. Haddy said he had never heard of cheese squirting out of a can.

"Like shaving cream," Father said. "Comes out like Reddi-wip. Disgusting. The ozone layer? It eats it up. And there's four things wrong with it — the processed cheese itself, the squirt, the can, and the sandwich."

He was still hammering the boiler.

He said, "I never made anything that did not exist before in a similar form. I just chose something, or part of something, and made it bigger — like my valves and my Metal Muscle and my Self-Sealer. I got the idea from human anatomy — heart valves, striated muscle, stomach lining. Listen, I made gas tanks punctureproof! But it was just a question of scale and application, and — let's face it — improvement. I mean, doing a slightly better job than God."

Whenever Father mentioned God, the people in Jeronimo glanced at the sky and looked very guilty and ashamed, and squinted as if they expected thunder. Father saw this and changed the subject.

"People talk about the invention of the wheel. What's so wonderful about the wheel? It's nothing compared to ball bearings, but there are ball bearings in nature — you've got a rudimentary one in each hip! The development of lenses? All optical inventions are plagiarisms — of the human eye — though I admit the human eye is pretty inferior by comparison."

Mr. Haddy said he had guessed that before. It was all eyes and noses going by different names. And the cranes and derricks on the pier at La Ceiba were the same as arms, except bigger and roustier.

"You're getting the idea," Father said. "And what's this?"

He had finished hammering the boiler and was dragging it inside Fat Boy.

"That is a spearmint," Mr. Haddy said. "And you ain't catch me in there."

"It's a human's insides," Father said. "Its entrails and vitals. Its brisket. Digestive tract. Respiration. Circulatory system. Fatty tissue. And why build it? Because it's an imperfect world! And that's why I do what I do. And that's why I don't believe in God — stop looking up, people! — because if you can make improvements, that doesn't say much for God, does it?"

But no one replied, and no one dared to go into Fat Boy alone. It was dark and too cool and full of iron pipes. No windows, the insulation made it clammy, its darkest corners muttered.

"It's nothing to be scared of," Father said, looking at me. I knew what was coming. He buzzed a rivet at me. "Charlie's not scared. Want to see him climb to the top?"

The faces in the clearing flashed at me like clocks.

"He wunt get out alive," Francis Lungley said.

"That's an ignorant remark," Father said.

Clover said, "Dad, why is Charlie shaking like that?"

"Charlie is not shaking."

So I had to obey.

I had been working the bellows. I dropped it and wiped my hands and looked at all the clock faces. They were saying three-fifteen with their worried squints, and I wondered why. Some were fixed on me, others on Father. If they had not looked so flat and fearful I would have felt better about going into Fat Boy. But they worried my guts.

I said, "Oh, rats," and went in.

Father banged the door after me and cut off most of the daylight. All I could see, through the floor joists that had yet to be planked, was the sun shining dustily down between the cracks in the hatchway door.

It was like being in a monster body, under the cold lips of its stomach tank. Iron pipes rose sideways around the walls. Greasy with sealer and smelling of fresh welds, they had the egg stink of fart gas and meat turned to mud, and the slippery look of human waterworks. Where the cracks of sun lighted some rusty pipes, I could see how these reddened blisters looked like flesh. The smallest movement of my feet made a booming belly echo. Organs was a good word.

A week before, I had scaled the outside with ease. But this was my first time inside, alone, with the door shut, in the dark, making for the top. I gulped my panic and looked up — the way up was the way out. I started climbing the pipes, through the midsection, from the tanks Father called kidneys, across the rusty gizzard, to the steel tube he called the gullet. The only sounds that penetrated the walls were Clover's and April's yells as they played with the Maywit kids — in the sunshine.

There was no fluid in Fat Boy's pipes. Because of the echo, it was like being in something gigantically dead. The shadows were cool twisted pipes that creaked as I climbed. I swung myself to a prickly grid that Drainy Maywit had made with his teeth, and crawled across it, finding my way with my fingers.

Just as I said to myself *Don't look down,* I looked down. And kept looking. I recognized what I saw. This was no belly — this was Father's head, the mechanical part of his brain and the complications of his mind, as strong and huge and mysterious. It was all revealed to me, but there was too much of it, like a book page full of secrets, printed too small. Everything fitted so neatly and was so well bolted and finely fixed it looked selfish. I could see that it had order, but the order — the size of it — frightened me. *Like the human body,* he had said — but this was the darkest part of his body, and in that darkness were the joints and brackets of his mind, a jungle of crooked iron, and paunchy tanks hanging on thin wires, and soldered-over scars, tubes like vines in monkey shadow, the weight of metal hoses forking to the ceiling, and everywhere the balance of small hinges.

It made me dizzy. I could not understand enough of it to feel safe. I thought, You could die here, or — trapped inside — go crazy .

I fought for the door at the top and pushed it open. Below the hatchway were straw hats. Someone — not Father — screeched up at me. They set a ladder against Fat Boy and let me down, and they all looked at my face pretty worriedly.

"He ain't bawling anyway," Francis Lungley said.

"You're next, Fido," Father said, and hurried Lungley to the door. "In you go! Take your time — get acquainted!"

One by one he sent them in, slammed the door, and made them climb through the pipes to the top hatchway, so they would not be afraid, except Mrs. Maywit, Mrs. Kennywick, and the children. They said they were willing, but Father said, "That's all that really counts — willingness."

He said he was sending the people inside so that they would conquer fear, and I believed him. But I also guessed that he wanted to amaze them with his Yankee ingenuity and give them a glimpse of his mind — the model of it inside Fat Boy. As for me, I did not mention this. I knew what I had seen. And I was glad Father had bullied me into going inside. He was making me a man.

Everyone compared the experience with something different. Mr. Maywit said it was like being up the bell tower in the Dunker church. The Zambus said it was like a certain slate cave in the

Esperanzas, and Mr. Harkins said he had had a dream like it once, but when he tried to explain, his voice cracked and tears came to his eyes. Mr. Haddy said, "Shoo! It like some of these banana-boat engine rooms. Boiler and narrers." Hearing all this, Jerry fussed to go in, but Father refused.

"I hope you all admired that mesh over the evaporator lungs," Father said. "That nice piece of work was Drainy's doing."

Drainy had fixed the mesh with his teeth, making it the way he made his wire toys, with clips and clasps and fastenings that he gnawed into place and pinned with his molars.

"And as you might have noticed, Fat Boy isn't breathing," Father said. "That's why I wanted you to see him now, before he's got some life in him. Then he'll be dangerous and off limits. He's going to have work to do, and we don't want anyone traipsing around his guts then."

The smooth mahogany planks of the enormous icehouse caught the green and gold of the sun in the jungle clearing and glowed like skin.

"You won't believe what this old boy can do."

Father was proud of it and glad there were people here as witnesses. No one doubted him, or anything he made. He liked leading us around in the morning, from the pump at the river to the bathhouse and through the fields, pointing out how trim everything was, the water gushing and wheels turning and the hybrids shooting up and vegetables heavy on the plants. We walked along paths we had paved, past plants we had planted.

What Father had promised the first day in Jeronimo was now there for everyone to see — food, water, shelter. It was all as he predicted, but more orderly and happier than we had imagined. And on these early-morning inspections, he took Mother by the arm and spoke to everyone by speaking to her.

He called this notch in the jungle a superior civilization. "Just the way America might have been," he said. "But it got rotten and combustible. Greed panicked the worst into doubledipping, and the best fell victim to the system."

The Zambus didn't know what he was talking about, but they liked the way he talked. He could make them laugh by shouting, "Rheostats! Thermodynamics! The undistributed middle!"

He said, "I was the last man left."

But even when he was not talking for fun, I had to keep my head down or he'd say, "What are you grinning at, Charlie?"

Yet who wouldn't grin at some of the things he said?

"We've got to keep our traps shut," he would say, "or everyone and his brother will be down here on top of us, all the movers and shakers, opening gas stations and drive-in movies and fast-food joints. Issuing catalogues. Oh, sure, they'd strap a facility here and another facility over there. Sock a K-Mart next to Fat Boy and get the floating buyers. And you can bet your bottom dollar they'd find room for a Toyota dealership up on the Swampmouth path. This would be all parking lots from here to the hills. Facilities! They'd be ramming them down our throats."

Mr. Maywit said, "Wish we had a Chinese shop."

"He wants a Chinese shop!" Father said.

Mr. Maywit flinched. "Buy some salt and flour and oil."

"Save your money," Father said. "You don't need any Chinese shops. The sea's full of salt — sea salt, the best there is. No additives. Flour will be easy as soon as that corn is ready: we're going to mill it ourselves. Look at it — wonder corn! I brought that hybrid seed myself, all the way from Massachusetts. It's three times the size of your Honduras varieties."

"He say oil," Mr. Harkins said.

"I heard him, and my reply is, 'Peanuts!' Next to the spuds, there's a half acre of goobers. But give them time. Don't rush them. Are you going somewhere?"

As soon as the potatoes and yams were harvested he was going to ban the planting of cassava. It was a lazy man's crop, he said. Like bananas. True, there was no weeding to be done, but cassava exhausted the soil and there was no nutrition in it. Growing it would turn us all into funny-bunnies.

Work continued on Fat Boy, the fixing and welding of more pipes, the sealing of the tanks, and finishing the firebox and the chimney. Now, no one feared it. In fact, the Zambus preferred to work inside it because it was so much cooler there. It had double walls, and the roof and south side were faced with polished tin sheets that bounced the direct rays of the sun.

"If those were solar panels, we'd be self-sufficient in electricity," Father said. "But we don't need electricity or fossil fuels — this is a superior civilization."

We tested it for leaks by filling it with water. There was a fine spray peeing from nine joints, which Father marked and sealed when it was drained. Then Father declared it finished and said that he and Mr. Haddy were going to Trujillo.

"Plasma — for Fat Boy," he said. He had arranged for some hydrogen and ammonia to be sent to Trujillo. He had not wanted it shipped all the way to Jeronimo for fear of arousing missionary curiosity and getting more unwelcome visitors, like Mr. Struss or anyone of the Spellgood persuasion, or Toyota dealers.

"Used to shine windows up the Dunker with ammonia water," Mr. Maywit said.

"Up the Shouter," Mrs. Maywit said.

"Never mind," Mr. Maywit said.

Mr. Haddy remarked that there wasn't a glass windowpane in the whole of Jeronimo, which was true.

"You can do anything with ammonia," Father said. "The ammonia clock is the most accurate timekeeping device in the world. You don't believe me?" — Mr. Maywit was frowning — "Listen, the tick-tock in it is the oscillation of the nitrogen atom in the ammonia molecule. Francis knows all about it, don't you?"

Francis said, "For true, Fadder."

"I employ enriched ammonia," Father said. "What do you think I was doing up there in La Ceiba? Spitting in the plaza, like all the other gringos? No, sir. I was juicing up my ammonia. That's my secret, really. The more enriched it is, the quicker your evaporation. You'll see."

Mr. Maywit said, "I hear that."

"He do it all himself for the spearmint," Mr. Haddy said, while the Zambus stared. "He richen it. That is the way."

"It's more toxic," Father said. The Zambus laughed at "toxic." "But once it's sealed into the system, there's no danger. And it's everlasting. Take the acids in your stomach. They're not toxic, but they're powerful substances. They could burn a pretty big hole in your shirt if they leaked out. And there's ammonia in nature — you know, rotting vegetable matter, seawater, soil, even urine."

Mr. Maywit said he had heard that, too. "You want I come to Trujillo? I buy some salt and oil for Ma."

Father put his hand on Mr. Maywit's flour-sack shirt, where it said *La Rosa* on the shoulder. "I need you here, coach. From now on you're my field superintendent. You've got to stay, so you can tell me what to do."

Then he spoke to everyone — Mrs. Kennywick, the Zambus, Harkins, Peaselee, the Maywits, and us.

"I take orders from you," he said. "You're in charge here. And if you want Fat Boy to work, you'll have to send me down the river to Trujillo. To get his vital juices."

Eventually, Father encouraged them to say, Yes, please go —

"In the meantime, pick some of those tomatoes. Him" — he poked Mr. Maywit's flour-sack shirt — "he wants a Chinese store!"

Mother asked him how long he would be away. Father said he guessed anything up to a week, "barring unforeseen circumstances."

The next day, the *Little Haddy,* streamlined for the river, left Jeronimo for the coast. Mr. Haddy was working the sounding chain and Father was at the wheel. Mr. Haddy said for all to hear, "But this used to be me lanch."

We ran along the riverbank, nearly to Swampmouth, but lost them in the deep green foliage Father had once compared to old dollar bills.

With Father away, Jeronimo was very quiet — no speeches or songs, and the hammering stopped. The only sounds were the flap and splash, the *prunt-prunt* of the pump tower on the bank, and the sloosh of water in the culverts. The rest was the usual murmur of jungle, as continuous as silence, birds and bugs and monkey squawks, which changed in pitch with the heat and became a pressurized howl after nightfall.

Mother did not take charge. When Father was around, we did things his way, he kept us jumping, but Mother had no inventions and never made speeches. When she did talk, it was often a gentle request for someone to show her the local way of doing something.

The pepper-drying was a good example. After the small red peppers appeared in the low bushes, Mrs. Maywit said they would have to be dried. If Father had been around, he would have blazed a ten-sided tub out of sheet metal and called it his Pepper Hopper, or something of the kind, for drying peppers, the way he had made the fish trap and the bathhouse and the bamboo tiles.

But Mother got Mrs. Kennywick and Mrs. Maywit to explain how to string the peppers and hang them. "You know best," she said. It was a day's work, this pepper-stringing, Mother and the other women squatting side by side on a mat in the yard, knotting the peppers on twine so that the lengths of them looked like firecrackers. Father would not have done it, and he certainly wouldn't have squatted. He would have made himself a chair, probably a recliner, with a work surface, pedal-operated, maintenance-free, out of steamed and bent saplings. "Look how she fits the contours of the body, Mother!"

Mother had the Zambus teach her how to gut and skin animals like pacas, and how to peg fish to a plank and dry them, and how to smoke meat. They were slow, dirty, traditional methods, but she was in no hurry, she said. And these became our lessons in Jeronimo — the household tasks of the jungle people, the preparation of things we picked or caught. She made sure that each of us understood the gutting and smoking. We were not free to play until we had mastered these chores.

This was different from Father's way. He was an innovator. He thought nothing of getting a dozen people to peel wood or dig ditches, and he would not tell them why until they had finished. Then he would say, "You've just made yourself a permanent enhancement!" Or he would ask them to guess what a particular thing was for (no one so far had guessed what Fat Boy was for), and laugh when they gave him the wrong answer. He had his own way of doing things, and he liked telling people that their own methods were just waste motion. "Now I'll show you how it ought to be done," he'd say, and as they gawked, he'd add, "How do you like *that* little wrinkle?"

He had never been a good listener. But he knew so much he did not have to listen. We had heard his voice going like the Thunderbox wherever we were, and since the day we arrived, Father's chatter had been as constant as the Jeronimo locusts from morning to night, and it was louder even than the *googn-googn-googn-googn* of the howler monkeys. But now his voice was gone. Nothing was built, there were no inspections, the forge went cold. No talk of "targets," no sessions in the Gallery, and we stopped hearing "I only need four hours' sleep!"

We cleared the fish trap, weeded the garden, and picked the first tomatoes. Mother ran things smoothly, offering suggestions, not giving orders. She made cassava bread, something Father had not thought of doing. Mrs. Maywit provided the recipe. And Mrs. Kennywick showed her how to make wabool out of rotten bananas.

In her quiet, inquiring way, Mother discovered an amazing thing. She had the idea that it would be educational for us to learn the names of the trees in and around Jeronimo. She asked the Zambus what they were called, and what they were used for, so that a little printed sign could be tacked to each trunk for us to memorize. She found out that a good few of the trees at the southern end of the clearing were sapodillas. Even the Maywits didn't know that. The Zambus called them "chiclets" and "hoolies" and explained how to extract rubbery sap from the trees and boil it and pound it into sheets.

"There's enough chicle here to make a ton of rubber," she said. She thought this was funny. "That's what Allie would say. Wait till he hears. He'll make us all galoshes."

Father's work was work, Mother's work was study and play, but mostly she left us to ourselves. We did not feel supervised as when Father was around, and little by little we ventured farther from the clearing, and even out of Jeronimo itself, away from the splash of our waterworks and the *googn* of our monkeys.

Leaving, hacking a path, and setting up a camp had been my idea. It was like one of Father's challenges, but I challenged myself to go by daring the others — it gave me courage. We dared the Maywit children, too, and called them names, and soon they were shouting "Crummo" and "Crappo" at each other. Alice and Drainy were not afraid, but the little ones, Leon and Veryl (who was known as Peewee), were timid and always lagged behind.

We found a path that led away from the river and into a part of the jungle that was thick with screaming birds — bill-birds and crascos. There were monsters here, Drainy said, and all the Maywit kids agreed that it was in places like this that you met your Duppy. Clover said they were crapoid for thinking that. We put up our camp near a deep pool in a little pocket in the jungle, about half an hour's walk from Jeronimo, through flame trees and lianas.

"They's munsters in the water," Drainy said, and none of them would go into the pool. But it was because they did not know how to swim, which we did. Swimming there while they watched gave us a superior feeling, and Jerry told them they were spasticated.

But they were not afraid of the water dogs or the snakes or green lizards. Some of those lizards were as big as cats. If we said, "There's your Duppy in that tree," they went crapoid, because they couldn't see it. But when we saw a hairy piglike animal snuffling in the bushes, Alice said, "Oh, that's a mountain cow." It looked like a monster to me, but this little girl was not afraid, so we couldn't be.

For our camp here, we made first a lean-to out of branches, then a hut, and hammocks out of vines. Clover and Alice made seats for us, dug a firepit, and picked flowers. Clover was not strong enough to do the hard work herself, but she knew how to get the Maywit kids working. I saw that she was just like Father. She was firm like him and would not listen and wasn't happy unless she was directing operations.

There was a certain fanlike plant here that was edible, Alice said — the roots of it. Clover got everyone collecting these roots in homemade baskets, and we ate them. They tasted like raw carrots and were called yautia. With these and the bananas and fruit we picked on the way, we could have meals in this camp.

Clover complained that Jerry and April never helped. Alice said, "Peewee's a crummo, for true. Always eating and never picking." Drainy said he did more work than anyone. No one squabbled in Jeronimo, but here everyone fussed.

So I decided to invent money. It was no good getting everything free. From now on, I said, we would have to buy our food at the camp store.

"Where's the camp store, thicko?" Clover said.

I said the first thing that came into my head — "You're sitting on it" — and pointed to her little bench. By making Clover the storekeeper I shut her up, and I explained that stones and pebbles would count as money, because they were in short supply in this mossy place.

Leon said, "Want to buy some food, Ma."

"Where's your money?"

"Ain't got none."

"Then start digging."

This was a new game and a good one. We set out in search of stones, and everyone gathered a little pile. It was easy for me, because by diving into the pool I could pick up all the stones I wanted off the bottom. I became the richest person in the camp.

Clover also ran the school, which was the first lean-to. Drainy ran the church — that was a tree on which he had fixed a wire cross. We made fences out of branches, and in one of the other lean-tos Drainy made a wire box he called the radio set. That was imaginary, but the telephone was real — two coconut halves connected by a piece of string.

"This is like back home," Jerry said.

But it wasn't. It was the way other people lived, with radios and schools and churches — and money. Yet I was happy here in the camp — happier than in Jeronimo. I liked this place for its secrecy and best of all because it was filled with things that Father had forbidden. Spending money at the store and talking on the telephone were pleasant things. And when Clover ran out of lessons, I became the schoolteacher. I showed the Maywits how to count money and do arithmetic and write their names. Jerry wanted to put up a No Trespassing sign, but I said that would only make people curious. Instead, I got everyone to help dig a hole on the path for a man trap, to catch intruders or even big animals like mountain cows. Drainy said there were tigers around — he meant jungle cats or jaguars — and I wanted to catch one. We embedded sharpened stakes at the bottom of the trap and covered the whole thing with a layer of branches and dirt, to make it look like part of the path. That was the Zambu way, Drainy said. Father would have killed us for doing this, but he was still on the coast.

We said prayers, we sang hymns that Alice taught us, and we held long groaning church services in the shelter of the holy tree.

We still helped at Jeronimo, gathering peppers and weeding and seeing to the fish trap and doing our other chores. But when this work was done and Mother was satisfied, we escaped to our camp in the jungle, returning to all the things that Father hated. This made up for everything we had never had in Massachusetts and it stilled a longing in me for the United States. In this way, I overcame my homesickness.

We called our camp the Acre.

The Acre helped me to understand something of Father's pride in

Jeronimo. Until we built our camp, I had not seen why he was so boastful of what he had made in Jeronimo. Father had insisted that we look closely at the garden and the paths and the waterworks. He wanted us to marvel at the way we could be bone-dry in the rain and cool on the hottest day and not be pestered by insects. He was happy, and at the Acre I knew why. I looked around and saw that the pattern of life and the things we had fixed ourselves were all ours. Even the Maywit children were pleased by what we had done. But I felt that ours was a greater achievement than Father's, because we ate the fruit that grew nearby and used anything we found, and adapted ourselves to the jungle. We had not brought a boatload of tools and seeds, and we had not invented anything. We just lived like monkeys.

It was Drainy's idea that we should all be baptized. He said we would all go to hell if we weren't, and he insisted that we do it the Dunker way, by getting into the deep pool while he said prayers over us. It seemed like fun, so we stripped down to our underwear and made ready for the baptism.

"I'm the baptizer," Drainy said. "I know how to do this."

"Only thing," Alice said. "Drainy don't know how to swim. He cain't be a baptizer if he cain't swim. He get et up by the munsters in the water." She walked away.

I said to Drainy, "If you're really afraid, we can forget it."

"I ain't afraid," Drainy said, and sat on the bank and dangled his feet in the water. "And you go to hell if you ain't get dunked."

Clover said, "We don't believe in hell. Only ignorant people believe in hell."

Drainy said, "If Alice pull down her bloomers and show her carkle, she go to hell, for true."

Alice was in the schoolhouse. She poked her head out of the window and yelled, "Drainy Roper, you get youself outta there!"

Then she clapped her hand over her mouth.

"That ain't his name," she said.

Clover said, "You called him Drainy Roper. Roper — that's what that missionary said before Father kicked him out."

"That is our name," Veryl said.

"You got a mouf!" Alice yelled.

Drainy pulled his feet out of the pool and said, yes, that was their name, Roper. The missionary was right. And he was a Dunker. "If he was here," Drainy said, "he could be the baptizer."

"If your name's Roper, why is your name Maywit?" Jerry asked.
"They've got two names," April said.
"We got one names," Drainy said. "And it ain't Maywit."
I said, "Where did the Maywit come from?"
"You father give it to us," Alice said. "And my father take it."
"If it wasn't his name," I said, "why did he take it?"
"He afraid," Alice said.
Drainy said, "Of you father."
"You're crappo," Clover said.
Drainy said, "You father can do magic."
"What he does isn't magic — it's science," I said.
"Science is worse," Alice said.

They would not believe me, and I was sorry, because Father had made them change their name. I said, "Sometimes I'm afraid of him, too."

Jerry and the twins laughed at me for saying this. But they did not know what I knew. Clover said that Father was kind and not to be feared. He could have made a fortune as an inventor, Jerry said.

"Why don't he get rich?" Alice said.

"Because he wanted to come here," I said, "to build a town in the jungle. More than a town."

This did not convince the Maywit children, and when I told them that Father had said there was a war coming in the United States they just laughed. This made me lose heart and talk hollowly, for why else would anyone ditch the United States to sweat his guts out in the jungle? And I knew more than that. I had seen the inside of Fat Boy. That glimpse came back to me, and now, whenever I thought of Father, I saw the hanging tanks, the wilderness of crooked iron, the tubes like a brain in a sleeve, and all the tiny hinges. It had been like seeing the inside of someone's house, and, by studying it, knowing them better. I knew a person best from something he had made, and in Fat Boy I had seen Father's mind, a version of it — its riddle and slant and its hugeness — and it had scared me.

It was because of this, talking about Father in these whispers, that we skipped the baptism altogether and went and collected crazy ants instead. We floated them on the pool and watched them struggle on the skin of the water's surface.

Returning from the Acre that day, we saw *Little Haddy* at the mooring. Some men were carrying tall bottles of gas up the path to Fat Boy, and others were rolling steel drums along logs that served as rails.

Peewee let out a yell when she saw Father. He was outside Fat Boy, working a hand pump, emptying one of the drums into a pipe. What frightened Peewee was his mask. It was a gas mask, for safety, but it gave him a snout and huge bug eyes. A skull and bones was stenciled on the drum.

"He always wears that when he's working with poison," I said.

This word *poison* had a worse effect on the Maywit kids than the weevil mask, and they ran straight into their house with their fingers in their mouths.

It had taken ten days for Father to get the ammonia and hydrogen from Trujillo to Jeronimo. Mother told us the story of his adventures. Threats in the town. Nosy people. Honduran soldiers accusing him of smuggling explosives. Arguments and almost a fistfight. "How many pushups can you do?" Trouble with vultures. A hard time on the river, which was too shallow in places. Scraping the boat bottom and being followed by unfriendly Zambus and more vultures. A slow and dangerous trip. Into Jeronimo with their keel dragging on the riverbed.

There were only four gas masks — Father, Haddy, Harkins, and F. Lungley. Because of the danger of fumes, we were not allowed near Fat Boy until the transfer of ammonia and hydrogen was made and the pipes sealed. Father worked all night without lamps or firelight. The full moon gave the clearing a milky-pink shine, like mother-of-pearl, and Fat Boy looked like a block of dark marble, a monument or tomb in the jungle.

The four masked men jumbled in and out of Fat Boy, and all we heard was the clanging of steel drums and gas bottles, and Father saying "Watch it!" and "Careful!" and "Move over!" and the howler monkeys they called baboons, their *googn!*

In the morning, Father was highly excited. If anything had gone wrong, he said, we would have been blown sky-high along with half the valley — probably ended up in Hatfield, in smithereens.

"I have just spent the most dangerous twelve hours of my whole life," he said.

"Sounds to me as if it was dangerous for us too," Mother said.

"Sure, but you weren't aware of the danger, so you could sleep in blissful ignorance."

172

Mother said "I like that," and turned her back on him.

"I am the only person here who knows how lethal that stuff is. I took full responsibility. Was I scared? No, ma'am."

"We might have been killed!"

"You wouldn't have known what hit you. I can give you my cast-iron guarantee of that. You'd have been atomized, with a smile on your face."

Mother said, "Thanks, pal."

"Don't worry. All the seals are on. In fact, this afternoon I'm going to fire him up." Father saw me listening in the doorway. "Quit grinning and spread the news, Charlie. I want everyone over there to watch."

"This is why I'm here," Father said, after lunch. "This is why I came."

He was standing in front of Fat Boy's firebox with a handful of matches. Mr. Haddy was next to him, and the Maywits nearby with their gray-faced kids. Clover and April sat on the ground with the Zambus, Harkins and Peaselee on kegs, Mrs. Kennywick in the armchair she had dragged over from Swampmouth. There were some other strangers watching from beyond the beanfields.

"I'll bet you still don't know what this is for," Father said.

"Cooking," Mr. Haddy said, and put out his teeth.

"No guesses," Father said. "You saw Lungley and Dixon put those trays of water on the shelf inside this monster. Now we're going to light a little fire here with this weeny match."

"Steam engine. Boiler work." Mr. Haddy clowned for the nervous people.

"Can it! But stick around. You won't believe your eyes."

He called Peewee over and said that as she was the youngest it was she who should light the first fire. "When we're all dead and gone, you'll still be around, Peewee. You can tell your grandchildren that you were here on this historic day. Tell them you lit the fire."

Father struck a match on the seat of his pants and showed her where to hold it. There was some kindling in the firebox. Peewee put the match to it and up it went.

The Zambus grasped their ears, Ma Kennywick blew out her cheeks, and Mr. Maywit said, "Never mind." No sound came for several minutes, only the fire pop. The birds and bugs of Jeronimo went silent. The people held their breaths and went shiny-faced with waiting.

A single *gloop* dropped inside Fat Boy, as of liquid plunging in a pipe's plump bubble, and we moved, turning from the fire to where the sound had glooped in Fat Boy's midsection. Now we could all hear each other breathe.

Mr. Haddy licked his teeth. "Shoo!"

"Wait for it," Father said.

More plungings, and the trembling of pipes, and the creak of swelling tanks — it was a sense, announced in muffled percolations, of loosening in Fat Boy's belly. It was not one clear sound, but rather a vibration in the plant and all around it. The ground hummed beneath our feet. Liquid was shifting, still rising, and there was a final surge that slowed the vibrations, and the whole plant seemed to stir. The surrounding jungle murmured to the same beat, which was like the throb of a vein in your head in the progress of an almighty bowel movement.

Mr. Maywit said, "They is queerness coming out from the chimbly."

"Smoke," Father said.

"He stop bellyaching," Drainy whispered.

Father said, "This is going to take a little while. Everyone get comfy. Sit down where you are and let your mind wander. But don't think about war or madness."

"They is just what I think about," Ma Kennywick said.

Mrs. Maywit put her chicken eyes on Father and said, "Kin we pray?"

"If you feel the need, go right ahead. But I honestly wish you wouldn't, because then you'll treat this as a miracle — which it isn't. Rather than as a magnified piece of thermodynamics — which it is."

But I could tell from their faces and postures that they were all praying. They sat compactly, with their necks drawn in, like birds in the rain.

From time to time, Father stoked the fire. But there was not much fueling to be done — it was a small fire, and after it started its whistles and sucks, he kept it damped down.

"This is where it's all happening," Father said. "This is the center of the world! You don't have to go anywhere — you're where it's at!"

A half-hour passed in this way. Then Father stopped talking and climbed the stepladder. He read the thermometer that stuck out, and he looked pretty satisfied. Fifteen more minutes, he said, and after that time had gone he mounted the ladder again and crawled into the hatchway.

"Hope we ain't have to drag him out by his stumps," Mr. Haddy said.

Some people hissed, and Mr. Haddy and others looked at Mother. She said, "Allie knows what he's doing — and here he comes."

Father's head was in the hatchway. He made a face — hard to tell what kind, he was so far up. He waved his hand. He was holding a white ball, like a lump of raw cotton.

"What Fadder got there?"

Father was shouting.

"Haven't you people ever seen a snowball?"

He threw it, and it mashed in the grass, whiter than a heron's feathers.

We ran to touch it — and as we touched it, feeling the sting of its crystals, it began to vanish. But by then, in triumph, Father was bringing out the cakes of ice.

15

ON THIS PART of the river, narrower and shallower than anything I had seen — twenty miles of it, before mountains and jungle twisted it into a trickle — people dropped to their knees on the banks and waved at us and prayed. By now, they knew who we were and what we carried. The news of Fat Boy had spread throughout the river valley.

"Anyone want a beverage?" Father called to those people on the bank who took us for missionaries. Mr. Haddy thought this question was very funny, and he wheezed whenever Father said it. So later on, even at the uninhabited parts of the river, Father caught Mr. Haddy's eye and yelled, "Anyone here require a beverage?" and made the man laugh.

But the kneeling and respectfulness at last made Father gloomy. "The idiots think we came all this way to honk Bibles at them!"

Five of us were on the boat — besides Father, Mr. Haddy, and me, there was Clover and Francis Lungley. It was not the *Little Haddy*. Our new boat, built in the weeks after Fat Boy began producing ice, was an adaptation of a pipanto dugout, needle-nosed, wide-bellied, and almost flat-bottomed. It was powered by a pedal mechanism that worked a stern wheel, something like the Swan boats in the Boston Public Garden. Because of its shape and its cargo, Father named the boat the *Icicle*.

Except for the pedals and the sprockets and part of the chain (they were from Mr. Harkins's bike — "I cannibalized his Raleigh!" Father said), the driving mechanism of the *Icicle* had been made in the forge at Jeronimo, and some small parts by the wire-nibbling teeth of Drainy Maywit. "That kid's a human micrometer!" Amidships, Father had outrigged an ice-storage vault. There were two seats forward, and two side by side in the stern, in front of the pedaler's cockpit, which Father called "the Wishing Well — because whoever's pedaling in it wishes he was somewhere else." Going upstream, Francis worked the pedals. It was the perfect boat for the upper river. Father claimed that it was so buoyant he could go cross-country in it, providing there was a smidgen of dew on the grass.

Mr. Haddy said, "These people never see no lanch like this one."

"You're joking," Father said. "They've seen everything. River travel is easy. This is a turnpike. Missionaries have been tooling up and down here in canoes for years. Frankly, I don't regard this as much of an accomplishment."

"Tell you one thing," Mr. Haddy said — he was shouting from the bow where he sat behind Clover — "they ain't have no ice with them!"

"That's a matter of conjecture —"

Francis Lungley screamed at the word.

" — but they were here."

Mr. Haddy shrugged. He was wearing one of the La Rosa flour sacks Mother had made into shirts. His back said, *Enriquecida con Vitaminas.*

"I want to penetrate where they've never been," Father said.

There were blue butterflies kiting to the ferny branches that overhung the river, startled by our noise. The tumble and splash of our foot-operated wheel sounded like a washing machine sudsing clothes. I could recognize some of the birds in the trees — the jays and the ivory-billed woodpecker, the cockatoos and crascos — and I knew the cries of the hidden ones — the sudden honk of the smaller pava, the shouts of the forest quail, and the bass-fiddle boom of the curassow. These same birds lived near our camp at the Acre, still our secret hiding place from Father and his work, and his speechy ambitions.

"I want to take a load of ice to the hottest, darkest, nastiest corner of Honduras, where they pray for water and never see ice, and have never heard of cans, much less aerosol cans."

"But Seville like that," Francis Lungley said, bobbing his head as he pedaled. He was wearing a La Rosa shirt too. His said, *Molino Harinero* and *45.36 Kgs Netos.* "For true, Seville is dirt."

He had been promising Seville ever since Father demanded the poorest place imaginable. This had started one of the first arguments in Jeronimo. Mr. Haddy, Mr. Harkins, and Mr. Peaselee wanted to take the ice downstream to Santa Rosa or Trujillo. Father asked, what was the point of that? Big ships called at those ports — those towns had more electricity than was good for them.

"You just want to impress your friends. No, we're going upstream."

That was when Francis Lungley said that he had once been to Seville, as far upriver as it was possible to go. Mr. Haddy and the others said they were not going to a stewy bat-shoo place where people had no respect and probably had tails. But Father was interested. Francis said he had almost died there twice — first from fright, next from hunger. It was a falling-down village, where the people ate dirt and looked like monkeys — anyway, ugly as monkeys. They had rat hair and most were naked. They were not even Christians.

"That sounds like my kind of place," Father said.

Then Mr. Haddy agreed and said, oh, yes, heathens were the best fishermen and the strongest paddlers and "Those boys knows how to work, for true."

But as we sudsed up the river (monkeys on the right, kinkajous on the left), Father said, "I find it hard to believe that some missionary hasn't been here before and bought their souls with Twinkies and cheese spread in spray cans and crates of Rice-a-Roni." He watched a monkey on a branch. "Hershey bars." We passed by. He looked back at the monkey. "Diet Pepsi." Now he turned to the kinkajous. "Kool-Aid." He flicked his cigar butt into the river. "Makes your mouth water, doesn't it?"

"You see Seville, Fadder," Francis said, pedaling harder, his La Rosa shirt black with sweat.

"I want to see a wreck of a village that hasn't got a name, where they've been swatting mosquitoes and eating rancid wabool for two thousand years." Father pointed to the mountains. "Over those baffles, where it's all hell and they're being roasted alive!"

"Too bad we ain't back of Brewer's Lagoon," Mr. Haddy said. "Some of them villages is rubbish."

We had started before dawn — so early, the nighttime mosquitoes were still out and biting us. But by noon, though we had gone miles, we were some distance from the mountains of Olancho that marked the end of the river, where Seville was. We tied up at a riverbank for lunch. It was so thickly overgrown we could not get off the boat. The bank was hidden under bush fans and yards of lianas. Mother had packed us a basket of fruit and cassava bread and fresh tomatoes and a Jeronimo drink that Father called Jungle Juice, made from guavas and mangoes. Clover said the juice wasn't cold enough.

"It's plenty cold enough," Father said. "Listen, no one's touching that ice!"

He checked the vault on the boat to make sure the ice was still holding up. The ice was wrapped in banana leaves and the vault lined with rubber we had tapped from the hoolie trees. He had not made us galoshes after all.

"You're bound to lose a little," he said. The ice had shrunk in its banana-leaf wrappings. "Seepage. Natural wastage. Friction" — he was plumping it with his hands — "owing to excessive agitation. Right, Francis?"

Francis Lungley was peeling a banana. He did it delicately with his fingertips, like opening a present.

"I mean, how are we doing?"

The village of Seville was some way off, Francis said. He could not say exactly how far. He squinched his face when Father asked him the miles.

"How many men paddling the cayuka when you were here before?"

"No cayuka," Francis said. "Just foots." He showed us his cracked feet. His ankles were oily from pedaling the boat.

Father blew up. "Now he tells us! He walked! For all we know, we might not get there until tomorrow." He yanked the stern painter from the branch and said the lunch break was over. "If you want to stay here, you can," he said to me. "But we're not going to hang around and watch you feed your face."

I stuffed the sandwich I had made into my pocket, and we cast off. Soon, with Father's barking, we sudsed along like a motorboat.

"What are you brooding about?"

I said, "I wanted to pick one of those avocados back there."

"You're seeing things," Father said. "There aren't any avocados around here."

But there were — small, wild avocados. We had eaten them at the Acre. Alice Maywit had identified them. The Zambu John had told her about them. We peeled them and mashed them with salt and planted the seeds. I looked at Francis, but his eyes were turned on Father.

"Ain't real butter pears," Francis said. "Just bush kind."

"If I've got so many authorities on board, how come we're making such slow progress?"

No river is straight. They only turn and go crosswise and sometimes lead you backward — the nose of your boat heading into the direction you just left. River travel is like forever being turned back and not getting there. The sun shifts sideways from the bow to starboard, where it sways until a riverbend brings it over to port. Soon it slips astern. You know you've been going forward, but the sun isn't in your face any longer — it is heating the back of your head. Some minutes later it is beating on your knuckles. Then it is back to starboard. Another reach and it is burning around the boat, useless to navigate by. All it tells you is how much time has passed. For coastal sailing, the sun is a good guide, but it was confusing here.

In the jungle, all rivers are mazes, and this one was mazier than most — it was something only a small cayuka or an ingenious pipanto like ours could negotiate. The bad part was not that we were going backward, but that we seemed to be going nowhere. We would come to a bank choked with water lilies and hyacinths and green ruffled leaves, and see a bend of open water. We would turn and follow that bend. After half an hour, as the hyacinths piled up and the branches at the bank swung against the boat and smacked our faces and pushed Father's baseball cap sideways, we would realize that we had come the wrong way. Or we were in a swamp that was packed as solid as land, or a lagoon surrounded by black trees, or knocking against stumps. Then we had to go back and suds our way through the thick flowers and logs we had taken for a bank. Once past these barriers, we would travel on what seemed a new river or a tributary, now narrow, now wide as a pond and no opening. So the sun went round and round, and Father cursed and said, why did you have to go fifty river miles to advance five land miles?

He mapped the river as we went, marking the shallows and the bends and the false turns, the sandbar crescents on the reaches, the swamps and lagoons — all the deceptions of its straggling course. It was more than a crumpled shape. It was a bunch of knots, tangled like worms in winter, that made no sense. Even Father, who liked complications, called it a so-and-so labyrinth and said that if he had a dredger and a barge full of dynamite he would twist the bends out of it and knock it straight, so that you could see daylight from one end to the other.

This was the subject of his speeching. When we were led into a swamp by the temptation of open water, Father said, "I'm going to do something about that" — and the islands — "I'll sink them, first chance I get" — and the ponds — "Strap a channel through here, canalize it — all I need is dynamite and willing hands."

Father was now at the bow with Clover, while Mr. Haddy took his turn on the pedals. "Clear all this obstruction away — make some kind of scoop that cuts this sargasso weed at its roots and lifts it free. Get this mess into shape. How very American, you're all saying — the man wants to bring permanent changes to this peaceful jungle! But I didn't mention poison, and I certainly don't intend to make it commercial. Gaw, I like to get my hand on this," and he grinned at the tangles and bends. "It really makes me mad!"

He was getting redder in the face, and, being tall, he looked uncomfortable squatting at the needle nose of this narrow boat. He kept his hands on his hips and swayed like someone riding a bike with no hands. Every so often, he poked his head into the storage vault and said, "At least the ice is holding up, which is more than I can say for the crew. Pedal, Mr. Haddy! Stop catching crabs. Are you looking for avocados, too?"

We passed a semicircle of huts. Francis Lungley called it a village.

"I see signs of corruption," Father said. "I see a tin can!" At another group of riverbank huts, he said, "It's all gum wrappers!"

There was only one more village, and it was hardly a village — a few open-sided huts and a stand of banana trees. This made Father hopeful. Two men sat at the river's edge clumping submerged stones with boulders. Francis Lungley said the men were fishing — stunning the creatures under the stones. They turned the stones over after they clumped them, and pulled out squashed eels and tadpoles and frogs.

"We must be getting close," Father said.

Francis slapped himself on the head. "I forgit! Them mahoganies!" He smiled at the trees as if he expected them to smile back. "It near here."

Father looked satisfied. "They didn't cut them down. Nothing to cut them down with. Primitive tools. Nothing to use the trees for. Just sit back and watch them grow. Now that's a very good sign."

Here, grass spikes grew out of the water, and the trunks of short cut-off trees stood in pools. Clumps of spinach bobbed in the river, and the lianas were black and dangling, like high-voltage wires blown down by a storm. It was all green wreckage and might have been the mess left by a subsided flood. In what was supposed to be river, there were shoots of fountainy leaves, and the land steamed with crater holes of scummy water. Mud and mosquitoes — and it was hard to tell where the river ended and the land began. There was no definite riverbank, and if it had not been for the tall trees behind it all, I think we would have turned around and gone back — we certainly could not have gone any further. Many of the smaller trees were dead, and on the deadest ones were brown pods, quivering under the branches. "Bats," Mr. Haddy said. "They's bats." He repeated his bloodsucking story to Clover, but she said, "You can't scare me."

Staring at some bushes, I saw human faces. The faces were entirely still and round and staring back at me with white eyes that did not blink. I was not scared until I remembered that they must have been there the whole time, watching us thrash our boat through the spinach and the weeds.

Father saw them. He said, "I've got a little surprise for you."

At his voice, and while we were still looking at them, the faces vanished. They did not move, they just disappeared — goggling at us one minute, gone the next. They had turned into leaves, but not even the leaves moved.

"Out to lunch," Father said. "Get the duckboards. We're going after them. You first, Charlie."

"Why me?" But I knew I should not have asked.

Father said, "Because you're the bravest one here, sonny."

This was not true. But the risks that Father made me take were his way of showing me there were no risks. On the rock in Baltimore, up the kingpost of the *Unicorn,* climbing through Fat Boy — it had all been a kind of training for times like this. Father wanted me to be strong. He had known all along that he was preparing me for worse, for this tiptoeing through the spinachy swamp on duckboards, and teetering past the scummy pools and the vine tubes.

"Stamp your feet, Charlie."

I did so and a snake, hanging in six bracelets from a low branch, gathered itself and dropped into the water and swam away.

After that, I stamped my feet every chance I got, and further on a short fat viper, surprised by the clomp of my shoe, wormed into a stump hole until only its gray tail tip showed.

Father was saying, "Never can tell about these people. They might be Munchies — haw!"

We got through thirty yards of this by passing the last duckboard ahead and repeating this process to make a walkway through the mush. It was hard to believe there had been people right here, standing in the swamp. How had they disappeared without making a splash?

We came to bushes like hedges, and past them the trees were taller and had trunks like thick skirts hanging in folds. Parroty birds, and birds so small they might have been insects, screamed around our heads. Above the tops of the mahogany trees there were bigger birds, perched or making shadowy flights, like flying turkeys. Their wings made slow broomlike brushings against the treetops. They might have been curassows — I heard bull-fiddle twangs — but Father said they were vultures and that he wanted to wring their scrawny scavenging necks.

"Seville," Francis said, and pointed to an opening some yards ahead — more jungle, except that it was dark here and sunny there. Gnats and flies spiraled in the light and speckled it.

Mr. Haddy said, "I ain't like this place so soon."

"What kind of houses are those, Dad?" Clover asked.

"That kind of dwelling, of course —"

He never admitted not knowing something, but these huts were not easy to explain. They were small tufty humps made from the same spiky grass we had walked through on the duckboards. A framework of skinny branches balanced the hanks of dead grass bunched on top. Not huts — more like beehives that needed haircuts.

"— that's probably where they keep their animals, Muffin," Father said.

"Got no animals here," Francis said. "I ain't see one."

"All the better," Father said. "If they actually live in those things, then we came to the right place."

Mr. Haddy chuckled and said to me, "The right places for Fadder is always the wrong places for me."

Father looked gladly on the miserable village.

Yet only the huts were miserable. This jungle, the start of the high forest, was tall and orderly. Each tree had found room to grow separately. The trees were arranged in various ways, according to slenderness or leaf size, the big-leafed ones at the jungle floor, the towering trees with tiny leaves rising to great heights, and the ferns in between. I had always pictured jungle as suffocating spaghetti tangles, drooping and crisscrossed, a mass of hairy green rope and clutching stems — a wicked salad that stank in your face and flung its stalks around you.

This was more like a church, with pillars and fans and hanging flowers and only the slightest patches of white sky above the curved roof of branches. There was nothing smothering about it, and although it was noisy with birds, it was motionless — no wind, not even a breeze in the moisture and green shadows and blue-brown trunks. And no tangles — only a forest of verticals, hugely patient and protective. It was like being indoors, with a pretty roof overhead. And the order and size of it made the little huts beneath look especially dumpy.

The village — if it was a village — was deserted. Without people there, it was like the crust of a camp, where some travelers, too lazy or sick to make proper lean-tos, had hacked some bushes apart, shoveled a fire next to a rock, and spent one uncomfortable night before setting off again to die somewhere. The only sign of life was a sick puppy that yapped at us from behind a pile of trash — fruit peels and chewed cane stalks — and didn't bother getting up. I gave the hungry thing the sandwich I had stuffed into my pocket at lunchtime. He tried to bite me, then he ate the sandwich. In the center of the five huts, all made of grass tufts, was a smoky firepit, and some broken calabashes. There was not a human here to be seen.

But we had seen faces back at the duckboards.

Mr. Haddy said, "I ain't blame them for fetching out of this place. Lungley, what you say is for true. This is dirt." He was glancing around and wetting his teeth as he spoke. "We could go home, Fadder. We could slap we own mosquitoes."

Father was fanning himself with his baseball cap. He said, "They can't be far away. Probably down at the drive-in hamburger stand."

He looked up and saw Mr. Haddy walking away, in the direction of the duckboards.

"Anyone here require a beverage?"

This stiffened Mr. Haddy like an arrow between his shoulders. He turned around laughing in a sneezing sort of way.

"Or, on the other hand," Father said — he had bent over and picked something from the ground — "maybe they're getting their flashlights repaired. Take a gander at this so-called consumer durable."

It was a crumbled flashlight battery, its rusted case burst open and the paint peeled off and barely recognizable, it was so squashed. It looked like an old sausage.

"Francis, you said they were savages!"

The poor Zambu, who maybe had never seen a flashlight battery — flashlights were forbidden in Jeronimo — just smiled at Father and showed his teeth like a dog hearing a door slam.

"But if they're using these gimcrack things, they probably *are* savages."

We sat down and waited and watched the wee-wee ants.

"Could be at the gas station, in a long line, waiting to fill up with high-test."

"Ain't seen no gas station round here," Francis said.

"You wouldn't kid me, would you?"

There was evidence that someone was living here — straw beds in the huts, flies rotating over the trash pile, and a tripod with a burned baby on it, or, the nearest thing to it, a roasted monkey with curled-up fingers and toes.

Father said, "How did you talk to them when you were here before?"

Francis opened his mouth and wagged his blue tongue.

"What language?"

Francis did not know what Father meant. He said he just talked to them and they talked to him. "They savvy."

This was a Jeronimo explanation. People spoke English, Spanish, and Creole, but they did not know when they were going from one language to another. It seemed that by looking into a person's face, they knew what language to use, and sometimes they mixed them all together, so that what came out sounded like a new language. I had the habit myself. I could talk to anyone, and often I did not realize that I was not speaking English. But everyone on the Mosquito Coast, no matter what he looked like or what language he spoke, said he was English.

Pacing the clearing with Clover, Father looked like a man showing his daughter around the zoo — impatient and proud and talking the whole time and sort of holding his nose. Then, from the other side of the firepit, we heard his loud voice.

"Okay, the game's over. We can see you! Stop hiding — you're just wasting your time! Come on out of there, we're not going to hurt you! Get out from behind those trees!"

His voice rang against the jungle's straight trees and high ceiling. He kept it up for several minutes, yelling at the bushes, while we watched. Clover peered at the ferns Father was beating with a stick. He looked the way Tiny Polski had when he was flushing bobwhites in Hatfield.

The amazing thing was, it worked. We saw we were surrounded by people, more than twenty of them. This took place as we were staring, and they appeared in the same way as they had vanished before, without a movement or a sound. One second, Father was shouting "Come on out!" in the empty clearing, and the next second the people were there and he was shouting the same thing in their faces. We did not know whether Father had really seen them or was just pretending.

The women wore ragged dresses and the men wore shorts. But these clothes did not hide their nakedness. They seemed to represent clothes rather than serve any covering purpose. We could see their private parts through the rips and tears. And the children — Clover's age and mine — were stark naked, which was embarrassing.

"Carkles and wilks," Mr. Haddy said, and stuck his teeth out.

Father said, "They don't look so bad to me. Are you sure this is the place?"

Francis said it was.

We expected Father to say hello. He didn't. He turned his back on the people, as if he had known them a long time, and he said, "Okay, let's go" over his shoulder — meaning them. "Follow me — we've got work to do."

Three of the men — they looked a little like Francis, except that they were nakeder and had bushier hair — followed Father to the duckboards.

"You stay here," Father said to us. "Relax, get acquainted, make yourselves known."

He went off impatiently, whacking at flies with his hat, and then we heard him kicking the duckboards to scare snakes. The three men followed him without a word.

Clover said, "He's right at home anywhere." She sounded like Mother.

The people stared at Clover through the haze from the firepit's smoke. They had gray blurred faces and wore scorched rags. Mud was caked on their legs.

"See-ville, man," Mr. Haddy said. "What a spearmint!"

Francis said, "Almost went dead here, Haddy. Two time."

Now the people looked at us.

"What you do to these folks, Lungley?"

"Ain't do nothing."

"How is it?" Mr. Haddy spoke to the people. He stuck out his teeth and opened his mouth to listen.

No one replied. "Must be ailing," Mr. Haddy whispered. The naked children hid behind their parents. We looked at each other across the clearing, and it was like looking across the world.

They turned their heads. An old man limp-scraped into the clearing from the pillars of the forest trees. He wore a pair of cut-off striped pants, wire glasses, and socks but no shoes — his toenails were yellow in the rips. A rag was knotted around his neck. There were broken straws in his hair. He wore a bicycle clip on each wrist like a bracelet.

"That is the Gowdy," Francis said.

"Look like he require a bevidge," Mr. Haddy said. "Shoo!"

The next words we heard were Father's. He was hidden and saying, "Careful! Steady there! Don't drop them!"

We had packed the ice so carefully in banana leaves that the blocks were like parcels, tied with vines. The silent men carried two parcels apiece. Father led them to the middle of the clearing and directed that the parcels be placed on the ground.

"Who's in charge here?" Father said.

"Man with speckles," Francis said. "He the Gowdy." He nodded at the man who stood slightly forward of the group of staring people. Seeing our eyes on him, the old man clawed some of the straws out of his hair.

Father shook the man's hand. "You the Gowdy?"

"Gowdy," the man said, and he giggled.

"We've got a little surprise for you," Father said in his friendly way. "Want to get those other people over here?" He took out his jackknife and winked at us. "I'd like to show them something."

When the people were close, Father cut the vines and pushed the leaves aside, uncovering one block of ice. He stabbed his knife blade like an ice pick and hacked off a corner. He gave this hunk of ice to the Gowdy.

The old man bobbled it, just as Tiny Polski had done back in Hatfield, not knowing whether it was hot or cold. The people gathered around to touch it. They laughed and pushed to get near it and stepped on their children. The ones who touched the ice smelled their fingers, or walked a little distance away to lick them.

Father was still winking at us as he spoke to the old man, the Gowdy. "What's the verdict?"

"Good morning to you, sah. I am well, thank you. Where are you garng. I am garng to the bushes." The Gowdy's wire glasses had been knocked crooked by the pushing people. "Today is Monday, Tuesday, Wednesday. Thank you, that is a good lesson."

He bobbled the ice as he spoke.

"Hasn't the slightest idea," Father said to us.

The ice was melting in the old man's hand. Water ran down his arm, leaving dirt streaks on his skin. It dripped from the knob at his elbow.

"Completely in the dark," Father said. He put his arm around the old man's shoulders and gave him a wide smile.

The Gowdy shivered.

"What's that?" Father said, and pointed.

"Hice," the Gowdy said.

"Jesus Christ Almighty!" Father roared, and gave the Gowdy a shove, nearly knocking the old man over.

But no sooner had he spoken than every one of the people, including the Gowdy, dropped to his knees. The sudden movement startled the birds. A great uprush of them, big and small, shook the branches overhead, and these birds alerted the roosting birds, which took off like turkeys from the treetops. The sick puppy yapped and stumbled as the people knelt low, pinching their throats and murmuring.

"Ah Fadder wart neven hello bead name —"

"Cut it out!" Father said. "Get up — off your knees!" He tried to drag them up, then he turned to Francis and screamed, "You traitor, you gave me a bum steer! Thanks a lot!"

Mr. Haddy was laughing softly, relieved that they were Christians. And maybe he was secretly glad that Father, who seldom made mistakes, had blundered by taking ice here, when Mr. Haddy himself could more easily have shipped it to the coast and made a greater impression. He went forward to calm the confused people, who were still gasping and praying, and said, "You is good folks, but this is bush for true."

Father was so angry he vanished in the way the people in Seville had near the duckboards. He went up in a puff of smoke, leaving only his angry smell behind. We removed the rest of the parcels from the boat and talked to the villagers. They said that they had seen ice four or five times. They said it was wonderful stuff and they described it as cold stones that turned into water. Missionaries had brought it to them, and they believed that we were missionaries, too, and Father was our preacher. They wanted to know where we lived and if we had any food or salt to give them. The Gowdy boasted that everyone in the village was baptized.

He said they were waiting — waiting to go to Heaven and see the Lord Jesus. Mr. Haddy said it was a pretty rotten place to wait, full of monkey-shoo, but he could understand why they wanted to leave as soon as possible, for Heaven or anywhere else. Father returned — too late to hear any of this, which was just as well.

"I walked around the block," he said.

He would not speak to anyone in Seville. He said only that Francis had betrayed him. When the Gowdy tried to get the people started on a hymn, Father yelled as if he had hit his thumb with a hammer, and then said he would wait for us on the boat.

We left Seville. The people had begun to quarrel over the ice.

Father's moodiness made the trip back to Jeronimo mostly silent. But it was a faster trip. The contours of the river were not strange to us anymore, and the current was with us. Father made improvements on his map and we did not take any wrong turns. I worked the pedals. Father sat in the bow with Clover on his lap, sulking over his map, because the Seville people had seen ice before and because they prayed. "They might as well be in Hatfield, cutting asparagus," was all he said. He hugged Clover, like a big boy with a teddy bear. Francis and Mr. Haddy knew they were being ignored. They crouched amidships in the ice-storage vault with nothing to do.

After a while, Francis said he saw pipantos. Someone was following us, he said. Father did not reply or turn his head.

"Little one," Mr. Haddy said, looking past me. "Pipanto."

I glanced around but did not see anything. I had the steering to attend to.

"Me yerry," Francis whispered. He began muttering like a bush Zambu. He said he heard six paddlers — three pipantos.

"Never see no lanch like this," Mr. Haddy said.

Darkness came. It seemed to grow out of the riverside. The trees swelled, fattened by the blackness. The high curve went out of the sky. Pinheads of stars appeared and brightened into blobs.

"They still back of us in the rock-stone."

And night was around us. The water still held a slippery glimmer ahead, and behind us was the paddle wheel's loose froth, spreading in the current.

Soon we saw the lanterns of Jeronimo and the sparks from Fat Boy's chimney stack. The lights were small and very still on shore, but they poured from the bank and leaked yellow pools into the river. I heard someone say, "Here they come."

In the bedroom that night, Jerry said, "I could have gone with Dad. But I didn't want to. We were at the Acre all day. Ma let us."

"I saw two snakes," I said. "One almost bit me."

"We built another man trap. You don't know where it is. You'll fall in and kill yourself, Charlie."

"Go to sleep, crappo."

Later, through the bamboo wall, I heard Mother consoling Father. At first I thought she was speaking to April or Clover, her voice was so soft. But she was talking about the ice, and the boat, and his hard work. It was all brilliant, she said. She was proud of him, and nothing else mattered.

Father did not object. He said, "It wasn't what I expected. I didn't want that. They prayed at me, Mother."

"I'd like to go upstream sometime," Mother said.

"We'll go. It's not what you think. You won't like it. It's bad, but in the most boring way. Oh, I suppose they're all right — they'll be able to use the ice for something. But what can you do with people who've already been corrupted? It makes me mad."

It was two weeks before we went back to Seville, and in those two weeks we kids spent more time at the Acre, in our little camp by the pool. It pleased me to think that our camp was sturdier than anything in Seville. We wove hammocks out of green vines. We ate wild onions. The hammocks gave us rashes, the onions gave us cramps. A water dog crept out of the pool one day and we chased it into a trap and beat it to death with sticks. Then we cut it into pieces and dried the meat strips on a tripod, Zambu-style. But the next day the meat strips were gone. Peewee said a monster had come and eaten them, but I guessed it was an animal, because the tripod was not high enough.

We collected berries. Some were to eat, and others kept mosquitoes away if you rubbed them on your skin and let the juice dry. Alice Maywit showed us a cluster of purple ones and said, "These is poison."

Clover said, "I don't believe you. You're afraid of everything. I bet they're blackberries or something."

"Want to eat one, girl?" Drainy said. He showed her his wire-bending teeth.

Clover looked as though she was willing to try, just to show off and prove she was right, but I punched her hard and told her to stay away from them.

"No hitting!" she said. "That's the rule — Dad said so!"

"This isn't Jeronimo," I said. "This is our Acre and we have our own rules."

That was the pleasure of the Acre — that we could do whatever we wanted. We had money, school, and religion here, and traps and poison. No inventions or machines. We had secrets — why, we even knew the Maywits' real name. We could pretend we were school-children, or we could live like Zambus. That day was a good example. Drainy suggested that we take off all our clothes, and he pulled down his own shorts to show he was serious. Then Peewee did the same, and so did Clover and the others. Alice yanked her dress over her head and dropped her bloomers, and I stepped out of my shorts.

The eight of us stood there giggling and stark naked, but I was so ashamed I jumped into the pool and pretended I wanted to swim, while the others compared bodies and danced around.

Alice was standing at the lip of the pool.

"Ever see a carkle?"

She knelt with her knees apart and pinched the black wrinkles in her fingers, and for a moment I thought I was going to drown.

"What's that?" She closed her thighs and listened.

I heard nothing but the usual noises. Alice said she heard horse-flies. She saw one coming toward her and she looked steadily at it and got very worried. She said it meant there were strangers about.

We quickly put on our clothes and left the camp by the river path. Minutes later, we saw canoes. They were Indians, Alice said. She had known that from the horsefly. The canoes were old and water-logged dugouts, and the paddlers looked like the Seville people, their thin arms sticking out of rags, and broken straws in their bushy hair.

"They're trying to spy on us," Jerry said.

But they could not see us watching them. We had outsmarted them, and we laughed softly — even April, who was usually afraid — seeing them struggling upstream in their old canoes.

"They're coming from Jeronimo," Clover said.

"Good thing they ain't see us naked!" Drainy said.

"They'll never find our camp," I said. "No one will find the Acre."

I was glad that we had this safe place in the jungle. And now, be-cause I had seen Seville, I knew that ours was a well-ordered camp — better than the villages made by real jungle people.

We mentioned the canoes in Jeronimo. No one had seen them. Father said, "Maybe Munchies! Maybe Duppies!" and tried to frighten the Maywits.

On the morning Father said we were going back to Seville, Mr. Peaselee, who was doing fireman duty, let Fat Boy's fire go out. The ice melted. Father said, "We might have to cancel the trip. Everyone to the Gallery!" He gave a lecture about responsibility and good habits, and did we think Fat Boy could live without care and atten-tion? Fat Boy was kind because we were careful, but if we were careless he would turn dangerous. If we neglected to do our duty, he would split open and take his revenge by killing us all. Father said, "He's full of poison!"

After Fat Boy was stoked and new ice was made and packed, I heard Father say, "You can't take your eyes off these people for a minute."

Mother said, "That's just what Polski used to say."

"Don't compare me to that turkey."

"You're getting shrill, Allie."

"Poison," Father said. "Hydrogen and enriched ammonia — thirty cubic feet of each one. You'd be shrill too, if you knew the danger."

"I'll get the food," Mother said, and walked away.

Father saw me listening. "I'm the only one around here carrying the ball. Why is that, Charlie? You tell me."

I thought, He really does sound like Polski.

We left for Seville — the Fox family, no one else. Father pedaled and talked the whole time.

"Don't think I'm enjoying this," he said. "The last thing I want to do is go back to Seville. I'd just as soon go back to Hatfield. But we're obliged. We can't drop them after one shipment. I thought we might inspire them, help them out, cool their fish and give them time for farming — do all the things that ice lets you do. That's the whole point, isn't it? Give them the benefit of our experience? But I know what they'll do with the ice — they'll cube it and dump it into their glasses of Coke and just go haywire like everyone else."

"You didn't say anything about Coca-Cola," Mother said.

"Give them time."

We made Seville in under three hours, Father pedaling furiously and shouting about how he was going to dynamite a canal through the jungle and dredge the hyacinths out of the river. In his angry mood he imagined the grandest schemes. At the mahoganies we were met by five Seville people — they popped out of the spinach and the grass and startled us. They had seen us on the river, they said. But we had not seen them. They danced around Mother, telling her to be careful.

"We didn't get a reception like this the last time," Father said.

"I think they want us to follow them," Mother said.

As before, I ran ahead, stamping on the duckboards to frighten away the snakes. Jerry was behind me, looking worriedly from side to side.

He said, "What's that thing?"

"It wasn't here before," Clover said.

It was a wooden box in the clearing of Seville, as tall as me, and from a distance it looked like Fat Boy. It was smaller, somewhat resembling the original Worm Tub. It had a chimney stack and a firebox. Several women squatted near it, stoking its fire.

This pleased Father. "Maybe we inspired them after all," he said. He called out to the Gowdy, who was waiting to greet us. "What have you got there?" Father said. "That looks kind of familiar."

He walked straight up to it while the Seville people gathered around.

The Gowdy said, "Hice!"

Father opened the door, but the hinges of tattered vine were so flimsy the door fell off and the corner of it caught fire when it banged the firebox. Father kicked the fire out. We looked inside. It was empty.

"What the hell is this all about?" Father said.

They had made a copy of Fat Boy. But, Father said, what good was it? Of course it didn't work. It was only good for boiling eggs or setting yourself on fire. "Who gave you this harebrained idea?"

They smiled. They treated this box with a kind of reverence and asked Father to lead them in hymns in front of it. This enraged Father. He began to smell of his anger. The Gowdy tried to present Father with the lame puppy, but Father said he had enough sick animals of his own, and sick people too. So we unloaded the ice, and without even unwrapping it we went back to the *Icicle*. He said to Mother, "I hope you're satisfied." He also said he would never again go to Seville.

"I didn't come here to give people false idols to worship," he said. But the idol was there for all to see, made of warped planks and fastened by lianas.

"That's the trouble, really," Father said. "Any sufficiently advanced technology is indistinguishable from magic."

16

"WHAT'S ice *good* for?" little Leon Maywit had asked. But Father did not mind silly questions from small children. He went on, "Mainly it's a preservative — it keeps food fresh, so it keeps you from starvation and disease. It kills germs, it suppresses pain, and it brings down swellings. It makes everything it touches taste better without altering it chemically. Makes vegetables crisp and meat last forever. Listen, it's an anesthetic. I could remove your appendix with a jackknife if I had a block of ice to cool your nerves and take your mind off the butchery. It doesn't occur naturally on the Mosquito Coast, so it's the beginning of perfection in an imperfect world. It makes sense of work. It's free. It's even pretty. It's civilization. It used to be carried from northern latitudes on ships in just the same way they carried gold and spices —"

We were on the Gallery, all of us, Foxes, Maywits, Zambus, Mrs. Flora Kennywick, and the others — one of Father's dinner gatherings. Father pointed his finger stump at the mountains rising behind Fat Boy.

He said, "And that's next. Injun country. We'll take them a ton."

The newer people looked at his finger, not the mountains, and just as he said "ton," there was an earth tremor and their eyes popped.

It was a noiseless wobble, a slow half-roll that made the Gallery quiver. It was twenty seconds of rotation, like the drop of a boat deck. Nothing fell down, though there was a human yell in the forest and a breathless bark of worry from the river. I had the feeling that everything had moved but us. The world's peel had wrinkled and made a little skid. That was the first shuddering stall, but its various shakes and smoothings lasted a full minute.

Father made a flutterblast with his lips and said, "Gaw!"

Mrs. Maywit said, "Oh, God, Roper, what we do?" and she and Mrs. Kennywick began praying.

When I heard "Roper," I looked at Mr. Maywit. He covered his face and sobbed, "Never mind!" The moment passed. I think I was the only one who heard.

"Pray if you must," Father said, "but I'd rather you listened to me."

Everyone except us looked worried, as if he might point again at the mountains and cause another earthquake.

"I'm just thinking out loud," Father said, "but if I had the hardware, know what I'd do?"

At this, Mother smiled. I guessed what she was thinking — why do anything?

It was plain from where we sat that Jeronimo was a success. We had defeated the mosquitoes, tamed the river, drained the swamp, and irrigated the gardens. We had seen the worst of Honduras weather — the June floods, the September heat — and we had overcome both. We had just this moment withstood an earth tremor: nothing had shaken loose! We were organized, Father said. Our drinking water was purified in a distiller that ran from Fat Boy's firebox. We had the only ice-making plant in Mosquitia, the only one of its kind in the world, and the capability, Father said, of making an iceberg.

Down there were cornstalks, eight-and-a-half feet high, with cobs a foot long — "So big, it only takes eleven of them to make a dozen." We had fresh fruit and vegetables and an incubator (Fat Boy's spare heat) for hatching eggs. "Control — that's the proof of civilization. Anyone can do something once, but repeating it and maintaining it — that's the true test." We grew rice, the most difficult of crops. We had a superior sewage system and shower apparatus. "We're clean!" An efficient windmill pump overrode the water wheel on the ice-making days. Most of the inventions had been made from local materials, and three new buildings were faced with Father's bamboo tiles. We had a chicken run and two boats at the landing and the best flush toilets in Honduras. Jeronimo was a masterpiece of order — "appropriate technology," Father called it.

We produced more than we needed. The extra fish we caught swam in a tank Father named "the Fish Farm" — his names were always a little grander than the things themselves. We harvested more than we could eat, but the excess was not sold. Some of it he gave to people in return for work, though he never handed out any food to beggars. What he preferred to do was cut the produce open — watermelons, say, or cucumbers or corn — and empty out the seeds and dry them. He would give these to anyone who helped him. There was always work to do — he was determined to straighten the river and clear it of hyacinths, for instance. "It could take a lifetime," he said. "But I've got a lifetime! I'm not going anywhere!" River workers were rewarded with blocks of ice and bags of seeds. "Hybrids! Burpees! Wonder corn! Miracle beans! Sixty-day tomatoes!"

We were happy and hidden. All you could see of Jeronimo from the river was Fat Boy's square head and tin hat and the smoking chimney stack. "Low visibility," Father said. "I don't want to be pestered by goofball missionaries in motorboats who want to come up here and ooze Scripture all over us."

It was now November, the weather like Hatfield in July, and Jeronimo was home. And for this, Father said, no one had said a prayer or surrendered his soul or pledged allegiance or dog-eared a Bible or flown a flag. We had not polluted the river. We had preserved the ecology of the Mosquito Coast. And all because we had put our trust in "a Yankee with a knack for getting things accomplished" — him. He often said that if it were not for white-collar crime and stupidity and a twenty-cent dollar and the storm clouds of war, he could have done the same things in Hatfield, Massachusetts.

All this was plain from the Gallery, which had just wobbled with the earth tremor, and where Father was saying, "If I had the hardware, know what I'd do?"

The others were still fearfully gray and did not reply.

Mother said, "What would you do, Allie?"

"Sink a shaft."

He singled out the Maywits and Mrs. Kennywick and talked to them, because they had been praying hardest and were in a way still quaking themselves.

"The kind of hole they make in the Santa Barbara Channel or the North Sea. Your diamond bits, your giant platform, your whole drilling rig. I'd drill down — what? — four or five thousand feet and tap the energy resources right under here." He stamped his foot on the Gallery floor. "Just the way your chicleros tap a sapodilla tree. Same principle."

"You make me a sweet li'l raincap, Fadder," Mrs. Kennywick said. But her voice told that she was still thinking of the earth tremor.

"The rumble reminded me. Why doesn't anyone else put two and two together? See, the mistake they make in drilling for oil is that they're missing a golden opportunity. They've got all the hardware, but as soon as the oil starts gushing they pump it dry and bore another one. Talk about foolish and short-sighted!"

"But Fadder ain't do that foolishness," Mr. Maywit said to Mother, as if he knew what was coming. He looked fearful, or perhaps he just seemed so to me because I knew his real name was Roper.

"I'd let it gush," Father said, "and go on drilling. Go past the shale, lengthen the bit, go past the granite — lengthen it some more — and penetrate the bowels of the earth."

"Shoo," Mr. Haddy said. "That is a spearmint for true."

"That earth tremor we just had was a geological crepitation, a subterranean fart, from the bowels of the earth. There's gas down there! Superheated water, steam under pressure — all the heat you need!"

Mr. Peaselee said, "Ain't we hot enough now, Fadder?" And Mr. Harkins said it was so hot it was bringing out the crapsies, though I had no idea what he meant by this.

"Dad's not talking about the weather," Clover said.

"Listen to that little girl," Father said.

Everyone looked at Clover. She basked for a while under their watery eyes.

"Geothermal energy! Don't laugh. There's only a few places in the world where it's practical, and you're lucky enough to be living in one. The whole of Central America is a repository of high energy. You're on a fault line — thin crust, loose plates — listen to the volcanoes. They're calling out and saying, 'Geothermal! Geothermal!' — but no one's doing anything about it. No one seems to understand how the modern world got this way — no one except me, and I understand it because I had a hand in making it. Everyone else is running away, or pursuing wasteful and dirty technology, or saying his prayers."

"We ain't praying no more," Mrs. Kennywick said.

"The promised land is in your own back yard! All you have to do is get through that flowerbed, and drill the crust and tap the heat. We've been on the moon, but we haven't been in our own basement boiler. Listen, there's enough energy down there to do our cooking until kingdom come!"

I had to grin. Only Father would think of cooking by drilling to the earth's core. "Won't cost a nickel," was his usual boast, "and think of the benefits — a great invention is a perpetual annuity."

Father was excited by the earth tremor and his idea, and he infected the others on the Gallery with his excitement and optimism — just those feelings alone, because I was sure they had not understood a word he said.

"I see a kind of conduit, a borehole," he said. "Down go the drills, up comes the heat energy. I've already proved I can make ice out of nothing but pipefittings and chemical compounds and a little kindling wood. That took brains. But listen, any dumbbell can dig a hole. Why don't we? There's a good reason — we haven't got the hardware. Not yet. There's certain things in this world you can't make out of bamboo and chicken wire. But I'll tell you something else. Siphoning off the geothermal energy — I mean, in a huge way — might put a stop to these earth tremors, or at least take some of the kick out of them. See, I am talking about nothing less than harnessing a volcano!"

He had them twitching with this speech, and they looked eager enough to snatch shovels and start digging wherever he pointed.

All except Mr. Haddy. He stood up and cleared his throat and said, "That is a good spearmint, but it take an awful lot of brains. Between times, Lungley and me want to ship some ice down Bonito and Fish Bucket."

"Still dying to impress your friends, aren't you?"

"Ain't got friends down there," Mr. Haddy said. "But I can use me lanch like the old-time days, loading and sailing. That is my occupation, Fadder."

"I take it you're not interested in geothermal energy."

"Interested, sure thing, for true. But that spearmint, man, is real large. We ain't got all them holes and poles!"

"Not yet," Father said.

Mr. Haddy stuck his teeth out and blinked like a rabbit.

"How much ice do you want to take downstream?"

"Coupla hundred pounds. Two-three sacks."

"Hardly worth the trouble," Father said. "Why not take a ton?"

Mr. Haddy laughed loudly in surprise and relief. "She sink me old lanch!"

"Ice floats, Figgy" — Mr. Haddy smiled at the word — "You can tow it."

"How we do that?"

"Take an iceberg."

"Icebugs and bowl-caynoes," Mr. Maywit said to me, but clear enough for Father to hear. "Fadder sure is a miracle man!" Mr. Maywit looked very frightened.

"We could make an iceberg before breakfast," Father said.

It was the sort of challenge Father enjoyed, something grand and visible — a task that was also a performance. He had objected to Mr. Haddy taking a few sacks of ice to the coast, but towing an iceberg — that was a different story.

I had visualized a pyramid, its sides submerged, its point sticking up, being tugged by *Little Haddy*. But Father's iceberg was egg-shaped, and as tall as he was, to concentrate its coldness and limit its melting. He calculated that a single block made from many smaller blocks would be reduced by only a third if they floated it to Bonito Oriental, and it would still look like an iceberg in Fish Bucket. It would not make the coast. "But we're just proving a point here — not trying to change anyone's life. We'll see how it shakes down."

He told Mother it was mainly a morale-builder. "I like it when you get an idea and no one laughs. They deserve an iceberg."

Mr. Haddy was very proud. The iceberg was his boast, and he would captain the Creoles in taking it downstream.

"I'm just obeying orders," Father said. "If Figgy wants an iceberg, he's going to have it."

All work was put aside for this. Fat Boy was stoked and all the pumps primed. We had been keeping Fat Boy purring, but we only removed ice when we needed it for the cold-storage room, where we kept dead hens and vegetables. "We're a thoroughly refrigerated settlement," Father said. But the truth was that ice was not a necessity so far. It was a novelty, like Father's idea of geothermal energy. Why drill five thousand feet down to get at a volcano's bowels? To provide Fat Boy with an endless heat supply. One scheme justified another. We could have done without them, but, as Father said, why live like savages? "In the end, Robinson Crusoe went back home! But we're staying."

He said, "Someday, there'll be a conduit here, self-sealing and perpetual, and this whole refrigeration plant will be operated by geothermal energy. We'll have ice coming out of our ears and won't have to chop another stick of wood. Think of the future!"

That was the day we made the iceberg. We pumped water into Fat Boy and kept the firebox full and listened to the fizz and bubble in the pipes. Father ran back and forth on the path to the riverbank, where the ice bricks were taking shape as an oval iceberg.

"It's pretty and it's free. You find me a better combination of virtues."

Every half-hour we froze a new batch of bricks, and by mid-day we were finished — a large blue-white iceberg lay steaming and sweating in the mud, with a tow rope frozen in its center. It was roughly the shape of a Volkswagen Beetle, but larger, on a platform of bamboo logs that served first as a sled and then as a raft. We had no difficulty launching it. The tow rope was hitched to *Little Haddy*, and its gunning engine got the ice down the bank and into the river. The Creoles — Harkins, Peaselee, and Maywit — were in the bow, and Mr. Haddy in the wheel house, the ice creaking, the bamboo groaning, and the muddy water splashing all around it.

Of all the strange pieces of anything that floated down this jungle river, this was the strangest by a country mile.

"Our message to the world," Father said. "I'd love to see their faces when it heaves into view — coming out of the hottest, sickest, most parched and bug-ridden jungle in the whole hemisphere. They look up from their laundry. 'What is dat?' 'Dat is a icebug, Mudder, and he heading dis way!'"

Mother said, "They'll think it's the end of the world."

"But it's the beginning. It's creation, Mother."

The iceberg, hog-backed and bobbing, went around the bend and out of sight. The children ran down the Swampmouth path to get another look. Mother headed into the house, and then I was alone with Father on the riverbank.

"I could have gone with them," he said. "But I didn't want to spoil their fun. They can have the glory." He looked back at Fat Boy. "Besides, I've got to see to him. He might have overheated. He's full of poison and flammable gas. Ammonia and hydrogen, Charlie — those are his vital juices!" He looked at his finger stump and added, "But there's danger in all great inventions."

I saw my chance to tell him about the Acre. There was no danger there, apart from the traps we had set. We had food and water and shelter. But I was afraid of what he might say about the praying tree and the lean-to school. He might have got me to admit that we had taken all our clothes off one day and compared tools. He would have been stinking angry, or else hooting and calling us savages. So I said nothing.

"You feel a little like God," he whispered, looking around. His clothes were soaked from the ice bricks and sweat. His fingers were red from handling the ice. His hair was long and his face like a hatchet. He turned his bloodshot eyes on me and went on in the same tired and wondering whisper, "God had fun making things like icebergs and volcanoes. Too bad He didn't finish the job. Ha!"

Little Haddy returned to Jeronimo at nightfall. Mr. Haddy was giggling with pride, but at last he confessed that the iceberg had started breaking up at Bonito Oriental. They had cut it loose and let the current take the fragments downstream to the coast. He was a little drunk, because at the Chinese store in Bonito they had traded some ice for a calabash of mishla.

But Father was smiling at the river, maybe imagining the ice bricks floating down to Santa Rosa, and people pointing and fishing them out and struck with terror at the thought of ice sailing out of the jungle.

"This was a field day," he said. It had not cost anything, and we were all happier as a result. He told us he had left the United States so that we could spend days like this, working together and putting our ideas into practice. It was what he had always dreamed about.

Outside the Gallery that night, the birds fell silent in the muddy twilight and the bats began chirping. Around us was a circular wall of insect howl. A light breeze quickened in the darkness, brushing the trees. We played Up Jenkins on the Gallery floor, to the flashes of heat lightning that separated the mountains from the night sky.

"That's next. Injun country. We'll take them a ton."

But when he pointed, the Creoles and Zambus held tight to the Gallery rails, expecting another earth tremor. And Mr. Haddy, being worried, was all the more rabbit-toothed.

Father did not notice them. He was staring at the mountains, waiting for another lightning bolt. It came. It flashed on his face.

"You feel a little like God," he said.

17

IN THE DAYTIME, Jeronimo was ours — our design, our gardens, the whops and claps of our pumps, the nut-sweet fragrance of our split bamboos, our flowers and mechanics. It was hot, but the heat and light burned it clean of stinks. And it was always in the daytime that Father said, "I declare this a success."

The coldest Jeronimo got was in the hour before dawn, like right now, when it was coal-black and clammy and so silent in the clearing you could hear the trees drip. It was foreign and all wild. The jungle odors were strongest, too, the wet itch of hairy vines, the wormy tree trunks, the foul smack of sappy leaves, and the river rotting as it swept past us.

These were the stinks and perfumes of early morning, dew-soaked grass, and wet petals, and they overwhelmed the civilized smells of Jeronimo. Everything was black under the black sky. The stars, which at midnight looked like a spillway of broken pearls, did not shine at this hour — they were holes of light, like eye squints in black masks.

Father had woken Jerry and me and told us to put our clothes on. "We're all ready," he said.

We waited in the dark, standing in the wet grass near Fat Boy's firebox, yawning and shivering.

"I've been up for hours getting this together," Father said. I could see the glow of his cigar butt, nothing else. "Hardly slept a wink."

"Fadder ain't need no sleep," Mr. Maywit said. So Father had been lecturing him, too.

As my eyes grew accustomed to the darkness, I saw Mr. Maywit fussing around a block of ice. It was nearly as big as the iceberg Mr. Haddy had towed downstream two days ago. Something in Mr. Maywit's jittery gestures said he was not coming with us. He was working too hard, out of breath and chattering to Mr. Peaselee, as if he was impatient for us to leave, sort of showing us the door.

The slab of ice — it looked like a fat lump of lard in the darkness — was being wrapped in a mitten of banana leaves. It was fastened to a narrow sled. The sled had a pair of close-set runners and was rigged to be pulled by men in harnesses.

"Don't talk to me about wheels," Father said.

But no one had said anything about wheels.

Rustling the banana leaves as they layered them over the ice block, Mr. Maywit and Mr. Peaselee were whispering between themselves. Father's cigar butt blazed.

"Wheels are for paved roads — they won't get you anywhere on these mountain tracks. Too inefficient. Just break or get bogged down in the gumbo. But Skidder here" — it was his name for the ice sled — "will merely glide over the bumps."

The ice no longer glowed like lard. The wrapping was done. It looked like granite, the hump of a tombstone. Mr. Maywit and Mr. Peaselee stepped aside, their white eyes wide open.

"How about it?" Father said. "Are you coming with us?"

"Kyant." Mr. Maywit was hesitant and backpedaling. "I am Feel Super."

Father laughed at him. "He almost forgot!" he cried. "If you're Field Super, you get those gutters scrubbed. I want them so clean I can eat off them. Where are you, Mr. P.?"

Mr. Peaselee said, "Fadder?" from a squatting position, and sprang to his feet, muttering.

"You coming?"

"No man," Mr. Peaselee said. "They always troubles there. Contrabanders. Shouljers. Feefs. People from Nicaragua way. Up in those mountains, they got ruckboos, for true."

"Quit it — you don't know the first thing about trouble." Father turned his back on the Creoles. "Where's my jungle men, where's my trackers?"

"Hee, Fadder."

It was a low brown growl, close by. The Zambus had been there beside us like black trees, listening the whole time — Francis Lungley, John Dixon, and Bucky Smart. Now I could see their round heads moving past the star punctures in the sky.

"Harness up and let's shove off," Father said. "Go back to bed, Peasie. Get your beauty sleep."

We started out of the clearing, Father in front, the Zambus pulling the sled, Jerry and me following behind. Father was still talking.

"Trouble, the man says. I don't call a forty-five–degree angle trouble, and what's a handful of no-goods? I could have that half-breed pleading for mercy. Fuel shortages, unemployment, moral sneaks in Washington, and muggers on every street corner! Kids in grade school sniffing glue, polecats in every pulpit, old-lady hoarders, white-collar punks, double-figure inflation, and a two-dollar loaf of bread. That's what I call trouble. Dead rivers, cities that look like Calcutta — that's trouble for fair. You don't take a walk because you're afraid of getting a shiv in your ribs, so you stay home and they come through the windows. There are homicidal maniacs, ten years old, prowling some neighborhoods. They go to school! The whole country's bleeding to death — *bleeding* —"

He kept on talking as we entered the dark path out of Jeronimo, and the birds flew up at the sound of his voice.

"Our technological future's in the tiny hands of the Nipponese, and we let coolies do our manufacturing for us. And what about those jumped-up camel drivers frantically doubling the price of oil every two weeks? Did I hear someone mention trouble?"

The ferny boughs blocked the stars overhead, and the path was so narrow the wet leaves brushed dew against our arms. In the daytime this track was a green tunnel, but at night it was the throat of a cave. Father went on talking about the United States. "It makes me mad," he was saying. We followed his voice and the creaking sled. Very soon we were climbing, and within a short time Jerry told me his legs were tired. Mine were trembling from this new effort of climbing, and my feet were wet, but instead of telling him this I called him a spackoid and a sissy — it was what Father would have said — and I felt stronger.

The path zigzagged through dim pickets of trees. We had never been here before. On the tight corners, the Zambus called out, "Hoop! Hoop! Hoop!" and turned the sled. Father had been right — wheels would have been useless here. The loose boulders and soft dirt would have jammed them. And Jerry and I were lucky. The sled moved so slowly on these bends that we could pause and get our breath. The sled's runners made deep ruts, and on the steeper parts of the track we could hear the Zambus' whispered grunts.

"Not to mention the Russians," Father was saying.

Dawn was breaking — lifting the sky and uncovering the trees behind us. It did not seem so jungly now, except that in the grayness just before the sunrise cracked against the treetops, there came the whistle-screech of birds and the hurrying of perhaps snakes or pacas or mice — the scuttling of small creatures, anyhow, beside the path. In the dark, I had felt I was burrowing, but sunup brought greenness to the path and made me feel tiny on the thinly wooded slope. Jerry and I had fallen back. When we caught up with the sled, we saw that Father and the Zambus had stopped and were looking down the valley.

"But there's no trouble there," Father said.

We were above Jeronimo and could see its bamboo roofs, the columns of woodsmoke mingled with the mist, and mattresses of morning fog lying in the fields. The sunlight that was full against this high slope where we stood had not reached Jeronimo. But its pattern was clear, even in the broth of mist. Its stone paths were laid out among the gardens like a star outlined on a patched flag. It looked wonderful from here, neither a town nor a farm but a settlement of precisely placed buildings on the river that was a twisted blue vein in the muscle of jungle. At greater distances, smoke rose from the forest trenches of other clearings.

"They just got out of bed," Father said, seeing the people stirring in Jeronimo. "There's someone going for a whizz — probably Figgy."

I could see Mr. Haddy's flour-sack shirt.

"Lulled into a false sense of security," Father said. "I blame myself. 'Contrabanders — feefs.' Of course Mr. Peaselee wants to go back to bed. He knows he's in Happy Valley!"

Jerry said, "There's Mrs. Kennywick."

She was moving heavily toward the chicken run.

"Feed them chickens, shuck that corn," Father said.

Fat Boy was a bright-lidded tower, its reflectors catching the sun's first rays in its tin dimples. It looked like nothing else for miles — marvelous in a valley that was itself full of marvels.

"Mudda," Francis said, and pinched his fingers at the smallness of Mother hanging clothes on the line.

"She's all business." Father slapped my back with pride.

But Mother was not "all business." She took things easy and always asked us if we were hungry or tired, or if there was anything we wanted. It was through Mother's encouragement that we roamed the forest and made our jungle camp at the Acre. Father treated us like adults, which meant he put us to work. But we were children — homesick half the time and afraid of the dark and not very strong. Mother knew that. It was Father who, in what you would have expected to be a coconut kingdom of sunshine and lazy days, was always roostering around and crowing for us to get down to business.

It was going to be an all-day trip today, and I knew that with Mother it would have been different. Father might say things like "I'm working for you" and "Tell me what to do," but he was in charge. He had made Jeronimo succeed — it was all his doing — and he knew it. Yet at times like this I wished that Mother was here. She would have walked behind the ice sled with us. We would have talked to her about the hopes we carried on our backs like parachutes. With Father, we listened and sweated.

"It's another mile up this crooked path, at a loose guess," Father said, looking up the hill. "We'll keep dragging this old Skidder. Once we get up there, it's all downhill."

He was pointing ahead to what looked like a mountaintop. It was a dome we could see from Jeronimo. An hour later, when we reached it, we saw that it was not a mountaintop at all, but the hip of just another slope. This mountainside seemed to go on and on.

Jerry said, "I want to rest. Will you wait for me, Charlie?"

"Dad won't like it. We can't sit down while they're doing all the hard work."

Jerry was hot-faced and blush-blotched and damp from the heat. His hands were dirty and his skinny legs were clawed from the brambles that grew beside the path. I told him I would run ahead and ask Father. I felt sorry for Jerry, but I wanted a rest too.

"Jerry wants to stop," I said. "He's tired."

"He *says* he's tired."

Father kept on walking. He called to the Zambus.

"We'll have lunch on top. Then we'll have a lovely postprandial glissade behind this baffle and sock this frozen monolith into that benighted wilderness."

Francis Lungley grunted.

Father winked at me. "You've got to talk their language."

But where was the top? These summits were as false as the ones beneath. They showed nothing but other summits beyond. Looking back, we could see the succession of crooked slopes that had appeared to us to be mountaintops until we scaled them. We had climbed the mountain's bum only to see, miles away, its sunlit shoulders.

"After this, it'll be all downhill," Father said, on the steepest parts.

The ice block jiggered and its leaf mitten crackled as it was dragged. Though I could not see them, I could hear the Zambus gasping. Their gasps were regular and harsh, like the scrape of a bucksaw in a log.

We were used to the damp shade of our own trees, the buggy riverside, the flat gardens and cool hollows of Jeronimo. Up here, the trees were thin and burned dry by the sun, the slopes were rocky, there was no shade or shelter. We heard dogs bark and now and then we smelled smoke. But we saw no people. Father was still talking, still promising us lunch and predicting that soon it would be all downhill.

Pretty soon, Jerry and I were walking in mud. Water was shaking out of the bamboo sled and drizzling onto the ground. The ice was melting fast — the lower portion of the banana-leaf mitten, all that insulation, was blackened with moisture. The angle of the track was so sharp that the ice sled was not pulled steadily but jerked, and water flew out from the runners with each jerk.

I crept with Jerry from behind the sled. The Zambus were bent double in their harnesses. They gasped in their wood-sawing way, and their chins dripped with sweat and their faces were twisted horribly. Crouched like this, struggling forward practically on their knees, they no longer looked like men. They had been turned into suffering animals by this hard pulling, with dog faces and bruised thumbs. Their nostrils were wide open and their eyes buried in squints. They looked so frightening with froth on their necks, we did not dare tell them the ice was melting. And we knew that if we told Father he would go into fits.

It was well past lunchtime. Father had hurried on to get a glimpse of what lay ahead. When he came back and said "Let's break for lunch," we guessed that we were near the top of the mountain.

Jerry and I were carrying the lunch in our knapsacks. We spread it on a rock — tomato sandwiches, boiled corn, guavas, bananas, and Jungle Juice — and Father began describing how much more useful a cable car would be on this tortuous path.

"Project a series of tripods, bearing a cable for slinging passengers and cargo up and down the mountain," he said. "It would be no more trouble to build than a ski lift."

And while the Zambus were panting and Jerry whimpering over his sore feet, Father cantered around the slope saying, "Section it — that's the way. Hoist some pylons here and get pulleys working. Your trolley simply swings up and over these little cliffs. If you had a system of finely meshed cogs, you could work it manually above or below, or counterbalance it on an opposing line and make it self-operating. Then your descending weight would hoist your hopper to the summit. That's not ordinary rock you're wearing out shoe leather on — that's potential ballast. Oh, Gaw!"

He had jogged over to the sled to admire its size, but he had seen that the ice was melting.

"We've got shrinkage! Charlie, you fruit, why didn't you say something? Come on, let's move out before it all goes to pieces."

And he ran ahead saying, "We should have put a rubber sock around it!"

The Zambus sighed, and harnessed themselves again.

By mid-afternoon we still had not reached the ridge. But Father shouted so much, the Zambus stumbled. And they tried so hard to please him, they rushed the sled into a boulder that punched it apart. With a grunt that was almost human, the block of ice cracked in half, splitting its mitten of leaves and fracturing the sled.

"That's wonderful," Father said quietly. "That is just what I need. Thank you very much, gentlemen. Now, don't mind me. I'm just going to take a walk around the block. You stay here, and if you're inclined to pick up the pieces, I promise you I won't stand in your way." He gave us all a weak smile.

He disappeared. A minute later we heard him scream from behind a rock.

Francis Lungley looked at me in alarm.

"He's mad," I said. "You'd better fix this."

The Zambus cut the ice free and, grumbling among themselves, made two sleds. It was almost an hour before we could set off again, but now Father and Bucky were harnessed to one sled, and Francis and John manned the other. This was worse than before, for Father was angry, growling at his work, straining and yelling. The broken ice had melted smaller, the two teams moved fast along the track. But we were no nearer to the ridge. Jerry and I scampered ahead, listening to the men breathing hard beneath us.

The next rise brought us to a bowl in the mountainside that was filled with white flowers and bees. The track, descending for the first time (but it rose again on the other side), gave Father and the Zambus a chance to take it easy. When they caught up with us, Father said, "Your hands and necks are filthy. What's the matter with you kids? Can't you keep clean?"

We explained that we had rubbed black berry juice on our skin to keep the flies and bees away. It was the trick Alice Maywit had shown us at the Acre. The berry juice was as good as insect repellent. The Zambus had used it too, only it was impossible to see the dark juice on their black skin.

Father had been bitten — his wrists and neck were pebbly from insect bites. I thought he might thank us for this information. It was natural medication, it worked, and it was free.

But he hated the look of it. He said, "You think I'm scared of a few bug bites? Ha! If you're scared of bugs, you've got no business here."

The bees swarmed around him as he spoke. He batted them away. "They know when you're scared! They can smell fear!" A little while later he was stung on one ear. His ear lobe swelled fat and shook like a turkey's wattle. He said he could not feel a thing.

The sun was ahead of us, dropping behind the mountain we were climbing. It dazzled us, but it had lost most of its heat. I wondered what would happen when it sank, because in all the time we had lived in Jeronimo — almost seven months now — we had always returned home at sundown. But we had not reached the village. Jeronimo was hours behind us. Father and the Zambus were still grunting in their harnesses, dragging the two sleds.

I said, "We'll have to go home in the dark."

"We can't go home until we deliver this ice!"

Deliver it where? I looked at the cargo on the sleds. The banana-leaf insulation fit loosely, like a man's clothes on a child. There was not much ice left.

"Why didn't I think to put a rubber sock around it? Those two buffoons insisted on those useless banana leaves!"

And now the sun was half gone, a segment of cold fruit, and Father's face brassy bright in its last glare. He urged the Zambus on, as if chasing the sun to the summit. But the sunset was quicker, and while they heaved the sleds along the track, the sun slice blinked behind the rocks, and its afterglow was a dusty pinkness in the sky.

Father's determination left him then. He stepped out of his harness and walked up the path to snarl at the dying daylight.

"All right," he said, "we'll make camp."

"Where will we sleep?" Jerry asked.

"Why, just over there, across the street, in the Holiday Inn! You two kids can lounge by the poolside while I fix us up with a couple of rooms. Want a king-sized bed? I know I do, and I sure hope they've got air conditioning and color TV —"

He was walking in circles and biting a new cigar as he spoke.

" — barbecue pit, Ping-Pong, cheeseburgers, and a funny-bunny piano player in the cocktail bar. Want a roll of quarters for the juke box, Jerry? Play some tunes?"

Jerry had begun to cry. He had knelt down to tighten one of his sandals and, crouching there, put his head against his knee and sobbed quietly. I pitied Jerry. All he had asked was where we were going to sleep, but Father went on mocking him with this speech about the Holiday Inn and have a nice hot shower bath and good long rest.

"There goes Charlie, off to buy a Fudgsicle. Careful crossing the road, sonny!"

I knew Father was disappointed that we had not made it to the Indian village, so instead of sulking or crying, like Jerry, I had decided to do something helpful. I said, "I'm looking for some wood to build a lean-to."

"Hear that, Fido? He's going to show us how to make camp. Like he showed us how to keep the bugs away. You've got to hand it to these kids."

"Charlie know how," Francis said.

"He's a hamburger," Father said. "He's got your number."

It was clear that Father had not planned to camp out. We had eaten most of the food. We had no tents or mosquito nets, no lanterns or blankets, and only one mess kit. The water bag was almost empty. But there were several things in our favor — it was the dry season, so we would not get rained on, and there were fewer insects up here, and all day we had seen pacas and birds on the mountain-side — we could eat those. Father had traveled light in the hope of rushing the mountain, but we had failed, and now it was evening.

"Don't just stand there," Father shouted to the Zambus. "Improvise!"

The Zambus built a fire, while Jerry and I made a lean-to out of sticks we had found nearby. Then we gathered dry grass and made a bed inside and tried not to disturb Father, who was cursing, hacking at a sapling with his knife.

He was no good at making temporary camps, and he was surprised at how quickly and well Jerry and I put up our lean-to. It did not need to be waterproof — it was only to protect us from the wind, which was strengthening up here as darkness fell. When Father saw our bed-nest of grass he said, "You planning to lay an egg?"

He cut five saplings, saying, "I'm going to make a proper shelter!" He started to lash them together, but before his first frame was complete it was pitch dark, which was a shame because his shelter would have been much better than ours if he had finished it. At last, he kicked it apart and said, "What's the use!" Seeing me with some yautia plants, he said, "Picking flowers, Charlie? That's the idea — you can put them into your scrapbook. Won't Mother be pleased?"

I told them they were yautias and that their roots were as tasty as carrots.

"Eddoes," Bucky said. Eddo was his name for yautia. He had speared a paca rat with a sharpened stick and was roasting it over the fire with the same spear.

"I'm not hungry," Father said. "Anyway, I don't eat rats and weeds."

He watched us eat and he told us how, traveling in Eastern Europe, he had been disgusted to find that everywhere he ate, the silverware was dirty. He had smeary knives, and stains on his spoon, and the tines of the fork always had bits of yesterday's food between them. At another place, he had found a hair in his milk. He went on describing the filthy silverware, and he made the Zambus laugh, but I kept thinking how strange it was that we were squatting here on this mountainside in Honduras, eating a burned paca and burned yautia with our fingers, while Father complained about the dirty forks in Bulgaria. Normally he did not talk about food at all, and he said it was indecent to praise it while you were eating it. But that night on the mountain, all he talked about were the tormenting meals he had eaten and the cutlery that had not been washed properly.

Finally he said, "You're melting my ice," and ordered us to put the fire out.

The Zambus obeyed. They had made their beds beside low windbreaks of boughs. They were not the men I was used to in Jeronimo. Here, on the mountainside, they had become silent and simpler and a little wild-seeming.

"I'm not tired," Father said, as Jerry and I crawled into our lean-to. "I'll just sit here and cool my heels until you're ready to move out."

He sat cross-legged near the ice. He had combined the two blocks to concentrate their cold. I could tell from the hot glow of his cigar that he was sulking — maybe thinking about dirty cutlery. But I also suspected that he was guarding the ice. He had warned us not to touch it. The Zambus muttered for a while, and then they sighed and lay like logs on the ground. "I wish Ma was here," Jerry said, but he was soon asleep.

The wind hummed in the bushes and dragged against the rocks and dry grass. That was the only sound, the wind, but later I heard another noise in this humming of wind. It was a *plink-plink-plink,* as if someone were striking the highest key on an old piano. It was the ice melting, waterdrops hitting the tin pan of the mess kit. I was painfully hungry and still thirsty, and the sound of water made me thirstier.

I poked my head out of the lean-to and saw Father beyond the dead fire, sitting in front of the ice block. The block with is clumsy cover was about a quarter of its morning size, but silhouetted in the starry sky it still looked like a tombstone, and Father like a white corpse that had crawled out of the grave. The starlight made his face like a skull's and gave him bony arms.

"I want to sleep in my own bed!" he screamed.

I tried to think of something to say. I decided, after all, not to ask him for any water.

"What are you looking at?" he said fiercely. "This is the first time since creation that ice has ever melted here. Think of it! And you're saying that's nothing?"

18

I WOKE UP tired in damp clothes and remembered we were still on the mountain — Father, Zambus, and ice. Father had fallen on his side and, slap on the ground, had gone to sleep with his arms folded and his baseball hat squashed against his cheek. But he woke quickly and denied that he had even dozed off. He said he had got bored, watching us snore. He said, "No, we haven't failed!" and told me to fill the canvas bag with the water that had dripped into the mess-kit pan.

"Don't bother to get harnessed." He was peeking under the cover of the ice block. He shoved the cakes of ice into the knapsacks. Each cake was about the size of a football, speckled with brown broken leaf, and had the rotten texture of a hard sponge. This was all that was left of the great ice block we had dragged out of Jeronimo.

"Don't say anything. Don't ask me any questions. I don't want to hear a peep out of anyone. Now let's march!"

He sprinted up the path, his knapsack rising and falling, bumping his back, whop-whop. Francis Lungley followed behind with the other knapsack, then Bucky and John, empty-handed, and Jerry and I, trying our best to keep up. I carried the long water bag. It slapped against my knees and prevented me from running.

It was a bright cool dawn, washed in light, with parcels of cloud lying against the mountainside like ghosts of dead mackerel. Up ahead, Father had halted near an outcrop of rock. I thought he was waiting for us, but I saw that he had reached another ridge of the mountain. It was the last ridge. Below us — but it was a plateau, not the deep valley we had expected — was all of Honduras.

Such an empty world. I did not think wilderness could look so sad.

This was a different country from the one we knew: limitless jungle, volcanoes, and no ocean. No rivers that we could see, no water at all. It was a surface of treetops and skimming birds. Its vastness made me feel small and puny. No smoke, no roads, nothing to say that people lived here. It was Olancho, but that was only a name. It was anybody's.

"It looks so desolate," I said.

"You've never seen Chicago!"

The treetops beneath us continued to the horizon, and the unbroken greenness gave it such a strong suggestion of depth that it hardly looked like forest at all. It was a brimming ocean of wild leaves, a tide so high it had risen to the mountain range. Father was smiling at it all, and yet it was Father who had told us that the deepest tides tricked you with their flatness — if you stuck your foot in them, they would drag you out and drown you in their undertow.

"It's all downhill from now on." There was no path. Father set off, running beside the trickle of a stony creek.

The Zambus said we were to look out for more bees. The Indians here were beekeepers and always had hives near their huts. And dogs — half-wild ones — they kept those, too. But we smelled smoke before we saw either bees or dogs, and when the creek widened to a stream, we knew we must be near a village. The forest was darker — we were under that ocean of trees we had seen, and moving down. My senses told me more than I could logically explain. The smell of stagnant water and woodsmoke and burned meat, and a hairier, dirtier, rancid-yam smell of latrines and dogs — all boiled together. It was a stew-stink I now associated with human habitation — not ours but other people's. Jeronimo's cleanliness educated my nose to these sharp odors.

We might have missed the huts. They were leafy and made of peeled sticks and were the same color as the trees dying near them. But the starved dogs had rushed up to us and Francis was saying, "Fadder! Fadder!" and two macaws croaked at him from a branch.

"Leave this to me," Father said. He saw some lemon trees and whispered, "Juice balls."

In the stream that ran past the village there were women kneeling in muck doing laundry, slapping shirts and pants on boulders.

"Those women are washing clothes," I said.

Jerry said, "So what?"

"No one's wearing clothes," I said. "Not that kind."

The Indian men in the village clearing were practically naked. Shorts were all they wore, and these were in rags — more like aprons.

"Maybe they've only got one pair."

The washerwomen scattered when they saw Father, but he did not pause. He splashed across the stream, then kicked the water from his sandals and kept going toward the Indians and the huts. These were not the sagging tin-roofed huts that river Creoles lived in, and they were much larger than the rats' nests we had seen in collapsing Seville. They were tall stilted rectangles, with protruding roofs and a sort of attic space beneath the grass and leaf thatching. There were ten of them. Father was saying, "No beer cans, no candy wrappers, no flashlight batteries —"

We stayed right behind him.

"And no bows and arrows," he said. "No weapons of any kind. We're probably the first white men they've ever seen. Don't do anything to frighten them. No loud noises. No sudden movements."

They were brown Indians, about a dozen of them, with Chinese eyes and heavy faces and short legs. Some had long hanks of hair bunched at the backs of their heads. Just this squinting fence of men — the women had hidden themselves, and there were no children that we could see.

"Raise your arms slowly," Father said.

We raised our arms slowly.

"Francis, you're the Miskito expert. Tell them who we are."

Francis Lungley looked confused. "Who we are, Fadder?" he asked.

"Tell them we're their friends."

"Friend!" Francis howled. "Friend!"

"Not in English, dummy. Tell them in Miskito, or whatever crazy lingo —"

The Indians watched Father and Francis quarrel.

"They ain't Miskito feller. They Paya or Twahka feller. Maybe we give them bunce banana."

"You're driving me bananas," Father said, and pushed Francis aside. Now he spoke in Spanish. He asked them if they spoke Spanish. They stared at him. He said in Spanish that we were friends —

we had come from far away, over the mountains. They still stared. He said we had a present for them. They went on staring under their swollen Chinese eyelids.

"Maybe they're all deaf," Father said. He shook the knapsack from his shoulders and went close to the men. "Go on, open it," he said, and spelled this out in sign language for the men, motioning with his hands.

An Indian knelt down and opened the knapsack.

"See? He understands me perfectly."

The Indian looked inside, then turned the limp knapsack upside-down and poured water out of it. He spoke one word, which none of us understood.

"Quick, Francis, give me your knapsack!"

Francis unbuckled the second knapsack and said, "She all water, Fadder."

"There must be some of it left — maybe a little piece."

The Indians watched Father and Francis sorting through the soup in the wet knapsack. "Got it!" Father said, and held up a twig of ice — all that was left of the ice block — maybe two ounces. We followed as he went forward to show the men.

He placed it in his palm. Maybe his impatience heated his hand, or maybe it was the small size of the ice twig. Whatever it was, the small thing disappeared. Before they could look closely at it, it melted away and slipped through the cracks between his fingers.

Father still held his wet hand out, but the Indians were staring at his finger stump.

"I don't believe this," Father said quietly. He started to walk away. For a moment, I thought he was heading back to Jeronimo. But no — he was mumbling in Spanish and English. He had left us facing these bewildered Indians. Now he returned and gave a speech.

He had brought them a present, he said. But the present had disappeared. What kind of present can disappear? Well, that was the interesting thing — it was water, but a form of water they had never seen before, as solid as a rock and twice as useful, good for preserving meat or killing pain. It was very cold! We called it ice, he said, and we had an invention over the mountains for making it out of river water. He had brought a block of it that had been as big as two men, but it had gotten smaller and smaller, and by the time we reached the village it was tiny. That was unfortunate, he said, because now it was gone, and a moment ago he could have showed it to them.

"But I'll be back," he said. "I'll show you!"

Most of the Indians were still looking at his finger.

Then one of the Indians spoke very clearly, in Spanish. His face was square, and he had the thickest hair bunch, which stuck out like a short ponytail.

"Go away," he said. His teeth were black stumps.

Father laughed at him.

"I said it was an accident, Jack. Have you been over there? Do you know how long it takes to drag ice that far?" Surprised by the Indian's order, he had spoken in English. In Spanish he said, "Don't blame me! Ever seen ice? Ever touched it?"

"Go away," the Indian said.

"Thanks. We haven't eaten since yesterday. We had to bivouac on that mountain. Our water's used up and these kids are dead on their feet. Thanks very much."

"Go!"

The word was sharp, the Indian's black teeth were ferocious, but he looked very frightened. Father had been talking and trying to explain about the ice. Maybe he had not looked closely enough at these Indians to see that they were frightened. Maybe he assumed that their bewilderment had something to do with the marvel that had melted and leaked away.

The Indians were clay-colored and they stood there like pieces of pottery about to shiver into cracks. Who were we? they seemed to be thinking. Where had we come from? Had we fallen out of the sky?

"Real savages," Father said. He had not seen their fear. "I guess I got what I bargained for —"

They looked at Father's finger stump as he waved it around.

"If the ice hadn't melted, they'd be all over us — thank you, you're wonderful, please give us more, et cetera. But gentlemen, our plan has melted —"

Now the Indians were showing their teeth, the way their dogs had — black teeth, raw lips, squinting eyes.

"— and I can't stand this Neolithic hostility —"

Bucky said, "We go."

Francis said, "Yes, man."

"I'm not moving," Father said to the receding Zambus. "What about you, Charlie?"

I said, "I'm not moving either."

"Tell them that."

He took my hand and pulled me in front of him, making me face the Indians and cloaking me in his anger smell.

In Spanish, I said, "I am not moving."

"You heard what he said!"

But had they? They looked as deaf as when we had first arrived. The Indian who had told us to go away stood there picking blister scabs of dead skin from his elbow. Then he looked up and hissed, "Go."

"Tell him we're staying here until we get something to eat. That's the least they can do. A little hospitality won't kill them. We're not missionaries or tax collectors."

I told them this. As I was talking, Father was whispering to the Zambus, "This place is stranger than Jeronimo ever was. What I could do here! They haven't got a blessed thing. But look at those huts. They know how to make strong frames." When I finished talking to the Indians, he turned to me. "Tell them we want something to eat," he said. "I don't want anything for myself — it's the rest of you guys that need some grub. We eat, then we go."

The Indians, hearing me say this, looked uncertain.

"And tell them it's too hot here in the sun. We want to sit in the shade."

I managed to explain this, though I had to ask Father some of the Spanish words.

The Indian who had spoken (but all he had said so far was "Go away") backed to the largest hut and went inside.

Father said, "He's going to ask the Gowdy if it's all right."

The Indian reappeared and gestured for us to sit near that hut.

"Friendly little critters, aren't they?" Father muttered as we sat down. "What are they trying to hide? My guess is that there's something here they don't want us to see. Frankly, I'd like to snoop around."

Tired and hungry as I was, I would have been glad to get out of this place, and I knew from Jerry's face that he felt the same. Father was unruffled, still the Sole Proprietor of Jeronimo, if not the King of Mosquitia, passing whispers to his Zambus with his all-powerful air. He did not seem to notice — or if he noticed, did not care — that the Indians had crept across the clearing and sat watching us from a semicircle with their drooling dogs.

"Sure, this place smells," Father was saying. "They've got no organization. But it's a healthy climate. Cooler than Jeronimo. Fertile soil. Not many bugs. Lots of hardwood. You could work miracles here, if — "

But Father shut his mouth when the food and water were brought. He seldom showed surprise at anything, so his sudden silence now was as startling as one of his howls. It was the men who carried the gourds and baskets to us. He gaped at them, and, with his teeth clenched like a ventriloquist, said, "Will you look at that!"

Three skinny men, not Indians, stood over us. They were pale gray under their dirt and whiskers. Father whistled softly as he sized them up. They were tall and bony and looked bruised. They wore ragged trousers and broken sandals. Two of them had headbands, the sort worn by some of the Indians. Their faces were feverish and sunken, their skulls pressed against their sallow-gray skin. Their beards and bones made me think of saints in a picture book. But they were almost smiling, and as they placed the food before us they watched us closely with curious eyes.

"What did I tell you?" Father said to us. "This is what they didn't want us to see. They keep white slaves!"

The food was boiled bananas, flat greasy corncakes, fritters, and wabool. The water tasted of dog fur.

"Now it all makes sense! Hey," he said to one of the men in Spanish, "do you let these Indians tell you what to do?"

"More or less." The man did not seem concerned. He kept his feverish smile.

"What do you do for them?"

"We shine their shoes."

Father laughed at this. "You haven't lost your sense of humor." He passed the gourd of wabool to Jerry, without tasting it.

The Indians looked on from across the clearing, their heads lowered. The only sound from that direction was the growl of the dogs chewing fleas out of their gouged and scarred hindquarters.

"What is your name?"

One man wet his lips at Father's question, but another with stringy hair said, "We do not have names."

"Hear that? They don't have names."

Father glowered at the Indians. All around us in the tall trees, birds tooted and beat the leaves with their wings, and the sound of the stream was like the sound of tumbling boulders.

"Probably captured them down the pike and made them prisoners," Father said to Francis Lungley. "So these guys do all the dirty work."

"Gringo," one of the men said, hearing Father speak English. His starved face gave him a fine-lined expression that was both haunted and kindly. "North American, eh? Are you from the mission?"

"Do I look like a missionary?" Then Father whispered to him, so that the Indians would not hear. "No. We've got a settlement over the mountains. If you could get over there — slip out some night — you'd be safe. That's the best way to the coast."

The man nodded and passed his hand through his beard.

"Why did you come here?"

"I was just going to say. I brought some ice — half a ton. Well, almost. These Zambus and me. Those two are my boys, Charlie and Jerry. Wipe your mouth, Charlie."

"Where is this ice?"

"Melted."

The man smiled.

"You don't believe me?"

"Ice," the man said in Spanish to the others, and now they all smiled. The three men knelt before Father, and the first man said, "Where did you get your ice?"

"Made it," Father said. He took a small suck of wabool from the gourd. "You should see what we've got over there. Gardens, food, water pumps, chickens, drainage, and the biggest ice-making machine in the country."

"You have a generator for electricity?"

"Don't mention generators to me. Tell him, Charlie."

I explained that Father had devised a method of making ice out of fire.

"Your father is an intelligent man."

"Everyone says that," I said.

Father said, "They'll work you to death here. Then, when you're not useful to them any longer, they'll kill you and feed you to the vultures. They'll get some new slaves." Father's face darkened. "You think they'll try anything funny with us?"

The man said, "Who knows?" and the other men nodded.

"I want to walk out of here wearing my head," Father said. "Do you think those Indians are listening to us?"

"They listen but they do not understand. They are very simple people. They are also very strong."

"So I gather. But you shouldn't be here, waiting on them hand and foot. They haven't any right to own you. You're prisoners, aren't you?"

The man who had done all the talking shrugged. The shrug shook his whole loose-jointed body. He seemed untroubled, or else beyond caring.

Father said, "Notice I'm not eating much? I'll tell you why. Because I've got an enormous appetite. By not eating, I do other things better. Solve problems. Work hard. That's a form of eating, too. You should try it. If I ate, I wouldn't do anything else —"

All this time, the Zambus were eating and hardly listening to what Father was saying. Father seemed glad for someone new to talk to. Maybe it took his mind off the failure of our expedition.

The men whispered among themselves, then one who had not spoken before said, "You are not telling the truth, are you — about the ice?"

"Practically an iceberg," Father said. "It melted to mud, but there's a whole lot more where that came from. We've got everything over there."

"Guns?"

"I've got no use for guns. If I needed them, I could make an arsenal. But that's desperate."

But, he said, they reminded him of how he had felt in the States — like a prisoner, close to despair, murderous, half loco. It was frustration at the way things were shaking down, something like slavery, because the system made men into slaves.

"What did I do? I picked myself up and went away. I advise you to do the same."

The Indians were squatting with their ugly dogs thirty feet away. They watched Father talking to the skinny men. It was impossible for me to tell what the Indians were thinking by looking into the smooth clay of their faces. The Indians might have been harmless, but the dogs were part of their group. The dogs' fierceness made the Indians seem dangerous.

"They want you to go," the stringy-haired man said.

"They don't know what's good for them," Father said. "They don't deserve ice, or anything else, if they can't show common courtesy. But you," he said, "you're friendly enough."

"That is our nature."

"My Zambus probably think you're Munchies."

"Ah, Mosquitia!"

Father said, "I wish I could do something for you."

"It would be helping us if you did not anger the Indians. If you simply went away."

"Listen, one dark night you ought to get yourselves out of here. Do that. Clear out." In English, Father added, "Get the drop on them."

"The Indians say there is no path over the mountains."

"They would, wouldn't they? Listen, you won't get a road map from them."

"How far is it to your village?"

"A day's march. More — if you're carrying ice. But that's our problem."

"You will be home by nightfall."

Father said suddenly, "I've got half a mind to blow this place wide open and get you the hell out of here."

"That would be very foolish," the man said, and did not blink.

"Then it's up to you."

"Go," the man said, "or they will punish us."

We were given a calabash of wabool, and water, and a bunch of bananas. While we filled our water bag from a gourd, the three skinny men went over to the Indians. The Indians remained squatting on the ground, but their dogs ran away as the men approached. They did not begin barking until they had reached the rooty edge of the clearing. Without their dogs, the Indians looked nakeder and even a little afraid.

We left them like that, the Indians squatting, the three slaves standing. The dogs bounded forward and retreated, chasing us to the stream. They barked and stretched and showed us their wild cowardly eyes. All the other men were motionless. They were small beneath the vast hanging forest, watching us walk away. The women had not returned. The men looked as if they were posing for an oldfangled frightening picture.

On the trail, Father said, "What I can't make out is how they got there in the first place."

"Twahkas, Fadder?"

"No. The others." He used a Spanish word, "The nameless ones."

Bucky said, "These jungles is fulla monkeys."

"Monkeys don't ask that many questions —"

Neither do slaves, I thought.

"— Something weird's coming down here, people."

We climbed out of the forest and behind the rock steeples and up the path we had made to the ridge of the mountains. Then, where we had made camp last night, we stopped again and passed the wabool around. We sat on the broken ice sled we had left, the remains of Skidder. Father said that someday a foreigner would find it and proclaim that a great civilization had existed here, and put Skidder in a museum. This made him laugh.

"And did you see those Indians' faces when they saw the ice?"

We looked at him.

"They almost keeled over." He began to chuckle at the thought of it.

Jerry was searching Father's face.

"They couldn't believe it," Father said. "They were goggling. Flabbergasted and confounded!"

Finally — because everyone else was perfectly silent — I said, "What ice?"

"The ice I showed them."

I believed he was testing me again. I said, "It all melted, Dad."

"That small piece," he said.

This was not true.

"You saw it, didn't you Jerry?"

"Yes, Dad."

I thought, Crummo.

"Your long-faced brother's trying to tell me we wasted our time. You need glasses, Charlie. You've got bad eyes. Probably an astigmatism, eh Francis?"

"For true," the loyal Zambu said.

Father put Jerry on his back and carried him, while I walked behind with the Zambus. The Zambus' tiredness showed in their faces. It had been a bewildering trip for them, the more so because they had expected the Twahkas to have tails — and maybe they did think the three skinny men were Munchies. There was a grayness on the Zambus' bodies, and smudges on the gray, like the cloudy surface of purple grape skins. As we walked, they became more certain that they had seen the ice and the amazed Indians. "It is smuck in Fadder's hand like a rock-stone."

Father said, "It's all downhill from now on."

19

ON THIS downward path, in the tortoiseshell twilight, I thought of Father's lie. I hoped he did not believe it, but how could he be rescued from repeating it?

Something like this might work — perhaps, in our two-day absence, things had not gone right in Jeronimo — perhaps some small problem had arisen, enough to interrupt him, not a disaster but a hitch, to prevent him from giving a loud speech saying our failure had been a success.

The Indians had not been flabbergasted! They had only squinted at us and at Father's wet fingers, and sent out their slaves.

His lie made me lonelier than any lie I had ever heard.

Yet he had spoken it confidently and said the expedition was a triumph and he couldn't wait to tell Mother. Again and again I tried to remember ice in Father's hands and amazement on the faces of the Indians. But there was none: no ice, no surprise. It had all been worse and odder than his lie. They had told us to go away, and then the skinny slaves were peering at us and the dogs trying to bite our feet.

"Gaw, I love to walk home tired at the end of a good day with the sun in my eyes!"

Ahead, on the path, Father went on talking to the Zambus and Jerry.

"You can pack a man in ice and crisp him like celery and snap him out of sunstroke. That ought to be a useful application around here. And did I ever tell you about the advances in cryogenics?"

His voice tore through the trees and exhausted me. His confidence was something I did not want to hear now. I dreaded the thought of Father repeating his story in Jeronimo. And his lie scared me. *Did you see those Indians' faces?* But the Indians' faces were confused, they had monkey wrinkles, and they had tried to frighten us away by showing us black teeth like their dogs. Once I had believed that Father was so much taller than me that he saw things I missed. I excused adults who disagreed with me, and blamed myself because I was so short. But this was something I could judge. I had seen it. Lies made me uncomfortable, and Father's lie, which was also a blind boast, sickened me and separated me from him.

"Charlie's back there doing the best he can, people!"

I loved this man, and he was calling me a fool and falsifying the only world I knew.

I prayed for a hitch. My prayers were answered. Things were not right in Jeronimo. It was what I had wished, but, like most wishes that are granted, more than I bargained for.

Jeronimo was struck with quietness and a thin flutter of leaves. It had always softened and collapsed in twilight: it was the way the sun was strained through the trees, the way it glanced in weak glimmers off the river. It was the dust stirring. It was the way people were round-shouldered after such a long day of light and no clouds.

But this evening it was deadened. It had an atmosphere of disappearance and hiding alarm that said something had just happened, like the silence after a howl. There was a low skreak and skrittle of lizards watching from the undergrowth, and on the branches birds locating perches for the night, their polite strut at sundown.

Father halted us and said, "Somebody's been here and gone."

Fat Boy was not alight. The Maywit's house was black — none of their normal lanterns — open windows, empty porch, no smoke.

"Allie." It was Mother — her white waiting face in the Gallery.

Father walked toward her and asked her what was going on.

She said, "I thought something had happened to you, too."

"Too?"

"The Maywits — they're gone. I couldn't stop them."

Father said "I knew it," and smiled at Francis Lungley.

But I felt responsible. I had prayed for something to happen, and it had. Anything to prevent Father from bursting into Jeronimo and lying about flabbergasted Indians and ice and you should have seen their faces.

Now Father was smiling at Clover. She had run from under the house and was hugging him and explaining.

"A motorboat came and took all the Maywits away. The man called you names. It was the missionary you sent back that day. Ma Kennywick yelled at him and Mr. Peaselee busted the pump and Ma said you were going to run wild when you hear about it. But you're not, are you? Dad, was it spooky!"

Father looked at everyone in turn and his mouth bulged with satisfaction. "Why should I go wild?" he said. "I knew it was going to happen."

Jerry said, "What about Drainy and the other kids?"

"They went away," Clover said. "All of them, in the man's motorboat."

"What did I tell you?" Father said. He was grinning at the Zambus and they were grinning back.

Mother had come down from the Gallery with April, who was moping. Mother said, "I did everything I could, but they wouldn't listen. They didn't hear, they didn't recognize me, they were so frightened."

"Don't tell me," Father said firmly. "I know all about it. The Maywits ran off with that moral sneak in some polluting pig of a boat. Figgy's friend. You don't have to spell it out. I took one look across the clearing and I knew."

Hearing "Figgy," Mr. Haddy came forward and said, "It were puppysho. Them people jump everyways and we ain't get a dum bit of peace. Ma Kennywick scared out of her skin and bellyaching ever since. Peaselee, he bawling too, about seeing some dum fool with ruckbooses. Man, we glad you here, Fadder."

Father waited, then said, "And I know something else."

He smiled and took a mouthful of the silence and swallowed it.

"Fadder know." This was Francis Lungley, telling Bucky.

"Those Maywits have got a lot to learn."

If he knew everything, why didn't he know their real name?

I said, "Maywit isn't their name. It's Roper. They're all Ropers."

"Who says?"

I told him what the kids had said, but I did not mention the Acre or that they were all afraid of him. Jerry, Clover, and April said nothing — they let me take the blame for knowing. Father was still smiling.

Mother said, "You should have said something before this, Charlie."

"I thought Dad knew."

Father said, "What else do you know?"

I was going to say — Those men you called slaves didn't look like slaves, and the Indians looked scared. The ice melted before they could see it. You wouldn't let us rest, you made Jerry cry by talking about the Holiday Inn, and it was a terrible trip, worse than the river trips and probably a failure.

But I said, "Nothing else."

"Then I still know more than you do," he said — but when had I ever doubted that? — "because I know they're coming back."

We went down to the bathhouse and stripped off our clothes. Father set the showers going — what a marvelous invention! It was like a car wash, with jets of water shooting from pipes on the walls. We were all inside, jostling in the fine spray, in the half-dark — Father, Jerry, the Zambus, and me. Fat Boy's fire was out, so there was no hot water, but no one minded. The busy harmless sting of the showers took off the mountain dust and the bad memories.

Mother said, "I wouldn't be so sure about that, Allie."

"She doesn't believe me," Father said. "Pass the soap."

He was proud of his soap. We had made it ourselves out of pig fat we had traded for ice. It was greasy yellow soap and felt like a handful of lard. "No additives," Father said. "Why, you could eat that soap!"

"You weren't here."

"Didn't have to be."

"It was horrible," Mother said. "That missionary — Struss."

Father said, "I know."

Hollering through the bathhouse walls, Mother said, "It seems he was up in Seville in his boat. I don't know what he saw there, but it must have been those ridiculous people praying. He came back accusing us all of blasphemy and spreading the lies of science."

"Soap up," Father said to the Zambus. They always washed in a squatting position, never standing up. Also, they kept their shorts on when they took baths. I couldn't see them in the dark bathhouse, but I could hear the water pelting against their heads, and their spitting and guffing.

"Could they have been on their knees, praying to the refrigerator?" Mother said. "Whatever it was, your Reverend Struss was pretty upset. He came in swinging. We were doing harm, he said, leading his people astray. He was mostly yelling at the Maywits — he called them the Ropers. He made them get down at the riverbank while he splashed water all over them. It was a service of purification, he said, washing them clean of the sins we had taught them. Mrs. Kennywick didn't know which way to turn, and Mr. Peaselee freaked out."

Father said, "I could have told you."

"I ordered him off the property. I said you were due back in ten minutes and you'd sink his boat."

"Good thinking," Father shouted back through the wall. "I would have, too!"

"They packed their bags. I mean bags. Paper ones. And they all left."

Father said, "So they ran out on us."

"They is scared," Mr. Haddy said. His mouth was against the bathhouse wall, his front teeth sticking through. "The preacher is yartering about soldiers and trouble and ruckbooses."

Father shut off the water.

"What soldiers?" he said, as we dripped.

"In the mountains. Over the hills. Down the river. Up the trees. With ruckbooses. Russians and what not. Peaselee hear them."

Clover said, "He said you were just as bad as the soldiers."

"Peaselee said that?"

"The man. The missionary. He called you a Communist."

Father led us out of the bathhouse. The Zambus hopped and danced and shook their fingers to get dry. Father wore a flour sack around his waist, his hair was dripping, and his body was as white as marble. He held one arm up, like a statue in front of a courthouse.

"None of this is news to me," he said. "But I'll tell you something you don't know. They'll be back, as sure as anything. Because this is a happy place, and the world isn't. The world is plain rotten. People are mean, they're cruel, they're fake, they always pretend to be something they're not. They're weak. They take advantage. A cruddy little man who sees God in a snake, or the devil in thunder, will take you prisoner if he gets the drop on you. Give anyone half a chance and he'll make you a slave: he'll tell you the most awful lies. I've seen them, running around bollocky, playing God. And our friends, the Maywits — sorry, Charlie, the Ropers — they'll be lonely out there. They'll be scared. Because the world stinks!"

He started up the path to the house, taking long white strides. "They'll be back — just you wait. Remember where you heard it. Remember who said it."

Mother stepped beside him and said, "How did it go with the ice?"

Father was still walking. He grunted. I listened hard, then I heard him say in a low voice, "We had shrinkage. I knew it was a mistake to lug so much of it that far."

So he did not lie after all.

And the Acre in the jungle was ours. It was not the same without Drainy preaching and Alice doing the cooking and Peewee and Leon making baskets, but now, with fewer of us, it seemed larger, and we were able to spread out. Each of us had his own sturdy lean-to. We brought a rope from Jeronimo and fixed a swing to a tree by knotting the dangling end and sitting on it. Father would not have allowed this in Jeronimo. It wasn't useful, because if someone wasn't swinging on it, it just hung there — that would have been his objection — and was the waste of a good rope.

We ate yautia roots and wild avocados, and we repaired the camouflage in all the man traps — four of them, the deep holes nicely disguised with boughs. One day, in a trap, we saw a snake eating another snake — half of it choked down his throat and both snakes thrashing their tails. The eater could not crawl away or stop eating, so we could study it in safety. We brought it back to Jeronimo.

"There's a perfect symbol for Western civilization," Father said.

A spider monkey passed through our church tree another day and sat there picking his teeth. He watched us with curiosity, as if he wanted to play.

Then he sniffed, leaped from the tree, landed near a bush, and tore a small fruit ball from it. On his upward bounce he was back in the tree, eating it. He gnawed the skin and sucked out the inside, then rolled across the bough and tumbled away, yanking branches.

That was how we discovered guavas. The monkey had shown us that there were several bushes of them on the far side of the pool, and that day we brought a basket of them back to Jeronimo.

Mother said, "We can make them into jam."

But Father said they were too small and sour, because they were growing wild. If he put his mind to it, he said, he could grow sweet ones as big as tennis balls, and, "Speaking of food, you'd better start picking and peeling, or there won't be anything for lunch."

We did what was expected of us in Jeronimo, the usual chores. But we always returned to the Acre to live like monkeys. We missed the Maywits — I still thought of them by that name — but without them we had no need for the school or the store. We had the loose pages from Drainy's hymnbook, but we no longer held church services. Anyway, it was too hot to think about hell.

We knew from the Acre that it was the dry season. No one in Jeronimo knew this, or considered it important. The gardens were still growing, but we were in touch with the seasons: we had no inventions.

The Acre was primitive, a ragged hollow in the jungle, but the grass was soft, the pool made it pleasant, and we had everything we needed. For fun, we could swim or swing on the rope. The pool was unaffected by the jungle drought. I guessed that springs fed it. But the rest of the area was very dry. We watched wee-wee ants holding funerals — processions of them with corpses and leaf parasols. Snakes lived in the roots of a dead tree at one corner of the camp. We kept clear of that tree, but tried to think of ways of dropping them into the traps, to turn them into snake pits. The snakes and the walnut-sized beetles did not frighten us. We learned that the fiercest creatures were predictable, and though once it had all looked dangerous here, now it seemed more peaceful than Jeronimo.

We came here to escape Jeronimo. Ever since the building of Fat Boy, Father had been visited by people who wanted ice. They were talkers. They had heard of Father. They paid him compliments. Father put them to work, gave them simple jobs to do, and they took the ice away in canoes. There were always strangers in Jeronimo, admiring Father's inventions or looking for ice.

"Ain't do nothing with they ices but cool they bunya," Mr. Haddy said. Bunya was a drink of sour juice the local people made from cassava.

Father said, "That doesn't matter. They can wear it on their heads for all I care. Once they get accustomed to the idea of ice, the uses will be revealed to them. Each person will do something different — one man will preserve meat, another will make it into a painkiller, someone will get the idea of refrigerating his fish instead of smoking it, and how many will it bring out of sunstroke? Sure, it may take a generation, but think of the future — no one else does. Fat Boy is forever. No moving parts, Figgy!"

Father often talked of things being "revealed." That was true invention, he said, revealing something's use and magnifying it, discovering its imperfection, improving it, and putting it to work for you. A guava growing wild was to him an imperfection. You had to improve it to make it edible.

He said, "It's savage and superstitious to accept the world as it is. Fiddle around and find a use for it!" God had left the world incomplete, he said. It was man's job to understand how it worked, to tinker with it and finish it. I think that was why he hated missionaries so much: because they taught people to put up with their earthly burdens. For Father, there were no burdens that couldn't be fitted with a set of wheels, or runners, or a system of pulleys.

But instead of improving the world, he said, most people just tried to improve God. "God — the deceased God — was a hasty inventor of the sort you find in any patent office. Yes, He had a great idea in making the world, but He started it and moved on before He got it working properly. God is like the boy who gets his toy top spinning and then leaves the room and lets it wobble. How can you worship *that?* God got bored," Father said. "I know that kind of boredom, but I fight it."

Father saw the river and said, "Let's straighten it." Dragging the ice up the mountain, he had talked of nothing but the cable car for passengers and cargo. He still spoke of sinking a shaft — tapping the steam heat in the earth's core. And inventions themselves revealed unexpected things that Father called "the unanticipated wrinkle." An example of this was an exposed pipe on Fat Boy's shin. This collected drops of moisture from the humid air. Father added more pipes and turned this into a condenser that dripped into a tank. It was the purest water imaginable, and now he boasted that he could create water as well as freeze it — with fire! He had not expected this cold pipe to behave this way. It was revealed to him. He called it the Hamstring.

We kids said that if Father saw the Acre he would have a fit, or else laugh at us. He was a perfectionist. I could not forget how, on the mountain, he had kicked his lean-to apart and sat on the windy ground all night and said, "I want to sleep in my own bed!" He would suffer rather than sleep in a badly made hut, and he often looked at the Zambus' food or Mrs. Kennywick's wabool and said, "I'd starve before I'd eat that" — and he meant it.

We did not dare to say that you could eat what grew wild and sleep on the ground. His mosquito traps, "Bug Boxes," invited insects through inescapable baffles and kept Jeronimo free of flying bugs. But you did not need nets and Bug Boxes if you knew about the berry juice that acted like citronella. "Afraid of a few bugs?" he sometimes said, and, at other times, "It's not that I don't want them on my skin — I don't want them within three miles of me." We could have told him that we had learned that most work was needless, and a bathhouse wasn't necessary if you had a pool or a river. Father's homegrown carrots were tasty, but wild yautia was just as good, and no trouble. He had outlawed bananas and manioc — "They make you lazy, and I don't like the implications of bananas." And the ice — it was a marvel, but like most marvels all you could do was marvel at it.

The more I thought about, the more sure I was that we kids stayed in Jeronimo because of the Acre. It lay in the jungle between the mountains and the river, at the dead end of a narrow path our feet had made. It was invisible, it was safe.

We spent every afternoon at the Acre, and we were sorry we could not sleep there overnight. We wanted to prove to Father that it could be done. But at the end of every day, we pushed the bushes aside and walked back to Jeronimo and heard the pumps, their whops and claps, before we saw the buildings. Father would be smiling, for in the coolness of the late afternoon he cleared Fat Boy and gave ice to the river Creoles or Zambus who had worked for it. There he was, with his tongs and his pulley, hoisting great blocks of vapory ice out of this monster cupboard with its firebox blazing.

And always, when we came back, Father said, "Where have you been? Fooling in the bushes?"

We would say swimming or hiking.

"Look at them, people. We're killing ourselves and they're walking around the block."

The "people" were Mr. Haddy, the Zambus, Mr. Peaselee, and

Mr. Harkins. They were his listeners for he never stopped telling them his plans. These days he spoke of freezing fish and rushing them inland where no one had ever seen big river fish. "Six-footers! Catfish! Could change their whole way of life. Especially if they're open-minded and not in the grip of some moral sneak who's preaching hellfire to them."

That was a frequent complaint. The Maywits had not come back. Father said it made him mad.

"And the funny thing about hellfire is, it's imaginary. But not Fat Boy! He's got more poison in him than a century of hells. Oh, gaw, I could teach those missionaries a thing or two about chemical combustion. If they saw hydrogen and ammonia get loose they'd believe in me, instead of the dead top-spinner! If Fat Boy blew his lid —"

This Jeronimo talk made the Acre seem happier. The camp was our secret. And we had learned things there that even Father did not know.

My birthday came and went — the month, anyway. The months had names, but the days did not have numbers. I was fourteen, but still smaller than I wanted to be. And now the dry season lay across Jeronimo. It was dust and dead leaves.

The river had begun to get narrower, and it stank. It turned into a creek between deep slabs of bubbly mud, with flies buzzing over it and green hair in it. It snored and pooped past the mooring. A little above us it had become a marsh, and there was now no way upstream to Seville. Our boats were shanked against the mud, and our pumps at the river's edge often gagged on the slime and weeds they sucked up. It had not rained for months, and it might be a month or more, Father said, before it rained again. Now Father was making only small quantities of ice, and all our drinking water came from the condenser on Fat Boy's shin, the Hamstring.

We had not mentioned the Acre to Father, so we could not tell him that spring water in our pool still brimmed to the grassy edge.

The Jeronimo garden was green, producing beans and tomatoes and corn — the cornstalks were as high as some of the eaves. But the pumps were still gasping. Father said he had been a fool for believing the river would go on flowing — it was as undependable as anything else on this imperfect earth. He spoke again of sinking a shaft, not the geothermal one but a simpler borehole to the water table. Whenever people came these days, they were put to work digging this hole.

The work was hard, and not many people were willing to shift dirt in return for a small block of ice or a bag of hybrid seeds. Father predicted that the Maywits would soon be back and Jeronimo working at full strength. He had been saying this for three weeks.

One day he said to Mother, "I'm putting you in sole charge of Jeronimo, honey."

"Are you going somewhere?"

"Nope. But I've got my Hole to think about."

He hated the river and its smell, and all he talked about was his Hole. "Going to work on my Hole," he said in the early morning. And he asked every visitor, "What are you going to do about my Hole?" He was either in it or at the edge of it, his face as red as a tomato, cursing the river and the climate and trying to devise a machine for moving dirt. "Say, on the same principle as a vacuum cleaner, that can dig and suck at the same time — give it teeth and lungs, fit it with claspers —"

He complained that he was working with caveman's tools. "If only I had the hardware!" He dug with the Zambus. He did nothing else. If there was smut on the corn, or worms in the tomatoes, or rot on the beans, he ordered us kids to see about it. There was no water. He kept digging. The task took hold of him like a fever. He said, "I never stop until I get where I'm going."

Then he shut down Fat Boy. The roar and gurgle of the ice maker had been so familiar to us that when he put the fire out one morning, it was like hearing my heart stop. I had to hold my breath to listen. Fat Boy wasn't wet and dripping anymore. It looked as if it had died, and Father stiffened a little, resembling his invention.

"What about the ice?" Mother said.

"What about my Hole?"

So the hole got deeper, and it was wide enough for four men to stand in, swinging shovels. It looked like the opening to Father's volcano hole, and next to it was a pyramid of dirt and boulders, "Which proves, if proof were needed, that even with primitive tools and a little muscle you can do something constructive about this gimcrack world we've inherited."

But still he had not struck water. We stopped getting visitors. The work was too hard. Father dug in the hole and ate practically nothing and said, "If I only had the hardware —"

The pumps only brought us a green trickle from the squeezed river. We had to water the gardens by hand, pouring buckets of water into the sluice pipe that siphoned into the irrigation ditches. Mother stayed knee-deep in mud at the river's edge, and the four of us kids, in what Father called the Bucket Brigade, passed pails of water from hand to hand up the bank.

We were on Bucket Brigade just after dawn one day when Mother looked up and said, "Mr. Haddy's in an awful hurry."

He was running out of the jungle toward Father's hole. No one ever ran here. Something serious had happened.

"Peaselee say they is some fellers on the path!"

He yelled this down the hole.

We watched. Father climbed out and chucked his shovel aside.

"What did I tell you? It's the Maywits."

"He run down to tell me."

"Where is he?"

"Still running. Maybe Swampmouth by now."

Father saw us watching him.

"Don't anyone say a word. We can't blame them for going. We're glad to have them back. We'll pretend they never left — they've had a rough time. You think it's dry here? It's soaking wet compared to the drought they've got out there. Listen, the world is a terrible place for anyone who's had a taste of Jeronimo. Those poor folks will need all the sympathy they can get. Be nice to them. Give them some peas to shell, put them to work. We've got some extra hands for my Hole!"

Mother said, "It could be some people who want ice."

"I know it's the Maywits," Father said.

But this time Father was wrong. The Maywits were not on the path.

"Men," Mother said, looking up. We crowded behind her. "There's three of them, Allie."

"I was expecting them, too," Father said, but his voice had gone cold. "They're slaves."

"Then why do they have guns, Dad?" Clover asked.

The Zambus seemed terrified. I heard, "Ruckbooses."

20

AT THAT MOMENT, I knew how the people in Seville felt, the river Creoles and the mountain Indians, or anyone else who watched us Foxes coming out of the jungle. We stepped into their villages like this, big and strange and uninvited. So we deserved this visit, but that did not make it easier.

The three scarecrows were dressed differently from the way they had been in the Indian village in Olancho — sweat-stained shirts and dirty pants and boots. We had not chosen them — they had chosen us. This was what savages saw. They were heading straight for us, not looking left or right. They seemed worse-off in clothes than they had half-naked in the village. One had a rifle slung over his shoulder, and the other two had pistols in their hands. They were listening and blinking, a little stupid and a little angry, as if they were out hunting cats.

Father's face twitched. It was not worry. He was doing a rapid calculation in his head, adding, subtracting, figuring odds, doing the algebra of what they might want. I recognized the men's clothes — they were the ones I had seen the Indian women washing in the stream. The Zambus watched from the lip of the hole with their round blackbird's eyes.

"Tell them to put their guns down, Allie."

"Let me handle this." Father met the men and said in Spanish, "What goes?"

The men smiled at him, but their hands stayed put. They glanced around Jeronimo, holding us silent with the guns. They wore no insignia, although their clothes were similar and looked like uniforms.

Their long hair and beards made them seem like brothers. I had remembered them as tall, but here they did not appear tall — they were Mother's height. One of the pistol carriers wore a belt with a large brass buckle. He seemed more intelligent, less violent than the other two, but maybe it was because the other two had teeth missing. And the one with the rifle had a bandage on his hand — it was a filthy bandage and could only have been covering an infection.

Among the Indians in that village they had been shifty, almost timid — they had whispered to us and brought us food and warned us about the squatting Indians. But here they had none of that sneaking slyness. They looked strong, as if they were used to entering villages and sizing them up. They took their time, they did not even reply to Father until after they mumbled among themselves.

"We did not think we would find you." It was the one with the brass buckle who spoke. His teeth were too large for his mouth, and now I saw that he was not smiling. It was just his big yellow teeth stretching his lips.

"Here we are," Father said flatly.

"How many are you?"

"Thousands —"

The men looked behind them quickly.

"— counting the white ants," Father said. "We're infested."

Mr. Haddy whispered to me, "I ain't like this men," and then, "Hey, Lungley."

But the Zambus had gone: climbed out of Father's hole and backed into the woods.

"You are just in time for breakfast," Father said. "Scramble some eggs for our friends here, Mother" — he was still speaking in Spanish — "they have a long trip ahead of them."

We all went to the Gallery, and there the men put their guns down. They sat on the floor and ate eggs and beans, while Father talked about the white ants. Termites, he said, had gotten into everything — food, plants, even the roofs and floors of the houses. "They are eating us alive!"

It was the first we had heard of the white ants, but no one contradicted Father then, because no one ever contradicted him. The men listened and wolfed their food. When they finished, they stared at us with pale skinny faces. Eating did not soften their expressions, it only made them look hungrier and more dangerous.

The man with the teeth, who had spoken before, said that they had run out of water and then lost their way searching for water. They had camped on the mountain.

"I know how it is," Father said.

Mother gathered the plates, and that same man — Big Teeth did all the talking — said, "Your husband told us he had water and food. He invited us here. He told us he has everything. Up there, over the mountains, they have nothing."

"It's the end of the dry season," Father said. "We're feeling it. Everything is dead or dying. We won't see rain for weeks. But the white ants are getting fat!"

No one reminded him of his boast that Jeronimo was termite-proof.

"If it goes on like this, we'll have to start eating the termites."

The man with the teeth said *"Pleh"* — the thought disgusted him.

"City boys," Father said to Mother.

The men were still breathing hard, as if with hunger.

"See, around here, if there's no rain, there's nothing to eat. Ask anyone. We're down to our last provisions. The ants are all over the place. Our river's turned into a creek. The next time you come, things will be different."

"Where are your Zambus?"

Father wrinkled his nose. "Probably thought you were soldiers. They saw your ruckbooses."

"We do not understand."

"Arquebuses — guns. You're in Mosquitia now," Father said. "I didn't have time to tell them you were friendly. I imagine they are out dipping their arrows in poison, aren't they, Charlie?"

He was casual in the way he said this. And I knew from his voice what he wanted me to reply. I said, "Yes."

"You sure had them fooled!" He had become jolly. He turned away from them and looked off the Gallery to where the river lay stinking and almost motionless. "Where are you going?"

"It is very pretty here."

Father faced them. "It is crawling with ants!"

"We do not see any ants."

"Of course. If you could see them, you could kill them."

"Where is this ice you told us about?"

"We are not making ice. Look at that river — it is like a sewer. We need all the water we've got for the crops."

The man who had done all the talking said clearly to the others, "He is not making ice."

"There is not much river left," Father said. "But there is enough to float a cayuka. This is the Bonito. It flows into the Aguan. I could draw you a map. It is about a day to the coast. You will like it there."

"We like it here."

"I wish I had room for you. But most of the houses have infestation. Ants. You're lucky — you won't find any ants on the coast."

"There is an empty house next door."

The Maywits' abandoned house — they had seen it.

"There is no roof on that house," Father said.

"You are mistaken."

Father turned to Mr. Haddy and said, "I told you to rip off that floor and roof, Figgy. Now get your crowbar and go do it — I want every rotten joist torn out."

The next noise we heard was Mr. Haddy crowbarring the Maywits' house apart — the crack and screech of boards, like pigs being slaughtered.

"Please excuse us," Father said. "We have work to do. No sir, we are not on vacation!"

The men followed him outside.

"My Hole," Father said. "You will have to stay here, above ground. I don't allow weapons in my Hole."

The man with the rifle said "Arquebus — ruckboos," and smiled.

Big Teeth said, "We will look around."

"Go down to the river. You will see a cayuka there. It is yours — paddle down to the coast."

"It is not necessary."

"That is what the ants say."

The men shrugged.

"I will tell you a secret," Father said. "We are self-sufficient. We can feed ourselves. But we can't feed anyone else. That is why I am suggesting you go on your way."

"We will consider your suggestion."

It occurred to me that the men spoke Spanish in a way I had never heard before. It was polite, some phrases were new to me, and no words were left out. They were educated men and seemed out of place here where everyone's Spanish was a jumble of Creole and English. I could not hear the men speak in their perfect Spanish without suspecting them of being dishonest. But that was one of Father's own suspicions — he always distrusted educated people, and I knew he hated these men.

"Good. I'll make you another one," Father said — his patience was wearing thin. "Put those ruckbooses away. They make me nervous. I am not asking you where you got them. I am just saying that I did not come here to look down the barrel of a gun. And I don't need another nostril, okay? Do you see any locks on these doors? See any fences? No? That is because this is the most peaceful place in the world. I want to keep it that way."

The men only smiled and held tight to their guns.

"Grab a shovel, Charlie, and climb in."

We lowered ourselves into the hole.

Father said to me in a whisper, "I thought those gentlemen were prisoners of the Indians. Seems it was the other way around. Kick me, Charlie, I'm a fool!"

About thirty minutes later, there was a noise above us — Mr. Haddy scrambling into the hole.

"Maywit house finished," he said. "I knock the shoo out of her. She look skelly, but I ain't see no hants."

Father's back was turned. He had a spade in his hand. He was shoveling and thinking.

Mr. Haddy said, "I ain't like them friends, Fadder."

"Not so loud, Fig."

"They sitting under the guanacaste."

"All right," Father said. "Take the roof and floor off your house and tell Harkins to do the same. If you can't find Peaselee, do his house, roof and floor. We've got infestation. We're going to ream these houses. Charlie, you get Jerry and take a bag of chicken manure and spread it in the cold store. Wet it until it stinks. Board up the root cellar and the bean shed. Tell Mother what you're doing — "

He gave us more instructions, and when he had finished he had named every building in Jeronimo, except one.

I said, "What about Fat Boy?"

"Don't touch him. Just make sure his fire's out."

Mr. Haddy gave Father a rabbity smile. "So if the hants eats everything and we pull down we houses, there ain't no way for the friends to stay."

"That's about the size of it," Father said. "I'm going to defuse the situation peaceably."

By lunchtime, Jeronimo was changed — Haddy house out top and bottom, Maywit house ditto, Peaselee stoop torn out and broken up, other houses unshingled, root cellar boarded, cold store boarded and manured, bathhouse plugged and manured, pumps tinkered apart — all of them wrecked, Father said, "in the interest of fumigation." Our house was still whole, and so was Fat Boy, but the rest were open to the sky or else shut down.

"It's war on the ants."

Mr. Peaselee and Mr. Harkins had not returned. This was probably a blessing, because their houses were in a sorry state and they would have been upset to see them. Mother said that Ma Kennywick had gone to Swampmouth to stay with her sister — the hammering and banging were too much for her. The Zambus remained out of sight, and yet I knew that although we could not see them, they were watching us from between the loops and chinks of the leaves.

It was drastic that Father had decided to pull most of the habitable houses apart. But it was not surprising, and none of us was worried. We knew how quickly he could build a house — we had seen him. He often said that destruction and creation were father and son. He had taken the *Little Haddy* to pieces and reassembled it in a sleeker form so that it could float upstream. We trusted his speed and ingenuity. But after so many months of laboring to make it work, who could have guessed that Jeronimo would be silenced and turned into a slum in the space of a morning?

The three men disappeared, tracked into the jungle with their guns. They returned for lunch.

Father was in a good mood now. He greeted them heartily and filled their plates with food. He said, "If you leave right after lunch you can make it to Bonito Oriental. There's a Chinese store there — Ling Hermanos. All the cans of Spam you could ask for, and probably some rum. Mishla and radio music. That's the place for you city boys —"

I was in the corner of the Gallery with Clover, April, and Jerry.

Clover said, "What's Dad done to all the houses?"

"Busted them up," Jerry said. "Whacked them apart. Charlie and me put chicken poo in the cold store."

April said, "It looks worse than when we came."

"I want to go to the Acre," Clover said.

"We can't do that," I said.

"Charlie's a spacky."

"I am not. Dad won't let us. He wants us to help him."

"There's nothing to do here. It's all crapoid."

Jerry said, "Haddy thinks those men are criminals and they're going to shoot somebody with their guns."

"They couldn't shoot us if we were in our camp," Clover said. "They wouldn't find us."

April said, "And if they tried, they'd fall in a trap."

This was a perfect day for our camp, and there was more water in our pool than in the whole of Jeronimo. I would have given anything to spend the afternoon there swimming. I wanted to leave this place, then come back and find the men gone and all the houses rebuilt.

But when I told the kids this, Mother said, "It's not polite to whisper."

Father had been talking to the men. Suddenly he stood up and said, "These gentlemen want to know how I lost my finger. That is an interesting story!"

He hovered over the men and began barking in Spanish.

"It was our first night here in Jeronimo. We were sequestered in this wilderness, believing we were well prepared — we had mosquito nets, sleeping bags, tents, real guerrilleros. We all went to bed and fell asleep. But I had my doorbell dream, my button-pushing nightmare. I was standing at the devil's door and trying to get in. I was pressing, and I didn't know it then, but I had stuck my finger clear through the mosquito net. In the morning, I woke up and tried to pull it out. Only there wasn't a finger there, but a stump! In the night, something had chewed off my digit — a rat, a bat, an armadillo, a peccary. We have creatures here."

He showed the men his stump.

"That is what I had left! It's a good thing I hadn't stuck my whole hand out — I'd be wearing a hook."

The men examined the finger stump. I could not tell whether they believed him, but Father had told the story vigorously and well.

"Look at the teeth marks! After dark, this place is crawling with creatures. You're not in the mountains anymore — this is the jungle, boys."

"We have been in the jungle."

"Not this wild — this is not Olancho, and it is not Tegoose. The people here are descended from pirates and cannibal Caribs. Spiders as big as puppies? Vultures that pick you clean? This is the Mosquito Coast! That's why I advise you to go downriver, where you can shut the doors and windows. If anyone slept outside around here, there would be nothing left in the morning — not even bones."

The toothy man turned to his friends.

"For example, where are you sleeping tonight?" Father asked.

They did not say.

"It better be indoors and far away from here. You could lose more than a finger!"

We worked through the afternoon, digging the hole, sealing the houses, and wishing we were at the Acre, while the three men talked among themselves. They were restless, they watched us work. They had hot nervous eyes in sick faces, and they moved in flicks like lizards, crouching whenever they looked around.

Each time they stared at Father, he held up his finger stump and said, "It will be dark soon!"

They crept away, ignoring him.

This excited Father — their indifference. "I am giving you a chance," he said. Now he was almost pleading. "I am offering you my cayuka. You would be wise to shove off. It gets dark around here very fast."

The men played with Clover and April under the guanacaste tree.

Mr. Haddy said, "Where I gung sleep, Fadder?"

"I've got a bed for you," Father said, then he shouted to the men, "Get away from those kids!"

He picked up his claw hammer and walked over to them, past the torn-open or blinded houses.

"I don't care if you stay here, but keep your hands away from my children."

"They are very intelligent children."

"They have intelligent parents," Father said.

"Yes. They are telling us all the wonderful things you can do."

Clover said, "I didn't say anything, Dad. It was April."

April said, "Clover was boasting about your shaft to get geothermal energy out of volcanoes."

"That's a water hole," Father said. "This dry season has turned us into Zambus. We're just fighting for water. Keep your trap shut, girls, and go do something useful."

The men slunk to the river. We could not see them, we thought they had gone, but at twilight they returned. It was the hour the mosquitoes and bats woke and began flying. The men were slapping at their heads, rubbing their ankles, and scratching holes in their shirts.

In their absence, Father's mood had changed. He sulked, he chewed his cigar. He did not speak to any of us, but instead walked around mumbling. He took his tools over to Fat Boy and stood on a ladder, hammering the upper walls near the hatchway. But when he saw the men again, he began laughing. It was dark now. Mr. Haddy brought a lantern from the boat. Flimsy insects skidded around the lantern's glass chimney. I stood watching with Jerry.

Father was still laughing. He said, "I am a fool. You said you liked it here, and I did not believe you. But I am fully convinced now. You meant what you said. You are staying the night here, aren't you?"

"Yes."

"I would not be surprised if you decided to stay two nights, or more. Maybe until the rain comes and we start planting — and that's weeks away!"

"We will stay until we are ready. Then we will go."

Saying that, the man had the face of an insect, one that settles on a bean pod and burrows until it has eaten its fill. Insects make little probing twitches, but they have no more expression than a pair of pliers. The men looked that way — pincer lips and eyes like rivets. Insects.

"I am not a savage," Father said. "I am not going to lay hold of you and make you prisoners. It was your choice all along. But it's dark now." He took the lantern and put it near their faces, bringing the insects near their insect eyes. "You can't go anywhere."

The men stared at the mosquitoes and jumping moths.

"You would be fools to leave now. We haven't got much, but what we have is yours. This infestation — look, there is a termite on the glass, see his jaws? — has left us short of houses. But we can provide food and shelter."

"He is a very sensible man."

"I do what I can."

"He understands."

"When I saw you up there in that — was it a Twahka village? — I took you for prisoners."

The men smiled and slapped the insects away from their cheeks and ears. Holding the lantern this way, Father was tormenting the men.

"I thought, 'Slaves!' "

The men laughed as they fanned the insects away.

"But you were the guests of those Indians," Father said. "And now you are our guests. Look —"

A mosquito had settled on Father's arm. He allowed it to stay there a moment, and then he brought his hand down on it. He showed the men the squashed mosquito, the smear of blood.

"Dead! But don't feel sorry for him. That's not his blood — it is *my* blood!"

The men stepped back. Father had wiped the blood on his finger stump.

"This is Mosquitia!" Father said.

"You are right. There are more creatures here than in the mountains of Olancho."

"The Mosquito Coast is full of surprises," Father said. "That is why we like it, right, Mr. Haddy?"

"I sleeping on me lanch, Fadder."

"You do that, Figgy. Charlie, you take Jerry into the house or you'll be eaten alive —"

We started toward the house, which was now the only complete building in Jeronimo. Jerry took my hand — he was worried, his hand was damp. He tossed his head to keep the mosquitoes away.

"— and you gentlemen can use the bunkhouse."

Jerry said, "What bunkhouse is he talking about?" — Father had said the word in English — "We don't have a bunkhouse."

The lantern was swinging — Father was leading the men to Fat Boy. In the circle of mothy light he raised the ladder to the hatchway entrance on top.

Some minutes later, Father was at the screen door of the Gallery, talking as he entered.

"They want food. Put it in this pail, Mother, and I'll bring it across."

He jangled the pail down, and Mother ladled wabool into it. Then she made parcels of beans and rice, wrapping them in banana leaf, and put them into a basket.

"We're stuck with them," she said.

Father's face was blank, his long nose raw with sunburn. He stared at the floor where we were eating. It was as if he had run through all his moods on this confusing day and now had none left. He lifted his feet, and, letting them flap, he moved around the room like a goose.

He said, "*Stuck* with them? We're not stuck with anyone. If I believed things like that, we'd still be back in Hatfield." His voice was flat, he was still stepping back and forth across the floor. "No one who has the slightest spark is ever stuck with anyone in this world, or has to endure a minute of oppression. We proved that, Mother. We all choose our own thunderjug and sit on it and take the consequences."

Mother was smiling.

"Thunderjugs," Father said. "That's what we used to call chamber pots down in Maine."

It was after midnight, still so hot the grass and trees howled with insects. Frogs bellyrumbled in the shrunken river, and I could hear the current sucking at the reeds. These were the noises I heard the seconds after I woke. Father had put his hands on my face. In that darkness, I thought it was one of the men who had come to strangle me.

"Get your shoes on and follow me."

We had no lights, yet there was enough moonglow in the clearing for me to see the empty houses and the stacks of wood that had been torn from the roofs and floors. Jeronimo had been like this months ago, when we were building it — purple pickets in an empty crater, and the barracking crackle of the jungle.

Father carried a thick plank under his arm, but nothing else. It was a very clumsy weapon, if it was a weapon. We crossed to the cold store. The smell of damp chicken manure hung over it. Father knelt in the grass and drew breaths as if he was keeping count of them.

"I gave them every chance to go. Even offered them my cayuka." He crushed a mosquito and showed me the black stain on his finger, as he had done before. "Don't pity insects. That's *my* blood."

I nodded. I was afraid of the sound my voice would make.

"But they refused. You heard them. They're planning to fasten on us like they fastened on to those Indians. Remember those poor pathetic men, squatting in the dirt with their crazy mutts? Charlie, it was the Indians who were the prisoners!"

"They looked scared."

"Did they?" Father hung his head. "I'm not often wrong, but when I am, I'm as wrong as I can be."

This was a confession. I could not think of anything to say to make it easier for him.

"I don't usually make mistakes. You know that. But this is a lulu."

He was now staring at Fat Boy. He hunched his shoulders, and in the old hoarse joshing voice he used for testing me, he said, "Can you get up that ladder and shove this beam through the brackets on the hatchway door, without making a sound?"

"I guess so."

"You'd better be more certain than that, Charlie, because if you wake those bugs up they're going to start shooting."

He handed me the beam. It was heavy, but it smelled sweet, a roasted-nut aroma — it had been freshly sawed.

"You could get us all killed," he said.

I wanted to drop the beam and run.

"Up you go."

We crept to the ladder, and he took hold of it. I climbed past him and received a wave of heat from his body, the reddened sweat of his worry, which was like a vapor of blood in the air. Then I was cooled by the light breeze on the midsection of the ladder. I was glad it was dark — I could not see the ground clearly, only the moon-white flickers, like doves pecking in the grass, and gobs of putty-colored light on the trees. The fingers of my free hand were pale. They trembled on the rungs.

Nearer the hatchway, I imagined that I could hear the men snoring just inside Fat Boy, on the upper platform, in the tangle of pipes. Months before, I had seen these coils and pans, and I believed I had had a glimpse of Father's mind. I could not separate them, and now it seemed awful that these intruders were there, stinking and waiting and refusing to go. Men he hated had penetrated this private place.

There were iron bracket straps fixed to the jamb. Father must have hammered them there this afternoon. I had never seen them before. We had no locks in Jeronimo. This was the first.

I lifted the wood beam, set it against the door above the brackets, and slid it down. It was a perfect fit. But as soon as I did it, I realized how final it was. It had sealed the door — barricaded it, as Father would have said. My legs went weak and began to wobble. I descended the ladder quickly, expecting that at any moment there would be a crash, and gunfire.

"Stand back."

Father moved the ladder away from Fat Boy and eased it into the grass. He put his mouth against my head.

"You didn't climb that ladder."

His breath scalded my ear.

"You didn't bar that door."

He took my arm and squeezed it.

"We don't have any locks in Jeronimo."

He had gripped my arm so tightly I thought the bone would snap. He was leading me to the firebox. We had no shadows.

"I wanted you here to test your eyes. My guess is that they're as good as mine. I'll bet you can see the same things I can. Look there."

Still holding my arm in his left hand, he motioned with his other hand. Beyond the blunt finger stump was the firebox.

"Somebody's left a fire burning," he said.

But there was no fire.

I said, "I can't see it."

My hand went dead. He was squeezing hard.

"Look," he said, and struck a match and put it to a packed mass of kindling. It was all prepared — kindling, sticks, twigs, cut limbs, and split logs on top. "Somebody lit a fire here — and I told them not to."

"Yes."

He released my arm, but I could not feel a thing in my hand. It was as if, in the dark, he had pinched it off.

"No fires, I said." His face was wild.

The kindling wood must have been soaked in oil, because it went *wheesht* as it burst into flames and set the sticks and split logs above it chattering on fire, louder than Father's whisper. It roared against the bricks, and when Father shut the firebox door, I could hear it in the chimney, and the faintly foolish glugs of the liquid stirring in Fat Boy's pipes — swallows and burps, so sad tonight.

"We'll just have to let it burn. It's chock-full of logs. There's nothing we can do to stop it."

His voice was smaller than the rumble around us.

"Some devil has done this."

"The men — " But what could I tell him that he did not already know? He knew the men inside would freeze solid. I wanted to say something, because I saw them clearly, stretched out and gray, with frost on their faces.

"Start counting, Charlie. By the time you get to three hundred, there won't be any men in there."

He said no more. He led me back to the house in silence. He was gulping, as if he was counting too. The crackle of the fire, the swelling of Fat Boy's pipes, the creak of joints — it was like the quickened tick-tock of measured time.

Before we reached the house, we heard a rapping, a hammering inside Fat Boy — gun butts against the walls. Father went on gulping and started toward Fat Boy.

"If they lie down they'll be all right."

The hammering became frantic.

"They're trying to smash it." Father was not alarmed. He had built it himself, of mahogany planks on a bolted frame. He knew how strong Fat Boy was.

Four gunshots popped inside, then more. But they were muffled by the double walls, and I was not even sure they were shots until Father said the men were firing their guns.

"Allie, are you all right?"

It was Mother, standing on the Gallery in her white nightgown.

Father replied, but his words were drowned by the very loud noise that followed the shots — a great slamming inside Fat Boy. It was like barrels bumping downstairs over and over again. The trapped men were trying to fight their way out, beating on the door. They fired their guns, and the metal rang as their bullets hit pipes — and still the barrel-thud on the thick walls.

"Keep counting, Charlie."

Clover, April, and Jerry appeared with Mother on the Gallery.

April was crying, and the others were saying, "Where's Dad?" and "What happened to Charlie?"

"What all this racky puppysho?" Mr. Haddy was behind us in his sleeping clothes — undershirt and striped shorts. He danced back and forth with fear.

"Get your head down, Figgy. Everything's going to be fine. A few minutes more —"

"What cracking?"

"Crickets."

But the noise grew louder, and there were tunnel yells, like buried-alive men screaming into dirt. That and the chiming of pipes. I knew those pipes — if you touched them, the cold metal tore the skin from your fingers. The whole building shook. The tin roof rattled. The noise in that darkness made Fat Boy seem huger than ever. The strangled echoes of so much drumming and fright, and the gunshots, made holes in the night air. The struggle was like hell in an immense coffin that had been nailed shut on people who were half alive.

"They're damaging him," Father said. He was not frightened, but hurt and angry. "They won't lie down. They're going to put a hole in him."

He spoke as though something in his own head was breaking.

The kids were crying, and Mr. Haddy still dancing in his striped shorts.

"No!" Father cried. He started to rush forward.

Then the explosion came. It filled the clearing with light that scorched my face. It brought color to every leaf, not green but reddish gold, and it gathered the nearby buildings — the cold store, the incubator, the root cellar — shocking them with pale floury flame and then pushing them over like paper. It lifted Fat Boy from the ground, broke it, and dropped it, shoving its planks apart like petals, as the fireball of flaming gas shot upward like a launched balloon.

Father had turned away from the blast. One side of his face was fiery, the other black. He had one red eye. It was fixed on me, and it was so bright it looked as if it would burst with blood. His mouth was open. He may have been screaming, but the other noise was greater.

The boom was over, yet the power of it still made the trees sway as they did before a storm, tossing their boughs. Birds woke, and mewed. The planks that had broken from the walls had caught fire, and fire clung to the pipes that shot jets of blue flame like a gas burner, and inside there was a griddle-fat sizzle and a choking stink of shit-house ammonia that pinched my nose and stung my eyes.

Father dashed toward the flames, then put his hands over his face and ran back to us. His mouth was black, and now I could hear him.

"Follow me!"

He went rigid. He did not move a muscle.

"Follow me!" he yelled.

Mother and the children snatched at him and hugged him and pleaded. I thought they would tip him over. "Dad!" they shouted, and "Allie!" They were weeping and trying to make him move, and we were all gagging on the ammonia fumes.

Mr. Haddy moaned. "We all gung die."

"We'll get out of this poison," Father said, but still he did not move. I wondered if he was injured. His face was streaked and dirty. "There's more hydrogen in the tanks, the ammonia's going to flood us. Cover your faces!"

Across the clearing, lighting what was left of Jeronimo, Fat Boy burned. I had not realized that such a bright fire could be so quiet. The houses flamed like baskets, but it was the birds that made most of the noise. The clearing itself, its fringes and trees, caught, too. The fire spread fast. It was not the flames or the light, but the sewer stink of ammonia that made this seem like the end of the world. Another gas tank blew, and caused a tremendous wind of heat and poison.

With terrible croaks, Father rubbed his eyes and pleaded with us to follow him. But he did not move. When I saw him this way, and his red eyes, I began to cry.

I said, "I know a place —"

As I started away, they followed, and soon they were right behind me, pushing me along the cool path.

All this took less than five minutes: I was still counting.

And then there were various shocks in the dark, the way doors slam in a house on windy summer nights.

III
BREWER'S
LAGOON

21

ALL THAT NIGHT, Fat Boy's fire showed over the treetops like a bright hat. Even the pissy snap of hot ammonia gas reached us here. The flames brought Jeronimo close. Rising sparks put the stars out and replaced them with flaming straws, and the climbing smoke clouded the sky.

I sat in our dark camp, the Acre, tortured by mosquitoes. I could not find the black berries we used for keeping bugs off in the day-time. The Jeronimo smoke was no help here in driving them away—and it seemed unlucky to build a fire so near to the one that had destroyed our home. It was still chewing, in the violent and greedy way flames feed on dry wood, and spitting the trees into the sky as ashes. The kids had crawled into a lean-to, where they hid and slept. Mr. Haddy's whimpering about his boat had become lazy snores. He had turned drunk and silly on sleep. Father had found a corner of the camp and put his head down. He slept like the others. He had not spoken a word.

"Get some sleep, Charlie," Mother said. She yawned. Soon she was asleep, and only I was left awake.

Sitting among these purring people, I discovered how long Father's nights were. He was usually the one who watched the night pass. There were rattles in the darkness, and the clash of dropping branches, and the brief gallop of falling trees. There were bat squeals and, because of the fire, some birds still mewing and others beeping like clarinets. These sounds — the birds' most of all — did not belong in the jungle. They were too harsh, they nagged and rasped in all the soft, black surrounding trees.

Disorder here was this noise, loudest at night, and the worst of it cracking out in the darkest places. Some of it was like spurts from a broken hose pipe. I listened to the jungle being torn apart. These hidden creatures, and even some trees, had voices. They sounded their loud wakeful fear throughout the night, stirred by the fire that was stirring the whole sky. I was blind and the world was falling down like the dew around me. There seemed no remedy for it, to plug it or calm it or make it sleep. It all roared at me. Hope left me then, and wide-awake I began to worry. This was not solitude but rather a nightmare of damage, an iron wheel that drove on and on, monotonous noise in the timeless dark, scattering feathers and claws.

But Father was wise to these crowding sounds. Nights like this, which worried me, had filled his head with schemes. So when dawn came, I knew him better and feared him more than I had at the stunning ruin of Jeronimo.

"Let him sleep," Mother said. I was amazed that he was still at it: I had never seen him sleep so soundly.

He lay on his side, in a hedgehog posture, with his arms over his face and his knees drawn up — a bundle of grumbling snores. Flies had settled on his shirt, and they scratched undisturbed on the wrinkles and seemed to play, he was so still. No one spoke, no one wanted to hear what he would say when he woke up.

It was day now. I felt sick and small under the quivering trees.

In the dry-season dawn, the leaves seemed to die as the sun hit them. The dew dried on the grass, and the blades withered and were lighted like gold thread under the rips of foil on the boughs. Freed of the dampness and dark, the dust on the ground penetrated the air with a yellow smell of decay that was sweet this first hour of daylight. The rising sun heated each live thing it struck, and stiffened it and gilded it with death. There were lovely brittle coins on the shining trees, and whole bushes of crisp gold flakes. As soon as the sun was sieved through the topmost branches, everything in the Acre was bright and dead around the black pool.

We waited, hardly breathing, for Father to wake. I dozed and watched the spiders near the pool, the way they plucked their webs like zithers to trap and tangle a struggling fly before they rushed the insect and wrapped it like a mummy. They hung the parcels of neatly bandaged flies in a high corner of the web, the way Indians here stored peppers and corn.

"Poor Dad," Clover whispered.

Mr. Haddy said, "His spearmint almost kill us."

"We're all right now," Mother said. "Charlie saved us."

"This isn't Charlie's camp. It's the Acre. It belongs to all of us," Jerry said. "The Maywit kids helped make those lean-tos. And Crummo gets all the credit!"

"You were blubbering last night," I said. "You were scared!"

"I wasn't!"

Mr. Haddy said, "But I were skeered! I was praying. I see death back there. That were wuss than a preacher's hell. Ruther have hurricanes and twisters than them fires. I see devils. I see Duppies dancing. I were so skeered I were glad to die."

Clover said, "What happened to those men, Ma?"

"They're gone."

"And if they ain't gone, we got trouble for true," Mr. Haddy said, and he repeated, "For too-roo!"

I said, "I saw them go."

"Don't think about it, Charlie." Mother hugged me. "We're safe now. Your father's going to be grateful when he wakes up."

"What's Dad *doing?*" April said.

His sleep made us helpless. It prevented us from moving. As long as he lay there we could not leave. It was then that we were reminded how important he was to us. We had only known him awake. It was frightening to see him so still. If he was dead, we were lost.

The sun, now overhead, was burning on his back. People sleeping give off an underground smell, a boiled root stink of dirt and food and sweat and wounds — the way I imagined corpses steamed, like heated compost. Father was motionless. He might have been making up for all the nights he'd stayed awake. But he looked and smelled dead.

April said, "Ma, are we going to die?"

Mother said, "Don't be silly." She found our baskets and helped us gather yautia and guavas and wild avocados. She praised our camp, she said it was a good job — it had saved our lives.

Seeing the yautia, Mr. Haddy said, "You kids like eddoes? Me ma make eddoes!"

Father swung over and jumped to his feet.

"Let's go," he said. He sank to his knees.

It was early afternoon. He had slept almost thirteen hours, but no one mentioned the time. "Liars, swindlers, degenerates who sleep till noon" — those were some of the people he hated. He had always told us that deep sleep was a form of illness, and he blamed us when we overslept.

He sat down on the gold grass and dropped his hands into his lap. "What are you looking at?"

His voice was flat, dull, different, almost drugged, and very small. He hardly moved his lips. He seemed very tired, and yet I had watched him all night, lying there sound asleep.

Mother knelt down and touched his face. She said, "Your hair is singed."

His eyebrows were stubble, his beard was burned and so were his eyelashes. It gave him a startled sausagey expression. One side of his face was pink and creased, with a sleep map pressed on it. One eye was redder than the other. He pulled on his baseball hat.

"I had an awful night. Hardly slept a wink."

Mr. Haddy said, "I see dogs twitch more than you done! You were sleeping like a slope — wunt he, Ma?"

Father said, "I've got no patience with liars in the morning."

Then he sniffed and came alert, as if he had just heard something. The smell of smoke and ammonia was still strong in the air, with burned bamboo and roasted tin. Father sighed. His face cracked. He smiled sadly, remembering.

"It's finished," he said, in his beaten voice.

"All your work," Mother said. Still kneeling, she started to cry. "I'm so sorry, Allie."

"I'm happy," Father said. "Jeronimo is destroyed."

Mr. Haddy said, "She went up like crackers."

Father said, "We're free."

Mother protested. "Everything you made is gone," she said. "All the houses, the crops, those wonderful machines. All that work — "

"Traps," Father said. "I should never have done it."

"How were you to know?"

"I'm the only one who could have known. It wasn't ignorance; it was subtlety. But that's always been my problem. I'm too elaborate, too ambitious. I can't help being an idealist. I was trying to defuse the situation peaceably. It blew up in my face."

"Allie, why — "

"And I deserved it. Toxic substances — this is no place for them.

I'll never work with poisons again, and no more flammable gas. Keep it simple — physics, not chemistry. Levers, weights, pulleys, rods. No chemicals except those that occur naturally. Stable elements — "

Mother sobbed, "But those men are dead!"

"Tempered in the fires, Mother."

Clover said, "That's what I was just wondering."

"But not gone. Matter cannot be destroyed. Ask Figgy. They requested the transformation. Scavengers like them deserve the turkey treatment — "

Mother had put her fingers over her eyes. She wept softly as Father stood up.

"I thought I was building something," he said. "But I was asking for it to be destroyed. That's a consequence of perfection in this world — the opposing wrath of imperfection. Those scavengers wanted to feed on us! And Fat Boy failed me. The concept was wrong, and now I know why — no more poison, Mother."

He said this in almost a whining way, with his hands locked together. He went to the pool and poked the water.

He said, "Anybody can break anything in this world. America was brought low by little men."

He sounded as if his heart was broken. He raised some water in his cupped hands and washed his face and arms. "Where are we? What is this place?"

"It's the Acre," I said.

"Our camp," Jerry said.

"Call this a camp?" His voice was still small.

"This is where we play," Clover said.

"Some playground. You had water all this time?"

I said, "It's from a spring."

"You can swim in it," Jerry said.

Father looked around. I knew he thought it was all unsuitable. I wanted to tell him that it had kept us happy. He saw the swing. "I recognize that rope."

"She me stern painter," Mr. Haddy said.

"It was Charlie's idea."

"Huts, too. And fruit. And little baskets." He spoke sadly. "It's pure monkey."

"Those are guavas in the basket," Jerry said.

"Eat some, Allie. You haven't eaten anything."

"Monkey food, monkeyshines," Father said. "I hate this. I didn't want this. Why did you take us here, Charlie?"

"He saved us," Mother said. "He found us food and water. Allie, we would have died!"

"He didn't grow the food, he didn't dig the water." Father refused to look at me. He said, "Let's go. It's late. You're just sitting there."

Mother said, "We can't go back to Jeronimo."

"Who said go back? Who mentioned Jeronimo? I don't want to see it."

Mother's lips shaped the question, "Where?"

"Away! Away!"

"We'll have to salvage something to take with us," Mother said. "We can't go like this."

"This is how I want to go" — but he stood before us with only his hat on his head and his arms dangling out of his scorched sleeves. He looked like what he was — a man who had crawled away from an explosion.

Mr. Haddy said, "You tools? You foods? You bags and erl? Me lanch? Ain't leaving me lanch!"

"It's all poisoned," Father said. "We had too much with us — too much junk, too many drums of poison. That was our mistake. Do you know what a flood of ammonia can do? There's contamination there, and what's not contaminated is burned to a crisp."

"Please, Allie, you're raving."

"What I'm saying is understatement. Now let's go — I want to get this stink out of my nose."

"To the river?"

"Mother," he said. "I killed the river!"

"Why can't we stay here?" Jerry asked.

"Smell Fat Boy's guts? That's your answer. It'll stink for a year and drive you insane. No, I want to get away" — he pointed east to the Esperanzas — "past those mountains there."

"They is a river behind," Mr. Haddy said. "Rio Sico."

"We know all about it, Figgy."

"She run down to Paplaya and Camaron. We could go to Brewer's. She me own lagoon."

"That's the place for us," Father said.

This was too much for Mother. With a pained, demanding expression, she said, "How do you know?"

Father moved the part of his forehead where his eyebrows should have been. He was smiling unhappily. "Because I like the name."

He tramped around the clearing, punching the bushes and peering between boughs the way a person might fuss with the curtains on a window. His impatience made him clumsy and useless. Finally he sighed.

"Okay, Charlie, I give up. Which way is out?"

I showed him the path.

"Just as I thought," he said. He started walking.

"I'd better go first."

"Who put you in charge?"

I said, "We dug traps here and covered them with branches. In case bandits came. You might fall in."

"I know all about traps," he said, and kept walking.

We followed, carrying the baskets of food and a jug of water.

Between the Acre and the river lay Jeronimo. There was no other way to the mountains. Father told us to walk faster, but Jeronimo was unavoidable — it smoldered at the end of the path.

Father bowed his head.

Mr. Haddy said, "Shoo."

Jeronimo looked bombed. It was mostly powder, a pouch of gray ashes, the trees around it burned to spikes. Because the fire had spread, the clearing was bigger, and craterlike. Fat Boy's pipes had collapsed and whitened like bones, and all the pumps had fallen down. There was not a house standing or a shed intact. In the gardens, the plants were scorched and the stems blistered like flesh. The corn was down, and the squashes and tomatoes had burst and were seeping juice — they had been cooked to rottenness. Some fruit looked like ragged purses.

But the ashy ruins were nothing compared to the silence. We were accustomed to bird twitters and screeches, to the high ringing notes of the crickyjeen cicadas. There was no sound or movement. All life had been burned out of Jeronimo. What birds we saw were dead, roasted black and midgety, stripped of their feathers, with tiny wings and ridiculous bobble heads. Slimy fish floated on the surface of the tank. It all lay dead and silent and stinking in the afternoon sun. Some thick hummocks still smoldered.

"You wanted to see it!" Father said angrily. "Feast your eyes!"

Distant birds cackled deep in the forest, mocking him.

He hooked across the black grass and picked up a machete with a burned handle. Then he went to our house and chopped the remaining timbers down, making the ruins complete.

We remained standing where the bathhouse had been. Heat had cracked the culverts and had baked some of the clay sluice pipes solid. The burned air stung my eyes.

Mother said, "Don't touch anything."

Mr. Haddy said, "Ain't nothing left to touch."

"I heard that!" Father had started toward us with the machete in his hand. I thought he was going to whack Mr. Haddy's head off. He sliced it at him.

"I'm left, they're left — you're left, Figgy. If you've got the strength to complain, I'd say there's nothing wrong with you. Show some gratitude."

Mr. Haddy put his teeth out. "Me lanch — she catched fire. She all wrecked."

"I lose everything I own and he worries about his pig."

"She all I own in this world," Mr. Haddy said. Tears ran beside his nose and dripped from his teeth.

"What good is a boat if you haven't got a river?"

"The river is *there*, Fadder."

"The river is dead," Father said. "It's full of ammonium hydroxide and gasping fish. The air — smell it? — it's contaminated. It'll take a year for this place to be detoxified. If we stay here, we'll die."

Father kicked at the ashes.

"He knew that. He just wanted to hear me say it!"

It was all as Father said. The air was sharp with the stifling smell of ammonia, and trapped in the weeds near the riverbank were dead fish and swollen frogs. They were more horrible than the roasted birds in the black grass. These river creatures were plump and had no marks on them. They had not been burned, but poisoned. We had to wade through them and push their bodies aside with sticks, to get to the opposite bank.

Father made three trips across, carrying the little kids. On his last trip, struggling through the mud with Jerry, his face and arms sooty and his clothes splashed and torn, Father began to cry. He just stood there in the water and did it. I thought it was Jerry at first — I had never heard Father cry before. His whole face crumpled, his mouth stretched and went square, and I could see the roots of his teeth. He made gasping noises and small dry honks.

"I know what you're thinking. All right, I admit it — I did a terrible thing. I took a flyer. I polluted this whole place. I'm a murderer." He sobbed again. "It wasn't me!"

He had splashed to the bank and dropped Jerry and led us into this forest, moving fast. After his crying, we had not seen his face.

It was high ground on this eastern side of the river. Within an hour we had left the buttonwoods behind and were among low cedars. Above us was a saddle between two peaks of the Esperanzas. The advantage of the dry season, those blue rainless days, was that the forest was scrubbier, easier to walk through, and there was more daylight. But it was also smellier. In very hot weather, when no rain had fallen, the jungle odor is skunky and as strong as garbage. Sour waves of it hit us as we climbed. Part of the way was familiar. I told Father how we had come here with Francis and Bucky, looking for bamboos.

He said, "They're sleeping in their own beds tonight."

He walked with his head down, like someone who has lost something and is retracing his steps to find it. I caught his eye — his face looked slapped.

He said, "Don't look back."

He walked away from the sun on the dried-out hillside among dead trees. Five miles up this gentle slope was the saddle ridge, and here we were within sight of a new range of mountains. Mr. Haddy said it was the Sierra de San Pablo. Between us and these mountains was the deep valley of the Rio Sico, which flowed northeast to the coast.

On our way to the valley floor, Father sat down. I was glad when he said we would spend the night here. I had had no sleep last night.

Mother said, "I wish we had blankets."

"Blankets? In this heat?" Father said.

To remind Father that his boat was gone, and maybe to rub it in, Mr. Haddy unfolded his large captain's certificate, and said "Shoo," and used it for starting a fire.

"We haven't even got a pot to boil water in," Mother said. "Just that jug. And it's nearly empty."

"The kids will find us a spring," Father said. "They know more about this monkey stuff than we do. Look at them. They love it."

We gathered dry grass for beds and made nests in the hillside. There we sat, listening to the breeze in the cedars, eating the last of the fruit we had brought from the Acre. Mother found some manioc growing wild and roasted it over the fire. Jerry said if you closed your eyes it tasted like turnips. At nightfall we crawled into our nests. There were flies, but no mosquitoes.

In the darkness behind me, April whispered, "I saw him crying. Ask Jerry." And Clover muttered, "That's a lie — he wasn't. He was just mad. It's all Charlie's fault."

Later, I was woken by Clover again. "Dad, Jerry kicked me in the back!"

But Father was saying, "You won't catch me eating any of that stuff. I'm no camper. Anyway, the trouble with most people is they eat more than is good for them. Especially starches. There's no goodness in that cassava — "

He had recovered his old voice. He was preaching again. *Don't look back.*

The three adults were around the fire, guarding us. I felt safe again. And I listened. Between the whistles of the crickyjeens, Mr. Haddy was talking about tigers. Father laughed at him recklessly, as if daring a tiger to show itself so he could jig it onto a tree.

He said, "This is the best part — skipping out naked, with nothing. We just walked away. It was easy!"

He had forgotten Jeronimo already.

But Mother said, "We had no choice."

"We chose freedom." His voice was glad. "It's like being shipwrecked."

Mother said, "I didn't want to be shipwrecked."

The crickyjeens whistled again and stopped.

"We got out just in time — I was *right*. We're alive, Mother."

22

LOWER DOWN the slope, the cedars and pitch pines gave way to hoolie trees — chiclets and sapodillas. They were full of gummy juice and they reminded me of our rubber making in Jeronimo, the boiling-sulphur smell and the sheets we had wrapped around the ice blocks. It seemed wasteful to pass by without slashing them. Many of the trees in this jungly part of the slope were usable — there were monkey-pot trees and palms and bamboos and even finger bananas growing among some deserted palm-leaf huts. But we kept walking through the high jungle. I saw it all with my Jeronimo eyes. We could have stopped anywhere and called it home and started hacking.

Father said, "I have no urge to do anything here. Those hoolies? I feel no temptation whatsoever to lacerate them and cook up pairs of matching galoshes. Spare those trees — let them multiply and become abundant. Yes, before I might have stopped here and done a little tinkering. But I have had an experience."

The path was a gully of dust, then pebbles and bigger stones. We heard a squawk behind us: the *voom* of a curassow. Mr. Haddy had beaned it with a club and stood there wringing its neck. He carried the big black hen by its feet, swinging it like a lunch bag. He said he would pluck it and roast it on a stick when we got to the river.

"Figgy hasn't changed," Father said. "But I'm a changed man, Mother. A man who refuses to change is doomed. I've had a satisfactory experience."

He talked about his Experience as he had once talked about his Hole.

"I had a breakdown back there. A breakdown isn't bad. It's an Experience. I'm stronger than ever."

Mother said, in a different voice, as if she wanted to change the subject, "I hope we find some water soon."

"You can go seven days without water."

"Not hiking like this, I can't."

"Pass Mother the jug, Charlie."

Giving Mother a drink, I asked her if Father had changed, and what did it mean? She said it was nothing — if he really had changed, he would not be talking so much about it. She said he was trying to keep our spirits up.

Father was still talking, but the thicker foliage muffled his voice and prevented any echo. This was real jungle, not mountain scrub anymore. The bamboo was dense. We were kept cool by the damp trees along the gully path. There were gnats and butterflies on the plants, which were like parlor plants but grown to enormous size — ferns and rubber trees and figs with spotted leaves, and some red and striped with black, and with a suffocating hairiness, as if they were growing in a bottle.

"Before my Experience, I wouldn't have thought of doing this. Listen, consider what we're attempting! It's staggering, really. I have nothing up my sleeve, and look" — he turned to face us on the path, and pulled out his limp white pockets — "nothing there!"

We stumbled along behind him, through the seams of green light. As always, his talk made the time pass. Mr. Haddy said if it wasn't downhill he wouldn't be going at all, and "We gung eat me bird."

Father said, "Why, I used to fix Polski's pumps and set out for the fields in the morning with more in my pockets than I have now. Or go into Northampton. Burdened with material things. Wallet full of money."

Clover said, "Don't we have any money, Dad?"

"What can you buy with money here?" Father said.

Jerry whispered, "We're poor. We're done for. We should have stayed at the Acre."

"Money is useless. I've proved that."

April said plainly, "I think we're going to die."

Father said, "Don't you love these clear skies, Mother?"

High empty skies, burning blue, and our tiny path beneath. It was stonier, and now bouldery — we were climbing over them, they were so big. Then it was not a path at all but a dry creek bed. The boulders had been sucked smooth by running water.

"This is the true test of ingenuity," Father said. "We are trusting to brains and experience. I'm glad Jeronimo was destroyed!"

Mother said, "Those three men might have been harmless."

"Scavengers!"

We looked up and expected to see vultures. But he meant the men.

"This is the way the first family faced things," Father said. "That's it, Mother. We are the first family on earth, walking down the glory road empty-handed."

"I'd hate to die that way," Mother said. She was still thinking about the men.

"There's a worse way," Father said. "The way they would have killed us. A scavenger takes his time."

The undersides of the boulders were mossy and damp. Here was a mud puddle, our first sight of natural water since leaving Jeronimo. Father said, "Water has a smell around here, just like everything else." But this water smelled stagnant, and dead insects floated in it like tea leaves. More was leaking from beneath the smooth boulders, and smears of it bubbled out of the bank and gave the clay edges of the path the texture of peanut butter. It drained on, became a trickle, and there was enough of it to have a sound like slow boiling in a pot. The water had a sickening smell of decay, but its plopping sound was hopeful, like a simple song. And there were animals and birds here — monkeys midway up the trees, and little agoutis beneath, and pava birds with crazy shrieks, and more curassows. If they could live here, so could we. In a dangerous place, all wild animals gave us hope.

We walked beside the creek for a while. The land was broken by level terraces. Father said, "This is how a river is born. You're seeing it with your own eyes. You didn't have to get it out of a book. This is the source of oceans."

It was as if Father had created the stream with his speeches, as if he had talked it into existence with the racket and magic of his voice. From will power alone, so it seemed, he had made the pleasant valley appear. We were in the open, under a strong sun. In the jungle I had not felt exposed. There were so many different kinds of tree cover. But this valley felt like outdoors — bushy walls on both sides. The stream, shrunken in the dry season, was a green vein running through the middle of a wide rocky riverbed.

"This is satisfactory," Mr. Haddy said, borrowing one of Father's words. "We can have a lanch here. Or one of them pipanto things."

There was a flat-bottomed boat in the shallow stream. It was a wooden trough, and a man was standing in its stern and poling it to a sandbank under some buttonwoods.

Father said, "I think I can take credit for inventing that boat."

"That a pipanto," Mr. Haddy said. "That a pitpan."

Father said that the fact that it was used by the Zambus and Miskitos made no difference. He had dreamed it up as the best design for our river, and he was pleased that the same design was used here.

"It took these people a thousand years or more to invent this boat. How long did it take me, Figgy?"

"We're being watched," Mother said.

The man had drawn his boat up to the sandbank. He stood there like a heron, with one leg drawn up, staring at us. He was very thin, not as dark as a Zambu, and had choppy teeth.

"*Naksaa,*" Father said. It was the most friendly all-purpose word, meaning hello, how are you, good day, thank you, and all the rest.

Mr. Haddy gave the man his dead curassow and made it seem as if we had left Jeronimo and walked all that way and camped on the slope especially to deliver this present.

"He look a little hungry," Mr. Haddy said.

The man was examining Father with shining eyes. He said, "Mr. Parks."

Then we knew he was a Miskito, because Miskitos could not pronounce *F*.

Father said, "He knows me. Which is surprising, because I've changed." He smiled. "I guess I have a reputation around here."

Mr. Haddy said to the Miskito, "Yep, that is Mr. Farkis."

The Miskito spoke excitedly to Mother. "This man give me my garden!" He began to recommend Father to us. He pointed past the buttonwoods to a hut and some tall cornstalks. "Big one right there. Big tomatoes, like this one"—he made a fist.

"The hybrids," Father said. "I practically kill myself making ice, and all I'm remembered for is the seeds I bought in Florence, Mass."

"And peppers like this!"

"You came to Jeronimo and did some work, eh? I paid you off in seeds? Too bad about the ice. It was a good idea, but a little unwieldy."

The Miskito was saying, "Yes, yes."

Father said, "I invented this boat."

"Everybody got pipantos," Mr. Haddy said. "And them that ain't, got cayukas."

"This is my boat," Father said.

The Miskito insisted on taking us to see his garden, so we climbed the bluff above the sandbar and walked to his hut. It was a rickety patched hut of grass and palm leaves, but his garden sprawled beautifully around it. It was tall tassely corn and unpropped tomato vines, peppers, string beans, and summer squashes. There were muskmelons, too. These vegetables looked out of place in an Indian's garden. There were no papayas, avocados, calabashes, or granadilla. This was like Hatfield; like Jeronimo. The Miskito had grown them all from seeds that Father had given him months before, when he had crossed the ridge to visit us. He had done a day's work, or more, and taken the seeds as payment. He had never known seeds to sprout so quickly and bear such plump fruit.

Father snapped a string bean and said, "Kentucky Wonders!"

There were bananas near the hut, the sort of plantains the Indians called "plas," because they were like flasks. But Father said the Miskito deserved no credit for growing them — they grew all by themselves.

We heard the sound of whipping. It was the Miskito's wife, thrashing rice stems against a frame and letting the rice grains fall on a cowhide mat. She stopped when the Miskito called her, and she served us wabool and fried bananas and roasted ears of corn. And she plucked Mr. Haddy's curassow and trussed it to a spit over the fire.

Father would not eat anything.

"Don't take it personally," he said, waving the wabool away.

Mother said, "It's their custom. You know that."

"What about my customs?" Father said.

I felt he had not changed at all, for he had always said this in Jeronimo.

He grinned at the Miskito.

"I'm saving up for later," he said. "Hunger's a good thing. Makes you determined. Food puts you straight to sleep. That thing you've got in your hand there" — the Miskito was holding the burned and greasy curassow — "that's a soporific. Sure, you knew that, didn't you? I'm not talking about starvation, but hunger. It's nature's mainspring. It's a kind of strength."

He smiled at us. We sat on the ground, gnawing.bones alongside the Miskito's pig named Ed.

"There's only one thing I really and truly crave," Father said. "Think you can fix me up with a bath?"

Speaking carefully and with sign language and noises, he explained that he wanted some privacy and hot water and a basket. The Miskito provided him with what he wanted. Father then hung the finely woven basket from a tree and had the Miskito fill it with hot water, so it streamed like a shower. This ritual took place behind the Miskito's hut. We heard Father encouraging the Miskito and spitting water and scrubbing himself.

Mr. Haddy said, "Fadder got customs, for true!"

"That shower bath was better than a meal," Father said when he was done. His face was pink. His ears stuck out. He jumped in the sun to dry. "And it's taken the edge off my appetite. I needed that. I'm ready, Mother."

The Miskito was bewildered by all this business and by Father's talk. As if to please him, he sent his wife into the garden to gather vegetables, about four bushels in pretty baskets. And as a last present, he handed Father the pole to his pipanto. Father went through the motions of refusing these gifts, but he accepted them when the Miskito loaded the baskets into the pipanto and waited by it, screaming softly for Father to go aboard.

Mr. Haddy said, "He saying 'lukpara' — ain't worry."

Father stepped in and said, "I'm just borrowing it, Fred. You can have it back any time you like."

That was how we came to be floating down the Rio Sico that day. Father poled and Mr. Haddy hung over the bow looking for obstructions. "Rock-stone!" he cried, when he saw one. There were only five inches of freeboard, but there was not a ripple in this river.

It was forty miles to the coast, and Father calculated that the river was flowing at four miles an hour.

"Not fast enough, is it?" he said.

As soon as we rounded the first big bend and the Miskito's hut was out of sight, Father beached the pipanto. He found some loose wood for us to use as seats, wedging the planks amidships. He took off his shirt and rigged up an awning, tucking the tails into the starboard gunwales and stretching it over bent benches. He secured it by its sleeves.

"Looks like an oxygen tent! That's so you don't get heat stroke." He picked up a bundle of twigs. "And this is to give us a little speed. This is a real witch's broom!"

He lashed the twigs to the end of the pole, tying them with vines and turning it into a broomlike oar, so that he could scull from the stern one-handed.

Then he made a smudge pot to keep the stinging gnats away, and, smoking, we set off again. He promised that we would be on the coast by nightfall.

"Anyone get a look at that Miskito's hut?" he asked.

"They all look like that," Mr. Haddy said.

"That doesn't make it lawful, Figgy. That pokey little thing will fall down in the first rain. He was a generous man and he had a spectacular vegetable garden, thanks to me, but that was some miserable hut." We passed more huts on the riverbank, more Miskitos, pigs, and dogs. Father said, "Pathetic."

"You've got a gleam in your eye, Allie."

"Because I've just worked out what kind of hut suits this terrain."

"You said you were through with inventions."

"I didn't come here to live in a grass hut," he said. "I'm not Robinson Crusoe. Give me a little credit, will you? Hey, don't touch those baskets!"

Jerry had taken out a tomato and was polishing it on his knee. Father ordered him to put it back.

"We'll stop and get monkey food, if you're hungry, but don't eat those vegetables. Those are hybrids. Eat those and you're living on our capital. When we get where we're going, we'll take them apart and use them for seed. They're ripe enough."

Mother said, "That's unfair."

"It's propagation."

"You haven't changed a bit."

Father swept his broom back and forth. He said, "My whole way of thinking has changed. No more chemicals, no ice, no contraptions. Jeronimo was a mistake. I had to pollute a whole river to find that out."

Mother said, "All Jerry wants is one lousy tomato!"

"That tomato represents a whole row of vines. It contains a garden, Mother. Use your imagination."

"Please don't fight," Clover said.

Mr. Haddy said, "Fadder having another speerience."

"Everybody shut up," Father said. Then, "Who said anything about brain damage?"

Father went on sculling us downriver with his broom, shouting the whole time. And he predicted that before nightfall we would be at Paplaya on the coast, within striking distance of Brewer's Lagoon. Mr. Haddy turned around and stuck his teeth out at the name.

"We could walk down that beach to Panama," Father said.

"We could walk up it to Cape Cod," Mother said.

Father laughed. "Cape Cod's been blown away. We got out just in time. There's nothing left — nothing at all. It's gone, don't you understand?"

Mother said, "What are you talking about?"

"The end of the world." Father pointed north with his broom handle. "That world. Burned to a crisp."

"Jeronimo is back there," Mother said.

"Jeronimo was nothing compared to the destruction of the United States. It wasn't only the burning buildings and the panic. Think of the people. Remember Figgy's curassow? The way roasting made the meat fall off the bones? That's what happened to millions of Americans. Their flesh just slipped off their bones. Then the scavengers came. Hatfield's all ashes."

The twins began to cry.

Mother tried to comfort them. She said to Father, "Look what you've done."

"I didn't do anything but rescue us."

Jerry said, "Is it true there's nothing left?"

"Nothing that you want to see," Father said. "You think it's bad being on this river? Oh, boy, this is a vacation next to that war in the States."

Mr. Haddy said, "Was they a war up there?"

"Horrendous," Father said.

"You're trying to frighten us," Mother said. "Stop talking this way, Allie. It's cruel. You don't know what's happened in the States."

"I know what I've seen. I know about the armies, the soldiers — all the burning and killing." He was beating his broom in the river. "They knew where I was."

Mother held the twins in her arms. They sat under the tent Father had made from his shirt. Mother said, "He's joking, girls. Don't pay any attention."

"Some joke," Father said.

He looked at me and winked.

"But we're safe now. This boat, this river — you think it's precarious, but I tell you, we're looking good. We're alive. That's more than I can say for some people."

It was now June. A year before, we had left Hatfield. Two nights ago, we had seen Jeronimo destroyed. In Father's mind, the United States had been wiped out in just the same way as Jeronimo — fire had done it, and all that was left was smoke and a storm of yellow poison. That was what he said.

"They were after me. It was a narrow escape."

I wanted him to stop.

I said, "This is a beautiful river."

"Now you're talking, Charlie! Hear that, Mother? He says it's a beautiful river. You bet your life it is."

He said no more about the war in America or the loss of Jeronimo, which were for him the same thing. He spoke calmly of how we could begin again. He said these close calls had sharpened his wits.

This was the proof. We were in a fourteen-foot pipanto and moving swiftly toward the coast. It was no more than a flatboat, but we had shade and seats and a smudge pot. Father had converted it into something comfortable and fast. He talked wildly, but his talk was like creation, and on that downstream trip he never stopped. I had been worried. Yesterday he had cried, today he was yelling about his experience and the end of the world. He was very restless and hungry-seeming and now less predictable than ever. But there was no man on earth more ingenious.

23

JERRY ROCKED on the beam seat Father had made. He whispered, "Dad thinks he's great," and looked at me with a scolded scowl.

Clover put her head down. "He *is* great."

"There are lots of inventors in the world. He's not the only one."

"He's not like the others," I said.

"Anyway, the world is destroyed," April said. "Dad said so."

Jerry said, "How do you know he's not like the others?"

"He has different reasons," I said.

"Like what?"

I glanced astern — Father's widening eyes dared me to speak.

In that pause, Jerry's whisper was harsh. "You don't know."

But I did. Father was ingenious because he needed comfort. He never admitted it, but I knew it from Jeronimo and from the spruced-up pipanto. He had not changed, he was still inventive, he still needed comfort — more than we did. He was dead set on improving things, but he was not like any other man. I could not tell Jerry while Father was listening. He invented for his own sake! He was an inventor because he hated hard beds and bad food and slow boats and flimsy huts and dirt. And waste — he complained about the cost of things, but it wasn't the money. It was the fact that they got weak and broke after you bought them. He thought of himself first!

It was why he had invented the hydraulic chair and foot massager in Hatfield. It explained his lack of interest in his industrial inventions — potboilers, he called them. And it also explained his mania for ice. It was the reason he wept when Jeronimo was destroyed. He didn't want to live, as he said, like a monkey.

His movements, his travel, were inventions, too. When it looked to him as though America was doomed, he invented a way out. Leaving the country on the banana boat was one of his most ingenious schemes. And Jeronimo had been full of examples of his ingenuity, gadgets he had devised to make life — his life — easier. These schemes and tactics were his answer to the imperfect world. But I sometimes pitied him. Discomfort and dissatisfaction made his brain spin.

A moment ago, hearing Jerry's whispers, Mother said, "He's a perfectionist."

"Don't be bitter," Father said.

Mother was looking at the jungle on the riverbank.

"What a place for a perfectionist," she said.

Everyone thought of him as rough and ready. But I was not fooled. He was the opposite of a camper! He grew prize vegetables because he could not stand the taste of bananas and wabool. He hated sleeping outdoors. "It's lawless and unnatural to sleep on the bare ground." He always spoke tenderly about his own bed. "Even animals make beds!" An everlasting supply of free ice was his reply to the tropics, a complicated system of pumps his reply to the dry season. He liked the odds stacked against him. He said it helped him think. But though he was ambitious for his own comfort, he had never tried to cash in on his inventions — only to live a life that others might want to copy. The royalties on his patents he regarded as "funny money." "I may be selfish," he said, "but I'm not greedy."

Selfishness had made him clever. He wanted things his way — his bed and his food and the world as well. His explanations of events were as ingenious as his inventions. Had there been a war in the United States? Were people after him, as he said? Was it a fact that he was being hunted because "they always kill the smart ones first"? We did not know. But if you believed any of this, you could be very happy here. You did not notice the heat or the insects or the darkness that buried you at night. Father's talk took away your sense of smell. After hearing him speak about America, it comforted you to think that you were so far away on the Mosquito Coast. It comforted him!

Here he was, shouting his plans at us and grinning at our bewilderment. It might be simple scheming, like improving the pipanto pole, or making a smudge pot out of a coconut husk, or describing the foolproof house he was going to make. Or it could be almost batty.

"What a thoroughly rotten job God made of the world!"

I had never heard a single person criticize God before. But Father talked about God the way he talked about jobbing plumbers and electricians. "The dead boy with the spinning top" was the way he described God. "And the top is almost out of steam. Feel it wobble?"

He seldom let up. It was like part of the jungle racket, after our escape from Jeronimo. Like the pava birds and the crickyjeens and the nighttime tattoo, along the Rio Sico and where we turned into the Rio Negro for Paplaya. But of all the jungle sounds that I heard, and that static could be very surprising, the clearest of them, and the most often, was the sound of Father's voice, crying out for comfort.

It took us several days of "coasting," as Father called it, to reach Brewer's Lagoon. After all the talk and boat towing and the halt salty breeze, I expected something blue — sand, surf, palms, a beach. But Brewer's was an inland scoop, and its haulover was a neck of high ground that hid the ocean and blocked the pleasant sound of waves sluicing the sand and making the pebbles jiggle.

We were in mud here. The lagoon was wide and flat and swampy. It was brown water stretching boggily to a brown shore. No ripples — it was a dirty mirror with some stubs of weeds, and cut-down palms like old lampposts. A film of mud and fine silt covered the banks around it, and flies gathered where green cowflap lay drying at the edges of the still, dark puddle.

"It's creepy," Mother said.

"Don't be unhelpful." Father looked at me. "She's bitter."

Mr. Haddy crowed when he saw Brewer's Village. His mother lived there. The huts were piled against the shore. They were shaped like belfries and stained the same color as the lagoon. Zambus paddled dugouts toward the jetty sticks. It was a steamy afternoon, the sun a purple hoop in the gray sea haze.

Father said, "This is where we part company."

"Ain't you coming with me, Fadder?"

"No. I mean, you're not coming with me."

Mr. Haddy gulped, as if trying to guzzle his fear. But it seemed jammed in his throat and fluttering like a chunk of Adam's apple. He said he wasn't ready to go ashore just now.

"Figgy's dragging his feet."

"They gung say, 'Haddy, where you lanch?' "

"You can tell them about your experience. I've got a wife and four kids and nothing else. You don't hear me complaining."

Mr. Haddy opened his mouth and took a big bite of air and wailed, "I ain't got nothing left!"

Rocking down the pipanto from stern to bow, Father slipped his watch off his wrist. It was an old expensive watch — gold with a gold strap. Father was proud of it. It had survived our flights and failures. Strong, waterproof, and accurate, it was the one valuable item on this boat. Father had often said that it was now worth twice what he had paid for it and each year its value increased. But more likely it had been a lucky find at the Northampton dump.

"It's money in the bank, Fig."

Mr. Haddy shook his hands into his trousers. "I ain't take you watch."

"I've got no use for it anymore — have I, Mother?"

He dragged Mr. Haddy's skinny hand out of the pocket and pushed the watch over his struggling fingers. And he laughed.

"Son, observe the time and fly from evil."

Mr. Haddy looked at Mother. He said, "Speerience."

"Keep it," Mother said. "You've been a good friend to us."

Smiling mournfully at the watch, and wetting his teeth, Mr. Haddy said, "But where you gung, Fadder?"

Father said, "We're going to paddle up the blackest creek in this lagoon. And we're going to find the smallest cranny of that creek, where there's no people or plagiarism. Trees, water, soil — the basics are all we require. We'll hole up there. They'll never find me."

"You ain't like Brewer's?"

"Too exposed," Father said. "I don't want to be visited by scavengers."

The pipanto had drifted toward Brewer's Village. It was belfry shacks and cooking fires and mud banks and wet Zambus and a dog.

"I want a real backwater. Solitary. Uninhabited. An empty corner. That's why we're here! If it's on a map, I can't use it."

"Laguna Miskita ain't on no chart."

"How small is it?"

"Fadder, it so small," Mr. Haddy said, "when you gets there you ain't believe you there."

While Father sculled the pipanto to the jetty, Mr. Haddy gave us directions: two miles along Brewer's shore to the cutoff, and then inland for three miles. "Go till you ain't go no more." Gratefulness made him prolong his directions, but when we dropped him and he slogged through the mud to his mother's hut, he did not look back. He was admiring his new watch, lifting his wrist, and soon he was surrounded by children, Creoles and Zambus, singing at him.

It was painful for me to see him go. He was not ours anymore. We were alone again — the first family, as Father kept repeating. But without our old friends — Mr. Haddy, and the Maywits, and our Zambus, and Ma Kennywick and the rest — it felt like the last family.

We had found the creek draining into Brewer's and made our exit. Father sculled to where it opened into a string of lagoons. The last was Laguna Miskita. It had to be — we could go no further. Except for another creek, which led sideways into it and was too small for even a cayuka, there was no more open water. It was nowhere, it was a dead end, there was not a hut to be seen. We turned over our pipanto on the shore and propped it up with poles. This was our house. There were herons and kingfishers here, and overhead some pelicans. In the low gray trees at the edge there stumbled some wild cows with cloudy eyes. The lagoon bubbled and streamed with stripes of decay. It was the color of cooked liver. Flies buzzed around us. Even the mud bubbled, and the pressure of rotten gas underground made holes on the banks, like the dimples on clam flats.

"We're alone here," Father said. "Look, no footprints!"

He said that from now on our life would be simple — gardening, fishing, and beachcombing. No poisonous contraptions, none of the Jeronimo mistakes, nothing fancier than a flush toilet. A vegetable plot here, a chicken run over there, a good solid hut that could take the rain.

"Chickens?" Mother said. "Where are you planning to get chickens?"

"Curassows," Father said. "Chickens is just a generic term. We'll raise curassows — we'll tame them."

"What else?"

"Nothing. That's the beauty of it. Survival means total activity. There isn't time for anything else!"

"It'll be an ordeal," Mother said.

"An ordeal is a square deal."

That night and for many nights afterward, we slept under the propped-up pipanto. It was cool at night and we made smudge pots to keep the mosquitoes away. Each day we worked at making the place comfortable. We had done it before, at Jeronimo, but until we started beachcombing we had no tools here, except the burned machete. We built a latrine and a cooking area and Father paced out a garden — the soil was so black and soft on the shore it would hardly need tilling, he said.

"It might be a couple of weeks before the rains start. In the meantime, we'll build a real house, a watertight one, and get those seeds ready for planting."

As soon as the new hut was underway, April got sick, then Clover, then Jerry, then Mother. It was the squitters, but they also turned pale and ran a high fever. They lay under the pipanto and groaned and made dashes to the latrine. Mother said it was all the travel and banging around and our diet, which was wild manioc and fish, and the carkles and whelks that we dug out of the mud.

"If it's the food, how come Charlie's not sick?" Father said. "Or if it's the hard work, why aren't I flat on my back?"

"How dare you accuse us of faking!" Mother said.

"Just asking."

"Don't bully us, Allie!"

Father went silent. It was scary, hearing them argue in the stillness of this gray lagoon, but their silence was worse. For two days they did not speak to each other, and, because of it, all we kids did was whisper.

Mother recovered, yet she was still weak. Father said, "The invalids can deal with the seeds," and they stripped the Miskito's vegetables and corn and dried the seeds while Father and I gathered material for the hut.

We had found an abandoned dugout. We patched it and caulked its cracks. "Some fool threw this away — it's a perfectly good boat!" We made daily trips down the creek and to Brewer's to gather driftwood — beams and planks that had floated through the coastal inlet and washed ashore. We found them stuck against the mud banks. Most of this wood had nails and screws in it. We removed these and once they were straightened used them for fastening the foundation of the hut. And beachcombing, harvesting what the tides deposited, gave us other treasures.

On the coast, all huts were belfries on stilts. Not Father's. His was like a small barge, the tublike foundation resting against the bank. He took great care to make it waterproof, tarring its cracks and then hammering strips of tin on it to seal it from rats and moisture. This barge-hut was bigger than a pipanto, but it was pipanto-shaped at its base.

A Zambu passed by one day. He did not see us until Father called him over. His face looked punched, but he wore a clean yellow shirt and a straw hat. His name was Childers. He was going to church. It was Sunday, he said.

Father said, "I wish you hadn't told me that."

Childers's laugh was mainly fright.

Father said, "If God hadn't rested on the seventh day, He might have finished the job. Ever think of that?"

Childers said, "You putting up a bodge there?"

"It's a house."

"Look like a bodge. Or a lanch."

It did — a roofed boat on the mud bank overlooking Laguna Miskita.

"When the rains come, I'm going to be dry as a nut. Think about it."

The Zambu considered this, then laughed again in his gagging way while Father faced him.

The difference between the two men surprised and scared me. The Zambu in his yellow shirt and straw hat and walking stick, and Father, tall and bony and red, with long greasy hair and a beard and wild eyes and a missing finger and sailcloth shorts. Father was skinnier than the Zambu! And I had not noticed until now just how wild looking he was. If you didn't know better, you would have thought he was the savage, and not the Zambu. If the Zambu had had hair and eyes like that I would have run for my life. But we had gotten used to Father looking like a live scarecrow, the wild man of the woods, and hollering.

Worry was making the Zambu chuckle as Father scampered around the hut, pointing out its advantages.

Notice how practical it was, he said. No poles, so it wouldn't shake down in an earthquake. No amount of rain could penetrate the tarred roof. It was made from the wreckage of ships that had foundered off the Mosquito Coast — each timber had been sealed and smoothed by the ocean. Two long cabins, adults and children, each with its own entrance. It had everything — privacy, strength, and grace. It would be standing here, Father said, long after all the palm-leaf shanties had been blown away by the summer storms.

"I want some bad storms, so I can prove I'm right. Then I'll curl up inside and laugh my head off. Thick walls keep it cool, and we get a breeze from end to end through the hatchway between the cabins. Plus, I can jack up the roof. I don't know why I'm bothering to tell you this."

Childers said, "Me roof ain't leak."

"We'll see. But frankly that's the big mistake you people make around here. Always talking about your roof, always concentrating on your top. What about your bottom?"

Childers had started to back away.

"Your bottom's just as important. You can't eliminate the problem by sticking your house on poles and sending it ten feet in the air. That only compounds it — makes you vulnerable, conspicuous, and temporary. Look at what happened in the States!"

Father's lecture had taken the Zambu by surprise. He did not reply. He was still walking backward along the muddy shore.

"This house is leakproof, top and bottom," Father said. "Is yours? Is your bottom leakproof?"

Now the Zambu saw Mother and the twins separating the seeds into piles. He tipped his hat in old-fashioned politeness.

"How is it, Ma?"

"Don't trample my garden," Father said.

The Zambu looked down. There was no garden. He tiptoed up the bank, crossing imaginary furrows.

"Now you're messing up my chicken run!"

The Zambu didn't see it. There was no chicken run. But he picked up his feet and framed his arms and frowned with fear, as if an invisible chicken run stood in his way.

"Remember this. Experience isn't an accident. It's a reward that's given to people who pursue it. That's a deliberate act, and it's hard work. You choose to go to church — funny place to go, considering the state of the world and how it got that way. On the seventh day, God left the room — why should you make the same lazy mistake? Why pray when you could be making a hut like this?"

"Got no tools." The Zambu was panicky. He started to run.

Father followed him, shouting.

"I don't have tools. Everything you see here I made with my own two hands!"

But the Zambu was gone. He disappeared along the creek bank in Brewer's direction. He could not have heard what Father said. It was just as well, because what Father had told him about the tools was untrue.

Father said, "I dislike that man for his malevolent curiosity."

We went back to work. Father had denied we had tools. It was a lie, another invention. It comforted him.

We had tools, and more than tools. The Mosquito shore provided us with most of the things we needed. We had found the head of a claw hammer on the beach and fitted it with a handle. By pounding the tips of heated spikes we had made screwdrivers and chisels. A rusty saw blade we had seen lying in seaweed was now gleaming from use. We retrieved wire and tin and bottles from the tide wrack, and torn nets that we patched, and enough sailcloth for Mother to make shorts for us all and a smock for herself. Her needles were bird bones. She could have had real needles from Brewer's Village, but Father liked the idea of killing birds ("Scavengers!") and sharpening their bones to make needles.

Beachcombing was dirty, exhausting work. Nearly every day during those early weeks at Laguna Miskita, in the crackling bat-haunted darkness before dawn, we took the dugout down the creek and across Brewer's to a shanty village called Mocobila. Just west of there, before the Zambus were awake, we searched the beach for usable items. We walked abreast, Father and I — and when they were well enough, the twins and Jerry joined us — picking through the tightly knotted mass of wood and rope and seaweed that had been deposited by the night tide.

We found more fishing tackle than we could ever use, and rope and rags and plastic jugs, and lumps of tar, and oars and canoe paddles and cooking pots and skillets. One day we found a six-foot ladder, and on two successive days toilet seats.

It was like scavenging in the Northampton dump, but scavenging was not a word I dared use with Father around. As in Northampton, the shore was always full of birds, and sometimes we had to fight them off the tide wrack in order to comb it. There were vultures on this beach, and one horrible day Father killed a vulture with a slingshot for no other reason than to show us how the rest of the vultures would feed on it.

"That's how it was in Northampton," Father said.

Jerry said, "You mean the dump?"

"The city," Father said. "All those school kids!"

We watched the vultures tear bloody lumps out of the dead bird's breast, while its wings shook like a broken umbrella.

The wood we found, and most fittings, had been washed clean and whitened by the sea. The metal was scabbed by rust or barnacles, but Father loved taking a bristling skillet and scrubbing it with sand. He restored the cooking pots, he mounted the toilet seats in our new latrine, and he made us sandals from rubber tires.

I was glad we were alone. No one could see our silly shorts and homemade sandals, or the junkyard we had made at Laguna Miskita. The Zambu Childers never came back.

"There's a kind of industrial Darwinism at work here," Father said. "The things that get to this beach are indestructible remnants that survived the storms and tides and the bite of the sea. They've proved themselves — stood the test of weather and time. By putting them to use, we are making a settlement that can't be destroyed. Your average Crusoe castaway lives like a monkey. But I'm no fool. Take those toilet seats. That's natural selection. The hoppers are gone, but they're everlasting."

He kicked aside the armless rubber dolls and odd sneakers and chunks of plastic foam. He railed at the ripped life jackets and rusted aerosol cans. We got used to him saying, "Now there's a perfectly good eyebolt — "

Mother called him a magpie. I thought it was his voice, but it was his beachcombing, all the junk collecting. He would bring things back to the camp that had no practical use — the horse collar was one, the light plug another — and say, "Their use will be revealed — "

Apart from his talk about the United States ("It was terrible" — why was he smiling?), he had not changed. But our circumstances had changed a lot. We had a house and food and a routine, and yet life here was difficult. It took all day. Total activity was good, Father said — the job of survival made you healthy. But we were often ill with the squitters and fever and sand-flea bites, and had to stay in the hammocks. Mother picked the nits and lice out of our hair. Every cut became infected and had to be scrubbed with hot seawater.

Father was never ill.

"I'm not boasting. I just don't give in. I fight it. Keep clean and you'll never be sick."

We had come to Laguna Miskita with one bar of soap. Father would not say where he had gotten it. I guessed that he had hooked it from the Miskito Indian on the Rio Sico, after his shower bath. This soap was soon gone. But there was a shop at Mocobila, run by a Creole named Sam. Father called him Uncle Sam. He sold flour and oil and axheads and fishhooks to the local Zambus. Father avoided the shop.

Uncle Sam saw us beachcombing one day and asked Father if he knew anything about generators. His was busted. Father fixed it but would not take money in return. At last, after Uncle Sam pestered him, Father agreed to take a case of cheese-colored laundry soap. It was the only thing we lacked at Laguna Miskita, Father said. "And by the time we've used it up, I'll have figured out a way of making some myself." He reminded us that we had made soap in Jeronimo out of pig fat. "Good for what ails you. You could eat it!"

This was not the riverside rain forest and cloud jungle that we had begun to like in Jeronimo. It was coastal and low, salty, hot, full of skinny flies. There were no tapirs or otters here, only lizards and ratlike animals and seabirds that turned greasy when they were roasted. We killed the birds for their downy feathers, not their tough meat, because Father wanted soft pillows. We were surrounded by swamps in which dead trees stood. The trees were naked and gray. Fungus grew where the bark had dropped off. At sundown, these swamps whistled with bats. There were palms. Father challenged

Jerry and me to climb them and hack the coconuts down. Jerry was afraid of heights, he cried before he got halfway up, and on the ground he told me Father was "a crapster."

"If you don't cooperate with him, he'll hate you," I said.

"I want him to hate me," Jerry said.

Sometimes I thought that now we were alone, we knew each other better and liked each other less. Father knew we were weak and afraid. There were arguments. There was nowhere to hide. We longed to be back at the Acre.

It was still the dry season — where was the rain? After three weeks here, we noticed that the level of the water in Laguna Miskita had been falling about a foot a week. Broken boats were exposed, holed cayukas in the shallows, and cow skulls and fish bones, black with mud. The gunwales of a rowboat appeared one day, outlined like a church window on the surface of the lagoon. We dragged it to shore and discovered a slimy outboard motor was clamped to it. Father took the motor apart and began cleaning it, piece by piece. We used the boat for a washtub — "That's all these missionary dinghies are good for."

Mother said it was pointless to tinker with an old outboard motor when there was so much planting to do. The seeds had just begun to sprout in the shallow boxes. They would have to be planted in rows soon.

This turned into an argument. If we had been nearby, they would not have yelled as they did. But we kids were in the dugout, fishing for eels. We used the kind of weighted circular net we had seen the man throwing into the sea our first day at La Cciba. I had felt sorry for him. But now we were like that poor fisherman.

From the cove, we heard Father say, "I'm not going to throw this Evinrude away. You never know when it might come in handy."

"The magpie."

We could not see them. Their voices skimmed across the lagoon. Splintered echoes reached us from the dead trees and the shore, where beached hyacinths stranded by the dropping water had started to curl up.

"This magpie saved your life, Mother. If it wasn't for me, you'd all be dead."

"You can't boast about Jeronimo. You endangered our lives in the first place."

"Who the heck is talking about Jeronimo?"

"Saved our lives — that's what you said."

"Jeronimo was just an error of judgment. I was too ambitious there. I thought ice was the answer. But now I know that self-preservation is the only important thing. I saved your lives by *taking* you to Jeronimo!"

"You blew us up!"

"I got you out of the United States. America is sunk, Mother. I mean that literally."

"How do you know?"

"This is the proof."

He jangled something we could not see.

"Trash," Mother said.

"Beachcomber's booty. It is the detritus of a dead civilization. The buoyant part. America has foundered, and these things have floated to our lonely shore."

"That's a crazy explanation."

"I agree. But the world ran crazy. And we came here. Do you know a better place?"

"Allie, you'll kill us here!"

Her voice shimmered, amplified by the water. We stayed in the cove, clutching the net and the paddles, listening.

Clover said, "Ma's starting trouble. It's all her fault."

Jerry said, "You're a crapster, too, Clover. Ma's right. It's miserable here. I hope she bangs him on the head."

April said, "I want to run away from this crummo place."

I told them all to shut up or I would overturn the canoe and make them swim for it.

"What if Dad's right?" I said. And we listened.

Now he was saying, "I am making life tolerable for you. More than tolerable! This is a bed of roses compared to the wasteland we left behind."

"In Jeronimo?"

"In the United States! There are only scavengers left! We're the first family, Mother. We know what happened up there. As soon as we get our crops in the ground, we'll be self-sufficient."

"Your garden is imaginary. Your chickens are imaginary. There is no crop. We haven't planted anything. You talk about livestock and weaving! There's nothing here but trash from the beach. All you do is fool with that motor. Look at yourself, Allie. You don't look human."

It was what I had thought when the churchgoing Zambu, Childers, came by in his clean shirt. So Mother had noticed, too.

"I'm asking you to look into the future," Father said. "Use your imagination. I'll be proved right. But I'm no tyrant. I won't keep you here against your will. If you're not satisfied, you can — "

There was no more. We listened, but all we heard was the cuff of water against the dugout's sides, and the squawk of herons. We paddled out of the cove and saw that the yard was empty, the fire unattended. The junkpile of wood and metal from the beach looked like storm litter at a tidemark.

Then we saw Father. He was alone, wearing a pair of mismatched rubber boots, tall and short. He did not speak. Had he guessed that we had overheard the quarrel?

He had started troweling the garden on the mud bank, just above the lagoon. We joined him and, without a word, helped him dig the furrows for the seedlings. We worked in a sulky and ashamed way for the rest of the afternoon.

Mother appeared at nightfall. She hugged us. She had been out walking, she said. But there was nowhere to walk. Her legs were muddy to her knees, there were burrs in her hair. And her face was smeared. She had been crying.

"Have a shower bath," Father said. "It'll do you a world of good."

Jerry said, "Ma, how long are we going to stay in this place?"

She did not speak. She stared at Father.

Father said, "Answer him, Mother."

"The rest of our lives," she said.

Father seemed pleased. He smiled and said, "We're in luck — looks like rain."

24

STRIPS OF glue-colored cloud streaked past the breaks in the blue sky overhead, but beyond our lagoon, in Brewer's direction, a dense cloud bank formed every afternoon. It stayed and trembled. It was gray-black, the texture of steel wool. There was a mountainside of it, and it hung and thickened until night swept across it.

Each morning the cloud bank was gone, and the strips and puffs of cloud were like gas balloons against a fine ceiling. The black cloud always returned later, looking crueler. There was no rain.

Father howled at us to help him plant the garden. He got madder by the day. He said we were bone lazy and slow and never showed up when he needed us. He was mad about the rain. He had promised it, but it had not come. He howled hardest at Jerry. Jerry had a new name for him: "Farter."

We expected the rain to be plumping down, the way it had in Jeronimo — black rods of it beating into the trees. But there was only the daily upsweep of black cloud, and uncertain winds. Father said it was squalls offshore and that at any minute we would be drenched. We worked and waited in the still heat, watching the high dark sky over the twiggy treetops to the east. The storm lurked and watched us with its hanging wrinkles. It came no closer.

Our lagoon water was still dropping. Lily pads swung on long stems. The land was so dry that the mud had hardened as stiff and smooth as cement. To plant our seedlings — the sprouted beans and corn and the tiny tomato seedlings — meant cracking the mud-bank crust and making troughs. We lugged water in buckets and dumped it into these creases, to keep the roots soaked.

That was our job, the kids' bucket brigade, while Father worked to outrig the mechanical pump. He made one that jacked water into wooden sluices, a series of gutters with handles that trapped and seesawed the lagoon water up the mud bank with a great flapping and banging of boards. But it took seven men to operate this pump, and Father was continually thundering at us, so we kept on with the buckets.

"Why does it just hang there?" he said, twisting his face at the black cloud. "Why doesn't it rain?"

Water carrying and food snatching were our only activities, and still the heat dried our ditches and withered some of our garden plants. In the evening we ate manioc and mudfish and boiled plantains. Father was secretive. He would not let us see him eat or sleep. "I'm waiting until things improve here. I won't rest until they do — and you won't catch me eating that stuff." He said that going without food he needed less sleep.

He used the night hours to rebuild the outboard motor. He chafed the parts and cut new gaskets for the piston assembly. But we had no gas or oil, and there were empty sockets in the motor where the spark plugs should have been. He did not seem to care. He greased it with pelican fat and yanked the starting rope, strangling it and making it chatter and choke. It gave off the smell of roasted pelican.

Mother called the outboard motor his toy.

"That gizmo's keeping me sane," Father said.

Hearing this, Mother held her breath and stared at him until he turned away.

"Rain!" he screamed at the black cloud.

His voice was so loud, so insistent and commanding, that we hunched our shoulders, expecting a downpour. But there was only the cloud and the shifting wind.

He shook his hands and said, "When I came here to the Mosquito Coast, I was appalled that these people had done so little to better themselves. They lived like hogs. I used to wince at their weedy crops and their pathetic houses. What do they eat — corn shucks? Do they chew their toes? Do they sleep face-down and let the rain run off their shoulders? What do they use to wipe themselves with? Where's their tools? Do they dream, and, if so, what of?"

We were down at the garden, drenching the plants. We held our buckets still in order to listen.

"That's what I used to think," he said. "Now, after a year, it amazes me that they've got so much!"

"Jerry says you don't respect the Zambus," Clover said.

Jerry, betrayed, looked worried and unhappy.

"I'm full of admiration for them," Father said. "Even though they do live like hogs. But that's not for me — living day to day, hand to mouth. That's not my style. This is a permanent settlement. I never promised it would be easy. We're laying proper foundations. This is an organism. When it's working, thing will be different."

"Thinking out loud," he spoke of rearing curassows like turkeys, and starting another fish farm, and curing meat in a smokehouse. The real problem wasn't food, he said — it was dirt. He wanted to fix planks over the mud bank, which was our yard, and make a deck, a section at a time, and turn it into a wide screened-in porch, with a bathhouse. Healthy food, cleanliness, plenty of hot water, and no insects.

"I see a hatchery here and a water tower over there, and a boiler. Lack of ice isn't a problem in the tropics, but lack of hot water is — who would have guessed that? I see a kind of intersecting set of walkways to a mooring, and trestles around the garden, with plants growing between them. All bridges and boardwalks — your feet never touch the ground."

We would make this lagoon camp into an enormous pier!

It was a good idea, but so far all we had was the small watertight hut on the mud bank, and a junkyard — a pile of wood and scrap metal, eight feet high, that we had dragged piece by piece from the beach. Father said that he intended to sort it out, but there was no time. The garden, our best hope for survival, kept us busy. And already rats had found the junkpile and were nesting in it and squalling with the kinkajous, the nightwalkers.

Our camp looked worse than any Miskito or Zambu settlement I had seen. I was glad we got no visitors, because I knew they would find it strange. If they did not laugh at us, they would pity us. It was clear that we had come here with nothing, and now owned only what we had found on the beach.

In the late afternoon, when the black cloud hung in the east and our smoke was rising, our settlement looked like a dump on a gray shore, where desperate people had come to die. "We're escaped prisoners," Father said. That's what he thought of America. But if we were lost, and trapped in this coastal swamp, weren't we still prisoners?

It was the feeling I had when I saw our hut and the junk from the dugout, from the middle of the lagoon. Jerry and I had learned the knack of using the circular net, and we were excused bucket brigade if we brought back fish or eels. We liked paddling to the far end of the lagoon, so we couldn't see what Father called home.

About a week after the storm cloud first appeared, Jerry and I were in the dugout, fishing, and heard a loud noise. It sounded like cannonfire.

"Dad's started the outboard," Jerry said.

It was what I had thought, or wanted to think — it would take an outboard to get us out of here.

We paddled to the settlement, where Father was standing on the dry solid mud. His eyes were empty. He was listening.

Jerry said, "You got the outboard going!"

"What if I did?"

"We can go home," Jerry said.

It was a forbidden word.

"Sucker!" Father said.

The loud sound banged again. It was not the outboard. It was the roar of distant thunder.

"Why don't you ever believe me?"

The thunder kept on, sometimes like cannons and sometimes, slowly and terribly, like brick walls collapsing into a cellar. Like a whole civilization keeling over and ruining itself on its own dead weight, Father said. It was out there, where the cloud was. He grinned at us. "War!"

From the opposite side of the lagoon came a loopy reply to the thunder — *googn! googn! googn! googn!* — and the same four notes again, but softer. It was a howler monkey. Each time the thunder roared, the howler monkeys drummed and googned.

There was an even odder result of the thunder. All around the lagoon, as if woken by the noise, creatures began to break out of their buried eggs. First the tortoises and iguanas emerged, then the alligators. The eggs were hidden in the mud, but when these slippery scaly things crawled out, they dragged the shells with them and left this broken eggshell crockery on the bank. Beneath the booming skies the lagoon came creepily alive.

During this thunder period, Mr. Haddy shuffled down the bankside from Brewer's approach. He was bright-eyed and grinning like a hatched iguana, with phlegm on his front teeth. He brought us a parcel of conch meat and a live chicken tied up with string, and a bag of sugar. He scratched his back by pushing it against a tree, all the while staring at our junkpile. Then he kissed the twins and said, "How is it? Is it right here?"

"Pass me that rope, Charlie," Father said. He showed no surprise at Mr. Haddy's visit, and when I gave him the rope he wound it around the spool of the Evinrude and jerked it, making it go *whop-whop-whop* and stink of bird fat. Father's hair flew.

"Brang you some conk."

"Do I look hungry?" Father then ignored him and went on jerking the starting spool.

"Wheep! Wheep! Wheep!" Mr. Haddy mimicked the noise very well. "That is a spearmint for true!"

"This?"

"A motor with no sparks and no erl!"

"This is just to keep me sane." Father made it spin again. "Helps me think. I'm planning my boiler and my walkways. You've got to keep the mud off somehow!"

"Brang you some sugar."

"White sugar," Father said. "It's the worst possible thing you can stick in your mouth. Not an ounce of nutrition in it, only calories that burn up so fast they fizzle every B and C vitamin in your body. It gives you cramps, causes kidney failure, makes you tired, and — did you know this? — it's as addictive as dope. Figgy, I came here to get away from that poison."

"I bring you gas and erl next time," Mr. Haddy said. "And a set of sparks."

"Don't want them."

"Why you burning chicken fat?"

"Because we're not going anywhere," Father said.

Mr. Haddy saw Jerry.

"How is it, Jerry-man?"

"Don't talk to him. He's in the doghouse."

Mother said, "I can't imagine how you found us."

"Come down the cutoff. Look this way and that. I have a speerience, then I hear Fadder's voice. How you like this tonda? Man, we gung get some storms, Ma!"

He looked around our camp and sniffed like a rabbit, taking it in. "Hell of a place this Miskita lagoon."

"We're still getting settled," Mother said. "It doesn't look like much at the moment, but Allie has plans. You know Allie."

"Spearmints," Mr. Haddy said.

Father did not smile. He wrenched the engine with his rope and said, "Back to work, people."

"You garden pretty close up to the water. That you bodge?"

"Hut," Mother said.

"House," Father said.

"House, huh?" Mr. Haddy traced its shape with his head. "House pretty close up to the water, for true."

"The water's over there," Father said, opening his mouth wide to say it plainly. He pointed down the mud bank to the lagoon shore.

"Gung be up here when this rain come. Gung be over that trashpile. How that trashpile get there? Howlies? Baboon? Jacketman?"

Father came close to Mr. Haddy with his rope, looking as if he was going to twist it around the poor man's stringy neck. He said, "Why are you trying to upset everyone?"

Mr. Haddy appealed to Mother. "I ain't trying, Ma!"

"Allie's just mad because it hasn't rained."

Father said, "I have no control over the elements. If I had, the world wouldn't be such a mess. Talk to me about things I can control. Like my temper. Which I'm controlling at this moment."

"It rain when it ready," Mr. Haddy said. "And when it come, you wants it to go way. That how it is. We gung get some rain for true. That gung be speerience!"

"You haven't stated your business," Father said. "What exactly do you want?"

"Say hello and how is it. Tell you about me new boat."

"Tell us how you lost your new watch."

So that was it. Father had noticed; none of us had. Mr. Haddy was not wearing the gold watch Father had given him. That was why Father was acting ratty.

Mr. Haddy said, "That the same story as the boat story. I swupped me watch for me boat. Not a lanch. Sailing boat. Couldn't work her through the cutoff in this low water, so I walked. Want to see her?"

"No," Father said.

"I call her *Omega*, like the watch. She a pretty thing."

"I had that watch fifteen years."

"It three — three-thirty," Mr. Haddy said, turning his pleading eyes at the halo of hazy sun, to prove that he knew the time without the watch.

"He just gave it away!" Father said.

Mother said, "I thought you approved of that sort of thing."

"For me boat," Mr. Haddy said. "She a *sweet* boat."

"A boat ain't the answer."

"I ain't ask no question."

"Try asking yourself where you're going to be in fifteen or twenty years."

"Tell you where I be next week — Cabo Gracias." Mr. Haddy turned to Mother. "Got me a job. Shipping conks and hicatees out of Caratasca. Take them down to Cabo Gracias. You know the place?"

Mother said no.

"That is the Cape, on Wonks' mouth. She is some river. Make this Patuca look like a piddle. Want to come down, Ma?"

Mother said, "I'd love to. We could bring the kids."

"I take you for a good sail, sure. Look at the manatees. Look at the turkles. Few weeks more and that place be crazy with turkles laying eggs. The sweet green water and the nice sand. Kids go swimming, we go fish, and all the world is right here."

It was what I had hoped for, but one look at Father told me that it would never happen. His face was black. He waved us away and howled at Mother.

"Will you please stop encouraging him! We've hardly started on the garden. We have the boardwalk to build, and the fishpond and the chicken run. I'm trying to lay a solid foundation here, and I'm getting no help at all. Figgy," he said, towering over Mr. Haddy, "can't you see that we've got work to do?"

"That is the other reason why I come," Mr. Haddy said nervously, gripping his wrist to hide the place where his watch had been. "This Miskita lagoon ain't no place for decent folks. It a swump and a bother. They got tails up here. Them baboons — hear them? They worrying about the rain, and they worrying for true. Cause when the rain come, they gung be frashing and you spearmint gung be all wet, Fadder."

"What are you suggesting?"

"Brewer's pretty decent for a family."

"He's suggesting it's indecent here. This savage, who gave my watch away, is insinuating — "

Mother said, "Don't be so rude, Allie."

"Someone sent him here. Who sent you, Fig?"

"No, man!"

"You go back and tell whoever sent you that this is our home now. We live here. This is a pioneering effort."

Mr. Haddy chewed his lips.

Jerry spoke up. "I want to go with Mr. Haddy."

"See what you've gone and done!"

Mr. Haddy tried to move. But his feet had become big and undependable. He dragged them — still holding tight to his wrist — he stumbled, he almost sat down.

"All right, Jerry — drop your bucket and go. Get a move on. But remember this. If you go, you go for good. Don't come back. I don't want to see your face again."

"Allie!" Mother said.

"That's policy," Father said to Jerry. "Are you man enough to do it?"

Jerry blushed and he looked away as tears came to his eyes.

"Then get back to work, boy." Father's voice was like sandpaper.

Clover said, "I didn't want to go in the first place, Dad," and Jerry glared at her.

"These conchs will make a lovely stew," Mother said. "Take a seat, Mr. Haddy."

But Mr. Haddy had not recovered from "See what you've gone and done!" He glanced down at his feet, perhaps wondering why they would not take him out of here. Then he eyed Father and looked afraid.

Father said, "And here it comes."

The black cloud had massed in the east while Father had been thundering. The wind dropped, and for a little while there was no air to breathe. Sweat darkened Father's beard.

"I hate that thing."

The cannon roar, the crumbling walls, the bricks booming in America's cellar.

"Tonda pillitin rock-stone!" Mr. Haddy usually worried in Creole.

"And I'll tell you something else. I know why you came here today — because you finally heard about the trouble in the States."

I wanted Mr. Haddy to speak. He was silent. Father took a step toward him. Mr. Haddy's body said no, but his face said yes.

"Admit it, Figgy," Father said, and another thundercrack shook the lagoon.

"I hear something about it," Mr. Haddy said.

"That it was wiped out!"

"Yes, Fadder."

"And you're scared," Father said. He was staring Mr. Haddy in the face.

"For true."

"That's why," Father said slowly — he was smiling — "I call this the future."

The barge-hut on the mud bank, the rowboat, the sluice pump that took seven men to work, the garden of seedlings, the trashpile, the flies, the rats jumping, and the howler monkeys drumming *googn! googn! googn! googn!*

When a person is suffering and afraid, his ailments are obvious and his injuries stick out. I saw a dent in Mr. Haddy's forehead that I had never seen before.

Father said, "Before you go, look around — tell me what you see."

Mr. Haddy glanced from side to side, and swallowed, and said, "You talking about that trashpile, Fadder?"

Jerry whispered to me, "Trashpile is right. This whole place is a dump. That's why I wanted to go. Didn't you?"

"I see a thriving village," Father was saying. "I see healthy kids. Corn in the fields, tomatoes on the vines. Fish swimming and pumps gurgling. Big soft beds. Mother weaving on a loom. Curassows that eat out of your hand. Monkeys that pick coconuts. A ropeworks. A smokehouse. Total activity! That's what I see. And anyone — "

Mr. Haddy had started away. He was hurrying now, driven by the force of Father's words. There were only words. None of the things existed. Then Mr. Haddy was gone, and Father was speaking to us.

" — anyone who doesn't see it has no business here."

Soon, he was snapping his rope at the outboard. It was like strangulation.

I was thinking of Mr. Haddy, stumbling on his big flapping feet in the dark, when Jerry said again, "Didn't you, Charlie? Didn't you want to go with him?"

"No," I said.

"Dad's crazy."

The way he said it gave me goose pimples.

"That's why I want to go," he said. He started to sob, but he put his face down. He did not want me to see him.

"If we don't help him, we'll all die," I said.

"I don't want to help him!"

Jerry was miserable. He squalled about Dad persecuting him and favoring the twins. Dad kept coming up to him and saying, "You're awfully dirty." He called him a slacker. He made him climb trees. Of all of us, Jerry had been the sickest with the squitters, and he looked it — pale cheeks, dusty long hair, and a skinny neck, and scabs where he had scratched at his fleabites.

The weather had affected Father. In the humid heat and silence of the lagoon, he had fallen silent. With the thunder he had begun to argue with Mother. He became moody, he yelled, he picked on Jerry. He knew that Jerry called him Farter, and now he would not leave the poor kid alone. Jerry was angry and helpless.

"I want to go home," Jerry said. It was the forbidden word.

"This is home," I said. I told him that as America had been destroyed, we had escaped just in time. There was nothing of it left, except what washed up on the beach near Brewer's Lagoon.

"That's what Dad says."

"Mr. Haddy said so, too!"

"I don't care," Jerry said. He scratched his bites. He had never looked sicker. "I'm sorry Mr. Haddy went away. He'll never come back."

"Don't you see? We have to trust Dad."

"I don't trust him. He's just a man who sleeps in our hut."

I could not cheer him up. And his anger gave me doubts, so — secretly, while Father was out hammering a coop for the curassows he planned to rear — I asked Mother. What had happened to the United States — had it been destroyed?

The question made her sad. But she said, "I hope so."

"No," I said.

"Yes." She pushed my hair out of my eyes and hugged me. "Because if it has been, we're the luckiest people in the world."

"I said, "What if it hasn't?"

"Then we're making a horrible mistake," she said.

I was too big for her lap. I knelt beside her and thought for a moment that Father's hammering and the thunder was the sound of her heart.

"But it has," she said. "You heard Mr. Haddy."

And I had heard the thunder. But that, too, was a promise without proof. Mother was asking me to believe her. It was like the weather, this thunder period that was all sudden noise, promises of rain and storms. No one knew when it would come, or what it would be like, or how long we would have to go on watering our straggly garden of flopped-over seedlings. No one knew anything.

25

WHEN THE RAIN did come, it was so thick it was as if we were being punished for doubting the thunder — and then I believed everything. It did not plump down, but fell like iron swords out of the black sky, slicing our backs and twisting branches from the trees. It tore into the sand, it cracked against boulders, it beat against the sea and made a clatter beyond the surf. It was not like water at all, but like blades and buckshot.

We were at the beach that day — Jerry, Father, and I — hoicking up wire for the coop. From the east there were waterspouts, five of them, then five more, and the cloud bank burst apart and came at us, bluish-black. Big hard drops were flung out of it, and skins of rain shook our way, and long mops of shower swished toward the beach.

Father's cap flew off and his clothes flapped and turned black and stuck to his muscles. His beard dripped and at his feet was a spackle and spurt as the rain dug pebbles out of the ground. He began shouting almost at once. He raised his fists. We listened carefully to him, and even Jerry was obedient — no talk of "Farter" now. We had not expected this, though Father was pleased and almost choking as the buckshot hit his face.

"This is it! What did I tell you? Grab that wire — look alive!"

We slogged across the haulover sand and headed back to our lagoon, fighting the wind, which was blowing from the jungle. Father was sculling like mad and grinning as the rain dashed the creek. There were three inches of water in the dugout as we left the neck of the creek, and there we saw the squall hit the lagoon and whip it, stirring lumps out of it.

"The wind's veering," Father said. "It's a rotary storm."

Jerry said, "We won't have to water the garden now."

Where was the garden? Where was the hut? The lagoon had gone dark. The white margin squeezed against the bank was the froth of waves. Then I saw it. Under the stooping trees, through the blowing glint of the rain, lay the huddle of our camp, drenched black, while everything heaved around it — flying branches, tattered leaves, fists of water.

Father said, "I'll find something for you to do, Jerry. This rain's put us back into business." He took Jerry by the arm and screamed, "Now do you believe me?"

The rain lashed Jerry's face, but Father's hand was under Jerry's chin, lifting Jerry's face to that fury.

"Yes," Jerry said, and the rain was in his mouth. "Yes, please!"

The shutters of the hut were down and latched. Mother and the twins were inside, but the bullet noise of the rain on the roof was so loud we could not hear each other speak. With the windows sealed, the air was flat and stifling. We sat cross-legged, eating fish and eddoes, listening to the rain batter our camp and burst against the hut.

Father smiled and made the lip motions of, "We're perfectly dry."

Mother frowned, as if to say, "It's all terrible."

"Ingrate!" Father yelled, above the storm.

There were noises all night — the scrape of loose boards blowing out of the junkpile, the crash of trees falling nearby, the sizzle-smack of rain on the tin patches of our hut walls. It excited me and made my heart beat fast. That flipping of my heart kept me awake. I imagined that the rain had driven the rats out of the junkpile. They were desperate, massing around the hut, their wet black backs moving like a greasy torrent, and they were gnawing our walls. The storm had made the country seem vast. We were not at the shore of a lagoon. We were a speck in the hugeness of Honduras, at the rim of its violent coast.

The shutters strained to open. It was the pressure of wind, lifting them and rattling the hinges. The four of us kids slept in the forward part of the hut. The other kids were asleep. I lay awake, as I had the night we rushed out of Jeronimo, and tonight the frantic sound of rain was like fire — flames cracking against the house, filling the air with the ashy stink of mud. I pressed on my heart to slow it, so that I could breathe and sleep.

One shutter was shaking worse than the others. I grabbed it, to steady it, and it banged my thumb. When I pulled my hand away, the boards began a fearful rattling and, before I could secure it, the whole shutter lifted, splintering one board and yanking screws out of the hasp. Rain shot through the window. I reached for the flapping shutter, and a cold wet thing closed over my hand. Before I could scream, another cold wet thing reached in and felt for my mouth.

"Don't bawl," a bubbly voice said.

My first thought was that it was Father, with a crazy nighttime idea. The sour fingers were on my teeth. I said, "Dad — "

But it was Mr. Haddy, his dripping face at the window and his wet eyes bugged out. He let go of me and whispered, "Come here, quick."

I slipped out wearing only my shorts. It was one of Father's Jeronimo ideas — wear as little as possible in the rain, Father said, because skin dries faster than clothes.

Mr. Haddy was standing in the mud with his arms hanging down. I could not see him clearly, but I could hear the rain beating on his hat.

"Busted you hatchcover," he said.

"You scared me." I was shivering with cold. The rain blistered on me and stung my skin.

Taking my hand, and putting his face so close to mine that the rain dribbled from his face to mine, Mr. Haddy said, "You ain't tell Fadder I come here in this" — lightning made his face go purple and his lips black and his teeth blue — "Mudder!"

"How did you get here?"

"Poled and rowed," he dribbled. "You a good boy for true, Charlie."

I had the impression that he was very hungry and that he was going to bite me.

"The creek's not wide enough for a pair of oars."

"She rising."

I saw his rowboat on the bank.

"Come in the hut and get dry," I said.

"Fadder inside?"

"Yes."

"I ain't gung." He slopped to the bank. "I got some parcel of cargo for you."

He heaved a barrel out of the stern of the boat and squashed it into the mud. Then he squatted near it and took a plastic pouch out of his pocket and handed it to me.

"This is sparks and that is gas-erl. You take um."

"It's raining, Mr. Haddy," was all I could say. It was midnight, and stormy, and he had broken a shutter and clamped his hand over my mouth — to bring these things. What were they for?

"Raining for true. That is why I come here."

"Dad's asleep." I hoped he was.

"He vex with me." Mr. Haddy rolled the barrel along the bank and pushed it into the junkpile and leaned a log against it. He said, "This is for Fadder's outboard engine."

"What shall I do with them?"

"You ain't tell him where they come from. Tell him you found um. Charlie, you wants me to die?"

"No."

"Then don't mention Haddy," he said. "Now help me lanch me boat."

We dragged the boat into the water and Mr. Haddy got in. The lightning broke over the trees at the far end of the lagoon. A yellow-blue glimmer swelled in the sky, stuttering like a fluorescent tube, and lit the ugly clouds. Now Mr. Haddy was hunched over his oars.

"She gung fill up. All the rivers gung be high and you garden gung be drowning. They gung be water everywhere. Then maybe Fadder fix his outboard engine and come down to Brewer's. We look after him. I take all yous to the Wonks. Do some fishing and turkle catching."

"He doesn't want anyone to look after him."

"You want to get drownded?"

"Father won't let us drown. He's got a plan. He wants it to rain. It's dry inside the hut. This is our home."

Googn!

"Them baboon just hear you, Charlie."

The howler monkeys were drumming in the thunder rumble

across the black lagoon, and the rain's boom and crackle made a deep cave of the earth and filled the sky with dangerous boulders, too big to see. And all around us in the wet and noise was this dark edge of monkeys.

It made me remember.

I said, "Mr. Haddy, is it true about the United States — has it been wiped out?"

"Hard! Hard! Everywhere! Look" — but there was nothing to see — "she flooding!"

"Are you sure? Where did you hear it? You mean, there's nothing — "

She flodden, he kept repeating in a terrified voice. He moved his arms. The propped-up oars helped me pick out surfaces.

"Everything gone!"

That was the last I heard. He splashed the blades and turned the boat aside and rowed into the rain, groaning indistinctly. The shore fell away. He took the lagoon with him, and all the trees, and left me standing in the sting of straight-down rain. The night's black was above and below me. The rain closed over Mr. Haddy and the kick of his oars. He was like a man rowing into a mountain.

It was all rain and monkey howls in this pit of unseparated darkness. *Googn! Googn! Googn! Googn!*

In the morning, steam rose from the cold boilings of the lagoon, and from the root knuckles and beaten-down grass and broken trees. The land was covered with pink worms. It looked shocked by the twelve hours of heavy rain. It lay thrashed and still.

Most of the sprouts in our garden were pasted against the mud as flat as stamps, or else floated in the troughs we had dug. Our whole shelf of furrows had slipped sideways down the bank and lay bunched at the shore. The garden was waterlogged: the smaller sprouts were drowned, the bigger ones tipped over and showing the pale hairs on their roots. Twigs, ripped leaves, and branches littered the lagoon.

Father said, "I'll be willing to bet that we're the only dry folks in the country, if not the world."

"It rains in our yard and he thinks the whole world is wet," Jerry whispered. "Why can't we leave?"

I took Jerry aside and showed him the barrel of gasoline and the spark plugs.

"We can bomb out of here with that outboard," Jerry said. He was happier than I had seen him for weeks. "We can find Mr. Haddy. He'll take us home!"

"We can't go home," I said. "It's gone. Dad was right — "

"No!"

"Mr. Haddy told me. He wouldn't lie. Please don't cry."

But he had started. He put his arm against his face to hide it.

"We'll go somewhere else," I said. "We'll go to Brewer's Village, or somewhere on the coast better than this." I kept talking to him this way to stop him crying, and then I swore him to secrecy about the gasoline and the spark plugs.

Clover was at the shore with Father and saying, "Our nice garden's ruined."

"It'll perk up in this sun," Father said, and he made us dig ditches to drain it.

Overnight the trees around the lagoon had turned bright green, their leaves washed by the rain. They glistened with a shine like fresh paint. The gray was gone from the whole place, and under the clear sky the lagoon was deep blue. The land was black. Bird honks skimmed across the water.

Driftwood had been scattered from the junkpile, but after Jerry and I picked it up and stacked it, the barrel of gasoline was hidden. I pushed the pouch of spark plugs under my hammock pad. What good were they to us if Father was determined to stay? But his outboard motor, which was the first thing I checked that morning, had not been shifted by the storm. It was still clamped to its stump, and was wrapped tight in plastic like a leg of meat.

Father said you had to admire this foolish waste of energy — nature running mad and drenching everything. It was a huge demented squandering of water, like an attempted murder that a quick-witted man could overcome by crawling into his leakproof hut: all that trouble for nothing, because we were still alive.

"But we weren't meant to die!"

The storm had terrified everyone except Father. He was impressed by the way it had destroyed trees, and he marveled at all the uprootings. He calculated that six inches of rain had fallen in the night. You had to admire that. And look at the beaten bushes. And think of the velocity. You could build a machine that operated on falling rain — the collected rain would spin a flywheel, the same principle as a water wheel but more efficient — no drag. Only the rain was undependable, because the world was imperfect. Nature tried to burn you, then starve you, then drown you, and it made you dig a garden like a savage with a stick. It surprised you and made you fearful that something was going to go wrong. That fear made people religious nuts instead of innovators.

"But it will be weeks before anyone plants a garden, and by then ours will be in blossom."

Mother said the damage scared her. We would have to fight to save the garden.

Father said, "I like a good fight."

In the course of that hot day, most of the plants perked up just as he said they would. Even the little shoots followed Father's orders, and what in the early morning had looked like the ruin of a drowned garden had begun again to grow.

The important thing now, Father said, was to protect the plants. It was not the amount of rain that was so bad, but its ferocity: the wind, the waterspouts, the erosion. "If we don't take care, the plants will be punched out of their holes," he said. "But we *will* take care."

We sawed lengths of bamboo and fitted some of the plants with collars, and others we banked with dirt to prop them up. Father said, Wasn't that ingenious?

"I'll believe it when we have vegetables," Mother said.

"Patience!"

Toward evening, the clouds sailed in and the first drops hit us like slugs. Father ordered Jerry and me to work naked at repairing the garden, and so we did, up to our ankles in mud, with the rain whipping our backs.

"He treats us like slaves," Jerry said. "I'd like to get that outboard working and escape from here."

"We've already escaped," I said.

"Even if America's burned — even if it's destroyed — it's better than this. This is a stinking dump. I want to go home."

"But the garden's all right now," I said. "When it grows, things will be different."

"Why are you always on Dad's side?"

"He was right about the rain — he was right about the garden!"

"It's still raining," Jerry said. Thunder compressed his face and gave him a frightened smile. The fat raindrops riddled on our little hut.

The next day, half the garden was gone. Some of the plants floated in the lagoon, where they had been washed with the storm's debris, and others lay broken in the furrows. The bamboo collars had done no good. They served only to bruise the plants under the strength of the falling rain.

"It's no use," Mother said.

"You make me laugh," Father said. "You talk as if we have an alternative! What we're doing is all we can do. There's nothing else. A garden is our only hope, Mother. Have you got a better idea?"

Mother said, "Why don't we just pack up and go?"

"Nothing to pack," Father said. "Nowhere to go."

"There's Brewer's Village. Mr. Haddy said —"

"Figgy is busy dying. They all are, except us." He had taken a shovel and was mucking out the furrows and replanting the stringy shoots. He saw us watching him and said, "Stick with me, people, or you'll die, too."

Jerry knelt down and said, "I hate him."

Clover heard. She said, "I'm going to tell Dad what you said."

"I want you to tell him, Crappo. I want to see him go buggy."

This made Clover cry. She ran to Mother and said, "Jerry just swore at me!"

"No one gives a hoot," Father was saying. He threw down his shovel and unwrapped the outboard. He spun it and throttled it with his rope, making it choke. Seeing him, I almost told him about the spark plugs and the gas. But he had said, *Nothing to pack—nowhere to go.* It would make him madder. He would ask me where I had got them, and why, and how. He would scream if I mentioned Mr. Haddy. I wished Mr. Haddy had never come and stuck me with that secret.

"That's to keep him sane," Jerry said.

I looked at Father tearing at the outboard's rope.

"It's not working," Jerry said, and he laughed.

We concentrated on what was left of the garden. But down here at the shore I could see that it was not the rain that had done the worst damage. The level of the lagoon had risen, as Mr. Haddy had predicted, and submerged the plants that had been near the water's edge. Jerry wanted to tell Father, to show him he had been mistaken, but before he could, it began to rain again. We stripped our clothes off and began bailing. It rained five times that day. At noon it was so dark we had to use candles in the hut to see our crabs.

A few days ago, it had all been dust and gray trees. Now we were in a wilderness of mud and water. There were frogs where no frogs had been, and snakes, and animal tracks everywhere. Lizards left their marks all over the bank, like bars on sheet music, with little noteprints above and below the lines of their tails. There were more birds, and crabs, and crayfish, all stirred into life by the rain. We caught them with ease. Mother boiled them on the cookstove. It made me think that we could survive without the garden.

Father came sneakily into the hut one morning. There was mud all over his chest and the front of his thighs, and gunk on his hands and dripping from his beard and on his nose. He was angry. He had not wanted us to see him. But we stared, and even Mother was puzzled.

"Pushups," he said, and snatched the rope of the outboard.

"The scavengers are back," Father said, looking up. The gray gulls and fat pelicans had flown inland to feed on the creatures that had sprung out of the mud. Vultures followed them, but instead of feeding they found perches in the trees and waited. Father screamed at the birds, to frighten them away. They screamed back at him. He hated scavengers, he said — hated their mad eyes and their filthy beaks, the way they pounced, the way they fought over garbage. And, as if in revenge — but what had they done to us? — he caught them by letting them swallow baited hooks, and he plucked and roasted them. He ate them. His hunger was hatred. He used their grease on his outboard motor, and left their blood and feathers in the mud. One morning we saw that he had killed a vulture and hung it high on a tree. It stayed there, lynched, until the other birds tore it apart.

"Know why I hate scavengers?"

Mother said, "Allie, please," and turned away.

"Because they remind me of human beings."

He denied the lagoon was rising. Even after the shoreline engulfed most of the garden and covered the foundation of the smokehouse, he still would not admit the lagoon was filling. He said the land was settling.

"It's a sinking effect. That's why I waterproofed the hut. I was expecting this!"

He hammered a marker in the mud, at the lagoon's edge. The next morning, the marker was gone — either submerged or swept away. Father said a scavenging vulture had mistaken it for a turd and eaten it.

The storms had tidied our camp. Destruction had made it neater. The half-made coop for the curassows was gone. The latrine was in the creek. The boards for the walkway were covered in mud. The seven-man pump had collapsed — it looked small and simple on its back.

And the hut had begun to sink. It had once rested high on the mud bank, on its own watertight bottom. But now the mud brimmed around it. It looked like one of those family tombs, the bunkers with doors that are half imbedded in the ground in old graveyards.

It worried Mother. She said she could not cook while she was kneeling in water, and what if the hut just went on sinking until mud came through the hatches? Father moved the cookstove inside and fitted it with a chimney. The hut looked more than ever like a little barge, and now the lagoon lapped against its front.

"Allie, it makes me nervous."

Father got a rope and some pulleys and, using a tree to brace the arrangement of tow ropes, tried to yank the hut away from the lagoon. He struggled, but it was no use. The hut was stuck fast in the mud. He left it tethered to the tree.

"That shouldn't be happening," he said. "It's not supposed to get bogged down."

He fitted logs to the sides, at the level of the brimming mud, to stabilize it and prevent it from sinking further. He said he was sorry we did not have time to go down to the coast — the storms would be washing lots of interesting articles onto the beach. The wildest seas gave you the best things, he said — iron chains, steel drums, yards of sailcloth. It was only the ordinary tides that brought you toilet seats.

But we stayed at Laguna Miskita and tried to secure the camp. We dug trenches, we bailed, we fished. The storms assaulted us. They crept up and darkened the day. They made us very cold, they drove us inside. They stole our wood, they broke down our trenches, they fouled the place with mud and excited the monkeys. The storms were always followed by flocks of scavenging birds.

"Sandbags," Father said. "If we had sandbags we'd be in good shape. I'll bet there are stacks of them down at Mocobila. They don't know what to do with them there. They're all busy dying on the coast."

The rain and the rising lagoon thieved most of what we had, and the wind burgled the rest. Now there was little more here than our hut. The junkpile was scattered, the barrel of gas had vanished. But this made me glad. I had no secret to keep. I would not get into trouble, and anyway there was nowhere to go. Jerry said that soon Father would give up and take us to live at Brewer's Village. He would have no choice — the camp was a failure, Father had been wrong to hide in this backwater.

Within a week, our garden was gone. Not a single sprout was left. There were no more seeds. We lived on land crabs and wet eddoes. We walked around with dirty legs. The mud dried on us and made gray flakes on our skin. "Keep clean," Father said, but the hot shower he had made was the next thing to go. The lagoon was under the front half of the hut, and now at night I could hear it like bones knocking beneath the floor. The hut was tilted forward, straining the rope. During the storms I heard this tether rope grunt.

"Any seepage?" Father asked. But there was none. The hut stayed dry. It was Father's one satisfaction — the hut did not leak. He boasted about it as the rain came down.

"There's water underneath the front," I said.

"Bow," Father said. "Underneath the bow."

He began saying things like "Get aboard" and "Go astern."

"We're roped to that tree," he said. "If the line breaks or the tree cuts loose, we'll take to the dugout. We won't be carried away! Jerry, swab the deck."

There was a strong current flowing through the lagoon. The sight of it panicked Father. In its muscles and boilings floated uprooted bushes and branches and coconuts and black fruit and dead swollen animals — all moving swiftly toward the creek and the sea.

The land had softened and turned to swamp. The trees stood in water, the paths were gone, and still the water rose, until what had once been a camp spread over a whole length of the lagoon's bank was now no more than a shallow island — our hut on a bar of mud. Creeks had opened in breaks on the lagoon's shores. There was not a living soul that we could see in this maze of muddy waterways. Birds flew around us. Father cursed them from our lopsided hut. He wanted to kill them all.

The world was drowned, he said.

He made a list of things we needed — chains, pulleys, fastenings for a paddle wheel and treadles, wood for boardwalks, sailcloth, more seeds, inner tubes, tin strips, wire mesh, salt.

"Seeds?" Mother said. "But there's nowhere to plant!"

"Hydroponics," Father said. "Grow them in water. Think of it."

He said he was sure that most of the things we needed were lying on the beach near Mocobila. As soon as the rain eased he was going to make a dash in the dugout for one last look at the Mosquito Coast.

"What if we die?" April asked.

"There are worse things."

Clover said, "What's worse than dying?"

"Being turned into scavengers." Father slapped his list. "It's already started to happen. I scavenged this paper, I scavenged this pencil. But I don't need this stuff — you do."

"Maybe they'll send a search party for us," Clover said.

"Who's 'they'?"

"The people."

"What people? You think the Coast Guard's down there waiting for us to send a distress signal? Search parties out looking for us in raincoats? No — they've all been torpedoed. Muffin, believe me, we're the last ones left."

Mother said, "Allie, why don't we leave together? We've still got the dugout. We could get down the creek, we could —"

"Down the creek!" Father grinned angrily. "With the current, the broken branches, the rotten fruit. I won't do it."

"Why not?"

"Because I'm not a broken branch. Dead things go downstream. That's a funeral procession on that creek. If we surrender to the current, we're doomed." He pointed his finger stump in the direction of the coast. "Everything tends that way. But we've got to fight it, because down there is death."

"We could live at Brewer's. You know that."

"Like savages. Like scavengers. I'll die before I turn into one of those garbage-eating birds. Hand-to-mouth? Me? No, Mother, I make things. And if I can't survive that way, I'll go up in flames — I'll turn myself into a human torch. Then the birds won't get me. Ha!"

Clover said, "What about us?"

"We'll all go up in flames! It's no disgrace to be the last ones to go. It means we've made our point."

He was still smiling. Already his face shone as if, inside, he had began to smolder with heat.

We guessed that he was serious, and so we were startled when Mother laughed.

Father challenged her with his fiery eyes.

She said, "Allie, we're too wet to burn."

"I've got fuel." He opened his mouth wide to mock her. He looked wild.

"We've got nothing!"

"Gas," Father hissed. "We'll take a bath in it, and pull the plug. One match and *whoof!*"

It was as if he had told Mother he had a weapon. She stammered and said, "There's no gas here."

"A barrel of it."

Mother said nothing.

"Found it in the mud. Some fool jettisoned it, but he was busy drowning. The barrel reached our shore. I roped it to a tree." He smiled at our frightened faces. "It's no disgrace to die your own way."

Jerry looked at me. I shook my head. I didn't want him to tell Father how Mr. Haddy had brought the barrel of gas to us. He said, "Charlie's got spark plugs."

"Charlie's got no such thing."

"Show him," Jerry said.

I got the pouch from my hammock and gave it to Father. He tore open the plastic and tested them with his thumbnail.

"I found them in the mud," I said, and glanced at Jerry, daring him to deny it.

Father was sweating. He came close to me. His face was hot, his lips white and cracked. I thought he was going to hit me, or demand to know where I got them — the exact place — and accuse me of lying. But he hesitated. Maybe he was ashamed of himself for talking about suicide, dousing ourselves with gasoline. He opened his mouth to speak, but before he could say anything, Mother screamed.

"Allie!"

Father turned to her.

With fear in her eyes, Mother said, "The house just moved!"

Father felt it — we all had — the moment he opened his mouth. It was a soft bump, a nudge against the floorboards, a sideways push under our feet. Father had already started to laugh and by then he had forgotten me. He rushed outside, saying, "I planned it this way!"

That night we were woken by a thunder sound that shook the hut. But this cannon thunder was the outboard, vibrating on the beam where it was clamped. It echoed all over the lagoon and the surrounding swamp. He killed the engine, and now I could hear bats, and the steady flutter of the rain, and the monkeys answering Father's noise.

Then we were afloat. I could feel it — the water shouldering the hut and tipping us in our hammocks. The rising lagoon had lifted the small watertight hut and turned it into a barge. In the morning the water was all around us, and we were lit by the muddy glimmer of the lagoon. The trees were distant, but our tether rope still held us to the solitary tree in the water. We were out of the current, and the outboard was clamped to the rail on the short deck behind the hut. The dugout, holding the barrel of gas and some junk Father had rescued, was tied to the back — the stern, Father reminded me.

"Who was right?" He took Mother's hand and said, "I couldn't die if I tried!"

Mother said, "What if it leaks?"

"Logs under us! We're stable — we're unsinkable! I planned it this way!"

Mother was at the cookstove, frying breakfast fish.

"Tugboat Annie," Father said. "Now I'm going to eat. I've been saving up for this — let it rain!"

But the hut still scraped the bottom, and when it rocked from our movements, we could feel the bump of the mud bank under us, the hut's bum sliding on soft soil. Father ate an enormous breakfast, then got his dugout pole and began pushing us further into the open water.

Jerry said, "As soon as we get to the coast, I'm going to find Mr. Haddy. He'll sail us to La Ceiba. We can get that banana boat."

Clover said, "Dad, Jerry says we're going to the coast."

"You want to die, boy?"

Jerry said, "But we're safe — you said so."

"Anyone can float down to the coast," Father said, and pushed his pole. "I could have done that without an engine. But I hung on. I fought it" — and he pushed — "I wasn't cut out to grow vegetables. I'm an inventor. I make things, Jerry. But that Mosquito Coast is a dead loss. That's the edge of the precipice. One false step and you're gone." He kept shoving at the pole, pushing the floating hut into deeper water. "There's death down there. Wreckage. Scavengers. Garbage eaters. Everything broken, rotten, and dead is on that stream and being pulled down to the coast. And that's the nearest place to the United States — how do we know it hasn't been poisoned? I've been fighting the current all along" — and he pushed — "and it's been a draw. I haven't given an inch. When did I say, 'Okay, let's drift and God help us'? Never! That's why we're winning."

Jerry said, "There's nowhere to go — that's what you told us."

"You're taking that remark out of context!" Father plunged the pole into the mud and hung on it. "You're misquoting me. Isn't he, Charlie?"

I said, "If we aren't going to the coast, where *are* we going?"

"I make things! I've got maps in my head! There are more safe places on those maps than you'd ever dream possible. Look at the house I made. She floats! Look at this outboard" — he circled its spool with his starting rope and got it blasting — "she works! Some jackass threw this away! Look at us, Mother — we're only drawing a foot of water, a foot and a half at the outside. We can go anywhere in this craft. We can get away from those birds. They're all dying down there, but we're going to live. Do you think I'd be fool enough to risk drowning us all, when the whole world is ours?"

And saying this, and more, he pointed the hut inland, toward the Patuca, and steered us against the current.

IV
UP THE
PATUCA

26

"I SAVED YOU from certain death," Father said.

Yes, we were alive in this waterworld.

"What are you going to do for me?"

What could we refuse? We owed him everything.

"You'll have to do as I say."

How else could we pay him back?

"Upstream," he said. "Downstream it's a toilet. You know that."

But even if this was true, it did not make our going easier. Every mile seemed like a mistake, because we were not free anymore. It was like the slow death in dreams of being trapped and trying to scream without a voice box. No one said anything.

In the space of a day our circumstances had changed. From a rained-on quarreling family, clinging with dirty hands to a mud bank and fearing worse floods, we had been turned into river people. Our main worry was that our hull would be sheared away by submerged rocks and we would sink like a brick. Jerry and I worked the sounding chain from the bow. The rutting and flapping of the outboard motor cleared the trees of monkeys — whitefaced baboons and ringtails here — and scared everything except butterflies.

The hard thunder rains of the lagoon and the ruination of our garden were nightmare memories. But the very moment we believed we were rescued and could make it to Brewer's to shelter safely in one of those stooping belfry-like huts, Father turned us around and began fighting us upstream.

Jerry said it looked dangerous.

I told Father I was scared.

Mother said, "Allie, why don't we take a chance on the coast? At least we know what's there."

Father called us savages. That kind of thinking had doomed mankind's carcass. Did we want our goose cooked? It was not the unknown that was dangerous, but the known. Only drowning people clung to wreckage. Those who bothered to seek the unknown were saved — but who bothered? Of course it was hard to get a heavy boat up a flooded river on one engine! That proved it was worthwhile!

He had been right in other things, so we went along with him in this, and found ourselves agreeing with everything he said.

"Dentists in the States had an interest in candy factories," he said. "Doctors owned hospitals. Detroit kept bankrolling oil wells. America had terminal cancer! I saw it was all leading downstream. Why didn't anyone else?"

An aerosol can of bug spray swept by us one day. Father did not question where it came from: he was too busy railing about it. And plastic jugs on the current. He railed more. He railed against fat people and politicians and banks and breakfast cereal and scavengers — there were turkey buzzards and muddy vultures right overhead. He bawled them out, he cursed machines.

"I look forward to the day when I can cut this outboard loose; turn it into the meat grinder it really is." All machines were gravediggers, he said. Leave them alone for a minute and they bury themselves. That's all they were good for — holes.

"I had a Hole once."

He smacked his lips, congratulating himself.

"I made ice out of fire!"

He named our floating hut the *Francis Lungley,* then changed it to the *President Fox,* and finally scratched *Victory* on its side with a nail. He said it was the world. It was twenty-seven feet long and six feet wide. He and Mother had the "master cabin" (the cookstove, the chair, the pelican-feather bed). With the excess weight of timbers thrown overboard or cut for fuel, our craft moved more easily in the water, with the hefty grace of a canal boat or a motorized barge in the Connecticut Valley. As soon as we were past the cutoff, where branches banged our roof, we plugged along the creek, staying midstream. Anywhere, Father said, as long as it was against the current.

We entered the Patuca that first day. We were surprised that this great river had been flowing all this time beyond the swamp to the east of our little Laguna Miskita — four hours' chug. But the river was hidden. We did not see it until we were almost on top of it. Father said he was not surprised at all: right again! The rain had swelled it over its red banks and into the trees, and made it silent and so wide that in some reaches it hardly seemed to flow at all.

Father worked the boat along the edge of the submerged banks, where the current was easy. We made slow progress, but, as Father said, "Where's the fire? What's the rush? This isn't a vacation — this is life."

At night we tied up to a tree and ate and slept with our smudge pots going, to drive off the mosquitoes. When a cloud of mosquitoes approached, its millions drooped over us like a terrible net and made a loud high-pitched hum, the sound a radio makes between stations.

With the river murmuring past us, slurping at our logs, Father said that in all the world we were the last ones left. If we yelled for help, no one would come. Oh, we might meet stragglers, we might bump into savages or even see whole villages on high ground that had been spared. But we were the only ones who knew that a catastrophe had taken place — the fire that had been followed by the thunder of war and the flood had been general throughout the earth. How could anyone here in Mosquitia know that America had been wiped out? It was man's narrow conceit that rain fell on him alone. But Father knew it was global. At each stage, he said, he had predicted what was to come. Even Americans themselves had seen the handwriting on the wall — they had talked about nothing else! But while they had sat and complained and twiddled their thumbs, Father had taken countermeasures to prevent our destruction.

"I may have exaggerated at times," he said. "But that was only to convince you of its seriousness, and get you moving. You're hard people to organize. Half the time you don't even believe me!"

What did it matter, he said, if he had been wrong about picky little things? He had been vindicated by great events. And what we had seen over the past year was the highest form of creation. He had outwitted the specter that haunted the world, by removing us from a fragile and temporary civilization. All worlds ended, but Americans had been sure that, in spite of the obvious flaws, theirs would last. Not possible! But Father would carry us safely upriver.

"Farter," Jerry said. "Farter, farter, farter."

Father did not hear him. He was shouting, "How can I be wrong if I'm going against the current?"

The coast was death. The current tended that way. So it stood to reason that it flowed from life — mountains and springs. There, among the volcanoes of Olancho, we would make our home.

This was what he told us at night, in the cabin, when we were tied to a tree and the frogs croaked and drawled outside. During the day he still talked, but with the outboard going we hardly heard a word he said.

The river seemed to swell out of the ground. It flooded the jungle. This was a wilderness of water. Tree stumps with crooked uprising roots tumbled past us. It rained less often — a sprinkle in the morning, a downpour in the afternoon. But, as Father said, we were waterproof. And we saved the rainwater to drink. The sun on the river turned the muddy current to brass. It gave the jungle a nice bright smack. Shining through the morning mist, it thickened the air with gold-spangled smoke that danced between the boughs. In places, there were clouds of white butterflies — regattas of them, tacking just above the water. Or blue ones, as big as sparrows, working their tottery wings so shyly they moved like beautiful scraps of silk flung out of the trees.

Two or three times a day we saw Zambus or Miskitos in cayukas, slipping quickly downstream. Often they waved to us, but the current took them so fast that no sooner had we spotted them than they were below us and around the bend.

"He's a goner," Father usually said as one went past. "He's a dead man. A zombie, not a Zambu. Going down to die."

They were wet, but they looked perfectly normal, paddling in their grubby underwear, riding across the fumbles of the current.

Jerry said that one of these days he was going to hop into our dugout and let the current take him to the coast. Father got wind of this, maybe from one of the twins, and ordered him into the dugout.

"In you go!"

Then Father cast it off and let it zoom downriver. Jerry was too terrified to paddle. He hung onto the seat and crouched with his head down and howled.When Jerry had almost traveled out of sight, Mother said, "Allie, do something!" and Father snatched up a line. It was attached to the dugout. He jerked it, toppling Jerry onto his face. Jerry was shaking as Father towed him and the dugout back.

"That was insane!" Mother said.

"I proved my point. I got my wish."

"What if the rope had snapped?"

"Then Jerry would have got *his* wish," Father said. "Anyone want to try it? I might just decide to let you go next time. Down the drain. Anyone interested?"

Another day, he caught me snoozing over the sounding chain. He punished me by putting me into the dugout and towing me behind the boat ("I sure hope that line doesn't snap! Better sit still!"), while my little canoe rocked and slewed in its wake.

We passed flooded villages. They were deserted — the wooden bones of huts standing in water, huts tipped over, others with fractured roofs, no more. These dead empty huts proved Father right. He said the people had been swept away — those were the folks in the long johns we saw paddling down the drain to be swallowed by the sea.

"They won't need these," he said, as he picked alligator pears and limes and papayas and plantains off their trees. We found bags of rice and beans in some of these empty villages.

Father said, "This isn't a raid. It's not theft. And it's certainly not scavenging. They don't need this where they are."

But sometimes the birds beat us to it.

"Scavengers!"

One day we thought we saw an airplane, but our outboard was so loud we could not hear the plane's engines. Father said it was a turkey buzzard. What human had the sense to come here? This was the emptiest part of the map. In the whole world, this part of Honduras was the safest and least known — the last wilderness.

"But don't praise me — praise this boat." Our *Victory* was like a wooden pig in the water, creaking and oinking upstream. "She's futuristic!"

The rain had watered the ants and made them sprout wings. At sundown, these flying termites flaked onto the roof of our hut-boat. The jungle was dotted with these winged ants feeding. The twins called them cooties. The river water changed its color with every change in the weather, and it was different at every hour. I liked it brassy, its daytime green, the red mud bank showing underneath like soaked cake, its shoving, slipping bunches of spinach, the way it moved through the unmoving jungle.

At twilight the air was sooty with insects, and swampwater diseased the dark spaces under the trees. The sky grew clearer as dusk fell. Shadows straightened up and stiffened. Then a dirtying of the sky, and it was night, nothing to see, the black so black you could feel its fur against your face. Without the hot sun to burn it away, the smell from the trees was like the hum of green meat. The full river snuffled like a pack of hogs, and birds lolloped in the branches near us and made loud cranking cries. We felt sick at this still, leftover time of day. We tied up and sat among the smudge pots of our wooden floating hut, and ate whatever we had managed to gather from the drowned villages.

"This is the future," Father said. He stuck his burned nose in our faces until we agreed we were cozy, we were lucky, we were having a good time.

"This is what it is," he said. "The fatal mistake everyone made was in thinking that the future had something to do with high technology. I used to think it myself! But that was before I had this experience. Oh, gaw, it was all going to be rocket ships."

"Monorails," I said.

Clover said, "Space capsules."

"Smellovision," Father said. "Video cassettes instead of school. Everything streamlined. Meals were going to be pills. Green ones for breakfast, blue ones for lunch, purple ones for dessert. You popped them into your mouth — all the nutrition you needed."

April said, "And space suits."

"Right," Father said. "Stupefied people with pointy ears and names like Grok wearing helmets and living in chrome-plated houses. Moving sidewalks, glass domes over cities, and no work except playing with computers and sniffing the smellovision. 'Get into the rocket ship, kids, and let's go have a picnic on the moon' — that kind of thing."

Mother said, "It might happen."

"Never. It's all bull."

Clover said, "I think Dad's right."

"Science fiction gave people more false hope than two thousand years of Bibles," Father said. "It was all lies! The space program — is that what you're saying? It was a hollow, vaunting waste of taxpayers' money. There is no future in space! I love the word — space! That's what they were all discovering — empty space!"

April said, "I think Dad's right, too."

"This is the future," he said. "A little motor in a little boat, on a muddy river. When the motor busts, or we run out of gas, we paddle. No spacemen! No fuel, no rocket ships, no glass domes. Just work! Man of the future is going to be a cart horse. There's nothing on the moon but ruts and pimples, and those of us who have inherited this senile exhausted earth will have nothing but wooden wheels, pushcarts, levers, and pulleys — the crudest high school physics, that they stopped teaching when everyone flunked it and started reading science fiction. No, it's grow your own or die. No green pills, but plenty of roughage. Hard backbreaking work — simple, but not easy. Get it? No laser beams, no electricity, nothing but muscle power. What we're doing now! We're the people of the future, using the technology of the future. We cracked it!"

He wanted us to feel, in our creaking hut-boat, like the most modern people on earth. We held the secret of existence in our smoky cabin. Now he never talked about changing the world with geothermal energy, or ice. He promised us dirt and work. That was glory, he said.

But after these short nights, he started the outboard and set the front of the hut against the current, and Jerry whispered to me, "He's killing us."

We stuck to the river's edge, creeping around the reaches and studying the flow of the current before we moved forward. We made five or six miles a day, and still had plenty of spare gas. And what did it matter if we used it all? We had the rest of our lives to get upriver.

I thought everyone except Jerry was convinced. But one day, as we furrowed along, the outboard went mad. It quacked, its noise climbed higher, became more frantic and animal, and soon it was shrieking. Birds exploded out of the trees. Then something snapped, and after a quack or two the engine went dead. But its echo continued to quiver in the jungle. The boat hesitated and became light and directionless. It tipped, it rolled back.

We were going downstream sideways on the river's tongue in silence under the dropping ants.

"Anchor!" Father vaulted toward the bow. "Get out the lines!"

Our anchor was beautiful — we had found it on the beach near Mocobila — a cluster-fountain of curving barbs on a thick shaft. But it was also very heavy. It took Father's help to get it over the rail, and by then we were moving so fast that it did not seem to take hold. Father jumped overboard and swam to the bank with a line. He secured us, the anchor caught.

We were in a curve of the river — the current swung us out on the line and held us gushing in the middle of the stream. Water plumed from either side, and the whole hut-boat tottered as we helped Father aboard.

We had lost the shear pin, he said. It wasn't much — only a cotter pin — but it meant the propeller had flown off and spun to the bottom of the river.

"Can't you make a new prop?" Mother asked.

"Sure I can. Pass me that lathe, the calipers, the machining tools, the set of lugs and files. What's that? You mean we only have spit and a screwdriver? Then I guess we'll have to dive for that old prop."

We looked upstream at the dark horns of waterflow pumping out of the river.

"Don't worry," Father said. "We have the rest of our lives to find it." He was smiling, biting his beard. He turned to Jerry and said, "What are you smirking at?"

"The rest of our lives. It sounds daffy when you say it like that."

"We'll see how daffy. You're going to dive for it."

"What about the alligators?" I said.

"You're not afraid of alligators," Father said. "You go after Jerry."

Mother said, "No — I won't let those boys go in there."

"Listen to me," Father said. "It's not a question of what you want. It's what *I* want. I'm captain of this ship, and those are my orders. Anyone who disobeys them goes ashore. Your lives are in my hands. I'll maroon you — all of you."

His large scarred hands were still dripping river water. His voice was a weapon — he was threatening to abandon us unless we jumped in — but what I feared most was being slung ashore in his raw fingers. His life here had made his hands terrible.

"Put on this harness," he said to Jerry, and gave him a line to tie around his waist. Jerry, with sick defiant eyes, kicked off his sandals and went to the side.

"It's somewhere in this dogleg," Father said. "We lost it near those trees. Probably hit a rock. The current can't take a lump of solid brass very far. Swim to the bank first, then go and get it."

Jerry held his nose and went overboard like a basket.

"I've been grooming you for this all along," Father said. "It's all preparation for survival." He pulled out a nail from his pocket. "This will do for a new shear pin. But we need the prop." He held the little nail between his fingers. "It's always something small that keeps you from savagery. Like those plugs. Like the prop. Like this. The shear pin held our whole civilization together. There's no better example of what a delicate balance there is between — " he looked upriver at Jerry's small white feet — "How's he doing?"

Jerry bobbed up and blew out water, but before he could regain his stroke he came downstream and caught hold of the boat.

"I can't see anything. The water's too muddy."

"Try again."

"He's tired, Allie."

"He can rest after he's found our propeller."

Mother said, "Let me go."

Father said, "What if you drown?"

"What if Jerry drowns?"

She said it in a slow suffocated way.

Father scratched his beard with his knuckles.

He said, "I need you here, Mother."

Jerry tried four times. Each time, the current pulled him back to us empty-handed. At last he was so tired he could not raise his arms, and Father had to tug the harness line to keep him from being taken downriver.

It was my turn. I swam to shore, then dived to the bottom at the place Father had indicated. I stuck my hands into the mud and raked it. The mud ran through my fingers. The churning river was like vegetable soup, with sunlight knifing into it and showing me long shadows I imagined to be alligators. As my breath gave out, I broke the surface of the river and saw that I had traveled almost to the boat.

"You're not serious," Father said. He made me swim back.

The sludge and weeds at the river bottom disgusted me. The dark current sucked at my legs. Mud floated into my face. But worse, being on Father's rope was like being a dog on a leash. Staying on it, I was in his power. But if I cut myself free of the rope, I would be swept downstream to drown.

It was a dog's life. I was glad Jerry had said the things he had. Why hadn't I told Father what I thought of him? A dog's life — because we didn't count, because he was always right, always the explainer, and most of all because he ordered us to do these difficult things. He didn't want to see us succeed, he wanted to laugh at our failure. And not even a gun dog could find a small propeller at the bottom of this river.

I told him I had swallowed water and felt sick and could not go down again.

He chuckled — I knew he would — and said, "Children are no use at all in a crisis. Which is ironic, because children are the cause of most crises. I mean, I can look after myself! I don't need food, I don't need sleep — I don't suffer. I'm happy!"

April said, "Dad, is this a crisis?"

"Some people might say so. We've got an engine we can't use. We've got a boat that won't move forward. We've got two cripples who can't find the prop. If the anchor or that line cuts loose we'll be wallowing down the drain. And it's getting dark. And this is the jungle. Muffin," he said, "some people might call that critical."

Mother said, "I want to try, Allie."

But Father was putting the harness around his waist. He tied the free end to the rail. He said the only thing he trusted to hold his life-line was one of his own knots.

He went over the side with a heavy splash. We watched him take a dive, expecting him to find the propeller on the first try. He came up — he did not raise his hands. He dived again. He was a strong enough swimmer to hold his own against the current, but when he dived a third time he did not come up.

We waited. We watched the water ribbing over that spot.

Clover said, "Where is he?"

"Maybe he sees it," Mother said.

A whining net of mosquitoes came and went.

April said, "He's been down a long time."

"It's dark down there," Jerry said.

We stopped holding our breath.

More minutes passed. I could not say how many. Time did not

pass precisely here. The day was light, the night dark: time was lumpish. Every hot hour was the same, silent and blind. He might have been under for an hour.

Mother went to the rail and plucked at the line. She lifted it easily and dragged it on board, coiling it, until she had its whole length out of the water. The end was kinked like a mongrel's tail, where the knot had been.

"He's gone!" Clover screamed. She became rigid. And she cried so hard she gagged, then cried more because she was gagging.

Jerry said, "I don't see him."

But Jerry had stopped looking. He was staring at me. His face was relaxed — very white and hopeful, like someone sitting up in bed in the morning.

Mother shook her head. She gazed at the torrent of water slooshing downstream. She did not speak.

I felt suddenly strong. A moment ago night was falling, but now everything was brighter. The sky was clear. Tiny insects fussed above the river. A quietness descended, like that sifting of gnats, and silvered the water and streaked it like a new tomb. This stillness sealed it.

"He's somewhere! He's somewhere!" But April's voice did not disturb the river or the trees. She clawed her hair. She held Clover and they gagged together on their sobs.

"We can drift," Jerry said. "We'll tie up tonight and go down the river tomorrow. It'll be easy."

I said, "What if Dad was right?"

"Don't be frightened," Mother said.

Jerry said, "We're not frightened!"

Mother said, "I can't think." Her listening face was lovely. It did not register a single sound. It did not hear April saying we were going to die, or Clover calling out to Father, or Jerry describing our easy trip down to the coast.

Little Jerry, set free, was scampering around the deck.

"Listen," Mother said.

The water trickling silver, the slouching jungle — it was an insect kingdom of small whistles, a world of crickyjeens.

A Zambu went by in a cayuka. That was like time passing, the duration of his coming and going. It was the only time here — a man's movement. This Zambu was alive.

"We won't die," I said.

Mother did not hear me, but I meant it. Our boat was small, and it hung precariously on a line in the middle of the river — on air, it seemed. But I had never felt safer. Father was gone. How quiet it was here. Doubt, death, grief — they had passed like the shadow of a bird's wing brushing us. Now — after how long? — we had forgotten that shadow. We were free.

"In a couple of days we'll be on the coast," Jerry said.

"We'll die there!" Clover said.

It was what Father had always said. I thought I believed it. But he had gone and taken fear with him. I heard myself saying, "We can get rid of this outboard. We'll build a rudder. The current will take us."

Jerry tried to make the twins stop crying. He was saying, "Don't you want to go home?"

Was it that forbidden word that did it?

There was a splash — explosive in this whistling world. There was Father's wet streaming head, his beard brushing the rail, the chunk of the brass propeller hitting the boards, and his howl, "Traitors!" Then all the light was gone.

27

FOR THE NEXT three days, as punishment, Jerry and I were towed behind the boat in the dugout. We ate in it and slept in it. It tailed and twisted like a plug trawled at the end of a fishing line. There was hardly room to lie down. The barrel was between us, and the fruity, sourly luscious gasoline fumes mingled with the burned-cloth stink of the outboard's exhaust and gave me a prickly headache. We knelt in the water that seeped through the splits in this hollow log and we killed time by dragging a hook off the stern, hoping to gaff a catfish.

Father sat at the end of the thirty-foot towline, on the stern rail of the hut-boat, his back turned to us. I hated his shoulders, his greasy hair, the slant of his spine. I imagined how it would be to stick a knife in it, just below his ragged collar. Sometimes I saw myself doing it. There was no blood in my imagining — no scream, no struggle. Just a grunt of released air as the blade slipped in and the hilt smacked against flesh. Then he was gone, like an inner tube with a rip. I saw it so clearly my arm ached, as if I had already done it — punctured him.

I listened to him, thinking that he knew what was on my mind, and felt guilty. But all I heard was Mother arguing, trying to convince him to let us aboard. He would not discuss it. He said we deserved worse. He was hard to hear over the motor roar. He prided himself on the fact that he had never spanked us, or laid a hand on us in anger. But it would have been better for us if he had beaten us yesterday. This dugout and the bugs and the heat hurt more than a whipping.

"Let's cut the tow rope," Jerry said. "We'll show him!"

Jerry wanted to set us adrift. Maybe Father was testing us, to see if we had the guts to do it. But I would not let Jerry touch the line. I was afraid that it might snap all by itself, or that Father would cut it. Often, during those days, I fell asleep and woke up frantic, thinking we were spinning down the Patuca in this flimsy dugout.

I said, "If you touch that .rope, I'll jump overboard and swim ashore. You'll be alone, Jerry. You'll die."

For the brief period of Father's disappearance, when I thought he had drowned trying to retrieve the propeller, I had not been afraid. We had the boat, and our hammocks, and Mother. But when he climbed aboard, he brought all the old fear with him. I was spooked again into believing that the storm had raged across the whole world and that there was death on the coast.

"I don't believe that cowflap," Jerry said when I told him.

Jerry was more violent in the dugout than he had ever been on the boat or anywhere else. Here, towed at the end of a line, he said forbidden things. He talked continually about running away and going home. What he said gave me nightmares, because he put my worst imaginings into words. We deserve to be punished in this dugout, I thought. We belong here.

"I hate him," Jerry said. "He's crazy."

I told Jerry that without my help he would never reach the coast.

"We won't make it upriver," he said. "It's impossible."

"How do you know?"

He kicked the barrel of gas, two thuds that echoed hollowly inside like the boom of a bass drum.

"It's almost empty. Dad can't run his outboard motor without gas."

"He'll paddle."

"He'll go backwards!"

Jerry laughed at the thought of it. He said he was glad I was worried.

"I'm going to tell him he's running out of gas. Watch him have a bird."

"Cut it out," I said.

"You're afraid of him, Charlie. You're older than me and you're scared. I'm not scared."

But his voice broke as he said it, and he had to swallow twice in order to finish speaking. This dugout punishment made him suffer. He had hardly slept, and he looked sick. When he wasn't complaining about Father, he was blubbering, sobbing like a baby. He sounded very young when he cried. He squalled into his hands, with his head down, so that Father wouldn't see him.

One night, hearing Father's laughter in the master cabin, Jerry said, "I'd like to kill him."

His voice came out of the darkness. Now he was breathing heavily, as if it had been a great effort to say that.

"He wouldn't be hard to kill." Jerry was panting. "We could sneak up on him. Hit him with a hammer. On his brain —"

"Don't say that, Jerry."

"You're afraid."

Yes, because you're saying the terrible things on my mind, I thought. I could feel the smooth handle of the hammer. I could hear it crack against his skull, and the skull part like a coconut — the leaking of pale water. I said, "No."

"I wish he was dead," Jerry said. He began to cry again. I was consoled by his tears. He was crying for me.

He claimed he saw a plane one morning, a small gray single-engine plane passing overhead. I did not see it. I told him he was dreaming. It was a turkey buzzard or a heron or a parrot. Any bird in flight here looked like a Cessna or a Piper Cub. Jerry cried because I refused to believe him. I sounded like Father, he said. Worse than Father.

"Mr. Haddy gave you those spark plugs and this gas. And Dad took all the credit! Who did all the fishing at the lagoon? We did! He was treating us like slaves, but what happened to his garden and all those stupid inventions? They got washed away. We saved his life!"

He was speaking my thoughts again and making me afraid.

I said, "If you tell him about Mr. Haddy, I'll tell him what you said — that you want to kill him."

This panicked Jerry. He knew he had gone too far.

"Anyway," I said, "he'll deny it."

"Because he's a liar. He's wrong about everything."

"You don't know that. There isn't any proof. He's probably right — Mr. Haddy agreed with him! You're eleven years old and your face is dirty. When Dad cut you loose in this dugout last week you cried your eyes out. You were glad when he towed you back."

"He tricked me. I wouldn't cry now. I'd go." But his eyes were red and crusted like two wounds.

Father looked astern, and, seeing us arguing (he could not hear what we said over the chatter of the outboard motor), he nodded and grinned as if to say, "That's just where you two punks belong."

Mother had said that if he was right, we were the luckiest people in the world. If he was wrong, we were making a terrible mistake. But she obeyed him. She was afraid, too.

"Maybe we'll find out if he's right or wrong," I told Jerry. "I don't want to go to the coast if it's a graveyard. And what's the point of talking about America, if it's not there anymore? Dad says it's not there — so did Mr. Haddy. What do you know, Thickoid!"

Jerry said, "We have a white house in a green field, with trees around it. There are birds in the trees. Catbirds and jays. The sun is shining. The noon siren is ringing at the Hatfield fire station. People walk by our house and look up the path. They're saying, 'Where are those Foxes?' "

"No," I said. But I saw it clearly. I saw the clouds over Polski's barn, and the valley hills and the corn. I smelled the goldenrod and skunk cabbage, pine gum, cut grass, the sweetness of dew on dandelions, the warm tar on country roads.

" 'Did their old man take them away?' That's what they're saying." Jerry looked at me. He was surprised and a little fearful. He said, "Charlie, why are you crying?"

I put my hands against my face.

"Please don't cry," he said. "It scares me."

At last, Father let us aboard the boat. We were so ashamed of what we had been saying that we went straight to the bow and started working the sounding chain. We were burned and bitten and had the squitters bad. Jerry had been contrary in the dugout, but here he just looked miserable and did not say a word against Father. Instead, he cursed the twins. He even bit April on the arm, and the teeth marks turned purple. I was glad. I had wanted to bite her, and Clover, too, for a long time.

Every village we passed was washed-out or deserted — sticks of huts and a few fruit trees and a rotten-sweet latrine stink like the smoke smell of burned toast. They were green ghostly places, crawling with wet rats, all the dugouts sunk, and new vines twisted around the hut poles. Where roots showed, they were like stubbed toes, bruised black and raw, and long weeds hung in hanks from the crooks of branches like witches' scalps.

But one morning, after eleven days of pushing up this Patuca River, we came to a village that was not washed out or even flooded. It was on a high red bank at a bend in the river. A child was squatting in the shallow water by the riverside, doing his business, with a faraway look on his face, like a dog in a bush.

Father craned his neck for a better look at the village. Then he smiled. He seemed to recognize it.

He said, "I know where we are."

"Where, Allie?"

"You'll see."

The squatting child heard our engine. He covered himself with the rag he was holding and bolted up the bank. Father cut off the engine and tied our boat to a tree.

Now, on the bluff of the bank, where we had seen smoke and the straw peaks of huts, there were about fifteen men. They wore rags and they stared down at us with empty eyes.

"Miskitos," Father said. "Indians."

They were black, they were brown, they were yellowish, they were very skinny. Their thinness was like suspicion. They did not move.

Father jumped ashore and put his hand out.

"Hi, there. *Naksaa!*"

He was soon shaking hands with the men and talking a mile a minute in the way he did when he wanted to charm strangers. We had not seen him energetic and friendly for a long time. He had a habit, when he was in this good mood, of poking his finger stump into a person's chest and sort of tickling him as he talked. It worked on wild dogs and cows. It had worked on Mr. Haddy. It worked on these Miskito men.

He jabbed their ribs and said, "You did it this time, didn't you? You're a smart cookie, aren't you? You're really pleased with yourself. Quit laughing," he said, as he tickled them in turn. "What's so funny?"

It made the Miskitos giggle and jump. Though they had looked fierce at first, they were now talking to Father with friendliness. They no longer seemed interested in eating us, although they still looked hungry. They beckoned us into the village.

Mother said to us, "Stay together. I don't like this place. Let Dad do the talking."

Jerry said, "That's all he's good at."

"Watch your mouth," Mother said, and left Jerry to sulk.

"This village is a mess," I said. "These people are starving."

"Dad knows where we are," Mother said. "Listen to what he says."

But what could he say? It was a dreary smoldering collection of huts made out of torn banana leaves and held together by knotted vines. The huts were roofed with bunches of thatch straw. There was savannah at the back, and jungle — like a smudge of mold — beyond that. The ground was muddy from the recent rain, and the whole place stank of dirt and old wabool and the smoke of wet firewood. We had seen villages like this before. It was Indian misery. Stalks of blackened plantains hung from some of the sorry huts, and nearby a lame dog chewed at a filthy fish head. A flat-faced woman was dragging a sled piled high with broken sticks. She muttered insanely as she went along. She spoke to Mother — something evil — then laughed through her tooth stumps. Another woman with wild hair, scrubbing rags in a tin basin, looked up and made a face, then went on scrubbing.

"What did I tell you?" Father was speaking to us.

Swarms of loud flies buzzed around the people's faces and around their big dirty feet and scabby ankles. They found the black plantains, they skidded on the three-legged cooking pots. I did not see any gardens, but there were clumps of banana trees and skinny maniocs near some of the huts. A loose pig snorted and pushed his snout at the rind of a papaya. In the middle of the shacks was a tin-roofed open-fronted shed. A sign over it said LA BODEGA. Jerry and I looked inside, but saw only empty shelves and some hung-up flour sacks and a lantern.

"See?" Father said. "I was right."

Two Miskitos were beating the bark off a log. One was using a wooden mallet and the other a hatchet. They stopped their work and eyed Father. Then it was all silent, except for the pig and the dead monotonous buzz of the flies.

"This is it," Father said.

A crowd had gathered. The people stared at Mother's hair — the river travel and all the sun had turned her hair streaky blonde —

but they were listening to Father. They had dry starved faces, the old-age look of hunger. Two men wore snakeskins around their necks, coralitos, red with black rings.

"This is the future!"

Father looked around in admiration.

The muddy ground steamed in the sun. The smoke and the smell of rotten roof thatch and wabool made me squint. Near their bony shacks, the ragged Miskitos squinted back.

"I've got to congratulate you people," Father said. "Put it there."

The Indians were surprised, but they shook hands again and smiled at him.

"You've got the right idea."

They looked pleased, as if no one had ever told them that before. Smiling, they looked less hungry.

One Miskito cleared his throat. He said, "We making a new cayuka," and pointed out the two men straddling the scarred log.

"That's the idea."

"You has a spare chopper?" It was the Miskito with the mallet.

"You don't need a chopper. A chisel maybe, to go with your mallet. I've got a chisel. We could come to some arrangement. You're going to have a nice boat."

"She hard work, uncle."

"I know all about it. But what's the hurry? You've got all the time in the world."

"You has a ripsaw, uncle?" This was one of the Miskitos with the peeling snakeskin around his neck.

"What do you want with a ripsaw? You won't get a ripsaw anywhere. There aren't any to be had. Buddy, believe me, you can live without a ripsaw."

A horsefaced man asked Father whether he had any sulfur for making chicle rubber.

Father said, "Don't mention sulfur to me, friend."

There was a wheelbarrow tipped on its side in a ditch. Father picked it up and righted it. He looked at it lovingly, as he had once looked at Fat Boy. He said it was a perfect piece of engineering, the fulcrum wheel, the handles that acted as levers, the built-in balance. A man could lift four times his own weight in it with a minimum of effort.

The Miskitos listened to Father praising this splintery old wheel-barrow and began to look at it as if it were enchanted.

"Ain't selling me barra!" The man who said this spat on his finger and wiped spittle on the handle.

"I don't blame you. That's going to come in mighty handy now that half the world is destroyed."

They were not looking at the wheelbarrow anymore. Father smiled at their open mouths.

"Haven't you heard?"

The holes in their eyes said no.

"Sure, it's practically all gone." Father waved his arms. "There's only a few of us left. Out there" — he gestured again — "they're all dead or busy dying."

Downriver — that was the world. They squeezed their eyes at it. The horsefaced man said, "Why ain't we dead, uncle?"

"Because you're too smart. And you live right."

Father complimented them. He told them what he had told us, that this was a village of the future, that they were people of the fu-ture, the new men. They were lucky, he said, just living the simple life, while everyone else had gone to hell. Listening to him tell them they were in heaven here in this miserable village with its scrawny roosters and its black fruit and its one pig and its torn huts, they ad-justed their rags and cheered up.

"They thought we were going to the moon," Father said. "Listen, no one's going to the moon."

They offered us calabashes of wabool, and Father ate some. Their coffee was made of mashed burned corn kernels, but Father drank it. They gave us bananas. Father said, "I draw the line at bananas." They handed him a stinking cigar. Father smoked it and said, "Best thing I know for keeping the bugs away."

And then they told us that it was not a village but a family. Their name was Thurtle. Every Miskito here was a Thurtle. They were fa-thers and mothers and children and cousins, in a complicated way, all Thurtles, big and small.

Father said he was not surprised to hear it. Families were the only social unit left. He introduced us and had Clover and April sing a song for them. The twins gave them "Bye, Bye Blackbird." The Miskito men did a slow heavy dance, stamping in a circle and clap-ping.

This village, the Thurtle family, was like twenty others we had seen and ignored. But that was months ago, and now Father was a different man. This was the proof that he was different. He was completely patient. He didn't ask them to change. He didn't turn up his nose at their sour wabool. He didn't call attention to their humming latrine or their thin crazy pig. He said it was a remarkable place. It was the village of the future he had described to us less than a week back, on the river. He praised the way these Miskitos lived, and said he much admired the knots on the vines that held their huts together.

While he talked, clouds gathered overhead and a light rain and a distant barrel-roll of thunder began. The Miskitos were afraid of thunder. This storm worried them. Father said that sense of fear had saved them — they had smelled danger, as he had.

He found a drum of gasoline behind the store. The Miskitos said it was for the generator, but the generator was broken. It had rusted out. They were waiting for a new armature.

"Don't waste your time," Father said. "What do you need electricity for?"

They said for the lights.

"What will you do when the light bulbs blow? You'll need new ones. But they can't be had for love or money. No light bulbs. Nothing!"

Father said they had what they had, and what they didn't have didn't exist.

The Miskitos understood this quicker than we had on the boat.

He told them if they wanted oil they could use fish guts or pig fat. And he needed the gasoline more than they did, because he was running low on outboard fuel. He was willing to swap them a chisel and a toilet seat for it, and he would throw in a mirror, if they really wanted one.

They said okay.

"Barter," he said to us, as he loaded the gasoline drum into the dugout. "That's how it's going to be from now on."

They should be glad he was taking this gasoline off their hands, he said, because it was nothing but a fire hazard.

"Admit it," he said, poking a man in the chest with his finger, "I just did you a big favor!"

The man giggled as Father poked him, and the other Miskitos laughed.

Mother said, "I think you've made a hit, Allie."

"I can't help it, Mother. I *like* these people."

Jerry whispered to me, "They're starving. They're dirty. Look at their houses. They haven't got anything. You can see their bones. Their noses are running. They're spackies."

I said, "This is what Dad said it was going to be like."

"It's horrible."

"Jerry, he was right."

And even Jerry had to agree that Father had predicted this.

Father was saying, "You know Up Jenkins?"

They said there was a certain Jenkins in Mocoron, but he had died from a bite of a bonetail.

"This Up Jenkins is a game."

It was the one we had played in Jeronimo and Laguna Miskita. It involved a person in one group hiding a coin in his hand, and the other group trying to find out who had it. The second group called out "Windowpanes!" or "Slammums!" or "Creepums!" The group that had the coin hidden among its players had to do precise things with their hands — windowpane, slam them, or creep them. Usually the coin fell out as they did it — before anyone could guess who was hiding it — and everyone laughed. It was a silly game, but the Miskitos liked it, and we played it on the counter of the shop until the rain let up.

Eventually, Father looked toward the Patuca and said, "Time to shove off."

They wanted us to stay. They were enjoying Up Jenkins and Father's friendly pokes. But Father said he did not want to take advantage of them. At the river, as they gathered to say good-bye, it seemed to me that Father's awful prediction had been right. They were Miskitos, but they looked like us. They were bitten and muddy and their rags were no different from ours. This was the future he had promised, and we were savages in it.

"You going upriver in you bodge?"

Father said yes.

"Mobilgasna?"

"How far is Mobilgasna?"

"Four hours."

"We're going farther."

"Wumpoo?"

"How far's that?"

"Two days."

"Then I'm going a month or a year. I'm going until I run out of river. I don't intend to stop until I get where I'm going."

On the boat, Father said, "Did he say Wumpoo?"

Mother said, "Something like that."

"Wumpoo sounds familiar. It means something. What?"

Mother said she didn't know. But Father was right. Wumpoo did sound familiar.

That night, moored below Mobilgasna (it was steeper here, the riverbanks piney and covered with boulders), we lay in our hammocks and heard Father boasting to Mother, "You just saw the future. It's not so bad. It just *looks* dirty —"

Then I almost fell out of my hammock. Wumpoo — *Guampu!* I remembered what it meant.

28

ONLY I REMEMBERED Guampu, that name, but I had reasons. I kept it to myself, sucking on the secret like candy. No one mentioned it again. The others were calm, or at least so depressed by the Thurtles' village that they were out of hope.

During the days we spent in the smell of hot mud, in the quiet reaches of this upper river, they figured we had come to the end of our travels. All this and only this for the rest of our lives, as Father liked to say. But I wanted to go on and keep floating, because of Guampu.

We saw more slubbery villages, where people had burned out scoops of jungle and hung up huts. We saw them weeding rice, scattering seeds, hauling clumsy carts, and sawing wood into planks. Mountains appeared — yellow-topped ranges to the north and west, with clouds blowing past them, as if the wigs of these peaks had slipped off. Between the villages were miles of unseparated jungle. Father congratulated himself on having boated us into the future. We were lucky, he said. We were safe, we were free, we were perfectly comfortable. Plenty to eat, and a hot engine behind us — maybe the last engine on earth. We were sailing through the wilderness in style! So he said.

But the Miskitos' oil was bad, water in it fouled the valves, and after a day of cursing it and coaxing it, Father threw the outboard motor into the river.

"Don't want it! Don't need it anymore! Just a headache! Give it a decent burial!"

It sank into the weeds and began bleeding rainbows.

We poled our hut-boat with long bamboos, throwing our weight on them at the bow and walking them to the stern. In this way we made quiet progress up the oozy edge of the river, and no waves.

The current was less swift and the sun shone all day, giving the water a warm buttery look. The trees in the tall forest were heavy with creepers and full of the clickety-click of monkeys and the hot frying sounds of crickyjeens. The flowers hung from some vines like bright bunches of rags, or with blossoms like shuttlecocks. There were clearings and beaches tucked into riverbends. Any of these places would do, Father said. We could stop anywhere and call it home.

"Why don't we?" Mother said.

"Fine by me," Father said. "How about this? Shall we put in here?"

Mother said yes, the twins agreed, and even Jerry was reconciled in a kind of stupid moody way. They were all beaten flat by Father, the heat had gotten to them — their brains were poached by the sun and river steam, like fish flakes in a skillet.

"No," I said, "let's go on." I swung my bamboo pole and pretended I was still full of beans.

This made Father glad. He used me as his excuse to keep going. He heaved his pole and said, "If it wasn't for you, Charlie, I would have made camp back there. Good drainage and a gravelly shore. I'm amazed. I think I've finally succeeded with you. Fourteen years old, and at last you're showing some backbone."

But I wanted to reach Guampu. How had Father forgotten that name? Maybe because he hated to think about the past, the mistakes and failures. Turn your back and walk away fast — that was his motto. Invent any excuse for going. Just clear out. It had made him what he was — it was his genius. *Don't look back.* Yet for me the past was the only real thing, it was my hope — the very word *future* frightened me. The future spoke to Father, but for me it was silent and blind and dark. Guampu was part of the past, and with this name in mind I pestered him to push further up the river.

Father believed we were moving into the future. I felt the opposite — as if we might get a glimpse of the past. Anyway it was not far, and even if I was wrong I wanted the satisfaction of knowing whether or not my memory had tricked me.

Five days after leaving the Thurtles' village, at about noon, we heard an airplane. Its rumble-buzz came near. Though we could not see it, it brought me a familiar feeling: a plane going overhead was like getting a haircut. I ducked when I heard it, and I felt its shimmying teeth on the back of my neck. Father denied it was a plane. Crosswinds, he said. But he went silent — his face looked as if he had just sat on something like wet grass or cowflap. I was more hopeful then about Guampu.

I stayed at the bow, searching the river. There were pools of oil slick, little striped and hairy bruises stretching in the current. I spotted a green bottle on the gravel bottom, and a can of Diet Pepsi floating upright, and a kind of suds, like the froth from soap flakes. I saw a submerged sheet of paper curling as it went downstream, and more, and I thought of home, because each thrown-away thing was part of the past. This was the trash of that other world. It looked wonderful to me.

That same day, I heard singing—music muffled by trees. The water picked it up, and so did the light, the heat, the changes in the sky. I waited for someone else to speak.

"Allie." Mother listened. She had heard it.

"Birds."

It was not birds. It was church music.

Jerry said, "Who's singing?"

"Savages," Father said.

I said, "But this might be Guampu."

We rounded a bend, the jungle fell away, the sun was full on the bank. Set back from the river were bungalows with shiny corrugated roofs of new iron that caught the sun and flashed at us. At the center of the large clearing was a wooden white-framed church, with a steep roof and a belfry. It was all glorious and orderly and clean, a white harbor among the loopy trees and wild vines, standing straight on this crooked river.

Father's face was black. Paper peels of skin had burst on his nose and cheeks and left hot patches. He had seen the bungalows, the church, the flowerbeds. He lowered his head, looking double-crossed, and sweat dripped down his neck like fury.

"It must be a mission," Mother said. Then, sensing Father's rage — the smell he gave off when he was angry — she said no more.

A mooring lay ahead of us. It was a little dock of planks fixed to a

row of oil drums. A Boston whaler with a fringed awning and some
smaller dinghies were tied up.

Clover said, "Where are we, Dad?"

Father's mouth was shut tight, but there was fire in his eyes, the
energy he called hunger. He clawed at his long hair and jammed his
pole into the river, pushing us nearer the place, nearer the singing,
and another sound — a generator chugging in a shed by the riverside. This was the back end of the mission. We saw a sewer pipe
emptying into the river, and a little hill of bottles and cans and colored paper — more hope.

The singing stopped. Now there was only the generator.

We worked our way to the mooring. How lumpy and black our
hut-boat looked next to the sleek hull of the whaler, with its yellow
awning. What was our boat except a tarred and floating wreck of
scavenged wood? It was ridiculous here, and made Father seem like
a madman.

"We'll see about this." Father's voice was sand in a rusty bucket.

Mother lost her nerve then. She said, "Let's go on — let's leave it.
It's got nothing to do with us. Allie, no!"

"They have real houses," April said.

"Look, there's a backboard," Jerry said. "They play basketball!"

I braced myself and said, "It's the Spellgoods."

"Booshwah!"

Mother said, "Tell us what you know, Charlie."

"The Spellgoods — don't you remember? They said they lived in
Guampu. Emily said so. That preacher, with the family, from the — "

"Who's Emily?"

"One of the girls. She was on the *Unicorn*. The people who
prayed."

"I knew it was savages," Father said.

"Allie, maybe they can help us."

"We don't need help!"

"We're filthy. Look at us."

Father said, "Those moral sneaks have been hiding here, polluting this place. You'd think they'd have more sense. There's no more
world left!"

He leaped to the mooring and rocked on the planks in anger.

"I've got news for these people."

We followed him — chased him — up the stairs to where paths
were laid out with borders of whitewashed stones. There were no

more than ten bungalows, but they were neat, with flowerbeds in front of the piazzas and a vapory shimmer of heat rising from their metal roofs. Beyond them was a runway of mown grass, a landing strip cut into the jungle. But there was no plane, and no people came to meet us. We saw no one.

But the shutters of the church were open, and now we heard what was certainly Rev. Spellgood's voice.

"Jee-doof," he said slowly.

"I'll knock his block off," Father said.

Jerry said, "Is this the future, too?"

"I'm going to remember that, sonny!" Father kicked at the white-washed stones. "Keep behind me."

"Let's go back to the boat, Allie. Let's get out of here."

"She's afraid," Father said.

"I've never seen you so angry."

"That's right," Father said. "Belittle me in front of the kids."

Spellgood was preaching in a high-pitched parroty voice, quoting Scripture. Sam-yool, he said, and something about ten cheeses and the Philistine of Gath.

"He'll wish he was in Gath."

We looked through the open window. I waited for Father's yell. It didn't come — only a hiss of disgust that traveled from deep in his throat, like poison gas escaping from a pipe, like Fat Boy on the boil.

The church was shadowy, but at the front, propped up on a table and being watched by a whole congregation of Indians in white shirts and white dresses, was a television set.

The set had a large screen, about the size of a car door, and there was Spellgood's face yapping on the screen. He was in color, but greeny-yellow, holding a slingshot and telling a story. Beside him was a giant green man with a gorilla face, plastic-looking, with fangs and a helmet. As Spellgood preached, he fitted a stone into the slingshot and made ready to snap it at the giant dummy next to him.

"They have TV here," Jerry said.

The Indians were so amazed by the program that they did not see us. It was a miracle to them — it was a miracle to me.

I said, "That program must be coming from somewhere. Maybe it's being relayed by satellite from the States."

"Impossible," Father said. His voice sounded tearful and thin, as it had the day he cried when Jeronimo was burned. "America's been destroyed."

"Where's the program coming from?"

"From inside that box. It's a video cassette. A tape, a trick, the old technology. The Indians think it's magic. Pathetic!"

He ran into the church and marched up the aisle and pulled out the plug. He started lecturing them, then "Wait!" he cried, for just as the picture fizzed and faded the Indians stood up. They filed out of the church. They were not startled, only bored and talkative when Father cut off the program. Before long, the church was empty and the Indians in white cotton were heading for the jungle.

The Spellgoods were nowhere to be seen.

"Back to the boat," Father said.

"Can't we look around?" Clover said.

"This place doesn't exist!"

He was not content to let us sit on the deck, watching the bungalows and enjoying this sight of the past. He ordered us into the cabin — the four of us kids — and pushed a board against the door. We sat there in the hut, wondering what was coming next.

"I think we're moving," Jerry said.

We were. I said, "He's taking us away."

But ten minutes later the cabin was still again. We heard the splash of the anchor and Father fumbling with ropes. He muttered to Mother, but none of his words were clear.

As the sun faded in the cabin's cracks and the air grew cooler, we heard a plane overhead. It came in low, as loud as hair clippers, then there was silence.

Clover asked me why Dad was acting so funny, and April said she wanted a drink. They annoyed me with questions, until finally they went to sleep. I fell asleep too, but woke up in the dark. Why not take the dugout ashore?

Jerry was already awake and ready to do whatever I said.

We crept through the hatchway that Mr. Haddy had broken the night he gave me the spark plugs and gas. We were anchored across the wide river, a little above Guampu. We could hear the generator and see the Guampu lights. But even without the lights there was enough moonshine on the river for us to see that the dugout was gone.

Jerry put his mouth against my ear and said, "He's taken it."

"Maybe he just cut it loose," I whispered. "So we couldn't leave."

"Let's swim."

We slipped over the side and made for the far bank, frog kicking and floating with the current so we wouldn't splash. All the lights in the mission were burning in a friendly winking way. I had never thought I would see an electric light again in my life. The only sound we heard was the generator down below, its chugging.

We started toward the bungalows, staying in what shadows we could find, then duck-walked to the largest house, where we saw a flickering light. It was the Spellgoods' parlor. They were all inside, watching television in the hypnotized way the Indians had watched the church-service program. The Spellgoods were eating ice cream out of big bowls, lifting the spoons to their blue faces. Off and on, they laughed. The show was puppets — a green cloth frog and a rubber pig with silky hair — and a real man in a suit talked to them as if they were human — the sort of show that gave Father fits.

Emily Spellgood was stretched out on the floor. She was only a year older since I had last seen her, but she was much bigger and skinnier. She had short hair and wore blue jeans and sneakers. Seeing how well-dressed she was, I got worried. Jerry and I had long hair. We were covered in river mud. The only thing we wore was short pants, which were sopping wet. I felt like a savage. I did not want to stay.

The Spellgoods were enjoying the puppet show, and even Jerry laughed until I made him sit down under the window with me so we could figure out what to do next.

We stayed there, listening to the program and the Spellgoods' remarks. After about twenty minutes, the program ended. There was an argument then, and lots of suggestions.

"Let's play Space Invaders," one of the little Spellgoods said. "I want to send your module into hyperspace!"

"No, let's run *The Muppets* again. I liked the part about the singing babies. They're cute."

"What about *Star Trek?*" Emily said. "We can see if they got out of that time warp."

Gurney Spellgood said, "No. It's late. We want something wholesome."

He clapped a cassette into the black box, and a program with organ music and preaching came on, called *World Crusade for Christ*. Then they all had more ice cream and sang the television hymns.

"We'll be here all night," I whispered.

"I don't care," Jerry said. He looked like a wolf cub. "At least it's real. I wish Dad could see this. Where is he, anyway?"

I was just going to say *I'm glad he's not here,* when the screen door banged out front. There was a skid of sneaker soles on the piazza, like rubber erasers. Someone was outside. I crawled to the piazza and saw a boy about Jerry's age looking dreamily at the bugs clustering around the lights — one of the little Spellgoods.

He was so neat and clean, with his wiffle and his white T-shirt, that he gave me a good idea. I shook my hair loose — it was down to my shoulders — and crouched below the piazza in the shadows. I gave a low whistle. The little boy jumped.

"Who are you?" he said. But he wasn't worried.

"Soy una amiga de su hermana, Emily." By whispering, I could give myself a girl's singsong voice.

He said in English, "What's your name?"

"Rosa," I squeaked. *"Emily a casa?"*

"She's watching TV."

I told him, still in squeaky Indian Spanish, that I wanted to talk to her.

"You're not supposed to be here," he said. "Twahkas aren't allowed at night."

I pretended to whimper, then said sadly — and I *was* sad! — *"Lo mucho siento, chico. Voy a mi kiamp,"* telling him I was very sorry and that I would go home.

"Aw, wait a sec," he said. He yelled "Emily!" and went into the house.

Emily came out a moment later, but while she was still looking for me in the dark, I stood up and said, "It's me, Charlie Fox, from the banana boat, the one who killed the seagull. Don't be worried, I won't hurt you. Remember me?"

She made a goofy face and said, "What are you doing here? Hey, this is weird!"

"That's Jerry," I said, because he had just come out from behind the house, like a wolf. "We're going upriver with my folks. We're kind of stuck."

She came near me and said, "Hey, what happened to you? You're all dirty. You got smaller. Is there something wrong? Your hair's gross!"

I shushed her and said, "Can we talk where no one will hear us?"

But it was too late. Gurney Spellgood was at the window. "Keep it down, Emily." And then he saw me. He said, "Your parents are going to be wondering where you are, young lady. There'll be plenty of time for talking tomorrow."

Only my head showed above the piazza, and a good thing, too, because I wasn't wearing a shirt. But I had an Indian girl's long hair.

"It's okay, Dad," Emily said. "It's just a couple of Twahkas who want to be baptized."

"God loves you," Spellgood said. "Take their names, sweetie, and give them a shower bath and some Kool-Aid."

"Follow me," Emily said. She giggled as she led us across the field to the church, which was in darkness. We went behind it and sat under a tree. "He thought you were Indians. So did I! Hey, are you in trouble or something?"

"Kind of," I said. "We got here this afternoon."

"We were holding a baptism in Pautabusna. It's real gross there. We all went in the plane. Did you see our plane? It's a Cessna Directorial, a nine seater! Dad's got a license. He's logged five hundred hours. It's real neat, with a radio and fans and everything."

"How did you get it?"

I meant *how in the world,* but she said, "Contributions. We bought it in Baltimore. Dad flew it here. We came back on the *Unicorn.* I thought you might be on it, too. I looked for you, I really did. Hey, the things that were going through my mind about you were really X-rated! Why is your hair — "

"Emily," I said, "is Baltimore okay?"

"It's sorta freaky now. They closed down Dad's drive-in church. They couldn't pay the taxes — not enough people. That's why they gave him the plane."

Jerry said, "Is America still there?"

"Are you nuts or something?" Emily laughed. "Hey, this kid's really strange!"

I said, "My father says America's been wiped out. There's no one left but us. Because we're here. That's what he said."

"That's stupid," Emily said.

A whole country rose up and began to shine the moment she

spoke those simple words. And Father seemed tiny and scuttling, like a cockroach when a light goes on.

Jerry said, "Yeah!"

"Gee, I thought my dad was weird!"

"That it all went up in flames," I said. "That's what he thinks."

"We were there three weeks ago. It's the same. It's real neat. I learned roller disco. But we had to come back here. If it wasn't for the plane, it'd be really bummy. But anyway we bought some new cassettes. We've got a video system, with games. And *Rocky*. Dad even lets us watch it. He says it has a wholesome message. It's about boxing — this real neat guy."

Jerry started hitting me. "I knew it," he said. "He was lying the whole time. The liar! I'm going home. I ain't going up the river in no boat!"

"Your brother's real strange."

I said, "Emily, we're in bad trouble."

"Really? That's incredible."

"Will you help us?"

"Sure! I want to. Hey, I used to think about you a whole lot. You can stay here."

"No. We have to get down to the coast."

"My dad can take you in the plane. It's only an hour and a half!"

"Isn't there another way?"

"The river."

"That's the way we came. My father would follow us. What about the roads?"

"There's only one. It's over there" — she lifted her hand and pointed to the darkness across the river. "It goes to Awawas, on the Wonks. That's where our jeep is, parked on the road on the other side. You can see it from the river. It's a Toyota Landcruiser. Four-wheel drive. Green, with black upholstery. We hold baptisms in Awawas. The Wonks is a real neat river. You can get to the coast that way. There's plenty of boats."

I said, "Emily, if you give us the keys to that jeep, we can get away. My mother will drive us to that place you said — "

"Awawas."

"Yes, and then we'll leave the jeep and get down the river somehow."

"Won't your father go crazy if you don't take him?"

"He's already crazy," Jerry said.

"He can do whatever he wants," I said. "That's up to him."

"Aren't you afraid?"

"When I thought he was right — yes, I was. Now that I know he's wrong, I'm not. Are you afraid of your father?"

"Mine's got a gun," Emily said. "It's a Mossberg repeater. Plus it's got a telescopic sight. It's for the Communists. There's millions of Communists around here. Hey, if you combed your hair it'd look kind of cute, like James Taylor."

"Give us the car keys, please. We'll take good care of it."

"It's not a car — it's a Landcruiser. Hey, did your dad really say America's been wiped out? That's really incredible, you know? The people on the ship were talking a lot about him. He's really strange, they said. He's the weirdest passenger they ever had. Hey, I hope you don't mind if I say that! If someone said that about my father I'd cry, even though it's sort of true. Everyone said you were living with Zambus and running around *nudo* and climbing trees. I wanted to write you a letter. How do you like my hair? I had hot-curls, but Dad made me cut them off. Not wholesome enough. Want some money? I've been saving up. I could give you fourteen dollars. Gee, I wish I was a boy — "

At that moment, with a silence that was like a sudden thud, all the lights in Guampu went out. It was as if a black lid had been clapped onto the place. The chugging of the generator had stopped. Now I could hear frogs.

"That always happens," Emily said. "It must be out of gas."

The voices from the bungalow were loud.

"They're real mad. They were watching *Crusade for Christ*. Hey, did I tell you about the video machine? It's a Sony. Dad preaches on it. He can hold services even when he's not here, like today. The Twahkas freak out when they see it — they like it better than the real preaching. Sometimes they only stay when Dad's on TV! They all want to be baptized now, so they can watch — "

"If you don't get the keys, Emily — "

"Don't worry, chicky," she said, and stood up. "I'll get them. It'll be easier in the dark, anyway. Better not crash it." She walked away, saying, "This is weird, for cry-eye!"

When she was gone, Jerry started fussing. What if she couldn't find the keys? What if Dad was looking for us? He cried, he laughed, he kicked the tall grass. He said, "Dad's a crapster — a liar!" and "Jeez, what are we going to do?"

"Go home."

"Hatfield's so far away. You don't even know how to drive. Maybe we should stay here. I hate him, I could kill him." He took my hand. "Charlie, I'm afraid."

"You said you weren't."

"That girl's right. He really is crazy."

Emily came back wagging a flashlight, jingling the keys. "There's a power cut," she said. "My dad's ripping. He just had the generator overhauled. The church sent a guy down from Tegoose."

She shone the flashlight onto her own face. She was whiter. She had put lipstick on, there was green dust on her eyelids. The greasy red on her lips made her look older. She smiled and said, "Like it?" She had flecks of red on her teeth. It scared and excited me.

"Hey, I was thinking. You don't have to go right off. You could stay here awhile. Maybe meet some Twahkas. A few of them are really neat. We could go up in the plane. And don't you want to watch some TV?"

I said, "My father would kill us."

"He's incredible — worse than mine. Hey, why is your brother crying?"

"Never mind him. But remember — all of this is secret. Don't tell anyone about us. You have to swear. Cross your heart you won't tell anyone — not even your father."

"I won't squeal, honest."

"What if they ask?"

"Dad already saw you. He thinks you're Indians! They took the jeep before. They're always doing crazy things like that. I'll blame the Twahkas. It'll be easy."

She walked us to the riverbank. Before we crept into the water, she said she wanted to kiss me. I couldn't do it with Jerry watching, so I told him to start swimming. When I heard him splash, I kissed her cheek. She grabbed me and put her mouth against mine. Her lips were soft, our front teeth nicked together, she dug her fingers into my back and bumped me with her bones. I kept my arms straight down.

I had been worrying about how to get back to the boat, but I was so glad to get away from her kissing, the river seemed easy. But the river was cold. I looked back and saw her little light and wanted to kiss her again.

29

MOTHER WAS AWAKE, standing outside the cabin, as we climbed on board.

"Where have you boys been?" She was trying to be angry, but she sounded scared. It is easy to know how people feel by the way they speak in the dark. Emily had shown me that, and now Mother.

"Over there," I said. "It was my idea, so don't blame Jerry." I looked for the dugout, but couldn't see it. "Where's Dad?"

Mother said, "I thought you were with him. I was keeping watch. Then all the lights went out."

"Their generator's busted." We strained to see the far bank, but Guampu was in darkness — just jungle, and the chalkmarks of white bungalows. I said, "He was lying to us, Ma."

I told her what Emily had said about Baltimore and America. *That's stupid.*

Mother said, "It doesn't matter."

"America's the same, Ma! There's nothing wrong!"

"He hated it the way it was. That's why he left. That's why we're here. He'll never go back."

"I'm not staying here," Jerry said.

"Neither am I," I said.

"There's no way out," she said. "We have to do as we're told."

"We're making a terrible mistake — that's what you said!"

In a sad defeated voice, Mother said, "I should never have said that to you. It's true, but we have to live with it. This is our life now." She was going to say more, but she was choked by her crying — it was small, like one of Clover's sobs.

"We can get out, Ma. There's a jeep parked right over there in those trees, on this side of the river." I showed her the keys and told her where I had gotten them. "You can drive us," I said. "The five of us — before he gets back."

"You mean, leave Dad behind? I can't believe what you're saying."

"It might be our last chance," I said. "Please, Ma. Wake up the twins and let's go. Hurry, or he'll stop us."

"You want Dad to come back to this boat and find we've run out on him? That's horrible, Charlie."

"I want to go home!" I grabbed Mother's shoulders and shook her.

"What about me?" she said. "Don't you think I'd jump at the chance to go? But look how dark it is. Dad's not here. I'm always so frightened when he's away."

She did not push my hands aside, but she was trembling so badly I let go. If she was not willing to drive, there was no way we could escape in that jeep. And yet I could tell she was weakening. She sounded as if she might agree. But she was scared. Father was somewhere out there in the dark — in the dugout or on shore.

I said, "Maybe he's left us."

"We can't do anything without him."

"He might not come back!"

Jerry said, "Please, Ma! Please!"

Mother's voice shook as she said, "I can't think straight in the dark."

"Tomorrow will be too late. Spellgood will be looking for his keys. He'll see our boat. We'll get arrested!"

A light leaped on in Guampu as I spoke. Now we could see the hard outlines of the bungalows. Behind them, like the bonfire of sunrise, something blazed. High flames turned the nearby trees green and gold, and wet them with light, and gave them frantic Zambu shadows. The fire set the birds squawking and scraping, and human shouts reached me at the same time as the stink of burning gasoline.

"Fire," Jerry said. The flames lit his face.

The generator was the next to go. The tanks went with a bang and blew the whole shed sideways into the river. Pools of fire and burning sticks moved quickly, dancing in the current. The people in

Guampu were shouting, and the whole jungle was awake with monkey noises and the sounds of birds' wings thrashing the tree branches.

Mother said, "Oh, God."

The twins woke up and started calling from the cabin.

Jerry made slow scared groans in his throat.

And Mother was whimpering, hitting the boat's rail with the flat of her hand and saying, "Oh, God, oh, God, we should never have stopped here. Why didn't we keep on going?"

"Jerry, grab the twins," I said. "Come on, Ma, let's get out of here!"

"Sit down!"

It was Father's voice. He appeared on the river, standing in the dugout, the flames behind him, his face a shadow-lump of menace.

"You're not going anywhere."

He was struggling with the dugout. He swept his paddle into the fiery reflections and swung alongside.

"Allie, what's happening?"

"The fire's under control. No one's hurt. They won't miss that plane. Good thing I saw it — did them a favor. Nipped it in the bud. Okay, spread out — we're moving."

"You're a liar!" Jerry said, and went at Father like a mutt. "You lied about everything! You said America was destroyed!"

"I was right," Father said. "Look at the flames."

"Liar! Liar!" Jerry said.

"Charlie, get this screamer into the bow. We're clearing out."

I said, "We're not going with you, not after those lies you told us. You made us suffer for nothing."

"Into the bow!"

"Allie, listen to him. He's got a plan."

"You!" Father said, and pushed Mother against the cabin. "You've always been against me. You always tried to undermine me. You're no more use than these kids!"

The firelight from Guampu, the burning plane, reddened his face and picked out his hairstrings and bored empty holes in his eyes. I was so afraid of his face then, and the twins crying in the cabin, that I grabbed Jerry and pulled him to the bow.

The boat still swung on the anchor. And there were two lines from the rail tied to a tree that leaned from the bank opposite Guampu.

We could hear the Spellgoods' confusion and the flames beating like sails in the wind.

"Let's kill him," Jerry said. "We'll tie him up and bash him with a hammer. Then he won't be able to stop us. He deserves it."

"All right," I said.

"You do it."

"How?"

"With a hammer," he whispered. "Bash his head."

I never imagined it in those words. Hearing him repeat them made it impossible. The words were harsh brutes (*hammer, bash*) and frightened me with blood. The shouts from Guampu were like my wounded conscience shrieking.

"I can't."

"If we don't, he'll come after us. He'll kill us."

"Don't talk — don't say — "

"He lied to us," Jerry said. "He's dangerous. He burned their plane and blew up their generator. He hit Ma. That's what it'll be like from now on, if we stay with him — probably worse."

"Pull up the anchor!" Father yelled. "Get that line off the tree!"

"Don't do it," Jerry said. "He wants to leave. He'll take us further up the river. And he'll keep us there. He's in trouble for starting those fires. We'll never get home"

"The anchor! Hurry up!"

"Let's just leave," I said. "We can hop to that bank and get away. Come on, Jerry."

"He'll kill Ma and the twins. I know he will."

Then Father was behind us, and shouting.

"What's eating you two? Here, give me a hand with these lines, Charlie. Jerry, get a bamboo and start poling fast. If these savages see us, they'll be down on us like a ton of bricks."

He stepped into the center of the coiled sounding chain. Before I could think, or stop myself, I yanked it tight around his ankles. He tried to move and tipped himself over. He came down hard and smashed his head against the rail. He was not knocked out, but stunned and half smiling.

"I'm sorry!" I said. I was terrified. I kept telling him I was sorry, and went to help him up. But by then Jerry was working at tying Father's hands, looping rope around his wrists and thumbs.

"Do his feet," Jerry said. "Help me!"

I wound the rest of the chain around his ankles.

"I'm not going to bash him," I said. "I'm not going to kill him."

"Then tie him tight," Jerry said, and went on lashing Father's hands together. Father had taught us these knots.

"Allie, they're coming!" Mother cried from the stern.

Father seemed to understand, but he remained on his back, still enough for us to get double knots on his hands and feet. He murmured and drooled in a dopey, disconnected way, while I apologized for what we were doing to him.

"They've got lights," Mother said. She could not see us. "Allie, what do you want me to do?"

The airplane was still flaming behind the bungalows, but the generator fire had been squelched by the jungle. On shore, in the darkness, we saw flickering lights — lanterns, spotlights — shaking on the far bank.

Mother kept crying out. Her voice roused Father, and now he opened his eyes and made a dive at us. But the knots held and tripped him. He banged his head again. He got to his knees and tried to work his hands loose. Jerry picked up an iron pipe from the deck and raised it over Father's head. I snatched it away from him and threw it overboard. Father had not looked up. He grunted over his knots, then gave a whimper of embarrassment and anger that he couldn't break the ropes in one hard pull.

"Hey," he said in a drunken way, and began biting at his wrists.

I did not want to be there when he freed himself. Jerry and I ran to the stern. I swung the dugout around to our side of the boat, away from Guampu, and told Mother to get in. She was holding the twins and crouching in the dark, looking toward the Guampu shore, where the small lights swung in the darkness and the distant plane burned.

A yell went up on shore. It was Spellgood, shouting in Spanish and also in an Indian language, maybe Twahka. His voice had a tunnel echo, as if he was shouting through a bullhorn or a megaphone.

"Get into the dugout, Ma. Please, hurry!"

There was a gunshot, not loud, but it had the malice of a poison dart and made a watery wobble and plop into the trees just behind us on the near bank.

"Where's Dad?"

"He's not coming."

Another gunshot, and more Indian squawks from Spellgood.

"Allie!" Mother called to him as she put April and Clover into the dugout. They covered their faces. They were so frightened they had no breath left to scream with. Jerry got in next, then Mother, who was still calling "Allie! Allie!"

I hopped in and shoved us away from the boat. We were only twenty feet from the bank opposite Guampu, but before we had gone halfway — one paddle stroke — a light settled on the cabin of the boat and lit it from behind. We were hidden by the boat, in its shadow, looking up.

Father stood and faced the light, and when he tried to cover his face, I saw that his hands were still tied.

"Communistas," Spellgood screamed. *"Satanas!"*

Mother said, "Allie — here! What's wrong with him?"

Father thrashed his tied hands against the cabin roof, beating the knots against the wood.

"Satanas! Diabolos!"

"Give me a hand here," Father said in a plain calm voice.

As he spoke, there was another gunshot. A moment before the far-off crack, there was a smaller sound, almost innocent, like a ripe plum dropping with a mush on the floor.

And Father went down on his knees saying, "I'm all right! It's okay! I'm alive!"

We had reached the bank. The kids jumped out, but Mother remained in the bow.

"Allie!"

"Don't leave me," he said. He lifted his tied hands. "I'm bleeding, Mother."

Mother snatched the paddle from me and in the same movement dug it into the river and shoveled us to the boat, while I held on.

"Who's there?" Spellgood said through his megaphone from across the river. He tried to find us with his light. "Who said that?"

Father groaned, and groaned again. "I can't move."

By standing up in the dugout on this safe side of the boat, we were able to roll Father over and topple him off the deck into the dugout. He gave an almighty yell, as if we'd broken his back, but we didn't hesitate. With one of his legs dragging in the river, and water spilling over the gunwales, we made it back to the bank, where the kids were waiting.

"Hurry," Mother said.

"I'm coming after you!" Spellgood cried.

Father said, "I can't get out of this thing."

Mother dragged him onto the bank and, still hidden from the Guampu shore by the shadow of our hut-boat, we untied Father's knots. But even with his arms and legs free, he could not move. He lifted his head, but the rest of his body lay heavily against the ground.

"Help me, Charlie," Mother said. "All of you — grab hold!" She yanked him through the bushes while we shoved at his legs.

There were more people on the far shore now. They must have heard the shouts. There seemed dozens of voices. They were calling out to us, and once or twice I thought I heard Emily saying my name. But the river was wide here, the Guampu shore fifty yards away. We moved along, not saying a word until we found the jeep. The voices continued from the other shore. It was as if they were lost and wounded and calling out for help in the darkness — not us.

30

DOWN THE DARK, leafy sleeve of road, with night pressing on our roof, the twenty-eight miles on the rutted track to Awawas seemed more like a hundred. Mother drove as fast as she could, slewing the jeep, grinding the gears. The rest of us sat in silence. We watched the birds roosting on the road and the kinkajou furballs with light-bulb eyes that froze in our headlong clatter. When Mother spoke, it was always to Father. "You'll be all right," she said. "I won't leave you, Allie."

Father did not reply. He was on the rear seat with his eyes half-open. The skid of mud on him from the riverbank gave off a stink like death.

Then, still dark, there was no road. We were thrown into a dead end of trees, ferns, bush tips against the headlights, the loud stomach of jungle. Mother shut off the jeep and cranked the brake. She climbed over her seat and made Father comfortable, talking to him softly, as if he was sleeping. She said, "You'll live, Allie."

With the headlights off we could see stars, the moonhole in the sky's blanket. The moon went down and branches laid cracks across it. There was no sun for a while, only a gray light that lifted and penetrated the trees like rising water, and waxed them with a blur of mist which, as dawn broke, was cut by straws of sun that thickened and blinded us. The surrounding jungle had changed each second, dark to watery, to misty, to waxy, to gray, thinly stripping the shadows from the jungle — a rising tide of light with a mirror behind it. It was as if, that whole time, we had been riding from darkness into light, slipping forward like scared people in a silent canoe, into this brighter place.

All the darkness had been bleeding out of the morning trees, becoming mud and water.

And dawn showed us that we were alone. The jungle at night was tall, and its cool gloom dripped darkness. But daylight here was pale yellow, broken by starved trees, with hot spots. This was a riverbank, and night foliage had become frail and top-heavy weeds. Ahead, where we had expected more jungle, was water, the Wonks, where all the darkness had been bleeding.

"Mother." His voice was like this fragile light.

I could not bear to see his goat-white face, the blood under his beard, the gluey crescents in his eyeslits. I walked to the river with Jerry, stepping over roots. There was a bullfrog at my feet. I wanted to jerk it on a spear. But after seeing Father, I couldn't do it. I looked for yautia and guavas instead.

Jerry said, "I don't want him to die."

We heard voices and looked back at the jeep. Two Indian men stood at the windows. They must have recognized it as Spellgood's jeep, because they were smiling and talking to Mother. We walked over as Mother got out.

"Find me a boat," she said. "And water. And food. Make it snappy!"

Only Father's head was alive. We knew that when we laid him on the ground. It was clear when Mother washed his wound. His head was alive, but his body was like a bag of sticks and seeds. The bullet had entered the side of his neck and burst out the back. His neck bone was not broken, but there were red strings and fat in the clawed-open wound, and a black bruise around it, like a large whelk of meat. Mother plugged it with cotton the Indians boiled for her, and then they put him on a plank and brought him to the river. They carried him feet first, like pallbearers, because they thought he was dead.

Mother propped him at the bow of the boat, which was a flatboat with a long-handled rudder. By this time, the twins' crying had attracted other Indians, and these people stood on the gravel bank, watching us and not asking any questions. Some of them ran back for more pots of beans and rice — English food, they called it — and wabool and jugs of coffee. One of the Indians told Mother that it was neither good nor bad if Father was dead — everyone died, it was the world's way, nothing you can do about it, so be happy, he said.

"You believe that," Mother said. "But I don't, so don't ask me to. Just get me out of here and give the preacher his car keys."

It was what Father would have said. She had taken on his determination in a kind of panicky way. She got us hopping for paddles and poles, and gave the Indians orders. She did not have Father's flair for gadgets, but she knew how to make these Indians rig up an awning for Father's head. And when an Indian tried to insist on coming with us, she told him firmly that she appreciated the offer but she didn't want his help. "And I'm not staying here another minute." One, more boastful than pious, had mentioned a church service. They were the sort of people Father had once called "Praying Indians."

Mother said, "I don't pray."

We pushed off in this flat-bottomed boat, Mother at the stern, holding the rudder handle, the twins in the center seat with the food, Jerry and I paddling on either side of Father at the bow.

"We going upriver?" Father knew we were afloat. He strained to see over the gunwales, but he couldn't.

"Yes," Mother said. "Upriver."

But she hooked us in the current and turned us downstream.

The rushing stew of this river was like the hurry of an oncoming tide, but perpetual. Moving water looked odd here, sucking along at the deadest, stillest banks. The last time we had gone down a river was on the Rio Sico, when we had escaped from Jeronimo. But the Sico was a creek compared to the Wonks, and that was in the dry season. The Wonks was fuller and wider than the Patuca even. We traveled midstream and went fast. There was hardly any need to paddle, except for steadying the boat on bends.

Father thought we were still on the Patuca, going upstream. He was happy — his head was happy, the rest of him was a sandbag. "Pull hard," he said. "Away from the coast, away from the savages. There's death down there. Listen, the Mosquito Coast is the coast of America. You know what that means."

We gave him water and wabool, but he resisted eating. He said he wanted to starve himself until he got his strength back. "I'm not much use to you as a cripple," he said. "There's something wrong with my legs." And his arms, too — he couldn't move them. We fanned the flies off his face.

His big head was fixed in the niche of the bow like a goat in a halter, raving at us as we sped down the river, telling us that we were saved because we were going upriver, and sometimes crying.

He cried most when he saw the birds. They were harmless birds at first, parrots and crascos, but he raved and they turned into vicious creatures. They got bigger. They grew plumes and claws. Storks now planed overhead, then fish hawks, and finally vultures, which he hated worst of all. We had never seen vultures like this before. They were black, rather than shabby gray, and huge, with ragged wing tips and plucked necks and hooked beaks. They hovered without flapping, like wicked kites, looking feeble and patient in the summer sky.

"Take those birds away!" It was his old horror of scavengers, but now that he couldn't raise his arms, he was especially afraid. He was fearful of other things, too. The way the boat tipped — he couldn't swim as a cripple. The way flies gathered on his eyelids. Sudden noises. Fire. And he would not be left alone. He hated stopping. When we put in that first day at a riverbank village called Susca for bandages and fresh water, he made Jerry and me stay by him until Mother returned. He was not surprised there were villages here, and boats passing us, and Miskito cries. "This is where the last of human life is — upriver."

But we were fifteen miles down it and sliding toward the coast.

"Cover me up," he said. He made us move the awning, so that he would not see the vultures that followed us. And he said he hated the empty sky. "If I was in jail, I'd never look out of the window."

We were lucky, he said. The river was a labyrinth — "Easy to get in, hard to get out."

He raved when he was awake, and when he slept he howled in his dreams. There was always froth on his lips.

Easy to get in? We could not have gone upriver against this current if we had tried. At night we moored our flatboat near villages. Some were Moravian missions, praying Indians, and people from Pennsylvania. No, America had not been destroyed. Mother demanded food and water and medicine. The people were kind. She got all she wanted. We stopped at Wiri-Pani and Pranza, and at a place called Kisalaya we saw muddy wagons. Mother was told we were only three days from the coast, Cabo Gracias a Dios, which they called the Cape.

The twins had nothing to do. They were sick with worry, actually puking with fear at the rate we were moving. Mother stayed at the stern, wearing a straw hat from Susca. She heaved the long tiller, not looking to the left or right but sort of staring downstream past Father's head.

She did not speak to anyone but the twins, and she was too far from Father to reply to the things he said. I wanted to tell her that I had not meant for any harm to come to Father, only for us to escape. We had escaped, but in the worst possible way, down a river we didn't know, with the girls sick. We were carrying Father's head to the coast.

Every five miles was a village where crazy-sounding Indians shouted English at us. The Indians got blacker as we neared the coast, and the hanging vultures bigger and wickeder. Sometimes at night there were alligators. They scuttled from the bank and moved against the current. But they were cowardly, they did not attack, and when they bumped us with their snouts we made rag torches. Often sudden light stopped them, and the flames near their green nostrils always did.

The river was murkier and twistier nearer the coast, and the land swampy, so that cranes stood out like shirts hung on fenceposts. It was hotter here. The heat made Father rave more. His raving made me remember again how, in Jeronimo, climbing through Fat Boy, I had had a glimpse of his mind. I had seen just how tangled it was. I had been stumped by the plumbing of all its turns. What he was, he had made. His ravings came out of those orbits and circuits, that teeming closet of pipes and valves and shelves and coils — the ice maker, his brainache.

What he harped on most was this imperfect world. Well, I knew that one by heart. But there was more.

"I'm hurt." He said it again and again, as if he had just discovered it and hardly believed it. "I can't move — can't do anything."

"You'll get better," I said.

"Man sprang out of the faulty world, Charlie. Therefore, I'm imperfect. What's the use? It's a bad design, the human body. Skin's not thick enough, bones aren't strong enough, too little hair, no claws, no fangs. Drop us and we break! Why, we're not even symmetrical. One foot bigger than the other, left-handed, right-handed, our noses run. Look where our heart is. We weren't meant to stand up straight — our posture exposes the most sensitive parts of the body, heart and genitals. We should be on all fours, hairer, more resistant to heat and cold, with tails. What happened to my tail, that's what I'd like to know. I had to turn inventor — I was too weak to live any other way. Look at me. Look where seventy-five pushups a day got me. Yes sir, I'm going to live on all fours from now on. And that's what I'm fit for — hands and knees!"

He went on and on like this as we raced downriver under flights of butterflies and the ragged shadows of birds so high in the sky I had to get on my back like Father to see them properly.

"It's worse for other people. Women, Charlie, they're in bad shape. They leak, they drip. It's terrible about women's bodies, how they leak. All that blood, all that useless fat. They carry these bodies around with them all the time. No wonder they're so mad, wondering what they're for. It's humiliating to have a body with a design fault. I thought I was the strongest man in the world. I'm just pulp. Weakness makes you clever, but no amount of cleverness can save you if all the odds are against you. I'll tell you who'll inherit the world — scavenging birds. They're fit for it, everything in their favor. They are nourished on failure. The sky in America is black with them now. They just hang there, waiting. Get them away from me! There's sand in my eyes! I'm alive, but I can't see, Mother!"

It was dreadful trying to paddle, with Father's screams in my ears. But it was so bad I hardly noticed the twists of the river, and it saved me from thinking much about what would happen to us on the coast.

Father insisted on his head being covered. He wore a hood, like a condemned man, and sweated in it. He did not see the lifting flights of ducks, the tumbling plovers, the flamingos, the seabirds that met us near villages with English names like Living Creek and Doyle. He went silent for long periods. His silences had always been worse than his howls. But now we thought he was dead. He still steamed of death. We knew he was alive by his skin, the way he came out in bites.

The sand flies got him. The tortoiseshell cockroaches in the boat bit him. Fevers shook him. He raved and struggled and opened his wound.

"Nature is crooked. I wanted right angles and straight lines. Ice! Oh, why do they all drip? You cut yourself opening a can of tuna fish and you die. One puncture in your foot and your life leaks out through your toe. What are they for, moose antlers? Get down on all fours and live. You're protected on your hands and knees. It's either that or wings."

On this flooded river, his voice cracked through his gallows hood. "Listen to me, people. Grow wings and they'll never get you!"

The river grew wider and lost its current. We had to paddle hard to move forward. With swamp at both banks there was nowhere to moor the boat, and all through the last hot night we kept going. Just before dawn, we saw a beacon — a lighthouse — and heard the slap of waves on the beach by the rivermouth. This was the Cape.

"What's that?"

He knew the sound.

"No!" And raised his arms for the first time.

He pulled down his mask and said, "Charlie, don't lie to me. Tell me where we are."

I bent down. I could not speak. Then I had to turn away, because with bared teeth I heard something violent in me urging me to bite his ear off.

"Vultures," he said, and then the terrible sentence, "Christ is a scarecrow!"

Yet it seemed as if everything Father feared was true. He had predicted this. The sky was thick with birds — ugly pelicans and gulls and vultures. They circled and soared, they swung across the great curve of tropical beach. And sometimes they hurried down and fed, for surfing through the breakers were large paddling turtles, with parrot beaks and baggy necks.

The turtles' shells were crusted with periwinkles and weedsuckers and hardened sea glop. More turtles worked their flippers up the shelf of sand, and others were backed into the low dunes. Blinking and brooding, they laid brown eggs. Their beaks were splashed with the soapy saliva of their effort.

They made no sound at all. Only the birds cried out, and when a turtle was tossed ashore on its back by a rogue wave, the vultures went for its unprotected neck and jerked it out of its shell. The gulls had the leavings. Sunlight made this nightmare more horrible — the massing turtle lids flopping along the shore and pooping eggs into the sand, the birds hovering in the sky, the heavy surf. It was the coastal hell Father had promised.

We chose a secluded spot in a palm grove down the beach, over-turned our flatboat, and made camp. And Father wept. Each time he tried to speak he burst into tears. It was the sight of the sea, the Mosquito Coast. His tears said we had tricked him, failed him, brought him here to die.

Black Indians came in cayukas to stare at us. Father howled them away. Mother walked into Cabo Gracias, the village, and tried to find a doctor. People said the doctors were upriver, at the missions, or in La Ceiba or Trujillo — not here. She told the people she wanted a boat, to take us up the coast. But the boats were all going south, to Bluefields and Puerto Cabezas and Pearl Lagoon. They laughed when she told them we had no money.

We killed a turtle, and while vultures strutted nearby, swishing their wings and watching us, we roasted the fatty meat over our fire. We believed that the whole of Father's prediction had come true. We were dying on the Mosquito Coast, in the hot sand, among scav-engers and scuttling turtles. It was worse than he had said.

America was safe — the Spellgoods' word had been verified by the Moravians — but we were far away, so what did it matter? Hell is what you can't have. The best memory we had was of living in the jungle. It was too late to go back — the river was impossible without a motorboat, and the vast expressionless sea made us feel small and lonely. We had escaped to the coast, but we were more than ever like castaways, clinging to this scrap of shoreline. We were tired and empty, and hardly spoke. Father could move his arms, but his legs were useless. He lay staring at the waves, the turtles, the birds. Every sunrise, he saw sea monsters gasping in the surf.

Yonder were sailboats, shrimpers, and fishermen. But none came near enough for us to see if Mr. Haddy was among them. No boats landed at this beach, and Father had scared the blacks away. The twins were too sick to stand up. They sat under the boat with Father.

Our hope was Mother. She still walked the three miles through the palms every day to Cabo Gracias, demanding medicine, and cloth for Father's bandages. "I'm not a beggar — I don't take no for an answer," she said. The people called her Auntie and said she was loco. Jerry and I collected turtle eggs and firewood. We listened to Father pleading to be taken upriver, we squashed the flies that settled on him.

"Which way is the river?" he said in a small voice.

He spoke in baby talk about living on all fours far away in Mosquitia, and about going to sea in a sieve. Usually he said nothing. He stared. Thoughts folded his brow. Tears gathered in his eyes and, without his making a sound, rolled down his cheeks.

Five days of this weakened us worse than the river had, and now this coast seemed a great mistake. Creatures here, the only life, fed on each other. We went around in our rags. The longer we stayed here, the more fearful we were of the ocean. Because of the turtles, we never swam, and because of the birds, we stayed under cover.

When I slept, I had food dreams. I dreamed of chocolate fudge cake and cold milk. I dreamed of our kitchen in Hatfield, how some nights I had gone down in the dark and opened the refrigerator to cool myself and look upon the lighted shelves, the cheese, the milk, the bacon, a jar of grape jelly, a jug of water, a pie, a pitcher of fresh orange juice. The kitchen was dark, but the inside of the refrigerator was bright and filled with clean food.

I was woken from this very dream one day by Jerry's shouts, and I was to remember that interruption. Jerry had seen a sailboat beating from the south. The wind was offshore. The boat tacked way out, then sailed in on a wave, its gray sail luffing, and plowed the beach.

"It's a boat, Dad!"

Father raised himself up and watched Jerry running toward the sailboat.

I said, "It might be Mr. Haddy."

"Where's Mother?"

I looked around. I had been sleeping. "She must be in the village."

The twins were asleep beside him. They slept holding hands.

"Go see who it is," Father said. He gave me a sneaky glance, his coward's glance, which was weak and wanting comfort and willing to ditch anything in order to get away — his blamer's look, which had a hint of sadness and self-hate in it. I saw his face. I did not size up his expression until later.

"Take your time," he said. "I'll be right here."

I left him with the twins and ran down the beach. Jerry had already reached the sailboat. He was talking to the man on board, who had turtles stacked around his mast and filling his cuddy like manhole covers. It was not Mr. Haddy, but he was willing to talk. He had broken his mainsheet, he needed some rope. He was talking about rope when we heard the yell.

"The twins," Jerry said.

It was a child's shriek, thin and complaining and pathetic.

"Mother! Mother! Mother! Mother!"

"You got trouble for true," the boatman said, speaking at the sound of the voice.

The twins were awake, rubbing their eyes, when we got back to the little camp. Father was missing, but we could see the groove mark of his body across the sand, like a lizard track, with handprints on either side. All fours.

"Mother!"

The strangled shout came from the other side of the dune.

He had dragged himself quite a distance from the camp. He had been hurrying. He lay on a slope of sand. He had been heading west, where the rivermouth was. But he was motionless now. Five birds stood over him — vultures — and they were attacking his head. They made cruel swipes at his scalp. They cast terrible shadows over him. They held parts of his flesh in their beaks. The birds looked up at me. I had interrupted them, I was screaming and waving my arms.

They were not frightened. This victory had taken away their fear. They hesitated, they hopped aside, they gave me a look at Father's head. I grabbed a stick from the sand, but even as I went forward, a vulture bent over and struck and tore again, like a child snatching something extra because he knows he will be scolded anyway, and this one had his tongue.

V

THE MOSQUITO COAST

31

WE MIGHT HAVE gone on starving there. Coasters died every day. But a white man's death was news — a missionary, they called him. How he would have hated that! It got around, it reached Mr. Haddy. He came out of curiosity, and stayed with us when he saw who it was. When he cried, his tears reminded us that we had not wept at all. Exhaustion was stronger than grief.

And soon the breezes that had scorched us on the turtle beach below Cabo Gracias a Dios pushed us north along the Mosquito Coast. We sailed in a fair wind, with a cargo of dying turtles.

After Father died, time changed. The days were long and unbroken like a sentence with no commas and we felt lost like this.

There were moments when we half-expected him to show up, although we knew he was dead; expected him to appear somewhere astern and fling himself aboard and howl at us, as he had the day the shear pin broke on the Patuca. Seabirds rested on this boat. I saw them, and heard Father's howls in the wind. Mr. Haddy expected Father most of all. It made us watchful. We never talked about him, not a word.

We sailed past Caratasca, and when we came to Mocobila we hardly recognized it from the sea. The haulover at Brewer's, where we had scavenged, passed our rail, then Paplaya and Camaron. I felt we were heading home. I also felt we might die at any moment. We did not deserve more luck than we had had, we did not mention Father's death.

At night we sailed under twanging sheets, and in the daytime the heat laid us low. The boat rose and fell, plunging in the green water, taking us wherever.

Once I had believed in Father, and the world had seemed very small and old. He was gone, and now I hardly believed in myself, and the world was limitless. A part of us had died with him, but the part of me that remained feared him more than ever, and still expected him, still heard his voice crying, "They'll get me first — I'm the last man!" It was the wind, the waves, every bird, every cry from the shore. Like him, they thought out loud.

We saw the lights of La Ceiba early one dawn. But the wind was wrong. It took us out and tipped us further west, past the shacks, then beat us back until we could only put in near some palms, at a beach like the one we had escaped three hundred miles away, where Father lay buried among buried eggs. There was nothing here. Coconut litter, sea garbage, huts on stilts, pelicans, a cow — another wilderness. Father was not here, but his voice still rang over us.

Grief is a later feeling, as the sadness sifts down and makes your memory heavy and hopeless. It was too early for us to feel anything except the shock of relief, the leftover pain. We had been skinned alive and were raw. We had come through a fire, we still burned.

No, he was not here. But the pain was so strong I could not mourn him.

We dropped the sails. We drew up the boat and walked through the palms. What we wore was all we owned. But Mr. Haddy was turtle rich. He helped Mother walk, touching her arm for the first time, then tucking it in his, supporting her and looking proud.

Beyond the palms was a paved road, a parked jalopy, a driver. Soon we were inside, on our way back to La Ceiba and home. The world was all right, no better or worse than we had left it — though after what Father had told us, what we saw was like splendor. It was glorious even here, in this old taxicab with the radio playing.

FICTION

Blinding Light *"A bravura performance ... enjoyable and worldly."* —*New York Times Book Review*
In this novel of manners and mind expansion, a writer sets out for Ecuador's jungle in search of a rare hallucinogenic drug and the cure for his writer's block.
ISBN-13: 978-0-618-71196-3 / ISBN-10: 0-618-71196-1

The Elephanta Suite: Three Novellas *"Stereotype-shattering."* —*Publishers Weekly*
The three intertwined novellas in this startling, far-reaching book capture the tumult, ambition, hardship, and serenity that mark today's India.
ISBN-13: 978-0-618-94332-6 / ISBN-10: 0-618-94332-3   HOUGHTON MIFFLIN HARDCOVER

Hotel Honolulu *"Extravagantly entertaining."* —*New York Times*
In this wickedly satiric novel, a down-on-his-luck writer escapes to Waikiki and finds himself managing a low-rent hotel. ISBN-13: 978-0-618-21915-5 / ISBN-10: 0-618-21915-3

Kowloon Tong: A Novel of Hong Kong
"A cleverly, tightly constructed, fast-paced book." —*New York Times Book Review*
One of many caught up in the hand-over of Hong Kong from Britain to China, Neville "Bunt" Mullard is forced finally to make decisions that matter.
ISBN-13: 978-0-395-90141-0 / ISBN-10: 0-395-90141-3

The Mosquito Coast *"A work of fiendish energy and ingenuity."* —*Newsweek*
In this magnificent novel, the paranoid, brilliant, and self-destructive Allie Fox takes his family to live in the Honduran jungle, determined to build a better civilization.
ISBN-13: 978-0-618-65896-1 / ISBN-10: 0-618-65896-3

My Other Life *"A seriously funny novel."* —*Time*
This wry, worldly, and deeply moving novel spans almost thirty years in the life of a fictional "Paul Theroux," who moves through Africa and between continents.
ISBN-13: 978-0-395-87752-4 / ISBN-10: 0-395-87752-0

The Stranger at the Palazzo d'Oro and Other Stories *"Masterly."* —*Vogue*
The intensely erotic story of an unlikely love affair leads Theroux's collection of compelling tales of memory and desire. ISBN-13: 978-0-618-48533-8 / ISBN-10: 0-618-48533-3

And don't miss Theroux's acclaimed nonfiction:

DARK STAR SAFARI: OVERLAND FROM CAIRO TO CAPE TOWN
ISBN-13: 978-0-618-44687-2 / ISBN-10: 0-618-44687-7

FRESH AIR FIEND: TRAVEL WRITINGS
ISBN-13: 978-0-618-12693-4 / ISBN-10: 0-618-12693-7

THE GREAT RAILWAY BAZAAR: BY TRAIN THROUGH ASIA
ISBN-13: 978-0-618-65894-7 / ISBN-10: 0-618-65894-7

THE HAPPY ISLES OF OCEANIA: PADDLING THE PACIFIC
ISBN-13: 978-0-618-65898-5 / ISBN-10: 0-618-65898-X

THE KINGDOM BY THE SEA: A JOURNEY AROUND THE COAST OF GREAT BRITAIN
ISBN-13: 978-0-618-65895-4 / ISBN-10: 0-618-65895-5

THE OLD PATAGONIAN EXPRESS: BY TRAIN THROUGH THE AMERICAS
ISBN-13: 978-0-395-52105-2 / ISBN-10: 0-395-52105-X

RIDING THE IRON ROOSTER: BY TRAIN THROUGH CHINA
ISBN-13: 978-0-618-65897-8 / ISBN-10: 0-618-65897-1

SIR VIDIA'S SHADOW: A FRIENDSHIP ACROSS FIVE CONTINENTS
ISBN-13: 978-0-618-00199-6 / ISBN-10: 0-618-00199-9

SUNRISE WITH SEAMONSTERS: A PAUL THEROUX READER
ISBN-13: 978-0-395-41501-6 / ISBN-10: 0-395-41501-2

www.marinerbooks.com